I would like to dedicate this book to Christopher Gibson.

Ann Patricia Turner-Savage

THE SAND CASKET

AUSTIN MACAULEY PUBLISHERS™

LONDON * CAMBRIDGE * NEW YORK * SHARJAH

A CIP catalogue record for this title is available from the British Library.

ISBN 9781528981309 (Paperback)
ISBN 9781528981316 (ePub e-book)

www.austinmacauley.com

First Published 2021
Austin Macauley Publishers Ltd®
1 Canada Square
Canary Wharf
London
E14 5AA
+44 (0)20 7038 8212
+44 (0)20 3515 0352

Special acknowledgements to Christopher Gibson who taught me anything is possible, and Clinton and Landon Peck.

Finally, Edith Piaf—

—who proved it.

Chapter One

People have as many opinions about dreams as there are dreams. We fall in and out of them without choice. They are, to me, old travellers with tales to tell by picture and by verse…and this is my tale of warmth and longing. Within the dream is an answer, a riddle and a confusion of the two.

My face is to the sun and I'm walking higher and higher. Ah, but already this is not quite correct, my steps are heavy and through sand. Rea ching the very highest ridge of a sand dune pushing forward, a slight bend to my body. I am dressed as a Bedouin woman – a close-fitting headcloth with some kind of ornamentation at the forehead. I am wearing a 'thob' a long cloak-like garment of deep dark blue and when I lie to rest upon the side of the dune, my anklets make a soft tinkling sound – as if shallow water is moving over stones. Around my neck is a silver cylinder which contains verses to protect the wearer from accidents and scorpions. Triangles pattern my garment and I have gold in my ears and on my wrists.

My right arm is flung back and I begin to rise above the dune, and I see myself below asleep and it looks as if I am waving to my other self in the sky. A buzzing surrounds me like music but it gets louder and the figure in the sand shimmers.

The alarm is buzzing and I reach across to shut it off. My cat, Delly, is sat on my chest again purring, and the purrs change to a growl of protest which goes into threat of attack mode very rapidly, as I struggle out of the warm duvet and manage to stand. I sway sit and then stand again. It's Monday and I turn to Delly, who by now is struggling out of the duvet and giving me looks fit to kill.

"Don't worry, Delly nuttle chops, I am already the grand recipient of several utility bills I can't possibly pay…and one that wears an almost triumphant air of Greek drama proportions from that horrible – dairy. Ah! Irony, 'tis irony that did for me; irony upon irony equals cliché equals torture by butter…"

A new milkman is swaggering up the path with more paperwork. I know exactly what happened to the old one. My once-upon-a-time delightfully light-hearted husband ran off with him. Ray or as I call him now, X-Ray…suddenly became a new *man,* who dyed his hair and visited the gym with the fervour of a man whose life depended upon it. He ignored me unless it was absolutely vital that he speak. Or he wanted his favourite casserole. Then, to add insult to injury…left, leaving a note on the top of his clothes stating, 'This is just not me anymore.'

I ask myself out loud with Delly furry knickers looking inquiringly from her cushion, "*So,* when did he become the dummy for the milkman to talk through. Ah, must have been all those extra creamy yoghurt drinks at the back door. Oh you have to watch them aphrodisiacs one and all."

Well, that was a little over three days ago. I'm still plucking up the courage to go to the cash point…oh and the bank, now there is a laugh of the black humour kind. It's going to take a few voddy's to get that visit dealt with. Voddy's that I cannot afford. I rang my grandmother Sunday morning. She only talks in philosophical phrases lifted from the script of 'Gone with the Wind'.

"You just have to go on being brave."

Knowing which scene this referred to, I said, "What make a dress out of the curtains?"

"Now, my girl, it's just that sort of smart-ass talk that's got you into this situation."

"Oh really, thanks, Gran, *bye.*" Rang Greta, my daughter who is at university trying to learn Japanese. She is trendily wicked.

"Oh, Mum, what a…"

"Yes, Greta, I think I get the picture."

"Right, I'm coming home."

"Well, darling, I much rather you stayed at university at present because…" Her mobile clicks off.

"There's no money, and my job does not cover all the bills and the mortgage."

I am talking to the cat or the air or a large plumped-up cushion…again. Knowing Greta so well, she will come home with a mound of washing and an empty bank account, each thing explaining the other nicely. Then with that razor-sharp brain of hers, will work out that while Mummy is vulnerable, she will buy me many lovely things.

The doorbell trills…it's that bloody new milkman again…I know it is. I can see the stupid delivery van in the lane. I won't answer the door and that will teach him to replace my husband's new lover with such indecent haste. He of the Errol Flynn moustache and masculine tendonitis thighs swinging and yodelling through the trees or whatever he does, swashing his ruddy buckle and grinning with victory.

I sit at the bottom of the stairs and switch my phone to silent mode. Delly sensing new things comes to join me.

I whisper, "This is our very own special sit-in, darling." I gently stroke her head.

Delly purrs approval.

Greta turned up during the early hours and prowled about without the lights off in high heels, no doubt with the sole purpose of saving electricity now it's all too little too late for such things.

When I called out rather angrily, I must confess, to "Take those bloody heels off and get into bed."

A few oaths were left dangling in the air. The morning came and although I was feeling very groggy, my job still demanded my presence if I wanted to continue to put food in front of the cat for her to disdain, and keep a roof over all our heads. So I braved a cold shower and that certainly gave me something to think about.

After placing a lovely, finely balanced, nutritious meal of flavoursome chicken in jelly – which to be honest I could have eaten myself – in front of Delly, I stood back and sighed. For she in true Delly pernickety pickle style, is staring at it as if to say, "This, this, this…is my breakfast."

"Well, Delly furry knickers, if you don't eat it, I will."

I truly feel like offering her my magnification glass so that she can really examine it in depth and write me a manifesto later.

To my amazement, Greta slops into the kitchen where I am applying spread to the driest cracker in creation.

"Hey, Mum, sorry I woke you up. I am here now though and want to be useful."

I notice she is wearing one of her errant father's good shirts, no doubt from the selection which is obviously I see now no longer 'him'. I try, and happily succeed, in getting rid of the image of him in a baby doll, orange tan, and a beard.

By now Delly has stalked with the air of a queen not wishing to smudge her newly-painted toe nails to sit with an air of pure – this is so beneath me – in the window seat.

Greta looks in the fridge tapping her teeth.

"Do we have any of that really nice yoghurt?"

"Don't talk to me about nice yoghurt."

I get up and hand her the Sunny Dairy bill.

"FFF."

"Greta."

"Sorry, Mum, but where did all this lot come from."

"Ah, I think that's what can safely be called your father's Parthian shot…that or whereabouts. And the point might be where has it all gone…"

"Don't you mean thereabouts…?"

"No, because that implies, I know where he is, but when I do, I am posting it to him – first class."

"Oh, Mum, that's brilliant…you stick it to him, girl."

I take it back smiling what can only be described as the smile of Atilla the Hun when he saw a peasant village in the distance.

I pop it back into the 'to-do' tray, which is really an old shortbread tin, but then I never did get a high mark in domestic science.

"You'll have to take in a lodger, Mum, it's all the thing now…you know…really hot."

"Greta, that's amazing."

"Mmmmm, don't say I'm not useful."

The washing machine is in full employment with its lovely slushy sloshy background bubbly routine which is oddly comforting.

"What's your plan for today?"

"Seeing Megs – you off to work, Mum?"

"Seeing as I'm suited and booted, so yep."

"What time should I expect you this evening?"

"Greta, that's very thoughtful – well, first I have to go up to the high street with my paper and comb, do a spot of busking for hard cash."

"Oh, bloody hell, Mum, just stick a few cards in a shop window for a lodger or whatever. Gran's room is lovely; I wouldn't mind it myself and this house is lush – some houses I've seen…"

"What about these houses, darling, what have you seen?"

"Oh, you know, Mum, some of the places students live in and people who live rough…Derry's."

"No, what's a Derry?"

"Derelict properties, Mum, wake up."

"Good God, Greta, please don't tell me you go in those. They can give way, you know, the whatnots and the electrics might be dangerous…floors give way…ceilings."

"No, Mum, duh. I don't think you will ever have to worry about living in one."

"That's good, darling. I can't see Delly in a Derry somehow, not her sort of thing."

"Mum, you know you are funny without meaning to be…that's probably why Granny Grumples can't get on with you. She has zero humour."

"Ah! That's an entry for the diary of a left wifey, thank you."

"*Good.*"

"Now, Greta, have you learned to play the tambourine – hard cash, remember?"

"Very funny, right, I'm off to Megs…big kiss kiss."

"OK, see you later. Now, Delly, you can take that scorn of the Valkyries of your whiskery chops. And guard the house and if you are really good, you can have some boiled fish later. Oh no, you can't, it will stink the house out. If I am getting a lodger, I have to boil up some cinnamon and vanilla to make the house smell lovely. And while I am at it, throw in eye of newt and toe nail of dog or whatever; they do in the magic potions books."

On the way to the car, I indulge in a witchy cackle by way of entertainment. And backing out of the drive, I catch a glimpse of Delly jumping down from her sentry duty seat in the window to gobble her food as noisily as possible no doubt there is something very 'Estelle' from 'Great Expectations,' in her personality.

"Yes, my girl, I knew you would go to it, before it would ever go to you."

At the office, Jean, best pal and confidante, comes to greet me with a lovely latte fresh from the coffee shop nearby called 'French Tarts'.

"Gotta love you for this alone, Jean, thanks."

I love my job – it's admin, and I have babied it along with as much good humour as I can muster and like to think I can cope with whatever comes along. Unless it is within the sphere of dairy products.

During lunch break, I dash round news agents and even drive to the next town to a little sweet shop I know.

Leaving cards in the vain hope that a lovely person is to become a lodger – or is it a lodgee?

Back in the breakroom, I drink a glass of water from the tap – which is all I can afford – and tell Jean, "I'm gonna try for a lodger."

"That's a brilliant idea. It's really popular these days."

At five, Jean waves from her desk, and I also pack up. Driving to the high street, I park up and with great trepidation, approach the ATM, which seems to loom up out of the misty rain like a great and menacing warrior at the head of the damned.

"Thirty-two sodding quid."

At home, I go through all my clothes. Then the cupboards – why is it always old tins of peas and beans at the back of the kitchen units. Then with gloves on, go down the sides of all the furniture.

Which happily yields £4 10p and a few fluffy sweets, two pencils of the old school variety and a rubber. There are also items which do not carry a valid description.

Then I had a brainwave and ran upstairs with Delly on my heels – she likes to think we are hunting and this is sort of in for the kill so to speak. I pull open the store cupboard door and after the usual cascade of old bits and bobs, sweaters with holes in ancient paperbacks with lurid covers has subsided, dig down, down, down until I hit pay dirt – the Christmas hamper.

Oh, glorious food. Pickles of various types; pickled onions like vacant eyes stare back as if in menacing mood. Yes, and wonder of wonders, those fabulous chocolates with boozy centres, a winning combination of chocolate and liqueurs, delightfully expensive with individual wrappers that remind me of being a little girl in France and making them into little wine goblets for a fairy castle with Uncle Mourier. A pack of stale crackers. Cheese in a jar that I open for Delly's inspection. She sniffs with great interest. To round off this treasure, 'we' find peaches in brandy, a must in all good circles and kitchens.

"Right, Delly darling, supper will be but the work of a moment."

Friday evening finds me with Delly as supervisor making up boxes for the 'boot it all out' stall. Our house has taken on the air of shell shock with nude walls, shelves and closets. I'm taking no prisoners. Ray's stuff is the first to go in the boxes. I go through his suits with a fine-tooth comb and search waistcoats and pockets for money. Not a bean. I must say though the house is looking elegant with minimum ornamentation. Delly enjoys sitting in the boxes. Bless.

I go to bed exhausted and damp from excessive exfoliation. Off with the old and on with the new. A sleepy glow is ruined by clomp, clomp, clomp. Greta home again, in high heels again, in the early hours again. Death of daughter will end up in local rag at this rate.

I yell from under the duvet, "Take those bloody heels off and get into bed, NOW."

Not a polite way to greet one's offspring. A few oaths hang like fine mist in the air. I return to sleep muttering, "Thirty-two sodding quid!"

Breakfast consists of peaches in brandy with a whisky liqueur. Cheese that could lay a road on its own, and a stale cracker. Eventually, Greta flops in wearing very little. I have learned to be silent and arch one brow. Not an easy thing to do.

"Sorry about last night, Mum. I keep forgetting you have work."

"It's Saturday, darling, I'm doing the 'boot it all out' stall. Anything you need to sell, now's the time."

"Oh right, good thinking. Oh bloody hell, Mum, these are Dad and Gran's things."

"Yep."

I escape further investigational reports and check the answer machine. A message of garbled accusations from Granny Grumblings punctuated with 'my girl'. I clear everything and reset it for my new lodger – or is it lodgee?

Waking up without Delly anywhere to be seen or heard is so refreshing – Greta has the unwanted cat breath in the face alarm. Somehow, I do get myself up and doing a fairly normal get ready. The other side of the bed is now looking rather odd. Then I recall who used to be there and is now in the arms of 'Dairyman Dan'…or whoever he is. My car is packed to the gunnels with what looks very like our entire home. Oh, but wait a second, it is our entire home – silly me.

Greta is up and although bleary eyed, is smiling…a knowing smile.

"Mum, what is all this stuff in the hamper. I'm not eating any of this garbage, it's all out of date and besides, we can get food there."

"Good morning to you too darling daughter…Delly get down from the draining board or I will sell you first.

FOR SALE:
ONE USELESS MOGGY WHO WON'T EAT ANYTHING BUT EXPENSIVE FOOD AND/OR CHRISTMAS HAMPER CHEESE ETC.
TWO POUNDS FIFTY PENCE."

"Oh, Mum, she's so sweet, look at her drinking the tap water."

"Yes, wonderfully clever, especially as there is a perfectly fresh bowl of water on the floor…on the floor, Delly, or is that alien country now!!! Greta, we can't have a lodger with such an awful cat, what will they think?"

"What time do you want to leave, Mum?"

"Ten seconds ago."

We drive to the appointed field and are alarmed at the amount of people. Greta is already hungry and only shuts up when I offer her a chocolate with crème de menthe. We set up the peculiar fold up and fold out and watch your fingers as you do so tables from darling Meg's mum. Something is alright in the universe, just not this universe. We sell Granny Grumplings' stuff very quickly and are chuffed to get forty pounds for the quilt she told us was made by nuns in a posh convent in France. Liar, liar pants on fire – I find a label saying 'made in China'. Thank you, Chinese nuns, is what I say.

A very smart man with furtive eyes buys nearly every book, each volume quietly checked by me in case the odd intimate letter or five-pound note has been left inside. No such luck. We are both starving hungry and as the coffers are filling, I relent and send Greta on a scouting mission for nice hot tea and cheap, filling food. When she comes back, she is triumphant with a man in tow.

"Mum, meet David, he wants to buy some of our scarves and old sweaters."

I love the way young people can rally round at times and the lovely David goes off totally happy with armfuls of scarves from the range on the table which looked like gaudy theatre-goers on a spree. The sweater pile is down to one manky green one. I march up to it and change the label to make it cheaper than a duster. This works and now I am alone, as Greta is doing what Greta does best: spending my money.

We actually get nearly two hundred quid for the day minus expenses, and turn a blind eye to the fact that my hubby's clothes bore the worst of the make 'em cheap brunt. We drive back home with laughter and singing. Delly is in meltdown and so I open her some tuna which we bought when stopping at the local supermarket and buying supplies. Greta is thrilled as she now can have her fill of cream eclairs and we laugh about this most unusual of days.

Well, we shan't starve or have to go and speak to bank managers or sell our souls, body bits or dress up as French maids or whatever has to be done to keep our home that we can't really afford to live in anymore. This fact keeps sneaking up on me and the thought of a lodger is the only hope – funny how a stranger quite possibly is out there somewhere who we don't know, could be the saving of us. Sobering stuff this. I fall asleep with Delly making a sultana cake in my back, which is brilliant as it's already easing off the aches from standing at 'the boot it all out stall' all those hours.

I suddenly sit up and text Greta, even though she is only across the hall.

'Greta, I am so impressed with all your help today…you are a natural at selling. Thank you, my darling girl. xxx Mum.'

A reply comes flying back.

'Just want to be useful, Mum…we make a good team…glad you did not sell your clothes, you will need them to find and get a new man in your life. Night night xxxxx.'

'They say many a true word is spoken in jest. Good night universe x.'

Monday. Another lovely wake up with the resident blackbird singing his little heart out, his own personal arrangements include a wolf whistle, and a pretty little tune that he stole from Mozart, which you could easily sing and 'how are you today' to. Followed by a car alarm mimic and even more clever, a mobile's trill – amazing. I am happy to lie there forever if need be and then the sounds of Greta in the kitchen followed shortly by the wonderful aroma of fresh ground coffee being made. I bound out of bed, because this can only mean one thing. Greta is up to something. My feet being caught in the duvet prevent the full bound that you see in ads.

By the time I enter the kitchen, the wonderful coffee is being poured and I settle with it before one word is spoken.

"Morning, Mum, you look refreshed."

"Good morning, daughter dear, I know you are planning something but all is forgiven with this very special start to my day. Delly, get off the bloody draining board, I won't tell you again!"

Delly of course stays right where she is and gives me her fierce and determined look followed by the defiant flick of her tail which I know so well.

A pretend yawn follows as a signing off of her dignity remaining intact treatment of my scolding her.

"Mum, I'm seeing someone today before I go back to uni." I greedily slurp the divine nectar of the gods.

"Now this wouldn't be a lovely, rather lanky honey blonde with a smile that can reduce women and no doubt men to pools of subjugation…"

"Mmmm."

"Greta, top marks, small wonder you're the first in the family to make it to uni."

"He's very beddable, don't you think, Mum?"

"I'm not so sure, young lady, you should be talking like this in front of the cat, she's beyond the pale as it is. Oh Greta, get her off the sink, she's cleaning her bottom now. If we get a lodger, they will think it a very dirty house with that sort of thing going on right where you lay your knife and fork."

"Come on, you naughty girly whirly, is you gonna miss your lovely Greta babes, yes, yes you are. Out you go, darling, go look for mice or whatever it is you prowl about for."

"You can't go back, darling, I need you here to make this delightful coffee. How come you are always so well ahead of the game."

"Must be in the genes, Mummy darling, don't forget I get most of them from you and Gran, and all sorts of people way way back in the mists of time, right back to the warrior queens. The house is looking very, you know…what's the word?"

"I think the word you might be searching for is 'empty'."

"Yes, Mum, but in a cool way, very elegant…good to clear the decks so to speak and you know without Dad's dreadful kitch and bricka bracka knicka knacks, it's like the house had a designer makeover."

"Well, it did, darling, it's called a 'boot it all out', works every time."

"No work today, Mum, or is it dress down Monday?"

"They are bringing in IT specialists to upload a new security system. There is a catch though, we have to work an extra hour every night for the next hundred years, which will no doubt be spent in useless gossip, talking about expensive handbags and the grand consumption of Maltesers."

"Why can't they do that at the weekend?"

"Cost; we are cheap to run but these wizards are ultra-costly, and they probably will hack into our e-mails and I shall be exposed as a drooling idiot who adores Brad Pitt. And talking of handsome sexy men, *don't* change the subject…where are you going with David or should I say where are you making him take you? He does not look very rich, darling."

"Watch and learn, I'm taking him to Granny Grumplings on the full awareness programme. She won't say no to anything I ask her in front of a complete stranger."

"What are you planning to ask her for…no, don't bother telling me, it's gonna be money…right?"

"Right, and right again. As I say, watch and learn; getting money out of Granny Grumplings is like falling off a log."

"Aha, with my history with Granny Grumplings and how much she hates me, the log would end up round my head. What you have is a divine power over her…it's the only way to describe it. You have a way with her, the cat, Megs, Meg's mum, and the Davids of this world. Can you not be bad at something?"

"Not very good with dads."

"Oh sorry, darling, that's not your doing, but it does throw a light on all that awful kitch he would keep bringing home and what was right there under our noses and just waiting in the wings and every gay cliche I know and some I don't know as well."

Greta has banished Delly to eating outside the back door and the weirdest thing, Delly tucks into it with what can only be described as gusto. No finnicky pinnickity today – how very odd. Must be me, perhaps I'm too solicitous and should just grab the tin, yank out a dollop, throw it in the bowl and stick cat and bowl outside the back door.

Greta leaves wearing the skimpiest outfit to take David to Grandma Grumplings' house, no doubt in a dark wood where nasties lurk round every five-thousand-year-old oak – why do I keep thinking in these terms? Could it be a kind of madness – sent nutty by absent husband, Mrs Gina Tantridge finally kicks the milk bucket.

I have no cat to talk to so will be talking to the cushion. Luckily at five thirty that evening, the phone trills…it's Greta.

"Hey, Mummy darling, we just left and I'm on the train back. Granny Grumplings was a pushover. She adores David but would keep telling me to wear more clothes, so I told her to back off. David thinks she actually loves you a lot."

"How much of the discussion had the heading 'Gina is a silly girl'. You could slip into the conversation that he left me for another man so it was not my fault unless I should have been born a man and then you would not exist."

"Have you been brooding, Mum? Look, it's all quite simple, she saw Dad kissing another man ages ago. He must have been, you know, going off women way way back, nothing you could have done etc. Also, Granny Grumplings cried; she actually feels very, very guilty."

"Oh, she still thinks she's Mammy from 'Gone with the Wind.' It's an affectation."

"Hilarious, well, an Oscar is well overdue. She said – and sit down with a strong g and t, Mum – that it was always so upsetting to see how he lived this double life and that she wanted to tell you and there never was the right time."

"This is strange and now why is she still attacking me and not supporting me."

"Oh, the train's pulling out. Look, Mum, it will be too noisy in a minny, so let David come and see you, he has our house number and he's a tonic mum no funny agenda. Bye, good luck with lodger, big kisses."

And she was gone, and the bombshell fallout was leaving me very light-headed. I ran a bath and while Delly furry knickers watched me swish the water with unusual concentration, I decided to go all out and make it a spa. Greta had all sorts of goodies and I dolloped into the water something very expensive and sent a prayer to the mermaids that she would not notice. Next, a glass of rosé with the last of the chocs placed carefully next to the soap dish. Delly watched every move as if she was learning the tricks of the trade.

"Better not mix up the soap with the whiskey choc, Delly dearest."

I was humming to myself very happily while drying off when the phone trilled downstairs. I threw on a bath robe and went, with certain care and consideration for the rosé, down to answer. A young man's voice.

"Hello, is that you, David?"

"Oh hello, I'm calling about the card in Terry's newsagent you are looking for a lodger. Is it still available, the room?"

"The room…oh yes of course, are you working locally?"

"I am with 'Hendrick and Lee', the law company in the high street. I'm in your village now, is it possible to come and see you? Perhaps you are busy."

"It's fine, come over, do you want the post code for your sat nav…it's WN12BB. I'll pop the kettle on."

No woman in the decades going back to Salome and the seven veils ever dressed so quickly! Could not alter my hair in time so I made myself decent and was forced to answer the door with a towel turban and blouse and skirt. No underwear to speak of and bare feet. When the doorbell clanged, it actually made me jump, which is a first. I opened the door to one of the handsomest men I have ever had the pleasure of looking up at.

"Oh, do come in. You were very quick; I had a bath just now so was only half and half."

Stop saying daft things, he doesn't want to know all that. My head is spinning and my legs are very wobblesome indeedy; more shocks and I might have to call a doctor. There should be a law or something to prevent nature from producing such male beauty to place before a sex- and love-starved woman such as myself. Delly has ran from the top of the stairs like a steam train and is now in the throes of rolling, yes bloody rolling, on the floor of the hallway exposing her tummy for him, the stranger. What a tart.

"Oh, isn't she adorable. What is her name?"

"Delly…well, Delilah really. You don't mind cats because this is a very naughty one as you can tell."

"Well, I do not care for the Luxor Street cat too much, we have the thousands but this one is so sweet and clean. Oh what a pretty girl, oh *azzizi*."

"Luxor, that's Egypt surely…is that your home?"

"Oh yes."

And with that he scoops up that wicked, wanton Jezebel cat and cuddles her to him as if they are long lost friends. My life is certainly taking a very strange turn indeed. We go through to the kitchen and I pull out a stool for my handsome new lodger.

"You have a way with her. That's the first time she has ever behaved that way. Do you have a cat at home?"

"No, no cat or dog, but we have many animals on our farm."

"You live on a farm?"

"We have several homes, one is in Luxor, that is where my family are living at the moment, but we have a farm to grow things for the 'kitchen', you say this is?

"Yes, this is the kitchen, I grow a couple of things in the garden."

"Oh, how lovely your house is, so neatly done. I looked at another house last week, they want a lodger also but the house was so full of rubbish of all kinds, it was hard to move and made me feel nervous."

He wanders out the back door with Delly sucking vigorously on the front of his shirt.

"Oh, she's making you all wet."

Bloody cat, what a letdown it is, I'm trying to be all businesslike and the cat's scuppering our chances…but do I, could I, actually sleep in the same house on the same landing as this most amazing man, so polite, natural, confident and – steady on, girl – wonderful from every angle.

While the kettle sings its little electrification song, I look through the papers my handsome guest has given me. His reference from the bank is fine and his company quite obviously value him. Besides being Mahmoud Hajib, he has about half a dozen other names, and is clearly from a high-class Muslim family. And there is my naughty cat sucking wildly at his clean shirt, purring her head off and kneading his chest as if her very life depended upon the sustenance within the fabric of his clothes.

I don't pretend to be a cat expert but a nagging voice says this might mean she is needy greedy or taken too soon from her mother. When I carry the tray of tea, milk, sugar and custard creams out to where Mahmoud and Delly furry knickers have decided to sit in the pretty area of our garden with table and chairs, I'm more or less decided that someone so loving gentle and tolerant will make an excellent lodger. The fact of him being so good to look at with huge black eyes has nothing to do with the decision. Right.

"Do you want me to take her indoors? I think we can suffer the deprivation."

He laughs loudly and without restraint.

"No, I'm getting a good wash and my shirt is close to shrinking but it's amusing, I love this garden."

"How many sugars."

"Four, and no milk."

"Help yourself to the creams."

"Oh, I have no problem with sweet things. My mother tells me I am, how you say, chocaholic…is this a real thing?"

"You're in good company here, we are all a bit that way I'm afraid and yes, it's certainly a real thing." I dearly wanted to relate the whiskey chocolates in the hamper story, but the thought came to me that he may not understand what it is like to be dumped by a husband for Dairyman Dan and have only thirty-two quid in the bank. Some desperate measures must be left in the secret cupboard. We also enjoy easy laughter together as crumbs tumble over the besotted Delly.

"Your number one fan I think, don't you?"

"I don't mind really."

"She thinks you are her Egyptian mummy, literally."

"I have been called many things in my life but this first time to be mummy to English cat."

"Welcome to the UK, Mahmoud."

"Thank you, does this mean you would like me for lodger?"

"I think anyone who is obviously so tolerant of the jezebel cat can safely be allowed to live in this mad house. When do you want to move your things in?"

"Friday, if this is also good for you."

"Fine by me, the only thing is I don't finish work until five this Friday, and will be here at six at the latest, but I will make a fresh meal for us and get some keys cut in the meantime."

We take a quick tour of the house and he is thrilled with everything, the way the young often are. Waving goodbye to him with a pitiful looking Delly standing in the drive, with what can only be described as acute withdrawal symptoms is sad. And not only are we both sad, we are, if honest, a little bit in love with Mr Mahmoud Hajib and all his charms. While he was in the house, we felt so much better.

I rang Greta, but it was answer machine country. Ah…! The essay obviously is in command, well, thank all the angels in long dresses and those without.

My time at work and at the key cutters is a slow-going process of chores to be got through, ugh! Not like me at all. Jean is away for a well-earned holiday break, so I can't inform her of my newfound impatience and wonderful new house guest with his many attributes. I have the faintest feeling Jean would tell me to be very calm and businesslike, which would fall with a resoundingly deafening crash on deaf ears now my new sense of self and optimism has the upper hand.

At last, the wonder day has dragged itself into the time and date on my computer and I feel the excitement of a child at the thought of him quite possibly being under my roof tonight and no doubt I can persuade him to wear clothes of an appropriate nature in an all-girl household. Delly, in true pernickety pickle style, is refusing every nourishment. So I use a few oaths of an alarming nature upon her innocent or maybe not-so-innocent head and grabbing a cheap tin of cat food from the cupboard which Greta thoughtfully placed there, I open it…and taking an old spoon yank a dollop out into her bowl, dump the bowl and her outside the back door with a falsetto, "Oh, what a lovely whirly girly babe's she is, the diddums pretty girl…and Mahmoud is coming soon…to give you his shirt…the babes."

And the daft cat eats it!

I have a shower and change into what can only be described as a not quite a mutton dressed as lamb outfit but as near as dammit, and I don't care! Every cliche has a use and in this house, they reside happily, especially now the daft ornament tribe has decamped for good money and the cushions are no longer talked to and the exfoliation has produced a healthy glow, and I will think of other things later. Right now, the doorbell is clanging and it's…

"David."

"Woweee! Greta said you were looking great these days."

"All handsome men paying compliments even if fibbers are welcome tonight."

He produced a rather sorry looking bunch of flowers.

"They didn't do too well on the bike, I'm afraid. Shall stick 'em in water before they really give up?"

"Yes, if you like. Do you want a beer or are you a strictly tea only when in-charge of a bike?"

"Na, beer is brill."

"Have you spoken to Greta at all, David? Every time I call, it takes me direct to answer machine. I have a feeling that the essay is paramount at present, which is most unusual in student life."

"Same for me, I'm afraid, so sorry, no can't help you there, Gina. By the way, Greta has the old ex hubby address and is texting you or emailing, I'm not sure which. She mentioned something about stick the bill to him, and you would know what that means. Great cool beer by the way."

"Here's to the future, David, may it be a rosy one. I'm waiting on a lodger called Mahmoud…! I think he might be moving in tonight."

"Quick work. Does he have the right credentials?"

"Yes, he is one of the handsomest men I have seen. But all jokes to one side, Mahmoud is only allowed with his working permit to stay for a year, and three months of that is gone already, so this means I can only at best have funds coming in for that length of time."

"Sorry to butt in on this, but what about the old ex? Surely while Greta…you know."

"Yes, partly responsible I suppose, but taking him to court or whatever I have to do is beyond my means. No guarantee they will look with favour upon me, and don't forget the house will most likely have to be sold to allow him his share."

"Marriage for some women is a rum deal."

"We marry with the best of intentions, and when the husband goes off you, David, it's regarded as sheer bad luck and if it's the milkman he prefers…well, that's tough, but life serves up these dirty curves. We just have to weather it. My husband was never very affectionate with me. After Greta was born, he seemed to feel neglected, I could tell, but what can a woman do…babes have to be fed and fussed over."

"Greta is such a livewire. You did a pretty good job, I would say."

"You noticed. Oh, David, do stay. I think that's a car, and Mahmoud is due any second, I bet you that's him."

"Oh, do you think he might like a hand shifting his gear?"

We all trotted out with Delly hot on our heels, at the sight of Mahmoud stepping out of his smart and very well loaded-up car, she shot forward and began 'talking' to him in such an endearing way, we all started laughing. For the first time, I loved her for this – wonderful beginning and breaking the ice. Delly, the welcoming committee…how strange.

"Hey, Mahmoud. David is a friend of Greta's and thought you might like a hand."

"Oh, my God. Yes, hello, hello everyone and the little Delly. Oh, how she talks. Oh, darling, you missed me?"

We soon had the car emptied and while they trudged to and fro with the last of the goods, I was happy to finish preparing the meal and added extra for David for his kind efforts. The footsteps and laughter overhead were filling the house with such happiness and youthful good nature, I began to feel my body actually relax after what seemed like nineteen years of apprehension. Now it was my, or I should say 'our', new lives opening out into the great unknown – and the best part of it was: I was happy.

They soon trudged down again with Delly in Mahmoud's arms of course sucking upon his T-shirt.

"Right, folks, wash up and get tucked in."

"Oh, nothing like a good hot spud. Do you have grub like this in Luxor, Mahmoud?"

"We eat many things like this. My mum has to make food without hot spice for me, I hate it."

"That's pretty unusual, isn't it?"

"MMMM, I suppose so, but I love the green food. You might say I like all green food."

"When I was at uni, we lived on all this terribly cheap food like kippers."

"Oh, kippers, what is this, I don't know it."

"Lucky you, they have so many bloody small bones you have to watch out and not choke to death."

"Yes, and I think David forgot to tell you, Mahmoud, that they are bright yellowy orange and stink when you cook them."

"Do you think I would like them?"

"Well, I find them tasty but salty, and some mighty smoky flavoured. The Scottish kipper is the best, wouldn't you say, David?"

"Anything is best when you're stretching a student loan for months…lost weight."

"But did you gain a degree?"

The laughter exploded once more into the house and Delly took fright and whizzed out the back door.

"Call of the wild."

And we all exploded with laughter again.

David helped clear up, what an angel he's turning out to be. What I like about him is how easily and naturally he's fitted in with us all and our new extended family. *That's it*, I thought, *we have a new family.* It's all bloody marvellous, I can't quite take it all in. Granny Grumplings should be flying in on her broom stick very soon and twitching her nose.

The house finally settled down to just the odd scuffle and bump as Mahmoud finished off his unpacking and Delly showed up like the bad penny – no, wait, she is becoming a real asset. I waved David off on his bike, and Delly began prancing round me for food, so I served it Greta style: a quick dollop in the bowl outside the back door…with silly falsetto voice.

"There is the little girly pearly whirly, diddums dafty dumdums, and she is so clever to chew Mahmoud's shirt into a useless rag."

Well, praise given where praise due I always say, and that nutty cat Delly furry knickers starts to gobble up the food, no more draining boards or fussy eating. Life has suddenly become very interesting and without the hubby…I am actually happy. Who could have predicted this?

Getting back on track and going to work the following Monday was a very different story however.

The whole office was in uproar. And the MD was on the war path about the huge cost of our computer security updates; the 'atrocious cost' was certainly banded about – and not like chocolates, I can tell you.

We were all called in one by one for various lectures, high jumps on the carpets, and a nasty line or two as well as every Anglo-Saxon alphabetical oath thrown in for good measure.

I mean expletives are very hard to take down in the minute book.

Jean was so pale, I thought, *she was ill*. But she was so terribly shaken up…poor dear soul.

Chapter Two

We are sitting quietly watching a fascinating documentary when Granny Grumplings decided to give her broomstick an airing. To make matters worse, Mahmoud answers the door in a T-shirt and sexy Egyptian cotton shorts which make him look like the centrefold of an upmarket girly mag and some downmarket ones as well.

From the lounge I hear, "Who are you?"

That's right, Gran, you pour on some old-world charm.

"I'm Mrs Tantridge's grandmother."

"Do come through."

"Hello, Gran, this is our lovely Mahmoud, he's staying with us while he studies International Law. He is a godsend and Delly wants to marry him."

"What rot are you talking now?"

"Manners, Grandmama."

"What sort of name is that, how do you say it?"

"Just as it sounds. Gina knows how to say it…very well. I will make you tea."

"What sort of name is that…why's he here, nobody tells me anything."

"Mahmoud is a lovely name and Mahmoud is a lovely young man. Please stop being so offensive, it's not as if there are people rushing in from all directions to help pay for the running of the house, Gran, and we feel lucky to have such a pleasant young person in the house! Don't know if you have noticed but hubby has run off with the milkman and I don't know what he is about to do. I have no idea where he is or how we are to move forward. So, in this crisis, ease off with the strange remarks."

"Oh, what about me, can't you talk to me?"

"Greta is the expert in that field."

"I'm sorry, Gina, it's been dreadful knowing that he was, you know, leaning in the other direction and truly, I have just not known how to tell you. Let's not act like this is an everyday sort of thing in our family. He's not normal. We were *fooled*."

"Thanks for that, Gran, but it seems to be happening more often these days than you could imagine, it's our new society, so let's try to be civil with each other from now on."

Mahmoud comes in wearing the smile that can melt ice. And quietly proceeds to pour Gran tea just the way she likes it and offers a plate of custard creams with a dusting of hobnobs.

"Thank you, dear, I will have to call you that. I don't think I'm quite up to funny names today. You have lovely manners. Where's your home 'cus it's not here, that I do know."

"Luxor."

Gran could have knocked us all over with half a feather with her next remark.

"I went there a long time ago; you want to know how and why, I suppose. I had a boyfriend serving in the British Army there and he was raving on about it so much. I told him to send us some money and I would save up the other bit and go there to see it for myself, and we went to the pyramids."

"Oh, my God, you have stayed in my country!!! This is very big news to me."

"I don't show off all I have done like some people."

"Did you like what you saw? What was your favourite place?"

"Hold your horses, dear. We only had a week to do everything and I went into the desert and rode a lovely creamy coloured camel. Oh, it was so funny; it kept breaking wind. Not the most romantic thing for a youngster like me to experience but my boyfriend, Jo, he was a bit of a card, you see. He negotiated a price with the keeper and we managed to go right over to this village on these camels. Mine was called *Habibibby* or some such funny name, and as for laugh, well, I think we had tears running down our cheeks from start to finish."

Mahmoud is open-mouthed and I am looking at her with renewed interest.

"Do you remember the name of the village?"

"No, bless you, I was too busy laughing and trying to stay on this camel, and Jo kept urging it to go faster, and the faster it went, the more its back end made these horrible noises and then when it saw some what must have been lady camels, it made noises at the front end as well and we had tears streaming. I have never laughed so much in my life! I—"

29

"Oh, Gran, stop, where are the tissues?"

"We had these funny men come up to us with things round their heads sort of wound round and round and one of them began trying to help me off this windy camel, and oh the racket 'cus all the people came forward and we had this big dinner in a tent on the floor, well no, not the floor, what I mean is like the sand, but it was covered in cloths and rugs and things hung up all very colourful. The food was like I never saw before and tasted really good. I was hungry I suppose. Do you have any more tea in that pot, dear, and only two sugars this time, thanks."

After this wonderful story, we went very quiet. Sipped our tea and I suppose the shock had to sink in so to speak.

"Well, dear, I have to go now. I'm meeting Edna for a walk round the shops. She's had a very big windfall and wants to buy a new television. You know the big screen type. She says it will be like being in the pictures, I can't wait 'cus I'm first to see this film she's getting set up…like you watch."

"You could get one just like it, Gran."

"Oh, I know but my set is still good and you get used to the size. These really big ones mean you have to move all the furniture about."

"We could help you do that if you asked us…just tell us. Thanks for coming, Gran, and for the story about the camel…I really had no idea you had such an adventure. Come and have a hug."

"I don't want a hug. You are too sloppy you know, Gina, it's your worse fault, you need to be more coolheaded."

And with that reverting back to her nit-picking old self, she donned her coat and walked briskly out to the hall. Delly was watching her slit-eyed from the stairs, as she allowed Mahmoud to open the door and without a backward glance, left.

"That was Gran."

"She is very much the secret person; I think you would say."

"Mahmoud, with your usual accuracy about people, you have hit it right on the head."

"I don't know if I could live with this lady but a small visit is very funny."

"Quite."

"Right, come on, Mahmoud, and let's look at this restaurant you keep talking about in Brighton. Did you say it's called Mascara?"

"Absolute. Gina, you will love it, they have very good dancers of Egyptian *baksa shabi* and the food is very good."

"Will it be authentic; you know all tasty and spicy?"

"They will make for you just as you like. But, Gina, do not ask for hot and spicy because for the first time it may be, you know, too much for you. I don't like for myself the too much hot."

"This is such a revelation for me. It just goes to show you can't assume anything and you really don't know people. Life truly is full of big surprises. Well, it is now. To be honest, Mahmoud, I'm really glad that my husband ran off with that daft milkman."

It's only Monday I keep reminding myself, for it really was as if the gods of the sods law had been having a meeting the night of my happy new life decisions. The outcome was as horrible as any outcome could be. Jean was waving wildly to me from the breakroom, not her usual calm self at all, and I was jittery for no reason at all.

"Hello, Jean, what's up?"

"We saw Ray with his new boyfriend, just as we were finishing off our coffee in the high street yesterday, you know in that brandnew place with all the fancy furniture. He came in with him. They were very distant I thought with each other."

"Did he say hello to you?"

"Oh no, we were behind one of those enormous plants they have as part of the decor. To be honest, Gina, it would have been very awkward you know for all of us, all round so to speak."

"Well, it's bound to happen. Greta has sent me an email with his new address. Granny Grumplings has called by for a tea and biscuits visit, empty-handed for all her supposed concern. She has been rude to Mahmoud already but did make amends for that. Admitted she had seen Ray with a man ages ago kissing him, and God knows what else. I am going to behave badly very soon and follow the cat's sluttish behaviour."

"I'm not sure what you mean. It's all been a terrible strain. I don't want to sound condescending and I know I just did."

"Oh, don't worry, Jean, it's not as if I am not already exposed to life's many dirty trick curves and anything else that can be thrown in the pot to make it spicy. I am prepared for a lot worse and the person who will be hauled over the coals next is dear husband Ray. I can forgive a lot, but the dairy bill he ran up with his lover will be sent to him along with a letter saying: 'feel we need a divorce.' He really has given me grounds for that at least, and 'he' can settle the cash at the courts. He can also pay for Greta to finish her degree because he volunteered all that when she first asked him. His decisions will have to paid for."

Jean had gone pale.

"You have found some backbone and that's brilliant."

"Thanks, you're a true pal. I must get on. Oh, are you alright, you looked upset the other day?"

"Had a dressing down for a mistake I had made in the accounts for that funny case we dealt with. Could happen to anyone. Timing was off because the MD had been on the war path over that huge bill from the computer security update. Don't forget we have to work an extra hour tonight."

"Oh, that's a nuisance. Mahmoud wanted to take me to Brighton."

Jean pulled a face and mouthed, 'See you later,' which meant the head of section was obviously in the building and heads would be parted from shoulders if normality was not in evidence. Normality being an empty break room and all at desks.

I sent a letter to Ray with all the points included that I had so succinctly laid out to Jean for her approval. My 'office head' being very different from my at-home head. You know, the one that's living with the nutsy cat and all its attendant virtues. The day went by so fast I felt light-headed and at the end of the extra hour which was well-spent for a change, I slipped the bill from the dairy in with the letter to Ray – photo-copied it kit and caboodle – and posted the strong missive first class for good measure.

Home life for me had changed beyond all my imagination. Mahmoud was also held up at work and by his text message, upset.

I sent him a quick message saying, 'You and me both.' When he did arrive back, I could see the exhaustion on his face.

"What a day we have both had. Shall I make us a meal here and now, and then we can both rest up. There's always the weekend, Mahmoud."

"Gina, thank you for the understanding of all this. My God, the case we are on now. We are all very fed up from it, but it's how the law is learned and understood, so although harsh, and it feels very harsh, we will have good outcome *Insha'Allah*."

"Same here."

We sat quietly that night just bloody relieved to have good food and a quiet restful time. I had even gone so far as unplugging the phone from the wall and switching off my mobile. Mahmoud sadly was not allowed this pleasure but luckily, he was not given any grief from his.

When we eventually climbed wearily to our beds, the temptation to hug him was so strong but instead I laid a hand on his shoulder and he breathed a huge sigh. I don't think I have ever been closer to any human in my life as I was with Mahmoud that evening. Life certainly takes some thinking out at times. I had not a clue this time last year that all this was about to be played out.

Those extra creamy yogurts have a lot to answer for.

Delly has sucked all the life out of yet another of Mahmoud's T-shirts – it's funny and yet not funny. Like when you hit your elbow in a certain way.

Mahmoud calls the soggy T-shirt collection his mummy-feeding bras. You have to love someone as tolerant as that.

To say I woke up excited on the day of our big night out in Brighton, meal and floorshow at Mascara, meeting Mahmoud's pal and other diversions, would be an understatement. My first thoughts were what the heck is that. That turned out to be a rare pummelling in the small of my back by – yes, you guessed it – the Delly furry knickers. She was making soda bread and lots of it by the depth of purr and all the frantic kneading required. Had Mahmoud finally snapped and given her strutting orders? I threw the duvet over her and laughed at her attempts to 'surface'.

Work was a doddle on account of all the bitter and rich being at a regional meeting. Jean and I were 'signing' across the giggling youngsters. A lot of sweety rolling took place, and handbags, mostly 'Italian', were discussed. I did warn you this might happen someday. Leaving was great and getting home and leaping into the shower even better. I was ravenous but only dare eat a snack as waistline would be in the serious to not fitting programme. I was dressing up and not before time. My hair upswept with tendrils and dangly earrings. How lovely life can be. Greta sent a cheery text saying she loved the new nickname of 'X Ray'. I had planted on her errant father. I had to admit in a totally childish smug manner that I was quite pleased with it myself.

Mahmoud showed up in the lounge looking like a redcarpet candidate. We both gawped at the same time.

"Gina, I think you look fabulous, what a wonderful dress. First time to see you this way and my God you are kicking some ass tonight."

Don't the young have a wonderful turn of phrase.

"Thank you, and woweee to you. I feel like I'm stepping out with a film star. Would you like some tea? I don't suppose you have seen the UK's version of the sultry siren…Delly furry knickers?"

"So sorry, Gina, I cannot risk her making this very expensive outfit her nursing bra."

"Quite."

Laughter once more rang through the house. The house is often in shock these days, I swear, what with a mass exodus of the cheap ornament tribe and the handsome lodger and the laughter. If walls could talk. Being happy for real is wonderful. Putting up a show all those years was not.

We drove off eventually with Delly sulking in the window seat. I think the general message was, 'Hate you…sod off…and don't come back.' We didn't really get a lot of traffic until Preston Park and then were obliged to change tack. Our arrangement to drive and park at Bassam's house was such a good plan, and we all bundled into the same taxi. Bassam had the widest cheeriest grin I have ever seen and had the habit of saying 'Are you alright?' Every few minutes, which I put down to nerves. As for Mahmoud, he was bubbling over with happiness that was obvious. He didn't hesitate to sit with me quite snugly in the taxi and when we piled out at the door of Mascara's, it was in the middle of giggles over anything and everything. We had a good table and as we sat down and were handed menus, a fabulous trill of Egyptian music took me unaware and I gasped with joy.

Mahmoud was so happy I thought he might explode. The dancer that came on was a jewel fest of colours, sequins and jingle jangles. At one point in the dance, she arched her stunning body like a snake before it strikes. She danced for each table in turn and we clapped until our hands tingled. The food when it arrived overflowed the table in all directions and we tried this and that, and Mahmoud and Bassam told me about *foul* and I was laughing at such a name. I mean who calls their food *foul*. The answer was shouted above the racket and clatter.

"Egyptians!"

Life in the fast lane as they say.

Bassam leaned toward me as the dessert was served.

"You would like to visit Egypt I think, Gina."

"Most certainly, Bassam, but I don't think it is all like this. I know it cannot be."

Mahmoud was being pulled to his feet by another dancer with so much make-up that it was melting with the aid of perspiration. He went out and gave a few erotic wiggles but would not be drawn further into the exotica of it all. Bassam and some other people gave a display which made the whole restaurant explode with laughter. I cannot say I have had more fun anywhere with anyone. When we took the taxi back to Bassam's place, we were exhausted from laughing and eating, and flopped gratefully into Bassam's arm chairs.

"Chai all round please, Bassam."

We were staying the night and that meant I got the main room and the lads made do with what was left. I only remember very loud snores. 'What a night' was all I could think before I entered a deep and very restful sleep. Driving back the next day, I was very thoughtful. Mahmoud kept giving me very funny side-long looks.

"Gina, you are sad I think."

"Far from it, Mahmoud, I am very, very happy and don't want to break the spell that the Egyptians have cast over me. Because it is a spell I know and it is an enchanted one."

"You are I think not used to such a time. It is normal for us in Egypt life, *habibi*."

"*Habibi*…is that a nice word? It sounds like a nice one."

Once at the office the following Monday, I needed every ounce of patience. The company was quite clearly on the war path of downsizing, and the bitter and rich were making the loudest whooping noises. Jean was in the office on the red carpet again and naturally I was totally desperate for her to come out and sign me good or bad. We had a little code set up over the years. My life was never more on the line than it is now. Everything I had understood to be, had shifted around. It truly felt like a giant was moving the axis of understanding. Problem-solving was now a constant rather than a rarity. Another email from X-Ray sent me up the wall and down the other side, and I found myself saying things I would not normally say to anyone. He was behaving so badly. His stupid email ran, 'Gina, you have not asked my permission to run the home I help pay for as a guest house. If you insist on this sort of behaviour, I will put it on the market and you will all have to leave. The alternative is you buy me out…HA HA, of course you can't, because you don't have the money.'

My reply was short and sweet.

'Dearest, when you decided to leave without any warning, I think you forfeited any kind of discussion concerning the welfare of your family. We married remember. This is supposed to mean something.'

What I really wanted to say was pig pig pig pig pig pig pig pig pig pig pig PIG PIG PIG PIG pig pig pig………PIG!

As you see, it takes a lot of energy to stay angry, so I went into the break room and waited for Jean. This was a blatant move which would make the bitter and rich haul me into the office, and boy was I ready for them. It's all very well for them to smash fists upon desks and threaten but they have some key workers here and I am one of them. Also, I will send Delly furry knickers into the fray, that will sort them. Of course, it's a childish outburst. Apparently quite common when the bloody hubby gallops off with the bloody milkman and his sodding yoghurts into the sodding sunset etc, etc, and other diction phobia driven nonsense. Sounds like the kind of superlative even Granny Grumplings would love.

To save me from tears, as the song goes, I had an email from Jean too, 'Please come to our house later, we eat at about seven and we want to you both to join us. Love, Jean.' She had obviously sent it from her phone during a lull in a horrible situation. I feared the worst. On-the-spot dismissal from bitter and rich. He was gone out now and the light in the office was on normal and no blood was to be seen. Obviously, the troops were resting or re-loading. The youngsters were all nose to grindstone, no doubt all having massive credit interests to repay and the thought of no more Italian designer handbags is enough to get anyone motivated under the age of twenty-two, and come to think of it, I had a horrible suspicion that Jean was still in trouble over the accounts issue surrounding the last big case we had dealt with. In the car park, there was not a sign of her car or the bitter and rich vehicle. Also, a little birdy told me to get home quickly, quietly and rescue someone with the aid of the voddy bottle – oh no, I was driving to Jean's. I arrived the same time as Mahmoud and we tooted a little foolish sweet message to each other in the drive. Oh, bless Mahmoud, a sane and lovely sight in a mad bad world.

"Oh Mahmoud, it's been the weirdest day. Do you have plans this evening?"

"No, not at present, why, what has happened?"

"Jean, you know Jean, has invited us to her home for a meal at seven because she needs to tell me all the news from work. There have been big shake-ups. It all stems from a huge bill sent to the management regarding our computer security update. Has to be done, you know, these days with all the cybercrime and hacking, and as you guessed we deal with some sensitive issues."

"But of course, I know she is a big friend to you and you stand by each other, which is rare these days. Don't worry, Gina, I will make a snack now for us both while you enjoy your shower."

"May all the angels in long dresses and those in short ones, bless you and keep you."

"You are funniest lady I know, Gina, and the other funny lady, what do you need me to feed her?"

"Oh, I will sort Delly pernickety ping pongs."

Mahmoud goes off in gales of laughter. Nice to know he's happy enough here. Can't be easy so far from home. Poor lad even has to drive on the other side of the road. Amazing how he copes so well with every new challenge. Lessons to be learned from him to be sure. I spot Delly waiting anxiously in the garden on her favourite bench seat, no doubt awaiting her beloved. I call her in and once more dollop her dinner without ceremony or fuss into a clean bowl, refresh her water and pile cat treats on top for good measure, it cannot be for good behaviour, that's an impossible ask. I use the silly voice.

"Oh the darling, the sweety neaty nutkins, there you are little Delly welly poppinuts…who's a lovely girly!!!"

She flies across the garden and for the first time ever, twines my legs in greeting. Mahmoud and I snack on some tasty rolls he made, and as soon as possible we pile into Mahmoud's lovely car. I don't blame him for not really wanting to drive my poor old staid but reliable Honda. A car I know so well and love but, like its owner, really has seen better days. David is outside in the garden when we arrive and shows us through into the hall.

"So glad you both could make it. Jean's putting the finishing touches, do you want to wash your hands, Mahmoud?"

While they go off in male bonding mode, I seek out Jean and hug her.

"How are you? I didn't know what had happened in the office, was he a tiresome pig again?"

"Well, he always uses all the wrong end of things to get his point across as you know. I decided to come clean with him to shorten my time in 'the presence', so to speak. David and I discussed it all and I'm working my notice while we prepare for a big trip to Australia…a sort of long stay…we have to apply for the right sort of visa…you know what I mean."

"Oh well, knock down and with a double feather whammy…wow, Jean, this is good and bad news all in one."

"We aren't getting any younger, Gina, and while we have the strength and even more importantly the cash to do all of it with certain comfort, why not. Does Mahmoud drink, you know…wine?"

"Ah, that's a no no, and he is driving so we live around that for comfort and ease of decision."

"Yes, I did wonder if he was you know, not allowed. You seem to get on really well together, it must be lovely having such nice company in the house. Any news of Greta, you said she had some major essay writing to catch up on?"

"That's right, all's well on that front. Just sent her the usual catch-up texts in 'Greta speak'."

"I like that, 'Greta speak'."

"I know, she makes me laugh with the things she comes out with. To be honest, Jean, I don't know how I would have managed without her, all the recent changes and the horrible way in which X-Ray, as I call him, treats us."

"Such a foolish way to behave on his part. I think he might be overcompensating probably due to outside influence, if you get my drift. Changing subjects, does Greta have a new man in her life?"

"Yes, and wait for this, his name is David, although Greta's very funny as ever."

"Ah, I wonder where she gets that from. Sorry, you were saying?"

"Calls him 'very beddable'."

"Oh, I see. Well, I am biased, but David is the very best of names and good men are called David."

"I knew you would feel like that. Good point."

We chuckle and carry in trays to the spacious and very neat dining room. After a splendid and quickly demolished meal, we took our freshly made coffee into the living room. Mahmoud was very calm about everything, and noticed I ate everything offered me in spite of the rolls we had demolished earlier. Note, appetite back to normal, note, hanging in there on all wings and prayers in spite of all efforts on X-Ray's part to rock the boat. I'm still wondering why oh why did I call him 'dearest'. I'm pretty sure Freud would come up with something. Am I deep down a scheming female or is it something to do with the fact of having slept with my husband for so long that I can't take on the true facts of the matter? He's just not interested in women. But he was once, a very long time ago, though he barely looked at me recently and showed so little affection. Oh, I won't think about it.

I'll go to crazy land without a return ticket. Also, a nagging voice in my head says, 'move on, move on,' while an even louder nagging and rather churlish voice says, 'thirty-two sodding quid.'

This must be the voice of reason.

We all watch a brilliant television comedy and unwind – telly's great for this, I don't care what anyone says.

We say our thank-yous and goodbyes, and I notice although Mahmoud is very happy and relaxed, there is a question hovering.

"Something on your chest, Mahmoud?"

"Ah yes, you are very good to see this. I am going home to Luxor for two weeks in July. This is not very good timing I think."

"Oh, when are you flying out? Do you have a date booked yet?"

"I have tried for the first Monday direct from Heathrow to Luxor. My mother does not like to be parted from her children for so long."

"I don't blame her; if you were my son, I would hate it."

"Thank you, Gina, but this is very big point don't you think, because I am not your son. I am, I hope, your very special friend."

A silence settles over the interior of the car. A silence loaded with all kinds of we know what we want to say but we can't or won't say it – a strange drive home. Mahmoud searches the radio stations for a while in his usual tranquil manner, something I have grown to love and admire in him. Eventually, he finds Bruno Mars singing in that sweet, yet strangely masculine magical way of his. We both smile at the words, as the sincere voice transcends the moment into the ether in what can only truly be called romantic. I am shocked at myself by this; we are driving on into quite a different world. One day ago was the 'before' and this most surely is the 'after'. I go to bed in a mood which is electrified and yet I understand its implications fully. The total lack of romance and love in my life after all these years has given me a tough outer shell…tonight the shell is broken… And how?

On Tuesday evening, I make the most wonderful meal I can dream up and include falafel and produce a salad taken from the internet called 'Egyptian salad'. If this does not impress, I will be very surprised. When it's all laid out, I go up and knock politely on Mahmoud's door.

"Come in, Gina, I am just finishing off this paperwork. Just one minute more."

I go in and the awful Jezebel cat is stretched out on Mahmoud's clean duvet like Cleopatra on a couch going up the flippin' Nile. Tummy up and all four paws extended, purling and plaining fit to wake the dead.

"Delly is very relax I think."

"That's one way of describing it."

Trust her to place a malicious paw into the potion of a happy life.

"Quick, Gina, before she sees us leave."

We run downstairs like children running from a teacher. Skidding into the kitchen, Mahmoud stops and laughs.

"Wow, this is brilliant, this is same as being at home."

"Oh, that's all the thanks I need. Do you fancy mango or apple juice?"

The phone trills and we ignore it, the whirrs and clicks sending the caller into the answering machine. Some things simply cannot be interrupted.

"I wonder what Delly is thinking right now?"

"Which one of my T-shirts she will turn into a rag next?"

Greta rang me late Thursday night. We chatted about things in general, and she was indignant still about what she called 'Dad's rough way of dealing with the situation he had created'.

"I don't think he is actually speaking; I get the impression his whole new way of living is very much dictated by a rather ill-mannered but wholly persuasive 'Dairyman Dan' personality."

"Way to go, Mum. God, you really have summed it up."

"What else can I do, darling, if it had not been for your brainwave, we could have all been living in one of those Derry's by now. Delly would have packed her puss-in-boots ensemble and we would be living like – I hate to think."

"No, Mum, you are much too resourceful. Have you seen my 'Mr Very Beddable'?"

"Oh, already claiming him I see…quick mover. Yes, and no, I haven't seen him for a couple of weeks but he's moving back to a mate's, so possibly this weekend. He contacted Mahmoud along those lines, so any day soon."

"Right, in that case, looks like the plan we put in place will be good. I want to come home for the first week at end of term but now he's moved, we will be sharing a room for nearly all of the summer break."

"Oh, is there any reason why you don't want to live here, darling?"

"Managed to get a job, which is literally minny mungoes from his new place and we can pool our resources and see how we can stand living together. He does snore a bit…well more than a bit. He is getting treatment for it and we hope to sort it sooner rather than later."

"What kind of job?"

"Oh, a monkey job, Mummy darling, but I must stick it as even peanuts can pay for some things."

"Well, you won't have far to travel and I suppose saving on fares there and back will be a blessing."

"We are saving too. David wants to visit his parents who moved to France about two years ago. Provence, no less."

The mention of parents and France together, stung me. I suppose coming out of the blue like that sparked it off – whatever it was. I barely heard the rest of the conversation, going on auto pilot. I said my goodbye's, but Greta, ever aware of every nuance in my voice, trilled out, "Oh sorry, Mum."

"Darling, you can't possibly be expected to prepare me for every word you want to utter. It's so long ago."

"Yes, but still, you have had to face a lot of loss. Granny Grumplings must be feeling weird too at present."

"Feels weird and acts weirder. Yes, it's this coming Sunday coming that marks the day of the funeral."

"Thoughts and prayers, darling Mummy, thoughts and prayers. I'm sending 'Very Beddable' round to you soon so stand by for crumpled flowers."

"You too, oh he is such a dear young man. I admire your choice."

"Oh, and what about your choice. Little birds, Mummy darling, little birds."

"Bye, Greta, see you soon."

"Ha ha…bye, Mummy darling, this is to be continued."

And with that she was gone. Ever the brilliant at the 'one-liner'. We know where she gets that skill from. I feel I may have escaped close scrutiny for now, but it will not last knowing my very skilful and playful Greta.

I went upstairs and pulled out the old case with Mum and Dad's things, photos mostly. God, how lovely and so terribly young Mum was. Her eyes shone with youth. Dad, lean and floppy-haired. Lean and floppy-haired…yes, there was no mistake, Greta's David greatly resembled my father. How very odd life was. Now it sort of made sense that he belonged with us right from the start. He really did. *Maktoob,* as the Arab saying goes – destiny.

The news was broken to me as I walked into the house after school. Granny Grumplings had to tell me that the best mummy and daddy in the whole world were killed in a nasty car accident – just one more vile statistic. The police, used to such things, were distant and correct in their politeness. Numbness was my biggest reaction followed by a disengaged mistrust and tantrums. I was only eight. Granny Grumplings did most of the caring although I did have holidays in France, due to my father's connections there.

I fingered the photos of their wedding lovingly, tenderly. So sweet, so very bittersweet. I put them away just as the tears came.

Mahmoud, the ever watchful, prepared supper that night. He didn't ask loads of questions sensing that whatever it was, could not be spoken of for the present time. He even suffered my favourite TV show. Bless him. Even little Delly, who obviously knew the signs, resisted the T-shirt routine and came and planked herself on my lap instead and while I rather roughly smoothed her pretty fur, she suffered the treatment until I calmed myself inside, then sat gazing at me with an expression which almost said, 'Look, you can tell me…you usually do.'

Work, work and more work would help, it has done in the past and it would now. My emails took on the slant of Jean's leaving gift and the office were happy to come up with all sorts of ideas. Penny, who worked in accounts with Jean, kindly let on that there was a certain stunning vase along the high street which she thought Jean would love. During lunch break, I zipped along and yes, sure enough, a wonderful richly glazed blue vase held pride of place in the antique shop. First things first, I made a beeline to the desk and was able to put it aside. Then with a quick photo, hurried back to Penny; she nodded and I buzzed off with a wave to Jean which greatly puzzled her no doubt.

Gradually, by every stealth method known to me, I managed to secure sufficient funds from the youngsters and even bitter and rich put in a ten-pound note which was most fortunate and surprising. He read the card and scrawled his name with good luck next to it and umphed at the choice of card, a rather battered [by now] huge kangaroo with a 'miss you' hat loaded with bobbing corks. As the last of the hours of her last week drifted to a close, my heart was heavy. Mahmoud knew all that was taking place and was given permission to attend the leaving drink due to his ever-winning charm which not even bitter and rich could resist.

Jean came up to me with a whisper, "Is it safe?"

"Oh sweetheart, of course it's gonna happen, you of all people should know."

"I did my best not to listen to the hushed scuffles whenever I showed up anywhere."

I began to cry.

"Oh Gina, look, we will be back in no time at all, you know how these things are. Then I will be in your hair for the rest of the time so you better enjoy this calm while you can. Penny knows her stuff and besides, a change is as good as a rest."

"I'm being selfish but you are the mainstay or whatever it is they call it…even bitter and rich is upset."

"Oh, I think the ship will plough on, dear. They just have to put up a new mainstay, and a crow's nest for good measure."

"Is David excited? Who will water the garden?"

"What's this? Twenty questions? Our neighbour is more than happy to nose around the flower beds and David has found a new lease on life and is packing like a fevered beaver."

We both laughed. I was still sniffing when one of the young lively boys from accounts came in shoving a loaded trolley with Mahmoud, bringing a bunch of very expensive flowers and the gift which was now wrapped beautifully in pale lemon striped paper, one of Jean's favourite combinations. The young man introduced the ceremony with great decorum.

"Ahem."

General giggles and laughter.

"Jean, we don't want you to go and we know that one by one we have begged you to stay, but those Roos need you to add up for them down under for a while – who wrote this speech anyway?"

"YOU DID!" was the chorus then the champagne popped and glasses were filled. Mahmoud was given sparkling apple juice brought in by me. Bitter and rich bumbled and mumbled about 'bloody hard to replace'.

Which was astonishing in itself. Because Jean is impossible to replace and I was blubbing and the girls were flirting outrageously with Mahmoud and the vase was unwrapped to a cry of 'can you see the cracks?' Which set me off again. It did not take an expert witness to see the genuine delight and astonishment on

Jean's face. After all the jokes and cake with good lucks ringing in our ears, I hugged Jean who gave me a tearful smile. Joking in the midst of it all, Jean came out with, "I should leave more often."

Mahmoud drove me home. Which set me off again.

"Sorry, Mahmoud, you must think me very—"

"Kind and human, this is one of the things I like so much in you. Are you sure you are not Egyptian, you are not very English in your responses, they are usually *so*—"

"Reticent, stiff upper lip, is the expression I think, these are the words that you are looking for, dearest Mahmoud."

"Yes, I think you might be right."

"Egyptians are easily moved and a very passionate race."

"Yes, Gina, a friend of mine was talking to an English tourist by the side of a taxi; she was sitting in the passenger side and the door was open. He broke down suddenly because his son of only twenty had just been killed on his motorbike. So bloody dangerous these machines in my country. He broke down and went to his knees in the road and placed his head on her lap for compassion. She said and did nothing, nothing at all, she just froze. She could not even respond like normal person; even a dog would whimper."

"Mahmoud, oh my God, that's awful, I have seen a lot of this in England. The emotional chip is missing somewhere. I am sure it's bred into the bone, and yet the English, oh it's impossible to work out. I'm too silly apparently; Granny Grumplings always said I was too like my father. Well, if that's the bloody case, I love him more than ever."

He held me close and comforted me, well, actually we comforted each other – what a week it's been, what a month what a year. Is there anything else waiting in the wings to pounce or jump out and surprise us all?

Greta arrived midday Saturday with so many cases, books and bags, I began to fear she had quit from her uni course. David as usual was her personal slave – how does she do it? Delly made herself useful by running up and down the stairs and doing her best to get in the way. In the end, I rescued poor David from her unwanted attentions and shut her in my bedroom where she commenced this horrible catterwalling or whatever it is they call it.

"Are you alright, David? You're sweating pretty badly."

"Oh, I think that's the last of it now. I could do with a tea, and then I have to rush off. Only borrowed the van from a mate for a couple of hours you see."

"Understood, over and out. Kettle on now."

"Mum, Mum."

"Yes, Greta."

"Don't baby him, I'm trying to train him and toughen him up."

"Oh darling, he's not a horse. David, don't let her boss you about."

"Ah, I think you might be a bit late for that, Gina, the saddle is already on, nothing I can do about that."

"NE NE NE NE NE NE. See, Mum, he likes me to crack the whip."

Oh, God in heaven. Greta is well on her way to tyrannical girlfriend country. Perhaps there is something in this 'treat them mean and keep 'em keen' saying. But I would hate it, *hate* it. David was finally given time off for good behaviour and flopped in a chair in the kitchen where I plied him with tea and sarnies. Delly was let out of prison and went silly billy call of the wild, round the house out in the garden and back in again skidding to a halt, then gave me a glare fit to kill and ran up my best curtains for good measure. Once at the top, she tried the fireman escape down the pole method which failed, and she was left hanging by a little claw and proceeded to enter her song for 'The Voice'. Mahmoud fetched the step ladder and I scurried for nail scissors. We met at the foot of the steps with David munching on his lunch and giving helpful instructions along with a pair of gardening gauntlets to Mahmoud, who brave as a lion tamer, went up to the mouth of hell and came back with a furious Delly who was mouthing obscenities in cat speak while she glared at me with pure venom and a big helping of 'it's all your fault and I hate you.'

She scarpered for the relative safety of Mahmoud's clean duvet.

We were all of course laughing, most cruelly by now, and Greta was giving Mahmoud what can only be described as the 'once over' – she is naughty sometimes.

When the giggling died awaym she sidled up to me in the kitchen and whispered, "Flippin' heck, Mum, you don't get many of those for a pound."

"Greta."

"Twelve out of ten, Mum, his eyes are stunning and as for his—"

"That's quite enough of your slap-and-tickle style, my girl."

And with that, she raids the fridge and saunters off with what can only be described as her saucy ha'p'orth glow. I sigh, and wish I had her dash, nerve and boldness. Alas.

Mahmoud and David are out at the van and Mahmoud in old T-shirt – one of Delly's castoffs by the look of it – is proceeding to fix the poor old battered van that now having trundled wearily many miles with all of Greta's goodies, is refusing to go further. Can't blame it.

Greta seizes her chance and comes to me with wine offering and cuddles my waist saying, "I think we cracked the code here, Mummy darling."

Nodding her head in the direction of the van where a curly black head and floppy blonde one has met under the bonnet amongst revs and shouted instructions.

"You'll come undone one of these fine days, Greta."

"Ha, not likely. Men need a firm hand, Mother. Watch and learn."

Greta bounces out to the 'boy zone' as she wickedly calls it, where she kisses David on the cheek and as the poor exhausted lad drives away, blows numerous kisses after him. Mahmoud washing his hands ready for lunch, gives me a playful grin.

"He is very under her direction I think."

"Oh, you noticed, Mahmoud, I have only admiration for my daughter's brave disposition, but at times it is all I can do to keep quiet. A very modern girl is our Greta."

"This is a way I see only now and then."

"Greta is a law unto herself and will always do well in her chosen subject."

"Oh, I see."

"Yes, there is no cure. I am only quoting her last class report."

"David adores her."

"Poor lad is led by the nose and there is nothing any one of us can do about it."

"He is very very clever man you know, he will be scientist. He's going on to be researcher, already has all the funding in place."

"And if he isn't careful, he will be a groom at a church and that research will last him a flipping life-time."

Delly saunters in and makes her way to Mahmoud who scoops her into his loving arms.

"Oh, little Delly, have you recovered? Shall we be married, darling? Oh, you are so so sweet, you would look very beautiful in a white veil."

"Yes, if she doesn't shred it first."

"I think she will look fantastic."

"Mahmoud, it's the owl and the pussycat that went to sea in a pea-green boat, to be wed with a five-pound note and stuff, not Mahmoud the Egyptian mummy with a ruined set of T-shirts and a *baksa shabi* dancer."

And with that we both laugh but gently, as I don't think even, I could deal with another 'call of the wild' today.

At breakfast the following morning, a calm had descended. Mahmoud was called by his boss, the rather charismatic [so I am told] Mr John Kendrick to attend a client breakfast meeting at a rather posh local hotel. Mahmoud looked tired but managed a lovely wave from the driveway. Greta had decamped, wearing a very flimsy dress – jeez, she must be freezing – to the delightful David's new roosting quarters. Delly was following me like my shadow. I was very worried about the amount of luggage Greta had brought back; on inquiry I was told in a jaunty manner that the landlord had evicted them all, something to do with neighbour's complaints.

Well, there's a surprise, and so at the first opportunity to legally nose around on the pretext of a fresh linen delivery, we entered the forbidden city. Ah! I was confronted by the minotaur's labyrinth. The narrowest of narrow paths led to the hand basin, one to the bed and another blocked by a huge suitcase which looked like it could have housed a bear, and finally a track of minute proportions to the wardrobe.

Delly, who loved adventure, skipped about, nose a'twitch, and after a few leaps here and there, came back to me with the expression that said 'all clear.'

"Thank you, Delly darling, what would I do without your leap ability. Well, I am not paying the admission fee of a bruised shin to get to the bed, so I will leave her clean things right here."

And with that, I planked them on the nearest books and boxes wall. We beat a retreat to the comparative safety of another coffee and a hunt about for any sweet things in the kitchen. We made a beeline with all our goodies on a big tray to the dappled seating area under the trees in the garden, where I exhaled and helped myself to an enormous piece of cake. What fib *is* this…what illusion am I working under now. My waistline would never survive. So, I reluctantly cut it in half and hid the other half behind the coffee pot for later. Delly found a few jobs to do in the garden and I joined in to root up a few weeds for all of ten seconds and flopped down again. Delly saw this as the sign for her to sit on the other seat and contemplate the antics of a small copper butterfly – *Lycaena*

Phlaeas. The only reason I recall it so well is the fact it sounds like lice n fleas, and as schoolgirls we were amused by this.

Bliss was king for a day and we relaxed until I heard a car door click. Mahmoud came through with a bag of goodies and a huge bunch of flowers; this is twice I have seen him recently with expensive blooms.

"Oh, what's all this lovely stuff?"

"My boss sent it over for you, *he's* taking his *wife* away for five days and thought these would spoil, it's all really fresh…"

"Wow! Finest butterscotch ice-cream, surely that could go in a deep freeze."

"Ah, that's my special treat for *us*."

We put the lovely top-quality organic farm chicken away with all the fresh veg and I scooped some of the delightful butterscotch into bowls – my poor waistline.

"Oh, my lordy lordy, this is lovely, *habibi*."

Once more the tray was the pied piper to the dappled area and this time Mahmoud was under close attention from Delly, who stretched out like a pig at a trough. This time I intervened and eased her off. She sort of stretched and stretched like elastic and we were trying not to laugh. I dumped her unceremoniously in the bathroom.

"This is a happy time for me, Gina."

"Good, me too."

"We are having many lovely times, you and I."

"MMM, honestly, I don't know how I will cope while you are in Luxor. Do you have a confirmation on your flight?"

"Yes, one week from tomorrow. Direct flight, Heathrow to Luxor."

"Do you want me to drive you to the airport?"

"No, but thank you, Gina, my friend will take me, he is meeting his brother from a flight in from Egypt so it's going to be easy all round."

"Well done, that's all worked out well."

"It will be a hard time for you I think, Gina, with Jean away as well."

"Mahmoud, I have learned to enjoy and live in the moment."

"I understand."

Yes, he does, and with that I reach over and hug him. He colours a little and so do I. Taking my hand, he leads me indoors and we climb the stairs and enter my bedroom. The world has blurred at the edges and we hold each other and I rest my head upon his shoulder. Happiness like this is so very rare. Letting Delly out of the bathroom was on a par with dealing with a demanding child. She promptly ran through to my bedroom and jumped onto the bed. From this vantage point upon proceedings, she 'talked' at us until we were in fits of laughter. We sipped our tea and when she calmed down instead of throwing herself once more at Mahmoud's T-shirt area, which for the present was very naked, she took on the role of tea-cosy-in-waiting.

Although I offered her tidbits and water and a game with a tassel, she was having nothing to do with us.

"I feel like I am in the headmistress's study for detention." Mahmoud cuddled me closer.

"Quite right too, you have been very naughty."

During supper, I heard the telephone clamouring – why is it some rings have a more 'you better answer me I'm important' rings than others? So, I hurried through and rescued it from death by vibration. Granny Grumplings was on a louder than normal mission.

"What's happening over there? This is the fifth time I have called you Gina, my girl."

"Just wor—"

"Don't hand me that phoney line. Greta has walked off her job. She told me you told her to walk into another one next door."

"Gran, until you calm down, I can't respond to you. This is all pure imagination on your part. Have you been watching a war film?"

"I'm not going to stand by and take this cheek from you, my girl."

"Well, best thing to do, sweety, is sit down for it."

Mahmoud was giggling as I went back to fixing supper, which God love him, he was steadily working on anyway.

"Gran!"

"How did you guess? Mahmoud, this is the nuttiest house you will ever live in and I can't see any improvements for the foreseeable future."

At work on the following Monday, I felt suffused in a wonderful glow and smugness was in evidence.

And about time too.

Quarrels and door-slamming were emanating from the bitter and rich neck of the woods. As if I cared. He obviously was held up at work from his golfing chums, and it was all of ten fifteen. Also, that tiny well-worn fact that he should be managing the accounts department which was in what can only be described as pre-launch of Apollo mode. I got my head down and got on with my work. I felt for the recording device that Mahmoud has lent me whilst he is in Luxor – miss him already and he only left this morning.

I placed it in position ready to press if my door should be flung back by a bitter and rich two-year-old tantrum. I did not have long to wait. First Penny came in on the pretext of delivering a delicious and slightly overpriced latte.

This, the latte, was most welcome but it felt like the nose of the monster was in the door jamb, funny feeling that. I gave Penny a knowing grimace and she kindly gave me two sweeteners along with a whisper, "I can't take it anymore, he is threatening me."

"Ah, and here he comes like a marauding buffalo."

I switched on the recording device and purposefully put my hands over my ears. Penny was behind me, I noticed, a bit like one mouse standing behind another mouse, but hey. "You all seem to forget who is in ffffffffffffing charge here."

"Ah well, yes, in that case, perhaps your presence should be required to prove it, instead of swanning off to play golf."

His eyes bulged and he began jabbing me in the sternum very spitefully.

I stood up and as he began threatening me with all kinds of dead and by his hands, alternatives to my living and standing in the company's office, I simply walked outside and calmly, while he ranted on to no one in particular, called the police.

I must say they were pretty nippy at getting to the scene…considering all the cuts the government has imposed upon them.

Bitter and rich, who I confess is really called Mr Shoreditch, was hauled off in cuffs. The fact of him showing his teeth and spittle ability to the biggest policeman as well as a jab in his sternum, may have determined the outcome. The office settled down into what can only be described as a whispered silence – a rather loud one of course. One minute it reached its high point, then it died away and then reached crescendo point again until lunchtime. Penny was repaired around the eyes by yours truly. Many jokes exchanged.

"Oh, Gina, do you think this place will ever be the same again?"

"I bloody well hope not, Penny."

A call from head office came through and we were all told to resume normal working status – *right*, as if.

Any excitement at the office was soon outweighed by the news at home. Greta had sweetly sent me a post card from Cambridge. The Backs. Her new waitressing job was not far from the colleges.

Sounds fun. All the river a'glitter and ducks gambolling in the weeds. Idyllic. Her script was jolly which did not always carry the real message knowing my daughter really well. It ran, 'Hey, Mum, this is boring, I know, but I wanted to show the Sunday walk we plan when David returns from Alaska. He is part of a team who were selected on merit. He likes to study fish as you possibly know. I hated the old job and told Gran who got hold of the wrong end of things as per. New job, reeeeely great owner, fun and looks after staff reeely well. Wise move. Xxx take care, love to you and Dellykins. Greta.'

This of course was written so small I had to employ my biggest magnification glass, which I have offered before now to Delly. Now everything more or less is slotting into place or being addressed, or corrected. Life is fairly calm in the kitchen. Any adventure beyond the welcome mat is probably not a good idea.

Gran was out when I rang, 'oh joy', so was able to leave a reading of Greta's postcard to her on her answering machine. Really wanted to say, 'Put that in your pipe' etc, but that's childish. So said 'bye' at the end.

No message from Mahmoud and a feeling of neglect has stolen over me. I tried calling him but a garbled message in Arabic was the only result. I have only just noticed all of his good clothes are gone and just a few odds and sods left. No car in the drive as his friend collected it. Delly, ever hopeful, sits mournfully on the most sucked and chewed T-shirt remnant, which was left on his duvet.

I am not so sad as I thought I would be. No, that is a lie. House not same, me not same. Delly not really aware of the loss as yet.

Some things are just wonderful because they don't last.

Doorbell ding donging brought me out of the nostalgic journey into the recent past. Delly shot up the hallway, skidding to a halt as I opened the door.

"Megs."

"Oh hey, Gina. Mum is having a little shin-dig as she calls them and wants to know if you will be free on Saturday?"

"This one coming up?"

"Yes, it's really informal, not a 'dress up to the nines' thingy at all. Have you heard from Gina?" I showed her into the kitchen and sat her down with post card and magnification tool.

"Jeez, she can write small."

"Yep."

"Oh, so she did get cracking then…told me she hated that other job and as for the owner he sounded such a prat."

"Well, Megs darling, we both know the extent of our sweet Greta's tolerance level to pratty men."

"And some…do you remember that bloke with the car that kept breaking down and him asking her to help out with the repairs?"

"Do I ever. I thought him very brav. She threw a tyre at him right here in the drive and told him to get his vile car and his dumb ass off the property asap."

"And did he?"

"He valued his life, so yes."

"Did she ever tell you about the one that took her to a fancy restaurant hotel and asked her if she would mind going 'Dutch'?"

"Oh God, yes…that's gone as an entry into the family history. I wished I could have been there to witness it."

"It was a really heavy shoulder bag she used in those days."

"It would have been an assault with a deadly weapon in some courts."

"I really wish I had her nerve."

"You are not alone there, Megs. Tell mum I will be there. Oh, what time does she want me to come?"

"Nine-ish should be okay I should think…not before…right, must get back…see you then, Gina, love you Delly."

And with that, Delly escorts our visitor to the door. As we wave, a pang hits me right in the solar plexus – a miss Mahmoud pang – of double helping proportions. Delly lingers looking down to the dosed double gates. My car looks utterly forlorn. Going indoors, I tell myself to buck up; this is the downside to being involved with a beautiful visitor from faraway exotica.

Life gives and sure bloody-well takes away.

Delly is curled up and reminds me of one of those fluffy animals you see in expensive toy shops. She is the picture of perfect bliss. They say you would keep fit if you followed the stretch activities of a cat. I have tried it before, but Greta said I looked 'bloody daft' well, as Greta is ensconced in a house near the colleges at Cambridge, and can't see me being daft will have a quick stretch. Ah! So much better.

Granny Grumplings left another garbled message about an hour ago. I have not had chance to decipher the shouted nouns and adjectives just yet. Might need a voddy for vigour. 'Tomorrow is another day.'

Tonight is the night I go to the house party. So should be fun. I lay out my most not-really-dressed-up clothes as per Meg's direction. The thought however did arrive in my noddle that this may be a trick. I dress down and everyone else resembles a hooker's tea party or a 'Hello' mag shoot adventure. In the end, I choose a plunging neck line – well, it's a plunge for me that is. Lots of hair brushing and some new makeup filched from Greta's room, it looks very expensive and I might need surgical help for any further aid to be achieved. When I leave, Delly has surfaced from furry toy looky-likey to a top-quality three penny tart cleaning her small change. No doubt Mahmoud is expected any hour in her pussy cat mind.

She watches me dollop out her food and treats and then rushes at it scoffing the lot before I have even opened the front door to leave.

"Er, Delly welly furry vest, that was supposed to last you until I get back… Oh well."

It's in full swing as I ring the doorbell. The door opens and I'm grabbed in by an excited girl I sort of know and yet until I focus eye and ear to proceedings, it's hard to tell. The front room is awash with crisps, boiled red faces and drink…sticky ones are underfoot mostly. Megs comes forward.

"Gina, come and meet a lovely bloke Mum lined up for you."

The bloke looks all of twenty – oh bloody hell, my fantasy world. It has come to life. My reputation has gone before me like the beacon of the damned. It's simply not fair.

"Derek, meet Gina…Gina, meet Derek." He is enviously clear-eyed and hopefully clearheaded and so clears off. No luck.

"I'm a family friend." I offer him my hand.

"Me too, hey, are you the one they tell me has this really clever daughter."

"Ah! Yes, well, that's a relief. Yes, it's Greta and she's at the University of London taking Japanese Studies. They get to go to Japan during the final year, or something on those lines. Are you a student?"

"Oh, that obvious…I am in the middle of changing from Engineering to something else, not sure yet. How much is her course fee?"

"Ooo, you have me there, I think it's nine thousand, two hundred and fifty; yes, pretty sure that's right. Will your parents be backing you? A loan can follow you through life…quite hampering."

"Oh, I'm sure Dad will pay most of it, he's a stockbroker."

"In that case, I will go now, as I am not in the same cash bracket and most likely never will be."

"Oh, come on now, we can take a light plunge in the warm pool of riches and false living. You look as if you can survive it."

"You have six whatnots."

"Do you mean the sixth sense of extrasensory perception?"

"That's the doggy."

"I think this doggy needs a voddy."

And off we trot over the crisp laden carpet and end up at the buffet near the booze. I feel all will be okay and we will talk rot and for a change rubbish and then when the fuzzy warm glow goes sour, I will slip off my high heels and walk across the road to the drive gates where I live and then I will manage somehow or another to scuffle my way into same heels and walk over the small stones saying, "Sod it," and "Ouch."

But not perhaps in that order.

Hungover or not, the problems of life would creep up on me, somewhat predictably. David rang and as soon as I heard the tone of his voice, I sensed trouble was brewing.

"Gina, it's David, are you well?"

"A bit hungover but apart from that, why has something happened? Your voice is a bit…you know…"

"Ah yes, Greta might call you soon. It's tricky."

"Ah, Greta is high maintenance, so it's always along those lines."

"You understand my problem then, I think. Greta really needs a Great Bustard and I am only a humble Oyster Catcher."

"Er, sorry, not quite with you there, David."

"Oh, you know someone more showy and with white puffed-up chest feathers?"

"Yes, with you now. Did you have a row?"

"She's cross with me for staying over in London with an old girlfriend I was at school with, and to really be honest, she has gone off in a huff."

"Ah well, she isn't here, but I will go into her room and make sure, give me a second."

I go up and peep round the door; lots of stuff still, but bed not slept in.

"No, not here, she's probably mooching about thinking it all through."

"Well, I would love to think that, but it's a case of Alaska and then this little meeting, it's made her feel very neglected."

"So you think she might be looking for a Great Bustard. Well, anything is possible. No one can truly predict the Greta's of this world."

"Spose' not. Did you have a lovely party?"

"I can't remember yet."

"Oh, they are the best kind. Must tell you before I forget. Mahmoud has been trying to contact you, he has this problem at present with all these different factions with the Internet and phone signals being apprehended and the signal is never that good when he is on the farm."

"Oh, that's what it is, I felt really sad. Every time I tried to get through to him, I got this message in Arabic, but working it out, yes that's probably what's happening."

"Oh God yes, he likes you a lot."

"I like him a lot too, and as for the cat…"

"Yes, don't worry though, he will keep trying. He could kick himself I think because he didn't get your email details."

"Well, it happens like that sometimes."

"Would it be too much trouble for you if I stayed a couple of days."

"Come down, David, any time. I have the spare room free while Mahmoud is away and if you prefer, there is always Greta's room…if you don't mind living in the middle of all her stuff."

"Thanks, I will be driving down tomorrow afternoon. Will six be too early?"

"Fine, David, see you then."

My e-mails were full of Australian photos and a lovely message – at last – from Jean who was smiling out with the most amazing tan. David, her kind, caring – yes, I am envious – husband raised a glass of beer and I was rather tearful in the office that day from missing my pal. Home was a massive tidy up zone as David expected at any time. Mahmoud also had sent me a parcel; great mystery and I was busily unwrapping this when the doorbell rang.

"Gran, oh come in, you're just in time for tea. How good of you to call round and bearing gifts I see, how kind."

"What I spend my pension on is good sensible food not none of your off-the-television nonsense recipes."

"Oh, we are in a good mood…cup of tea?"

"Yes, but only two sugars. What's that you're unwrapping? Oooh, can I have the stamps for that little lad that calls round with the cubs?"

"It's from Mahmoud in Egypt, and no, you can't have the stamps, it's a gift for me."

"No need to get shirty. House looks very smart and presentable I must say."

"Mahmoud, how lovely."

It was a dear little perfume bottle in the style of a white phial with a gold screw top. The perfume was warm, exciting, musky and yet still retained a floral note. Even Gran approved.

"That's nice of him, is he gone home then?"

"Visiting his family in Luxor."

"When is he coming back?"

"Oh, according to this little note, next Friday."

"Well, you're a very lucky girl. Where's this tea you promised? Oh, the cat is looking a bit scowly, don't you think? Is she off her food?"

"No, not at all, but she is booked in for her check-up at the vet's soon, so he will tell me if there is a problem."

"That tea needs to brew longer."

And on and on. I won't tell you of the abject joy and perverse satisfaction I had when she finally donned her witchy cape and hailed a broomstick.

Yes, goodbye, you miserable old bat. I love you deep down, I am sure, but as you wind me up something rotten, glad you cleared off before I had chucked the remains of the bloody teapot over your daft head. I do approve of keeping up with family, don't you?

Of course this was all addressed to the drive which she was fast moving down and had no idea I was saying it under my breath.

Greta sent a loving text, if somewhat mystery-laden and short.

'Mum, I love you so much…life sucks.'

I returned with 'Darling, I love you too. David has called me…you must let him work and make his own decisions who he can meet. Otherwise, he will resent you. This is logical, I think. You may disagree of course. Xxxx darling girl of mine.'

Delly sends a silent mew. Gran's just left on the six pm broomstick express with warts akimbo and mad cackle fully in tune.

The return text made me laugh out loud.

'She is sending me money every few days which I spend on frilly bras. It's because she requests, I get good food with it and warm underwear, so does a burger come under that heading.'

'Yes, if you get the frilly bra with matching knickers.'

I am in the middle of hunting for my own bedraggled mismatched undies when the doorbell goes yet again.

"Can't a woman rummage in her own knicker collection in peace these days?"

"Obviously not," comes the reply outside the door

"David."

David is festooned with letters, gifts and parcels, and sporting a plant which is unscathed.

"Oh, how fabulous is this bribery and corruption?"

"Yes…and da da…"

He nods to the drive, where a neat little van stands. Without a rust patch or a dent patch in sight.

"Oh…no more motorbike then?"

"Present from Dad, he gave it to me to haul my research equipment and dive gear up to Ullapool."

"What a relief that is all round! Oh, it's very new, darling."

"Yes, let me show you later, I have some goodies for us."

"It's the day for goodies. Mahmoud sent me a parcel with some perfume. Come in and have some food."

How lovely life was again, with David tucked up in the spare room. My heart soared with true pride to see the glow of the light under the door and faintest of music coming forth. Delly was not interested in David as surrogate mummy. Which really tickled me for some reason. When supper was cleared, I wound down with a book about the Arabic language. Not easy to pronounce without the expert guidance of Mahmoud…well, any excuse will do to include him in proceedings.

After a shower, I allowed Delly 'in with me' on threat of removal of T-shirt and or death if she dare be a nuisance. Luckily, she settled with paws gently kneading the small of my back and me saying, 'Left a bit, Delly…mmm…that's better.' That was the night she made several trays of fairy-cakes, which need a light touch.

I met up with David in the kitchen next morning, both a bit bleary-eyed. He, bless his muddy old researcher on the riverbank boots, was making fresh coffee, dressed in old faded cords and one of X-Ray's cast-off sweaters; correction, one of the collections of 'boot it all out' fame. How very odd to see it here again.

"Good morning, David. This is the way to a woman's heart."

The coffee was handed over without stint or ceremony.

"Enjoy…good morning, Gina. Do you have plans?"

"Delightfully nil…nothing, now."

"Good, we can chill together."

I handed him Mahmoud's gift with wrapping and pointed to the date on the note.

"Told you…likes you a lot."

"Mmmm, I'm sort of bathing in the glow of being cared about by a young stunning Egyptian with credentials."

"I won't laugh out loud, Delly might zip up the curtains again."

"She's as mad as a box of frogs, last night she came in with me and kneaded my back, very restful."

"Delly the cat masseur has to be a first."

"David, if anything is to be a first, this house will no doubt accommodate."

"Have you ever thought about going to Luxor for a holiday?"

"Oh, how wonderful. Would have to sort out my passport."

"Easily achieved I should think…it's about sixty quid these days."

"Changing the subject, has Greta finished mooching? Or will she be coming here with tales of drunkenness and cruelty?"

"The latter. Forgiving is low on her list for chatting to any girl. I have to be very careful. Even in Cambridge it was a no go."

"I suspect your lovely blonde hair and gangly good looks plus intellectual prowess attract a lot of attention. Is that too much flattery for a morning?" His laughter produced a startled Delly who was poised now for flight. Front paw raised and pointed toward curtains. I playfully nodded in her direction. David replied in hushed tones.

"I keep forgetting…that's such a funny cat. Do you think she was a nervy prima donna in a past life?"

"Several nervy prima donnas I should think with a scatty actor thrown in on Sundays just for good measure."

"One thing is sorted; I have not snored for a while. Did Greta tell you about that bit?"

"Oh sorry, I will not tell a lie, it was mentioned in dispatches. Perfection is high on the list with our girl."

"It's not easy, Gina, I think you are very tolerant of her quirky demands."

"I always worry about her cheeky ways, but she seems to be very good at getting away with everything. My admiration is common knowledge."

"The thing is, Gina, I really have fallen for her very quickly, but I have to work for a living and there are criteria to be met if I am to get a good qualification."

"That's well understood on my part."

"Thanks, I didn't come here to be creepy and chatting up Mum, but I wanted you of all people to know how the land lies and if we can get Greta to see that if she's pushing everything in a poor direction…"

"Yes, you did the right thing. You cannot be manipulated by anyone. Ever. Your work is paramount and a balance must be found. How long will you be in Ullapool?"

"Two to three weeks, it's as long as it takes really, but we are very much working around the weather."

"Oh yes, of course. Well done for getting the funding in place, David. My advice is, tell her the facts plainly. If you back each other up at hard moments in your lives, like this, you will both do well. You have to do your critical research. I will remind her this end at first opportunity that if she wants someone there twenty-four-seven, then she should look for a robot. Or a Great Bustard."

We both laughed at that. I don't like talking about Greta in this way, but I fear her strong personality might scare off this clever young man, who obviously cares deeply for her, and we will all be the worse off for it.

When David left, the house settled into a quiet torpor and I felt rather lonesome. So, rather than brood, I grabbed up a raincoat and went for a long walk. Delly watched from her sentry post as I closed the gates with a click.

The trees were moving with the sudden change of the wind, but it was a comforting sound without menace.

Life is a fascination.

59

Walking invites thought. I have this experience, other people have theirs. I stop and look at leaves very closely, admiring the intricacies of pattern, the delight of holding it high to see the sharper green between tiny veins. Flowers have a certain lostness if they are picked, so I leave them alone today. My thoughts are with my child. If Greta doesn't calm down, she might lose this delightful young man so full of promise.

I do wonder of course if X-Ray's behaviour has triggered some of this. Naturally he has made her very vulnerable. I remind myself I am loving all the attention from Mahmoud, and Greta must be enjoying all the attentive sweetness that comes with a young man in love. So, why is she acting up? I am also wondering if going on this long walk is such a good idea. I'm brooding out of doors as well as in the house. Conclusion jumping. The whole point of this was to relax.

I am happily saved by a lovely expansive field, lush and green. Inviting as a lover. The field says, "Hey look at me, I'm a brilliant clean page start. So start me."

I walk over the swish and seedy fronds of its grasses. Hope rising. It's singing to me.

"Just walk over me, dear one, I have all the answers."

So I do so.

Chapter Three

When eventually I return home, I see a taxi in the lane, a tearful Greta, an impatient taxi man tapping imaginary fingers of impatience, by his grimace, as she counts out what is probably the last of Gran's pension. Or is it? I run up and gather her in a hug.

"Oh darling, what's wrong?"

The taxi leaves with a scowl; you would think he would be used to tearful students by now. We scrabble for Greta's bags which seem to be gaining followers with every visit.

"I'll put the kettle on, sweetheart."

"Oh Mum," Is all that she can manage.

We dump all the baggage of the cast of 'Exodus' in the hallway and Delly rushes up to greet with empathy mewing. Greta grabs her up and turns her into a hanky of sorts.

The sobs gradually turn into sniffing and I find her a box of tissues and give her a hot tea. With my arm around her, I wait.

"Oh Mum, I've messed up."

"Nothing that can't be put right. He only left a few hours ago. You must stop controlling everything he tries to do, especially for the degree course. You are making a mistake. So, stand back and take a good look at this scene and tell me what you see."

Greta looks at the kitchen table for a while and gradually, thankfully, with a few more sobs and many gulps of tea, she comes into the present moment.

"How does that work? Sorry, Mum, am I being dim here or something?"

"When it comes to decent good men, yes, you are a bit dim. They are thin on the ground. You just got very fortunate, my love. Appreciate him."

"Oh God, do you really think that's true?"

"Come on and eat some of this, it's all highly fattening but will do the trick."

We tuck into two of those microwave dinners which are supposed to provide no nourishment but taste great and right now I am not in the mood to cook. Too much at stake to peel spuds and soak pig's trotters or whatever it is all the best cooks do in Hertfordshire and Wiltshire.

"Where did this lot come from?"

"David brought the plant and all these 'you gotta try me before you die' dinners, and I have to say he loves to buy in supplies. Did you know he has a new, white, rust-free van?"

"Oh, he got it? His father came over and they went off together, made me feel like a fifth wheel that did. His father is awfully posh. He asked about Dad and what he did for a living."

"Oh, grief of nations, what did you come up with on the spur of the moment?"

"Mum, don't be angry."

"Greta, I'm worried, what on earth did you say?"

"Well, Mum, I felt a lie would come out later and scupper all chances of trust between us, so I told the exact truth."

"How exact, sweetheart? No, don't tell me milkman and yoghurts, handsome Egyptian lodgers and a cat that sucks T-shirts. Yes, we are talking about you, Delly, you should blush, you scarlet harlot."

"Yes, and I threw in the hilarity of the car boot for good measure. He already knew most of it from David. We all thought it marvellous how you came through such a shock and how life brought us all together."

"Thank you, all angels, in long dresses."

Monday was a revelation, not only were we the recipients of a huge basket of fruit and massive box of chocs from head office but a new and very interesting looking Managing Director, a Mr Paul. We were requested to be present in the breakroom where an outside caterer had set up coffee and nibbles. Balloons and flowers were very much in evidence. Also, we felt cosseted and generally made a big fuss of. Everyone was laughing and the youngsters were throwing choccy wrappers at each other. I managed to snaffle a few soft centres before the wildebeest herd with the helping of the locusts finished everything.

Penny as usual at my side. Bless her.

"Oh, it's not a bit like the old days, is it, Gina?"

"Well, I think they found that didn't work out too well."

"Oh, Jean said you were really funny and always chirpy. Look, try this special croissant, it's great, and they haven't stinted or anything, have they? Don't you think this new manager is a bit of a dish? I think he is very, you know, glam, and he looks as if he understands the role here much better, don't you?"

"Penny, that's the most I have heard you say without crying and I am thrilled with it all as much as you are. Oh, watch out, the speeches have started."

"Good morning, everyone. Thank you all for showing up, I think that's always a good start for a Monday, don't you?"

"Well, it would be if we could have a lie-in on Mondays."

General giggles and laughter all round and munching noises.

Mr Paul thankfully had a sense of fun and replied with, "Oh Derek, are you wearing your pj's again? Very stylish."

"Now some of you may know me from the London East Branch but I feel it is important that we all raise our coffee to this branch and the brave souls who work here. Especially, I would like to say a big thank you to Mrs Gina Tantridge for bravery in the face of adversity."

Well, you could have knocked me down with a quarter of a feather. I quickly swallowed a mouthful of coffee and wiped the croissant crumbs of my face.

"Would you kindly come forward, Mrs Tantridge?"

My knees would not work terribly well and I went forward very cautiously with all the departments smiling and watching. Thank you, all the mermaids of the deep, I had my best suit on and clean footwear. As I drew nearer to Mr Paul, I saw he was holding a little scroll and a small velvet box. It was all so toe-curlingly embarrassing and by the time I had arrived in front of him, I knew I was flushed and would probably mumble like a nitwit.

"Mrs Tantridge, it truly is a pleasure to finally meet you, they warned me at head office that you have a wonderful sense of fun and fairness. It gives me the greatest pleasure to present you with a small token of our appreciation for your quick thinking and for helping the younger members through a really nasty experience."

He handed me the box which was now opened and a lovely chic gold watch lay on the deep blue velvet. The scroll was also handed to me.

"SPEECH, GINA, SPEECH."

"I truly thank you all for such generosity…this is a huge surprise."

"Down the pawnbrokers tonight then, Mrs Tantridge."

General laughter, which I was grateful for because it gave me a chance to get my next line ready. My God, this was so exciting and unexpected. It was a first for me and all my usual jokes and snappy remarks had decamped.

"Thank you, Andrew. We can go to the cocktail bar later as usual then. As you can all imagine, this is such a big surprise and all my usual cheeky remarks have gone on holiday somewhere. But the most important thing is we know now that we will be treated fairer and allowed to get on with our work. The croissants are pretty delish too."

"I haven't had any yet," Andrew piped up, to more applause and laughter.

I manage to continue as the noise settled again, "Thank you very much, Mr Paul, and I am sure I speak for everyone and Andrew of course."

More laughter.

"That from now on we will be much more relaxed and able to get on with things in a…you know what I am trying to say."

Everyone clapped and gathered round cheering and generally making a huge fuss of me. It was wonderful, and my pride soared with my work pals patting me on the back; it was hard to hold back the tears I can tell you.

Later at the vets with Delly in her special carry basket, I felt a small swell of pride coming up from a very deep place. I suppose I had sort of done okay in the past few months but not being of the turn of mind to rely on my luck holding. I took the cat basket through to the vet with the determination to watch out for any rough water up ahead. But secretly was happily smug. No doubt darling Delly had plans to change all that.

There is always plenty of activity at Mr Anthony's. Delly is safe in the back of the basket for the first few minutes after our check-in at reception. This is all terribly exciting for her; she never yowls or yodels because she is too busy watching proceedings.

The scuffles, snuffles and wuffles fascinate her. By the time our name is called, she is up against the grid of her little 'transport 'em to the vet holdall' or pet carry – moggy mover. Mr Anthony is assisted by a sulky looking girl, who gives off the air of 'I should be in charge'. In fact, she's lovely and very good at what she does. Books and covers, I suppose. I help Delly out and we settle her on the big counter, where she sits like Queen Boudicea and is obviously drinking in the attention.

"Hello, Mrs Tantridge. Is there anything you are particularly worried about?"

"She tends to suck the T-shirts of my lodger every chance she gets. Gets very excited if we laugh and runs up the curtain…has to be rescued by at least three people."

"Oh, all the normal domestic cat behaviour."

"Really? Well, that's a relief."

"She's a rescued kitten, I believe."

"Yes."

"Well, I suppose we can read a lot into the sucking at the T-shirt mostly due to being taken from the mother cat too soon is usual cause. Nothing we can do about that, Delly. We could say she has landed on her feet and is content."

"She is also, and please don't laugh, in love with a young Egyptian lawyer who is staying with us; it's a big crush, I suppose. We call him her Egyptian mummy, it's very amusing."

Mr Anthony picks up and cuddles the purring Delly.

"Well, young lady."

Delly purrs come thick and fast as result of Mr Anthony's strokes and general examinations.

"Perfect condition, just a little tartar build up on the back teeth. Perhaps you would like to book her in for a quick once over on them, it certainly saves a lot of problems further down the line. Apart from that, the curtain thing is probably excitement. Neurotic, possibly. We can connect a lot of dots about feline reactions – at least she is fit enough to do it. If it becomes daily…is it daily?"

"No, it's when the house is full and people are laughing. We just say it's call of the wild."

"Yes, more than likely, does it include running around at dusk sort of letting off steam?"

"How did you guess?"

"She's in perfect health and her claws are fine, so all good at present, Mrs Tantridge."

"Thank you."

We go back to the car and I'm nearly home and have to turn back for milk. Bad move. There is Ray in the High Street outside our local mini market. I wait in the car in dark glasses. Childish possibly, but it is my first sighting of my husband since the butter and yoghurt fiasco.

Of course, what a dolt I am. I'm in my car so he would know it was me. All the dark glasses on the subcontinents could not hide me. I stay put though,

65

because it really looks as if he's not looking round and after packing the shopping away, he simply drives off.

I wander around the shop for milk and a few other bits and bobs like some dreary, moping old hen. It's the shock I suppose. Waiting at the till, I read the notices placed by customers. My eye automatically is drawn to my husband's name. What and what again! Handyman available, for cleaning guttering and windows, gardening maintenance etc, then his name and yes, his mobile number and a land line.

I don't know. I take down the number of the landline, pay for my groceries and leave. To say I am astonished is an understatement. My husband is a consultant in marketing and a darn good one. What mystery is this. My nature, and my line of work is solving them. Sharp as sharp, I call the landline number – no answer – my God they don't even run to an answer-machine service. Ah yes, at last someone answers; the call is picked up by a voice I don't know.

"Hello."

"Hello, I'm trying to get in touch with Raymond Tantridge regarding some consultancy work."

"Raymond Tantridge is no longer in that line of work. Is there anything else you need help with?"

"Oh, what company is he with now?"

"He's doing maintenance work these days…gardening, odd jobs mostly. Do you want to leave your number, I'll get him to call you back?"

"No, it would only be within the consultancy field that I would require his help. Thank you."

I close my mobile and carefully drive Delly and the groceries home. I rush in with the moggy mover and let her out in the kitchen. Delly picks her way daintily around the kitchen as if she has no idea where she is. I hear Greta thumping down the stairs.

"You okay, darling? I just picked up some choccy eclairs and extra milk."

"Oooo la la, dangerous yumminess is afoot."

"Vet's was fine, but she needs her teeth cleaning, she won't like that. I had to book her in for next month when I have two weeks off, so that works out okay. You will need to sit down for the next piece of news."

Greta is caught mid bite of escaping cream from eclaire activity, and is all attention.

"Yes. Thought that would cause cream moustache. Are you sitting comfy…here, have a kitchen towel, sweetheart."

"MMMMM."

"X-Ray was in the mini market. I stayed in the car and watched him pack his shopping away. It's not his car though but a cheapo thing that he would not normally be seen dead in. And he left a card at the shop advertising himself as an odd job gardener."

"No way, Mum, oh and you sold all his old clothes. Jeez, does he have to do gardening and stuff in his exec suits?"

"I called the new land line number and I think it might have been his new man that picked up the call. He said that, wait for this, Greta, Raymond is no longer doing marketing consultancy."

"Who was it? Do you think it might be his lover? Oh sorry, Mum."

"No need for sorry, Greta, he's simply moved career. His choice, and he wants a complete change of lifestyle. Hence, no more fabulous car with all mod cons and sun roof going back like in a James Bond action movie, just a cheap car that you can get off a second-hand forecourt…for nine n ninepence."

"Oh Mum, you are a laugh. I don't know where you get such upbeat thingameebobs from, it's certainly not from Gran's side."

"Ah darling, the alternative is vodka with lemonade, gin and hitting the skids, so I keep my pecker up. Oh, and the wonderful Mahmoud is coming back very soon."

"Oh, he's wonderful, is he? Well, I suppose he is, I'm thinking looks of Elvis and Italian waiter's bottom may be playing a role there."

"Don't forget to add eyes that go on forever, and what's the matter with the kettle, it seems to be going on forever."

"Ah, think you might have to get a new one, Mummy darling."

"Nothing lasts these days, where is the receipt…oh, come to think of that particular purchase, it's probably ten years old by now and they have a sort of built-in 'I refuse to work after ten years agreement'. It's in their job description."

"Talking of jobs, I must talk to my boss, he's so good-hearted, I don't want to take advantage."

"Go back then, darling, keep busy and write your essays and the time will whizz by…next thing you know, David will be in your arms again."

"Oh, you're quite the romantic these days, Mum. Is this anything to do with Derek, the teenage admirer from Gillian's party?"

"Who is…oh I remember…oh no, Greta, no matchmaking, he's a lad of twenty no more."

"But the lad of twenty stopped me in the lane and asked after you."

"Oh goodness, my reputation will be all over the tabloids."

"You will be famous at this rate, Mummy kindos."

"Oh, it's ages since I heard you call me that funny name. If I recall, it was when you wanted something; what is it this time, more money for saucy knickers?"

"Oh, don't, I am for the first time in my life ashamed of spending so much on such things."

"No, you're not, and look upon it as a sort of nutty investment. Very few men can resist a pretty girl in pretty undies in their bedroom."

"I'm going upstairs. You are quickly becoming a fast lady and a naughty mum. It's that Derek, he's turned your head."

"Greta, tea please!"

"Sorreeee."

After tea, I sort myself out for work. This is a big week with a haircut at the top of the list. Extra shopping to be bought in and hell's bells, a bloody kettle. Oh, it's too bad. At this rate I will be heading for another boot it all out stall – luckily, the tea makes for clarification and I prep myself for battle. Well, that is within the confines of my budget which would make a squirrel dig up all his nuts and some other squirrels nuts besides. I head for the shops and get in supplies and the petrol tank filled. Drive home and help Greta sort herself to return to her Cambridge abode, job, essays and all the other zillion pillion jobs that arise out of breathing in and out and being a woman in twenty seventeen. Trump is on the telly and the terrorists are up to no good again. We live in the dearest little lane and supposedly have smug values.

Delly is on tap watching duty and therefore gives that one hundred percent of her concentration.

She doesn't notice anything around her when on this mission and it's always made me wonder where do cats' brains come from. Planet Catatonic, perhaps.

When the reassurance of work comes round again, I spend my time wisely and crack on with unravelling the latest tangle. I am a bit like a kitten with a reverse role. They give me a mess and I weave in and out and undo it. No one told me I could do this; it was a weird discovery. Jean used to be so good to talk to about all this as her job was in the same sphere. Penny, bless her, is still in the stage of panic and panics quickly when things get out of hand. Perfectly reasonable I'd say.

Mr Paul is a doll…well, I'm only repeating what's being bandied about as office sex chat material. Chat that must never leave the building but might extend to the local cocktail bar. He's not crossed any line with flirtations. Yet.

The girls are drooling over him – and of course some of the boys – but I suppose after the vile bitter and rich era, a pit bull would seem a comfort.

During break time, I manage to email and catch up with Jean as scandal and intrigue always go down well with kangaroo soup I say. Jean does not respond very quickly; my guess is they are on the move and Oz is enormous, perhaps they have taken a diversion across the Gibson Desert and are in need of my dropping supplies.

No, it's okay, they are shacked up in a first-class hotel in Sydney. Their pictures have turned me green with envy. Both with Hello magazine tans and smiles to match. Grrrrr.

Text messages from Mahmoud. I sneaked a peak at them under the desk and my heart started to hammer like a woodpecker with bright green plumage up a tree in a dark forest. Oh no, we're back in the forests again – what is it with me and dark woods. Must have been an owl or something in a past life. Well, too whit too wooo. Mahmoud is coming home. I can't wait to see him. The sting of him being away was always haunting me in the background. Being forced by circumstance to get on with things did irritate. I wanted to be rich and run after him, take plane and go up the Nile – oh, what a lovely thought. Well, reality is here in the shape of my nearly empty bank account again, awful nails again, and skin like a rhino on my shins again.

I go into the break room looking for snacks that the youngsters overlooked. Yep, one browning banana. It will have to do, but it's a step up from tap water of the good old days. The hairdresser looked at my hair the way someone looks at a Christmas present they have just unwrapped and it's the very thing they hate.

When I leave the hairdressers, I trail behind me a strong whiff of the Parisienne salon, or is it the Parisienne puton. I'm not sure which. I even dare to catch glimpses of myself in shop windows at the new look. Never a good idea on our little high street due to pavement furniture. Just to finish off my day nicely, when I park in our drive, there is Granny Grumplings in her oldest 'I am a martyr' raincoat, sitting as squat as a toad waiting for a storm or impending doom, or both.

"Hello, Gran, do you want a cup of tea, will you be staying for supper?"

"Hummph! You look younger, what have you had done? I've been here ages waiting, where have you been?"

"That's a lot of beans, Gran."

"Don't be silly, Gina, it's your worse fault."

"Right and right again, Gran, it would never do to have any actual humour in our lives, would it? Silly am I. What's silly is you giving far too much money at one time to Greta, she is a lovely daughter and I know you love her very much, but she's wasting most of it."

"That's between me and her, and I suppose you're jealous."

Deep breaths, just take deep breaths. I open the front door and head for the kitchen to unwrap the new kettle and while I go through the boil and rinse procedure, I wait for the old kettle which battles bravely on its last kettle legs. Eventually I produce two cups of fresh tea. Then head for the downstairs cloakroom and change from my office suit into sloppy jumper and jeans. Refusing to cry from the sheer frustration of it all.

Returning to the witchy old toad, or is it the toady old witch who is perched on one of our lovely kitchen stools with a scowl fit to burst a pipe. I continue deep breaths routine and sip my tea. Delly is at the back door going through the aria from Carmen – my favourite – wondering why the cat flap isn't working. I slip off my stool and let her in. AGGGH! I see a huge mouse is hanging out of her mouth…the tail is a pretty pink and grey, and ears ditto.

Mischievously, I let her pass and she wanders over to Gran's stool, where Gran obligingly gulps down tea and shrieks.

"It's a gift, Gran."

"You horrible girl, Gina, get it away, I hate these things."

"What, cats bearing gifts, or does that only apply to Greeks bearing gifts?"

"You're…you're horrible, you always have to upset me!!!"

With this parting remark, she headed for the hall and swept her mangy toady raincoat off the coat stand and with a flurry around the front door, was gone. I naturally peeped out to say, 'Do call again,' but both toad and broom had whisked into the night…as in all good scenes.

Peace at last. My visitor was in the kitchen all of twelve and half minutes. The post cheered me up, a lovely card from Jean and David, the Australian sky a stunning blue of course. A long-awaited phone call from Mahmoud saying he's on his way, just stopping off for some last-minute shopping. I shower wearing a supermarket plastic bag over my hair to keep the style. Which is so fabby, I feel like dancing around…so I do…I'm ravenous so I nibble some feta and bagel while reading text instructions from Mahmoud not to cook as he has some really tasty takeout for us…and ends the message with 'just relax *xxx.*' Viva la difference.

Between his caring about me and the toad on the broom scenario, life is so very odd. The phone trills and it's Greta.

"Greta."

"Oh Mum, are you alright?"

"Yes, thank you, angel, just nibbling the corners of bagel and cream cheese, yumkylish. Mahmoud is due this evening and is bringing in takeaway, bless him, so I don't need to cook."

"Gawd, that's nice of him. I'm glad you have someone nice coming, Mum. Gran rang and told me a lot of rot about you being mean to her with a dead mouse! Told her plainly that it must be a lie. It's a lie, isn't it, Mum?"

"Delly brought in a mouse while we were having tea in the kitchen. I'd only just got back from the hairdressers, poor woman thought I'd emigrated. Gran was camped out in front the house."

"I knew there had to be an explanation."

"Yes of course. Job going, okay?"

"Oh, lovely people, Mum, I prefer it to uni actually. Mum, would you be very cross if I changed courses? The Japanese studies are truly boring and not a bit as thought it would be. I have got way behind with the essays and my lovely boss here says I am a natural with the food and the customers. I do get lots of praise for the dishes and people are always generous tippers."

"Oh."

"Yes, the owner Yanos says I could consider a course in Mediterranean dish preparation…it's so healthy and I am so happy with this lively atmosphere, what do you think?"

"So you want to learn Greek and give up Japanese? It's your life, darling, but if I were you, I would work through the essays that had been set. Otherwise, you will get a reputation of not having the discipline to see things through, which does not look good on a CV."

"Do you really think so?"

"Yes, I do."

"Gran's mean to you, isn't she, Mum?"

"Since I was eight years old, sweetheart."

"Oh God, how awful!"

"I'm more or less fine about it now. A lot of her generation didn't know how to show love and affection, the war years I suppose, and grieving. If it had not been for lovely Gran and Grandpapa in France, well, darling, they were my saviours in every way. They invited me to spend nearly every school holiday with them in their dear little place in Nice."

"We are part French, I knew that, but as so much happened I never like to pry."

"It's a lot to take on board, my darling girl. We must go there very soon. Let's make a big party of it by driving down to Nice, you will love it, eighty miles of beaches, the Cote d'Azure I think it's called. Grandpa Mourier was the owner of the local paper, and we can see all the wonderful things. They were the best. They even left me money, but I miss them more than I ever could say, that's how we were able to put such a generous deposit down to buy this lovely home."

"Mum, that's the most I have ever heard you say about that part of your life."

"Well, you're old enough to know more now and besides I'm happier than I have ever been."

"Brilliant. You know Gran sent me another load of money?"

"How much this time?"

"Seventy quid – yes, I know – so, I changed it up and sent back half with a note saying thanks Gran but it's too much to give me all in one go all the time and that she can't buy my good opinion of her if she's going to be mean to you."

"Oh, Greta, you are developing backbone, that's a good sign. I am proud of you. Don't be surprised if that particular money tree loses all its leaves suddenly."

"I want to be strong, Mum."

The doorbell was very busy, not two minutes after Mahmoud had arrived and we were hugging each other, laughing and kissing when it went again. Mahmoud, followed by a very vocal Delly, went into the kitchen with all the goodies. I opened the door once more to a stranger, or so I thought.

"Mrs Tantridge?"

"Yes, can I help you with anything?"

"I am Gordon, Gordon Elder. I deal in rare books. You quite possibly don't recall that I purchased a lot of books from you a boot fair some time ago. It's taken me some time to find you and then one of the other books contained a label with this address…a school book, if I recall. My apologies for taking so long."

"Oh, please come through and have a glass of wine with us, my friend is back from Egypt and we would be delighted for you to join us."

"But you have planned all this in advance I am sure, I don't want to intrude."

"No intrusion. What kind of wine do you prefer? I have mostly French but I am sure there is a glorious Californian sweet somewhere. Mahmoud, meet Gordon Elder, apparently he bought most of the books from the boot fair we held some time back."

"Oh hello, good to meet you, sit down, there is so much and we want you to enjoy it with us."

"Mrs Tantridge, I feel guilty enough as it is…look, do you remember these?"

"Oh, the French books, they are sweet I know. Did you find some old French notes inside?"

"In a way, yes."

"Ah, but they don't have any value now with the Euro taking over. I must admit, I used to love having French money in my pocket as a little girl."

"Do you have a big connection to France, Mrs Tantridge?"

"Oh yes, I spent nearly every school holiday with my French grandparents near Nice. My grandpapa was Mr Mouirier, the owner of a local newspaper."

"That explains it then. You see, these are rare volumes, the set here of four are in wonderful condition. *Recherches Statistique Sur La Ville De Paris* – their approximate value in sterling is around one thousand seven hundred."

Mahmoud was mid munch and I was mid gulp of a fine Merlot. We both stopped and stared first at Gordon Elder then at each other and last of all the books…that I had in total ignorance discarded as a job lot with all the bric-a-brac on the fold-up and fold-out tables. I must have been very upset to do such a foolish thing.

"Let me get this right, these are very rare books, and you bought them but have brought them back. My goodness, you are a very good and honest person, Mr Elder."

"I could not sleep if I had not done all I could to restore them to you and ask your opinion if you wish to sell them yourself, of course that is your choice. Oh yes, they were mine for a while, but I am not so foolish as to think you had not known what they were and now you have explained their provenance…as you know it…of course. Books are my life. My heart would be heavy from now on

73

if I had not disclosed to you their real value and I knew of course it had to be a mistake. My apologies, I should have spoken out at the time."

"You have spoken out now, Mr Elder, that is good enough for me. We were very hard up at the time and I was so upset. Not that it excuses me for such foolishness, but it goes a long way to show what can happen when the heart is involved."

"I will of course sell them for you if you so wish. Rare and antiquarian volumes of this nature belong in a specialist market, which I am probably more at ease with than you. I will of course only charge a very small fee for the work to in some way redeem myself. This is my home address and telephone number. Also, I will give you an 'acquired to sell on behalf of the owner' receipt. This is a correct procedure I think."

Mahmoud offered him a plate of food.

"Mr Elder, please eat with us. All good and best business is conducted with food. Or it is in my profession."

"Oh indeed, you are right. This is a pleasant tradition. What is your profession? You are not a lawyer, I hope?"

We all laugh at this correct conclusion and all its connotations at this table.

"Yes, I am in England to study the English counterpart of International Criminal Law."

At this remark we all roar with laughter which sets Delly on a call of the wild mission extraordinaire. My life is so very different now, and how odd that an ill-judged decision while clearing out books could lead to meeting such an interesting old world and yet wonderfully educated man such as Gordon Elder.

This was such exciting and timely news. A part of me remained cynical and I doubted the possible good fortune coming. The mortgage was a constant concern and naturally as X-Ray had proved himself incapable of telling us anything regarding how we should be moving forward.

I called Greta.

"Hello, darling, how is the essay coming along?"

"Oh Mum, so glad you called, I feel a bit of a chump."

"Nothing to feel chumpy about surely."

"Saying I wanted to change courses. I have put too much effort in to do such a thing. Have you had any good news? Is Gran behaving? Oh, oh of course, the wonderful Mahmoud is back. You must be in a very happy mood!"

"I'm more than pleased about your Japanese studies. Have you seen the news how North Korea has been sending missiles over Japan? It was on the news just now. Nearer to home and some brilliant news for us. A chap came to the house the same time as Mahmoud arrived. His name is Gordon Elder and he bought books from our 'boot it all out stall', do you recall him at all, darling?"

"Can't say that I do."

"He brought my grandpapa's books back. Apparently, they are rare and French and worth about…wait for it…somewhere in the region of one thousand seven hundred pounds."

"How amazing! Did he get a guilty conscience or something?"

"Spot on, not only that, we all had supper together. Mahmoud was wonderfully gracious and filled up a plate of food and gave it to Gordon with great ceremony. This is something I love about the Egyptian hospitality. He had spent a lot of money on making this meal just right but he included the stranger bringing us good fortune."

"Wow, sounds like he really likes you, Mum."

"Who, Gordon Elder or Mahmoud?"

"Ha ha. Both, I should think."

"Any news on David or from David?"

"He concludes his part of the research on Wednesday and then after a brief visit to his tutor, he's coming directly here. We did have chats on Skype. He said to thank you for your intervention on my daft decision on changing courses."

"Mum's have their uses. I couldn't let you throw away all that effort to get into uni and work so hard, not on a whim. You had a lot going on in your life and that must have thrown you off course…almost."

"Thank God you did intervene, Mum. I feel so lucky having you…for a mum, you know."

"You will make me cry in a minute. We have had a rough old time of it, Greta, but some good things and wonderful people have come out of it all. Our lives are enhanced by the changes. Mahmoud has just walked past with some freshly ground coffee. With the little shadow dancing not two feet behind him, he's already had one T-shirt gnawed near to ruination."

"Bye, Mum, let me know any more news. Oh by the by, my tutor is taking us all to Japan on an exchange thingy. We will have to work some of the time though, what do you think?"

"Excellent, go for it, darling. Speak soon."

We end the call with laughter on both sides. Mahmoud hands me a lovely cup of best brew as I sit down in the lounge.

"I could get used to this pampering. Thank you."

"Greta is happy I think."

"Yes, David is back next Wednesday or Thursday and her tutor at uni is taking a group of them on an exchange visit to Japan."

"If Japan is safe."

"Oh, good point. Oh, he's much too sensible to endanger his own students. A really excellent man."

"Our lives are so strange sometimes. I must speak with you about my family."

"Delly, leave Mahmoud alone for five minutes. Oh, she is such a pester to you, I'm sorry."

"No, don't worry, it's fine, she is so used to doing this, and it makes me feel part of the family. I'm missing home so much."

"I can understand that."

"She's so cuddly soft and warm."

"Soft in the head you mean."

"Yes, that too."

"You were trying to tell me about your family, Mahmoud."

"Yes, my father is very sick at present and my mother has arranged for my uncle to drive them to Cairo to a hospital there that has a specialist. The doctor has told us that my father has a severe form of cancer in his throat and he has to drink special meals through a straw."

"Oh, I am so sorry, Mahmoud. I'm not surprised you feel sad and far from your family. Do you think it's a good idea to be so far from him?"

"It is his dearest wish that I follow him in our company law. He wants me to get the best chance."

"Oh, and this is a good country for your best chance. Surely you would rather be near him at such a time."

"He wants me to carry on as much as normal. If he becomes more sick, I will have to go very quickly I think you understand this, Gina."

"Mahmoud, I have not known you a long time but one thing is clear, you always take the right road and do the right thing. If I can do anything for you in any way shape or form, please don't hesitate to ask."

"Thank you."

Loud sucking noises and extra purrs of pleasure are coming up from Delly who has both front paws kneading Mahmoud's chest with great vigour. We can't help but laugh softly, as we finish our coffee.

"Have you told your boss here, Mahmoud? He comes across as a very understanding person."

"Yes, I called him and tomorrow we are setting up a plan of action in case I have to fly home."

"Good thinking."

We looked at Mahmoud's mobile gallery and I felt very protective of him as his face lit up to show me his handsome fine father and mother. His elder sister who is a teacher and the younger ones in the family.

"One day I hope you meet them, Gina."

"How wonderful that would be, especially if your father is fully recovered again."

"I pray for this all the time, Gina."

"You look so like him."

"We sound the same on the telephone, many people mistake me for him."

"He is taller though; I think you told me once."

"Yes, and he is man of importance in Luxor."

"Well, if he is a lawyer, I can imagine he has a good reputation."

"Yes, this is something my family have always done. It is our family company! I will be lawyer."

"I think you love and honour him very much. It is only to be admired, this family loyalty."

"To Egyptian people, the family is everything."

We clear up and go to bed. Mahmoud is tired and so I hug him and tell him to sleep well.

It stands to reason the axis of our lives will change. No paradise can be forever in an ordinary life. The news is very sobering all round and I can only be there for him if he should need me. I cannot force any issue. Nor would I betray a trust. Life is always a complication.

We leave our doors open and I call out goodnight to him. But he is already asleep. I slip over and peep round the door to make sure all is well. Delly is cuddled as close to him as she can get. Her dainty ear tips just visible.

Her purring like an engine going full throttle.

Our lives were taking a new course. X-Ray was obviously not earning much anymore; the drop in his salary gave me great cause for concern. If I go to the bank and get a mini statement, it would in my mind be the sensible way forward. I wasn't due at the office until ten-thirty Monday morning and so that would be the first port of call for the good ship, I don't flounder now.

To my utter relief, a payment had been made. We would not be homeless. Mahmoud's money went straight in and that too made me feel a whole lot better. The office, by the time I had arrived and hung up my jacket in the stifling over weekend build-up of warmth, was abuzz with news. Crumples, what could possibly have happened now to cause such a chattering. The youngsters all gaily called out to me and I went into the breakroom after switching on all my office gadgets which seemed to be having electronic babies everywhere.

"Mrs Tantridge."

They all squeaked. As we assembled ourselves around tea, coffee, and bought bits and bobs from the cut price 'quick scrounge it now before it goes' tray. Something was most definitely afoot. Even Penny was with us, dressed smart as fresh paint in a lovely new suit.

"Hello, everyone. Penny, you look fantastic!"

"Oh don't, I knew it would draw attention but I had to get rid of the other one, it had bad memories round it."

"What is it this morning that everyone is in a hullabaloo?"

"Well, you might call it that, Gina, Mr Paul told Derek that old bitter and rich…is for the high jump."

"No surprises there."

"He's to, and wait for it, Gina, he is to go before a tribunal with the head office people and is at present suspended without salary."

"Oh, the grounds for that no doubt are not actually working for his salary and assault upon his own staff as well as foul language. The golf club will be one member short; he can't pay the extortionate fees and the life of Riley anymore."

"Well, no and not only that, he lives in an enormous house and the mortgage and that, well, how will he pay it? His car is a real gas guzzler so that might have to go."

"There's so much to a life of high salary than just a few numbers and words. He will be bitterly regretting his tyranny if I am any judge."

"Oh, I don't think he will. He's not one for regrets. He probably blames everyone else."

"Penny, bloomin' good point, you are a different woman these days."

"Oh, I don't want to come across as spiteful and serve him right."

"Not spiteful, Penny, that's never been in your personality, more realistic is the expression I would go I for."

"Do you really think so?"

"Yes, much more in tune with it all. Confident and chirpier."

"If only I could stop getting anxious, it's so easy here to feel everything is running away with you."

"Talking of running away with you, look out, Mr Paul is now in the main office. We better live up to our efficient reputation in front of younger members."

Mr Paul was beckoning me and I quickly followed him into the main accounts department. He was such a glamourous figure of a man. One you would not mind descending red carpeted stairs with. You know, the ones that curve down into a relaxed spiral, a true curve of beauty, and beyond into the ballroom where you whirl and twirl. I tried my best not to smile like the Cheshire cat in 'Alice'. But it was very hard.

I am in dangerous territory in this office with its panoramic views over the litter trimmed hedgerow and also the local supermarket car park in the distance. With blackbird quaintly perched in a small tree.

"Oh, do take a seat, Mrs Tantridge, I am aware of our younger staff members being excited today, and you have probably been filled in about Mr Shoreditch and the tribunal. It's easy for me to say here that his attitude to you all was beyond acceptance, to put it mildly. He has been suspended."

"Does that mean he will not be able to upset or hurt anyone ever again in this company?"

"Oh, yes, we can safely assume his actions will never allow him to work with any member of our staff again."

"His lifestyle will be altered a great deal I should think."

"He should have considered this…ummm for himself."

"Speaking of a tribunal. Would I have to attend?"

"I hope not. We don't want to expose you to anything which is detrimental to your good working relationships within the company, that would be self-defeating, putting it into logical terminology."

"Good."

"In the light of all this, would you tolerate a strange request or interesting errand, connected to your role with us?"

"Do handsome men come into it somewhere along the line?"

"Oh excellent, sadly no. This is a direct reference to a new problem we have found ourselves facing. Would you accompany me not as an assistant but more as an interested observer of human nature? I am attending a business meeting and a goodly round sum of money could come into the company funding if we could land the job."

"Ah, Mr Paul, I sense a 'but' hidden in the bushes of a grand garden scheme."

"Right on the money, Mrs Tantridge. Do you think you could wind up the present muddle we have placed on your desk…let's see…by this Thursday?"

"I will give it all I have got, Mr Paul. I shall be driven along by intrigue. Thank you for that alone."

"Ah, right then, I leave it in your capable hands. I will tell you more as I learn more. How does that sound?"

"Excellent. I will get on now if you don't mind."

"Ah indeed."

And with my curiosity up to boiling point, I left his office in near exultant mood. My eyes were obviously all a'glitter with the prospects ahead. One, I was to be given extra trust. Two, an amazing task. Three, it looked like a salary raise might just be in despatches. Well, yippee doodddly do.

The cat has got the flu…

We were all abuzz at the office and in the middle of everything, Mahmoud called me about poor Delly. She would need a tooth taking out and she was in great discomfort. They needed my permission as her owner to go ahead. I nipped back to my office and called them from there as I did not want her to suffer. They explained the prices and procedures. I agreed and went back to the main office. Mr Paul met me in the hallway.

"Ah, Mrs Tantridge, are you free to come along now, it's only a business lunch and as far as I can tell, it's at the better hotel with the better menu."

"What exactly would you want me to look out for, you said it was more of an observational role?"

"I'll brief you in the car."

With that we hurried into the car park where his stunning old MG sat all gleaming in the rain. The weather had taken a nasty wind- and rain-driven turn.

"You probably have guessed at part of the errand we are running. We need a replacement for the accounts management team."

"Right."

"Our job today is to observe someone that another branch has whipped up. This does not mean he will be suitable and that's where we come in. We have the dubious honour of looking him over."

"Why would they want me to see him? I'm not personnel."

"This is my idea. You helped us a great deal recently and I think you have a certain skill that money is unable to purchase."

"Feminine intuition."

"Spot on."

Due to the rain, the entrance was busy with guests tutting and showing great reluctance to make a dash for their cars and people arriving hungry and thirsty for fine wine and whiskey. We manage to run the gauntlet of the raising brolly as going out brigade and the wet coats shuffle of those newly arrived. The restaurant was wonderful and all a'glow with lovely lighting of the gold and rose-pink style. Staff all bustling with trays of balanced glasses fizzing. Food went past our noses and we were *oflfer* grinning at each. Mr Paul actually pulled my arm into his as we were shown to our table.

Not by way of ownership or any silly thing like that, or that I needed the aid. No, this was a gesture to give us both courage and dare I say a great deal of camaraderie.

"Ah, here we are."

We sat at a large table already heaving with bottles and as I sat down with the usual formalities, I noticed that one of the men was decidedly furtive. Don't ask me why I thought this. I just did. It was not long before he began chattering away and I got the 'hair raising' signal at the back of my neck.

Now I knew why I was here. He was a decidedly unpleasant character and all his confident bluff and brag did not change this for me while we all sat there. No, not one iota. He could have worked at it all night; my opinion was set. Sorry, Mr Kay, it really ain't your day. Because it's ours, we need to get this right. The meal was wonderful and ill thoughts of waistline inspections later, went out of the window. Well, they would have done if it had been open. The rain lashed on with a seemingly excited fervour. I was chuffed as a duck with new tailfeathers. My lovely gold watch glinting in the warm fuzz of golden lights. The wine – ooops, steady on, gal – was a fine rosé but of course. My favourite food if I could afford it was fresh trout and new pots with baby peas with a fine sauce. I really did need to get the menu just to take home and prop up on the mantelshelf to recall the yummy luxxxy wuxxxy of it all. Bliss and no washing up. We had a dessert which Mr Paul ordered saying, "Who's for Eton mess?"

"Oh, how deadly dull," I teased.

"Of course I eat it every Thursday."

The other man, the quieter one, was a delightful looking man called Mike Kemp, no airs or graces but common civility nonetheless. He had the finest eyes of light blue and a dancer's or athlete's physique. We hit it off very quickly and it was poor Mr Paul that wound up being sleazed over by the Kay character. Poor Mr Paul.

During a lull while the other men had nipped to the gents, he said very quietly, "Any ideas yet?"

"Mr Paul, all the hairs stood up on the back of my neck. He's too bluffy and blustery and the remarks are over-compensating."

"Right, I agree. Let's talk of the weather…subject returning."

We turned to look at the rain which was buckets ahoy and shiver me timbers now. Locating my mobile, I checked to see if any news had come through from Mahmoud or vet's or both. Luckily, all was clear. I was stuffing in the Eton mess just in case some passing waiter wanted to clear plates in an over-zealous manner, when Mike Kemp said something which made us all laugh.

"Now, Mrs Tantridge, I'm sure they have plenty more in the kitchen if you're still peckish." I had to struggle not to spurt out a crumb or three of meringue.

"Now, not even you can be sure of that kind, sir."

The bill was duly paid and the waiter brought me a little takeaway case of Eton mess due to the really embarrassing request of Mike Kemp who was an utterly lovely man…and so funny.

We all said polite goodbyes and that odd feeling came over me again as Mr Kay shook my hand. Back in the car, I felt the axis of my life had shifted yet again. I could not really say how or why but this was a defined moment. No doubt time would reveal.

As it invariably does.

Home again with the holiday mood already. In happy clothes and a little lighter headed, not leg-less or anything silly like that of course. Mr Paul sent our report as soon as we returned to base camp. Felt lovely to know I was actually appreciated. Nineteen years of service having given a result at last. All my happy thoughts melted. No silly lovely Delly nutkins to run up to me. This will teach me to call her inappropriate names. Or will it, no, she is a tuppeny tart whenever

Mahmoud has a duvet to throw down for her to purr upon. Oh bless. Mahmoud not home yet so I call him. Text comes flying back.

'Court debrief. Delly recovering but has to stay at vet's. You okay after hotel lunch?'

So I text back. 'Fine, have eaten too much and miss Delly, I should never have called her soft in the head. Ashamed. Gina.'

'But she is. See you later.'

Greta rings as I leave the shower so I grab a towel and manage to shuffle to the mobile.

"Mum, hey, you okay? Guess what?"

"Japan, David, Gran, money, new knickers, are you drunk or sober?"

"Love you…you're nuts. You've had wine, haven't you?"

"Guilty as charged."

"Dirty stop out."

"That's me hie."

"Darling Mum, flippin' heck, Granny Grumples has sent me…wait for it…you better sit down for this, only sent me a thousand quid."

"Oh, is that all? Should be up to at least five though by now. Think of all the Japans you can visit."

"Only is an odd word to use as one of many descriptive possibilities."

"What a hoot. I'm keeping it for my trip."

"When is your flight, will David get upset do you think?"

"No, he is going to be in Denmark for a month."

"Oh, how lovely."

"But he's planning to come and see you before he goes. Will that be okay, Mum? I know you have two weeks off work and may be planning something."

"Yes, huge cruise to the vet's. Delly has had to have a tooth out, poor lambkin. Then I plan a huger cruise round the weeds in the garden finishing off in the attic to check there are no more fab French thing we can flog."

"I will tell David, he adores you."

"How lovely. I have to wait until I'm going seedy and blurred at the edges. Then I get love, kisses and Eton mess."

"You're nuts, you had rosé wine, didn't you? You always get like this after rosé."

"Right, and right again. A thousand quid, how lovely. Enjoy it, darling, try to keep something back. We might have to let out the attic at this rate."

"I think it's all turning out well. Gran wants to talk to you…you know, pop round…she's sorry."

"Did you have a heart to heart?"

"Oh no, just feel as a family."

"Gracious na, let her recall all those birthday parties she never gave me and the time someone gave me a watch for my birthday and she promptly took it. I was only fourteen and that hurt dreadfully."

"Oh, I think I'd much rather say. Mum's looking for her watch that someone gave her for her fourteenth."

"She's strange and no mistake. Let it go…as they say darling, let it go. I must make some supper for Mahmoud; he's held up with a court de-brief."

"Can you be trusted with utensils in your condition?"

Much laughter over the phone.

"Cheek. Well, I can always send out and I mean go into the garden and get the last of the lettuce that the bloomin' slugs and snails have not demolished. Wash 'em and hang 'em up to dry with a French something or another. Not the snails n stuff. Just the lettuce."

"Ugh! You French people eat escargot I know for sure. I better go, love you, speak to you or text you soon, tell me how Delly welly nut wits gets on. Love you, bye."

"Yes, will do, bye, love you."

I quickly dried off and dressed in something silky and cute. The garden beckoned with all its bounty.

One good lettuce left and several wonderful tomatoes. Does silk go with lettuce?

Mr Paul called me Tuesday morning, a total relief due to my job along with Mahmoud's rent being our source of income for mortgage as well as living and breathing expenses. Greta is a student and that's that. My desire to do right by her has been the main challenge. Shock upon shock can produce tiger people or mice people. I am not averse to cheese. But a bloody good leap from boulders with fangs is preferable.

"Mrs Tantridge. Good morning, it's Mr Paul. I am aware it's your holiday, are you jetting off somewhere so can't talk?"

"Oh, lovely morning to you too. I can talk and will be jetting off to the attic with my cat Delly who has had a tooth out recently and is a diva." Loud masculine laughter.

"Do cats get seat belts on jets?"

"Yes, they are called 'feline restraints', to give them the correct pc description."

"Wonderful, I have good news. Mr Kay did not get the position. Mike Kemp is filling a new role which will be the best for this branch. He will be our legal advisor as well as head of accounts."

"Why did Mr Kay have such influence?"

"Ah, this is for your ears only. He was a friend owed a favour. The very worse person to gain such a trusted role. He was as you and I know not the best material."

"Speaking out of tum…he was a bluffer and a blagger."

"Quite. Do you have a lot of little trips planned? My wife prefers gentle exploration in local beauty spots. Airports are a nightmare these days."

"I'm with her on this."

"The next piece of good news being you are in for a major salary hike and I will be sending confirmation of all the details in the post to you. They should be with you in a day or two at the very latest."

"Fabulous and timely, the trip to the attic will be done with a sprightly step."

"Well done, that's the spirit. I wish you a good holiday."

"Thank you for putting my mind at rest, Mr Paul. Bye."

"Bye, Mrs Tantridge."

Dancing along the hallway, I dived into the downstairs cloakroom and found old clothes and trainers. Then tackled the loft via ladder dressed in old long-sleeved tee, a Greta reject. Even older jog bottoms, ownership never established, ditto trainers and Greta's vile yellow bobble hat with white somethings tacked clumsily on – obviously something daintily stitched by a blind emu.

I took my smartphone up and as Delly did this peculiar creep creep run run up the ladder, caught a shot of her on the top step. One dainty paw testing a shoe box. Followed by a sneeze and a jump.

"Quite right too."

We spent a dusty time in my rubber gloves and feeling in dark corners. The light switch revealed more horror and I cleaned the tiny window which sent shafts of sun and dancing dust motes everywhere, hence more photos of Delly.

Then I got stuck into the pure junk which only seemed to be hiding even purer junk. In the end, I cleaned a sufficient patch and dragged down one box of ghoulish delight and dragged up the hoover. This of course sent Delly packing with her new name of 'get out of the bloody way'. And my new name of 'Gina the adventuress' puts fear and loathing into spider corpses. Some had adorned the window ledge. Obviously mental prisoners of their own delusions. Now I felt that I was really getting somewhere and it included the bent utensils and chipped plates. Mahmoud called and was breathless.

"Hey, Mahmoud, I am up a gum tree."

"How lovely, is that the one in Australia, or wherever, or the attic?"

"Okay, clever clogs, the attic one. You, okay?"

"Wish I could see you."

"I look like a Womble."

Much laughter.

"What nuttiness are you up to now? Are you okay…is Delly fully recovered?"

"I have just given her a new name. 'Get out of the bloody way' is taking the popularity poll just now. She's beat, a cowardly scared of spiders bigger than pinhead's retreat and is now at unknown destination. No doubt we will be treated to the evening performance. Call of the wild."

"Do you think I might get a new name one day?"

"Working on it."

"Ah, Delly is back up the ladder sneezing, do you want to speak to her?"

I lower the phone and I can hear Mahmoud singing out her name in his rather soothing melodious Egyptian accent.

"She's staring and has sent you three dead mice and a leather jacket, that's the insect, by the way…it's coming by special delivery."

"You're nuts."

"Yes, but I'm not the one who just talked to a daft as a brush cat over a smartphone."

"True. I will see you later. About sixish."

"Have a lovely afternoon. I have just spotted a huge chest. See you soon."

The chest turned out to be a tricky thing to shift. I am not one for kneeling but I had no choice lifting the lid. I saw a cut-out picture of a beloved kingfisher and the stab of longing it delivered made me catch my breath. For some strange reason, I thought of those girls giggling when Mahmoud so tenderly kissed the top of my forehead outside the coffee shop. I felt pierced by the beauty of it all. If I was to be pierced, I would at least be clean, and dragging down another box of rubbish to sort, I dumped it in the back by the bins weighted with brick Sr1he wind was rising again1cool and strangely Autumnal.

I fed Delly who now had the appetite of three lions and a whippet. Stroking the top of her head by way of saying sorry for calling her 'get out the bloody way'.

I ran a bath and poured in smelly stuff and sat in with door bolted and a face pack. Mistake – had to get out for a glass of water. I recall my life has come a long way since that little girl of nine pasting in the kingsisher. Its skimmering, shimmering flash of beauty and youth. Another realisation dawns.

Chapter Four

Returning to our attic was a strange journey. I, the lone passenger, was entering the past. Something we do alone. Kneeling like some supplicant…with Delly padding about, her little paw prints adding to the dust on the letters. Carefully sifting them until I had satisfactorily found all the legal documents among family letters. I set them aside and looked at the faded memories of childhood. Wonderment, yes, but also sadness. Few photos remained and I took them up like the treasured possessions they had now become. Life delivers strange echoes… Perhaps I was not wise to be alone.

I called the local library and asked if Mrs Devas was available; luckily, she was. I asked if she could look through some old French notaire documents with me. She was delighted and gave me permission to meet in her office. I agreed at once, locked up the house with a mystified Delly watching from her window cushion.

I arrived within about fifteen minutes of the call with the documentation all present if a little dusty.

"Mrs Devas, it is very kind to see me so quickly, I feel very privileged."

"Oh, it's my pleasure, Mrs Tantridge. It's so rare I get such an opportunity."

"They are a little dusty but totally clear, and please call me Gina."

"Make a little nest for us here, Gina…we won't be disturbed. The library is always so quiet this time."

We read quietly through article one of the orders dated second of November nineteen-forty-five, which laid out that the French notaire is a public officer who operates in every area of law including family, property, inheritance, asset, company law and local authorities. He acts on behalf of the state, is appointed by the Minister of Justice, and the fact that a deed is drawn up by a French notaire are rested with prerogatives of official authority which they receive from the state.

The documents were of a specific nature in that they allowed for me to access a trust when I turned twenty-one. For my sole purpose. I looked at Mrs Devas.

"I have never seen a penny of this. My parents died when I was just eight years of age. My French father must have set all this in motion when I was very small. I spent all my holidays with my French grandparents near Nice. It was strange that my English grandmother never spoke of it."

"We can write to the district notaire for Nice. Would you like me to email him outlining what we want to achieve?"

"Yes please, Mrs Devas, my French never reached beyond phrases used locally (did not absorb as much as I would have liked). It certainly did not reach legal standards of speech."

"I think they would be pleased to give us an answer."

We compiled a short introduction and the main request of why had I not been told of all this, explaining my grandparents had died when I was a teenager. This left it to my English grandmother to inform me. The chest of papers were sent from France on the death of my French grandmother Madame Mourier. We added dates and my present address and telephone details. Also the actual notaire's document registration numbers.

We felt very tired afterwards. I invited Mrs Devas to coffee and a snack, which thankfully she accepted, and we wound up the session and filed away the beautiful documents. We walked to the nicer coffee shop without crumbs on the seats. I had noticed Mrs Devas was as chic and beautifully turned out as French women have the reputation for.

"I certainly think, Gina, if I may speak freely, that there is something amiss, not within the notaire's work but perhaps within your family network."

"I have suspected this for some time now. My grandmother on my mother's side took over the care of me. She consistently resented this inside the home but was clever and sadly still is clever at hiding it outside to 'le monde'. I have such terrible experiences with her. Our relationship has broken down of late and even more tragically she is giving a great deal of money to my daughter who is at university. Gran only has her pension. It's all a bit odd."

"My role is to help with the French legal language. I would hate to overstep this and make assumptions. However, I can see you are suspecting her of something. Perhaps it is a good idea to get everything sorted before…mmmmm, can I speak openly?"

"Of course."

"She does something regretful."

"We can't assume, you are right. I hope it is a simple thing that can be explained and that the notaire will arrange for me to access my trust. My goodness, Mrs Devas, it would help us no end as a family."

We wound up the meeting and I hurried back to the car. Time had been stolen away by now and I wanted very much to make a lovely evening meal.

My woods and forests hauntings may have been an inner warning that my subconscious was nudging me with. Gran was naughty, I got that, but was she evil? I saw her in the cottage in the wood with her frilly mob cap and long nose. Her skinny fingers counting money that was meant for me. I had no right to suspect her of anything. I must be patient and go ahead when I had the facts. My decision not to tell Greta was an interesting one. In the circumstances, I felt I should apply all the knowledge gleaned from my work, to this cause; the first rule, discuss with no one. The second, trust no one. When the facts were all laid out, would be time enough.

She had only looked after me for appearance's sake. I was now aware of this. I hated to feel ingratitude. My lovely French grandparents tried time and again to get sole guardianship of me. She would not hear of it. Why had she so doggedly hung on when there was no affection for me? It did not make sense. A horrible thought crossed my mind. I knew the lovely Mouriers were the most loving, loyal and fun people any child could spend time with. My 'life' was with them. My misery with Granny Grumplings – hence the name – that was not accidental.

When Mahmoud arrived, I had applied a jaunty air to the proceedings and we enjoyed strangely one of the best evenings ever. He had enjoyed his time in court and felt more relaxed now with the English judicial system – dare not speak of the French.

Mahmoud was off very prompt the next morning. He wanted to clear up as much as possible. Plans were being laid. Not for his early departure to Luxor, thankfully, but a trip out somewhere and a picnic. We are both fans of sitting outside and enjoying what is left of the English summer. Leaves tumbling down, wearing colours of sharp singing orange and gold.

Meanwhile, the attic called me back and like some marionette, I did its bidding. My knees were cold and stiff within ten minutes and so I massaged them into some sort of semblance of normality, and with Delly nutkins 'get out of the bloody way' as chief bridesmaid, we returned to the kitchen. I text Gillian inviting her for lunch the next day and then scooted into town.

Gillian sent a text asking sweetly, 'Do you need me to bring anything?'

I replied, 'No, just yourself.' Sweet.

Town was nice and I set my head carefully 'eyes front'. Past all the tempting clothes now freshly in for the winter selection. Ran the gauntlet of chocolate shops and shoes. Oh to be able to buy some glorious new ones. I dropped off several pairs of office footwear and prayed on one knee that he could do them again. Thankfully, he said yes and they wandered to join a pile of desperado styles also in need of a dustbin but not yet retired.

Sent off the lovely photos of Delly in the attic with Lionel Feininger style dust mote shafts. One to Greta who had sent a lovely postcard of a geisha. One also for David who had cheekily sent a picture of a snail. Greta can be very naughty at times. The last one to Mr Paul, Penny and the youngsters at the office – the wording was amusing. 'Much love to all from my attic where I am spending quality clear-out time with Delilah the family moggy. Best wishes, Gina Tantridge.' That will stay on the staff message board for at least a year.

Bought salmon and all sorts of things for lunch and picnics, sneaked to the wine counter and chose a rosé of immaculate pedigree which was on offer. How I love offers. Then I gave all other places the slip and zoomed back to the car before something happened to my purse ie, became empty. On returning home, the postman had delivered a lovely creamy dreamy envelope with our office logo. My excitement mounted the curb of elation and ran amok in the fields of – bloody salary increase at last! Yes, and yes again.

When Mahmoud arrived back in with beads of perspiration on his brow, I was finishing off an experimental evening meal. He looked pleased with himself as Delly rushed for him like a steam engine crying tales of beatings and name calling mew, mew, mew.

"Oh, have they hurt the little girl again, oh where are they?"

"They are right here and she's just a little liar."

"Oh, we have to pretend…it's funny. Did they lock you in the attic with the dead spiders? Oh. Oh, poor little thing."

He goes for a quick shower and she dances along behind him. Cute really, in an irritating way. I hear the shower which means she is sat in the doorway of the bathroom watching him apply sponge and soap to his perfectly toned swimmer's body. She has good taste. I have to admit that much.

Next day, Gillian arrives. I am still trying to forget the kingfisher moment – not easy…with all its implications. I cannot speak of it to anyone, especially as my darling Gillian is very good-hearted but is gossip mistress of the well in the square. Button it, I tell myself. She arrives on time and the salmon is popped in for its quick cook. Wine is poured and Delly is looking in the oven with an appreciative tilt to the corners of her mouth.

Gillian is wealthy beyond my wildest dreams. Her hubby, Bob, gets seemingly tubbier by the month, works in the cut and thrust of the stock market world. Gillian is sporting a tan which is now a rich orange and she is very heavily made up. Her clothes are wonderful. I can't help but tell her.

"Oh, come in, Gillian, that outfit is a show stopper."

"Oh, it's the latest fad, darling, amongst the county wives. You look well and your eyes are very twinkly. Of course with that fair skin you have to be careful what you wear. I'm jog about Wendy Wooo these days and I have become the most dreadful gossip."

"No, I don't believe it, Gillian, for shame. Have a wine?"

"God, yes, stick it here. You know, this house has become really classy since that awful stuff of Ray's has gone. I use the word gone because I know it's a delicate matter. Oh, look at Delly, she's so sweet. Is your lodger here? My God, I bumped into that dreadful Kate woman, she said he is like Elvis Presley."

Sharp intake of breath.

"Yes, just like Elvis, Kate says, and you know how critical she normally is about anyone. Oh, I like this, I hope you haven't gone to too much trouble, darling."

"Well, I still haven't thanked you for sending over those tables…such a long time ago. My apologies."

"Oh, think nothing of that, my dear. This tan—"

Holds out orange arm.

"—is called Hawaii Dream Girl. More like tangerine in bloody Tangiers if you ask me. The girl said it will fade in. Be grateful you are not rich vain and silly like me. Oh, you know Mrs Bonner is dead, don't you?"

"No, I didn't. Oh, poor lady, she was always blanking us I'm afraid. She disapproved of Greta's wardrobe…the looks, the looks. Anyway, how do you know all these things?"

"I'm a nosy cow, it's that simple. I have nothing better to do than jog and gossip then jog a little more and I'm always asking questions. Can I give a bit of this lovely salmon to Delly?"

"Of course, but please not on the counter…put it in her dish…she's already queen of the draining board."

"She's a darling girl that's what she is, the sweetheart. I'd love a cat but Bob's so allergic. It's a pity he doesn't develop an allergy to food. Gawd, it's like going to bed with Bluebeard these days."

We laugh our way through lunch. I'm very fond of Gillian; for all her gossip, she is fun at least. I ask her if she knows of any handyman. My gutters must be cleared…it's vital.

"Yes, darling, here you are. Call him now…get it out the way."

I call him and luckily, he has a cancellation. When he arrives, we are laughing because of strong wine and not having to go anywhere in a car. Legless, in other words. We look out of the lounge window as we try to sip boring coffee and sober up. We gaze amongst explosions of giggles and utter silliness upon what can only be described as The Convoy. First, a van shows up and leaves the drive gate open. A lad begins unloading ladders and marches whistling up to the house, then a man in his late seventies follows on a huge old-style butcher's bike with a basket of tools balanced precariously. The last in line is a mangy cat with one of his eyes almost shut from fighting, gunge, or quite possibly a marriage of the two. Delly is all attention as we crease up with laughing on the coach. He is obviously some sort of Romeo in cat kingdom.

We had supper and cleared away, I thought I'd better explain to Mahmud about the key under the garden bench, and David arriving. We may be out and I didn't want the lad hanging about. We made our plans to set off early for the picnic so that we could get right over to the Seven Sisters. The walks there being very fine. Plenty of different views and a decent car park. We set off around 9 am and took a lovely clear road out; after all we had gone through, this felt wonderfully liberating.

Sometimes, just a few hours away can do most good.

"We are lucky to get such a clear day, Mahmoud, this mist has burnt off quickly. I don't suppose you noted a really scruffy tom cat hanging around."

"No, I didn't, is he Delly's boyfriend?"

"Good grief, I hope not, I've dubbed him 'puss in fleas'."

"Well, you are expert at names and does he have fleas?"

93

"If he gets near our little girl, he might pass them on."

"Can she have kittens?"

"No, I took her to the vet's to be spayed. It's the best fifty pound you can spend for the cat's well-being, unless you want to breed from her."

"This they should do more in Egypt…we have the thousands."

"Who feeds them or are they strays?"

"They go to rubbish bins and bags. It is horrible thing to see…I hate it."

"Are you missing Egypt very much, Mahmoud?"

"More than I can say. When I return…which I must…it will also be hard missing you. Why not try to come out? You will love the Nilos and all the temples. People are mostly good kind and friendly."

"It sounds such an exciting place but you call it another name. I know you do."

"*Misr.*"

"Look, there's one of those little roadside places, do you fancy a hot coffee?"

"Of course, we can enjoy anything we choose, this day is our day, Gina…we do what we like."

If anyone asked me to describe the whole day and part of the evening out, I would have said we lived the dream. Magical. My heart told me to enjoy everything. This precious time with him may be all I ever have. Correction – all 'we' ever have. He will return to Luxor one way or another, and trying to hold on to what we have in England, how would that pan out. I could not see how. Also, I feared for his father. Mahmoud's elation upon his post-op recovery I felt was to be short-lived. I feared and felt the worst was coming. I would say nothing. Why upset him…nothing to be gained from that. Nothing at all.

When we drove home, happy and dog tired with a bunch of drooping wild flowers wrapped up on the back seat, there were lights on. Alarmed momentarily, I quickly turned off the engine and ran up to the front door…of course it's David.q11

"Cooeee, David, it's only us."

"Hey, you have sixth sense, I just put some water in the kettle to boil…tea all round."

"Hello, David, dear friend, how are you?"

I leave the boys to do cave-dwelling hugs and back-patting, and rush to the loo.

"We have had the most fantastic time."

I hear Mahmoud giving account of some of what we got up to. Please God, I hope he knows what to leave out. Yes of course he's subtle enough when needs be, plus he's a lawyer.

We soon settled with a light supper David had kindly prepared and began catching up with news.

"Have you had much contact with Greta? She sent me a card but I presume from the postmark that it was her pre-flight posting at the airport."

"Yes, we sent off stuff the same time. I drove her there. She had so much baggage."

"That's my girl."

"Sorry about the snail…she made me do it."

"That's so Greta. Yes, and I have eaten them, they are fantastic in garlic sauce with garnish." A chorus of ugghhhs.

"Where's Delly? She usually runs at Mahmoud like an American freight train and ignores me, unless she's hungry of course."

"Oh, I fed her and she's…sorry to tell you…laying out on Mahmoud's duvet."

"So, what's new? Delly waiting for her lover and naughty Greta frightening Japanese people with her near to nude outfits."

Soft laughter to avoid any 'call of the wilds' which would be quite an experience if they commenced from upstairs.

"Oh, she sent some photos of the girls she's staying with…and they are dressed the same."

"Oh, can I see?"

Mahmoud pipes up. He reaches for the laptop with a sparkle in his eyes while I sulk and watch. A sharp ping of jealousy rushing right through me – oh no, not the jealousy thing. I have not had one of these horrible things since I was a teen. Oh no…no, no.

"Oh, they are very tiny girls like dolls."

Mahmoud loses all interest. He likes – I am now more than aware of – very toned and quite muscular girls. Breathe out again. He's also funny about faces and loves girls with ultra-short hair. Modern men, modern men. Then queen of the duvet, Cleo-bloomin'-patra herself struts in with a very stiff-legged gait and leaps upon Mahmoud. Now I know we are really at home with modern men.

We all sat outside in the dappled area for breakfast. It was something I could never do before with company. Greta, when she is at home, only gets up early to take action. Quietly contemplating is at present alien to her. Perhaps, and it is a big perhaps, the Japanese meditation teachers will teach her the value of a quiet moment. David is soon called away by his mobile which se13\.lp a clatter indoors.

"Sorry."

He pleads…and trots off.

"Were you jealous yesterday, Gina, when I looked at those girls? You became very pink there." Mahmoud softly spoken points to his face. Delly does a saunter over from what's left of the cabbage patch, where she has been studying entomology. This being a most recent pastime…we do not expect any real knowledge and in truth it might be said the huge yawns she is already displaying may be an early sign of boredom. I think it's an improvement on T-shirt sucking and Puss in Fleas' admiration.

"Oh yes, I am very normal in that region of womanhood." He reaches over and touches the side of my face.

"I am man…this is normal, man looks always at pretty woman."

"In this country, man looks also at man. You must have picked up on this by now. Yes, I am jealous."

"Do you get jealous over me or do you get jealous over many things? I only ask to see what you feel."

"I am only jealous over you. It's childish, I know that, but the threat of loss is raw at the moment. I am honest in this, Mahmoud. Don't forget my husband of many years ran off with someone…who has totally changed all our lives."

"We could say that this brought us together." I drew him close to me and caressed his arm.

"Yes, we could."

"We could also say that yesterday was fabulous and I want it to be this way forever."

David was returning and Delly took a fit and flew out to the front of the house. I managed to gain the use of my wobbly legs and strolled, hopefully in a feminine manner, to see what she was up to. The front of the house was a scene not unlike the Battle of Waterloo…but for cats. Delly was arched like a comic character and was spitting and hissing from the top of the drive gate – cripes, she can move fast when needs be. Her sparring partner was a pathetic Romeo tom cat, none other than the terrible but now sadly even more mucky Puss in Fleas. Mahmoud joined me and we both hid our laughter behind our hands as the hissing competition got under way. Horrible gurgle growls came from the normally Cleopatra reclina-like Delly. While softer pleadings to be merciful came from the hilariously lovetorn Puss in Fleas.

"I think he wants to date her." Mahmoud is laughing softly.

"Oh, she is behaving very angrily, I don't think there is much hope. What if I arched my back and sat on the gate and spat, would you find me irresistible, Mahmoud?"

"I would be very nervous."

"I notice she is cutting off his escape route…or that might be part of the courtship. If so, she has lousy taste in cats."

David has joined us and is holding a sweeping broom. "Are you planning to sweep him up?"

"I know animals and this is bad sign. Best break it up before she is injured, he is not a nice cat."

"Oh David, yes of course, we hadn't thought of that outcome, we thought he was trying to woo her."

"No, he is displaying a sort of double bluff. She will soften down and come over eventually and then he will attack and he is already between her and the house."

With that, I grabbed the broom and shoved the unsuspecting Puss in Fleas in the rear end. He leapt up in the air with alarm, landed, and scooted as if all the dogs in creation were on his tail. He cleared the gate and vanished in a flurry of manky tail fur.

Delly jumped down from her perch and came back to me of all people and twirled around my legs in a grateful pirouette. We all returned to the house where I made a coffee to settle my nerves. Mahmoud had to be at court, so now it was just David, Delly the queen of the draining board, and me.

I dragged David into the loft and we managed with that daft bloody cat insisting on 'helping' to get the chest down, it was a tricky affair. We plonked it down and I managed to clear it and clean it up.

"Wow, Gina, it's rather on trend, don't you think…all sort of faded and genteel with an air of shabby chic."

"It's terribly French don't you know. Would you like to see some photos of long ago and far away? It's really nice to have you in the house. I may be risking a wallop from Greta, but I see you as family now…am I barking up the wrong tree?"

"I'm flattered. I would like to think this, but Greta…well speaking openly, she can be very—"

"Difficult and bossy I think are the words you seek. Very good in a crisis though is our Greta. Well, I want you in the family no matter what so there."

We go through all the memorabilia with a fine-toothed comb. A nagging voice tells me that the letter from the French notaire will be here soon and I might have to burgle Granny Grumplings' abode for more evidence of her withholding my inheritance from me. Right when we need it most. It's truly annoying that at present I cannot take anyone into my confidence about all this. I should be used to this by now from my working role. Home is not the office, but accusing the daft old girl of such a horrid deed is also not on until absolute proof is in my hands and even then, a perverse loyalty keeps me silent.

I need access to her house without her knowledge and that can only mean one thing. David could be persuaded to take her to tea on the pretence of catching up with her and telling her of all that Greta is doing. I could be joining them for lunch in town after I have – yes, yes, after I have spring cleaned a bedroom…weak as water, that excuse. Umm, ah, I had to run an important errand at the last minute. Yes, that would do it. David was more than happy to take Gran to lunch and I waited for her to pose an objection.

No, she fell for it. Off he went in his lovely white van and I insisted he have money to clean up the van at the car wash with her in it. Telling him whoppers like 'Oh she will love it.' I promised to join them at the 'Little Wheelbarrow Cafe'. A suitable and boringly twee place. I told him to text me the minute he picked Gran up. He was puzzled but put it down to me being me. Obligingly, he drove off with a puzzled as anything expression about the workings of the female mind, uppermost no doubt.

I grabbed my burglary gear, which is the same I use to clean attics. Packed my good clothes, shoes, handbag, perfume, lipstick and brush into a case and hurried out to the car. Slapping my thigh like Calamity Jane for good luck. I had to run back and lock the back door. Silly me.

Off I drove to Gran's house…there is a lane close by and I parked there; luckily, the text came through quickly from David. They were on their way to the car wash, and Gran was very happy. Well, free lunch with lovely David etc.

Getting in the house is easy; I have a spare key in case the old girl loses hers or locks herself out. Once in, I head for her bedroom. Gran is no writer and any paperwork will be hidden upstairs. I search thoroughly and without luck. Under the bed is a case however and a quick shove tells me it's heavy. I am going through her private things like a gerbil making a nest when the doorbell rings. I ignore it. The thrill of the ring goes through my guilty senses like a hot wire.

"Oh no, this is hopeless."

I say it out loud, and guilt, frustration and the thrill of the chase all combine to make my hands tremble. I am about to give up when I spy a cardboard box. Ah! This is promising. I remove it and carefully open – ah yes, letters in French and some are official. I grab the whole box and empty the contents complete and unabridged into a plastic bag. Replace the box, shuffle the paperwork – mostly old bills – back into some semblance of order.

The top layer I place very carefully. With care, I shove the case back under and then spot to my horror grooves in the carpet which leave very telltale signs of disturbance.

Yikes! I run downstairs and find brushes. Run back up and carefully brush and smooth my way around the room. Then with care I grab up the plastic bag and do a sort of tango step out, erasing my footsteps as I go.

Phew. I hurry down and out making sure I wipe door handles; probably not needed, but you never know. Once back in the lane. I alarm three blackbirds and a sparrow by changing into glam gear, locking all the attic and burglary outfit into the boot. I brush my hair using the side mirror and apply lipstick and gloss, perfume and finally step daintily into my best shoes.

Driving into town to meet with poor David who must be truly wishing he had not succumbed to my charms by now – Gran is not an easy companion. I park a street away from the Wheelbarrow and as I turn the corner, I wave as if I have not a care in the world have not just rummaged in Gran's bedroom and certainly not scared perfectly innocent birds by changing gear in the lane. Why did I do that? Oh well, it is done now as, the donkey said as he got wed. David appeals with his eyes. 'Rescue me now'.

"Hello, all sorted, thanks for waiting. Have you ordered me something, David?"

"I don't know who you think you are keeping us hanging around, my girl."

"Ah Gran, I see you are well, that's good. What's on the menu, David? I really like the look of the mint and pea soup."

"Luckily, that's the one I thought you would like. I also ordered cottage pie. Why do they call it that, it's not like a cottage, is it?"

"Oh, I know, it's a case of recipe's handed down, I suppose, and it would have started in a cottage…perhaps easy for them to find the ingredients."

Gran thankfully is tucking into the soup. A rare peace falls upon us from heaven. David is learning bad habits from me with eye-rolling expressions and looking quickly at Gran as if I must read a whole essay of longing to be elsewhere. Which I do. Thankfully, more food arrives and we are too busy eating to even go into small talk.

I settle the bill much to David's surprise, but I will let him take Gran home. In fact, we go to her house in convoy and he drops her off faster than the magician pulls a rabbit out of a top hat. Well done, lad, you're learning.

Once we have high-tailed it through back lanes home, we arrive laughing into the drive and only just manage to park as there is a car already in situ. Sat on the little bench by the front porch is X-Ray with Delly, who although sat next to him, is making a statement by having her back to him and training to be a tea cosy. She is very successful. He jumps up at the sight of us both.

I send a prayer to Darby O'Gill and the little people that my temper will hold out on this most peculiar of days. All we need now is Mahmoud, and cats and pigeons…here we come. They follow me in and I head for the kettle. This is the best move for most conversations which come from the bloody awkward as hell corner. Would the little people commence planting four-leaved clovers…now…please?

They greet each other in a gruff man-to-man thing. No slapping of backs here. David does not approve of the offhand and cavalier approach X-Ray has taken.

"Greta is in Japan so I gather then, Gina."

"Yes, Gran gave her a thousand pounds and while she is there the college has arranged for her to do some teaching as part of the visit. This helps with her Japanese conversation…gives her a fair chance, so to speak."

David is tense from this confrontation. I whizz through to the cloakroom and change into casual clothes, sending him a text message saying, 'Yes, I know… I am as surprised as you are…just hang in there, darling…and I will gain strength and merit from you.'

They are sat as far from each other that my kitchen counter allows. I make tea and find biscuits in a vain attempt to look normal. Well, I try. They are both looking at their own mobiles. David reads my text and his face changes, becomes more relaxed. We, the conspirators, pour tea and hand out nibbles for the elephant in the room.

"I was rather hoping to talk to you alone, Gina."

"David is part of the family, Ray, he has been for some time, helping us in every way that he can. I want him here."

"Okay."

He looks at me and then at his cup of tea…shrugs.

"Gina, I am simply not in the same salary bracket any more, in fact I am building up a little handyman garden cum paint and repair business…it's all new to me. I need my share of the house."

I am not going to be angry. I simply sip my tea which is hot and sweet – how lovely…the best is yet to come. I deliver my bombshell.

"I want to stay here in 'our' home so if you would be reasonable civil and fair for a little longer, I will be able to hopefully, and I underline hopefully, will be able to buy you out."

He's stunned that's obvious.

"Oh, I see."

"This is Greta's home you see…as well as my home."

"I am aware of that, Gina."

I start clearing away and pick up David's mug and my cup and saucer, and walk away into the lounge. David gets the cue and follows. Delly also catches the spirit of the message and follows with her…I am a very dignified cat gait. We sit in the lounge and I reach for the TV pinger. Fuming inwardly. But outwardly calm.

Ray, obviously sensing the interview is at an end, leaves the house without another word. Well, what else is there to say? We hear the car leave after a few gear shifts due to the tight parking. Then David lets out a huge sigh. I join him. Then we laugh.

"Oh, what a team we could be on the set of Ironside, darling. Oh, David, I am so glad you were here, it all went so much much better than I ever could have anticipated."

"How could he, it's about what he's done. He simply does not care about you two at all."

"David, he hasn't cared for a while. He used to be so light-hearted with us. Greta could tell him anything. Now he acts as if she doesn't even exist. He only raised the subject of Japan to talk of finance. I am amazed at him."

"But he is so strange…he acts."

"Yes, that's it, David, he is an actor. He lived with us for years pretending he was one thing when really, he was quite another. This new man must be great in the sack."

We both laugh out loud and Delly pulls her 'I warned you not to ever do such a thing again' face and whizzes out of the lounge, negotiates with well-timed skids, the kitchen and cat flap, obviously turns on her heel – do cats have heels? – well, she turns on her paws, comes back through the cat flap, back again into the lounge with ears flattened and goes right up my good curtains again.

Delly, of course, is stuck. This time by two claws. She cries most piteously. Not from the pain but because Mahmoud is not here to croon loving nothings into her daft little pink-tipped left ear.

"David, it's action stations. Step ladder if you don't mind, sweetheart."

I locate the gauntlets.

The next few hours we spend in the world of genteel old French photographs. David is so intrigued. He has connections to France and promises to get all the family information he can. From his side. We make supper for Mahmoud, an especially nice one. He has already sent me a text which warmed my heart.

'I saw a dear little bird in town, she was cute and very bouncy I think the word is. She reminded me of you.'

You gotta love someone who sends things like that. I replied with a mischievous smile.

'We are preparing the bird seed right now for the cute birds, mate…which is the Perty Bottomed Egyptian Hawk…or thereabouts. Xxx'

Yes. We are being silly but life is short and love is…

We spend an evening watching football. Or rather David and Mahmoud have a lads' night in. I am very happy to hear the shouts, cheers and general laughter while I work through the letters that Gran had hidden from me. The case is getting more and more obvious. She has been attempting and failing to gain access to my trust fund for many years. The notaire has not budged. I am lucky in that at least. They are not fooled by her capers. Pleading poverty and artful excuses have not worn them down.

Our lives are all so different now. I put everything in the files I have set aside for the task ahead. I will eventually have to go to Nice. I cannot see any way around this journey. I look forward to it immensely. Setting up my laptop, I find all the info I need to know about passport renewal and flights etc. Then run upstairs to find it. I glimpsed it yesterday, I'm sure of that.

Delly sees this as a special treat laid on for her; anyone running in the house is quite obviously playing a game. She prances like a kitten ahead of me and then blocks the top of the stairs, eyes wickedly widening.

"Come on then, trouble, let's go hunting."

We spend a few minutes with me in a cupboard peeping out and trailing a string mouse outside and then at the last second pulling it in…she loves this of course. Eventually, I sigh and let her have the mouse, and locating my passport, wander downstairs again only to be outrun by a skidding through the hallway, Delly nutkins with pink ear tips all aglow. She takes the 'mouse' into the lounge and obviously does something quite horrible with it because Mahmoud and David both yelp together.

Triumphant, she returns to me. Stiff-legged and queen of the cupboards, string mice, and all Egyptian persons.

My life would be complete if only I could wrangle the truth from Gran and get X-Ray off my case. Literally. The two people I should be able to trust are untrustworthy. Life is a manoeuvring business. I should be used to it by now. Greta cannot be told anything at present. In her youthful firework display of emotions, the shock could lead her to have a shouting match from Japan. Costly and in no way beneficial to any party.

I go online to check flight prices. I spot a round trip – I wish to God I could run away there with Mahmoud and stay there forever – ah, but the responsible head is back on my shoulders…so the price is one hundred and thirty-four sterling.

We wave David off to his next assignment. I have never seen such reluctance to don the garb of the final year student. I feel the parting deeply. We all get on so well…that to break our new family, if only temporarily, is becoming increasingly hard. Mahmoud passes a comforting arm around my shoulders as we go back into the hallway. Delly scampering ahead. Her little life with Mahmoud cuddles still intact. This sweet time is however short-lived as I drive into the village to post off my forms and old passport to get everything renewed. Gillian is waving wildly. I pull into her small lane.

"Oh, my sincere apologies, Gina…waving you down like a hitchhiker. I really need a lift into town, hubby had to take my car, his has developed some ghastly fault. Do you mind?"

"Absolutely not, it's a pleasure to be able to help you for a change."

"Oh, you are sssssssweet. Saw the marvellous Mahmoud and the divine David. Christ, you have a houseful of handsome men. How do you do it?"

"I'm afraid one of the handsome men has just gone off on a student assignment, bless him…he is such a good man. Greta better hang on to him, otherwise I will shove her in a nunnery…with no key."

"You have to hand it to her, fancy landing a course with a trip to Japan. Apparently, my girl says she's lapping it up."

"Yes, David arranged a link through Skype. We all had tears rolling down our cheeks as she danced to Japanese punk rock music. I am still recovering from the write-ups. The band she likes is apparently a cooler version of the Sex Pistols…and as for Vice and Friction. The music makes your ears bleed apparently. Our little house is still in shock. Delly was about two inches from the laptop when she saw Greta dancing."

"Oh no, it sounds like she's escaped our petite bourgeoisie income bracket for the wilder side of Japan. You will have to send David out to get her back. Oh, come to think of it, he might stay there."

"Ah, but you see, you need the same capitalistic income base to pay for it all, the trips, the clothes, the hi-tech…the whole kit and caboodle."

Gillian is flummoxed by this. Being wealthy through her marriage, she, God love her, has no idea how finance and social interaction works. She just spends it…she does not make it. I hate myself for thinking like this. Truth has its sting. Greta also is still only able to earn a little here and there with English conversation and short stints of waitressing. Life.

We say our cheery goodbyes in the village and I tell Gillian to text me if she wants a lift back. The rate Gillian spends money on shoes, her favourite pastime along with tanning salons, nail salons, facials of strange concoction from wise veggie plants grown under regulated and organic conditions salons. Hair salons, yoga salons and breathing. By the time she has visited all these alternative planets, I will be tucked up in bed with hot chocolate and other wonderful comforts.

Mahmoud that evening is very attentive, we cook a dinner together and Delly is delighted to get in the way with impunity as Mahmoud allows far more naughtiness than I ever would. We all sit in front of the tv, Delly begging titbits. Me scolding. The shrew in the stew.

"Mahmoud, she will get terribly fat, it's not her sort of food. She's eating it out of her nutty mistaken identity of being your girlfriend."

This sets him laughing.

"You are the other jealous girlfriend, Gina."

"Well, this is the limit. I am not putting up with cat hairs everywhere."

We laugh behind our hands to prevent up the curtain and call of the wild during the evening meal.

Peace of course is only temporary. We have just started the clearing up when the doorbell jingles, and jangles my nerves. It's Gran. Mahmoud lets the witch into the living room. I fear a showdown and wonder if all the carpet marks were erased. Oh hell.

"Oh, hello, Gran, we just had supper but I can make you a snack if you like."

"Hello, Mahmoud."

Patience…count to ten, go and put the bloody kettle on for the old…

"Your car's nice, Mahmoud, they must pay you good money at that law place you work."

Oh, that's nice and subtle, Gran, I don't know why you don't run special courses in social niceties. I make the tea. Any excuse to be out of the room where the daft old bat is holding forth on her virtues and everyone else's marked deficiencies. Charming. Mahmoud, God love him, is like David. He is ultra-polite around her. If they only knew. Having all these cannons in my personal arsenal is doing me no good at present but there will come a time very soon when I will, if required, to save the house and Greta. Drop the old girl right in the pan. I have a tiger in me somewhere and this horrible grandmother and all her nasty, mean, 'cut every corner, deprive and mistreat me' ways will come to a sudden end. Roll on the day.

I carry the tea tray into the lounge with aplomb. No one would ever know of the personal seething with fury at the sight of her sat there on my sofa in my lounge with my cushions etc. Mahmoud pours the tea and hands it to her with gentle politeness. I smile with the smile of a tigress just about to pounce on a goat tied to a stake. Believe me, the pleasure will be all mine.

My last few days of holiday ran away like a freight train. David rang from Denmark. He sounded so very fed up and lonely. I think he wished he was here or Ullapool. At least this experience narrows his choices down regarding where he will seek a placement when he completes his degree. Perhaps some of the problem lies with the separation from Greta. Huge distances and love. I was to find out for myself over the next week. The changes would come quickly and without much warning.

Took Delly into the office on my first day back. She adored the attention in the breakroom. I made an appointment to see Mr Anthony in my lunch break and was back on time luckily at my desk. She had a slight ear infection. Her antics over the tablet taking with her food were very un-queen-like. In fact, I would go so far to say they were a demonstration outside the houses of parliament on the rights for cats. The looks she gave me after that could be described…near to swearing as any cat can get.

Office routine does wonders for the insecurity I have had creeping over me of late. Probably nuts but I am what I am. The in-tray was bulging and I began the careful sort through by date and then by date. Oh, and finally by date. Importance was always on red alert and urgent. So the thrill of the chase began in earnest.

Mr Paul, by now, had a fan club. He was unaware, married very happily and was not a flirt. He displayed a brotherly air of camaraderie. I thoroughly approved of this.

Mike Kemp was quite different, single, blonde and athletic. He attracted Penny, who soon came in flushed and in a miniature panic, her new haircut glam and rather sensual.

"Hey Penny, you look good enough to meet your new man. Who is setting your heart aflutter?"

"Oh, dear Gina, welcome back. I was on a late start today so this is the first chance I have had to say hi to you. Wow, you look so refreshed and smart."

"Thanks, Penny, you are a doll. I had a lovely holiday in the attic and my old shoes re-cobbled, oh and the guttering cleaned. Does wonders for a woman's morale."

"We loved your photo of Delilah. It's been very lively here while you were away. The new man v sexy. Seriously though, did you manage to have a real break? You know, like go away?"

"Yes, a couple of day trips…one with Gran. That was a strange success."

"It's been a hoot here. The youngsters are nearly all in love with Mr Paul. They wanted to know how it all went with you and him."

I got up and rushed and closed the door which was still partially open. Penny, thinking some juicy sex chat might be in the offing, drew her chair closer.

"Oh, nothing untoward, Penny, they are naughty to ever say anything. I feel it's probably creepy to say this but he is a gentleman and an excellent role model. We had a very genuine business lunch and Mike Kemp who is already making a beeline to my door, darling Penny, was also present."

"Crikes, I better get back to my job. He's already told me to get something done as a matter of urgency. Give me your sharpener quick."

I hand it to her with my best professional smile. Acting role: One – always look busy. Two – be helpful to working colleagues. Three – keep an eye on the clock for breaks. Survival of the fittest. Penny is like Flash Gordon getting out the door and Mike Kemp with a playful grin does a sort of matador side cape thingy without cape of course, oh and no bull. Unless you count Penny, who is petite and weighs about an ounce in high heels.

"Hello, Mrs Tantridge, you know it's ages since we last spoke."

"Good afternoon, Mr Kemp, yes, I think we had a contretemps over a lovely Eton mess, which I hasten to add was utterly delish. How are you settling in?"

"Oh, very busy, but gratefully so. You had a holiday and spent it in the attic with the cat?"

"Ah, guilty as charged, but I did manage a couple of day trips and wonderful they were too in their way. Your secretary is waving wildly…it looks like an urgent wave…we can talk more tomorrow hopefully."

"Ah yes, she is rather frantic, better hop it. Look forward to a real talk with you, so I will schedule you in for a formal office catch-up."

"Sounds good to me, thanks for calling by. If you need any help, just say."

"Oh indeed."

I could not be sure but as he left, the words left in the air sounded like, 'Can't come soon enough.' But it could have been my imagination.

At home, I made Delly comfy with food and enforcement of tablet taking, all accompanied with yodelled curses and threats of a cat revenge, no doubt to be taken up later. Smoothed her fur down and lay her on a blanket with her favourite cushion or should I say, cushions. Mahmoud gave her lots of affection and she slept as the tablets took effect. Poor rumplesnutskin.

"My mother called me today. Gina, it looks like my father is becoming sick again."

"Oh Mahmoud, no… I thought they had cleared him."

"They thought so too. It is an aggressive form of cancer! Love him so much. Life will be dreadful if he gets worse."

"Mahmoud, forget all about what's happening here. Book a flight home, be with him, be with your family. This is torture for you, I can tell."

He left the room and I heard him crying upstairs. I walked up very quietly and stood by his door. I could hear his dry sobs. Knocking softly, I called, "Mahmoud."

There was no reply. I felt helpless but he probably needed to be alone. He knew me well enough to ask if there was anything I could do. Bravery came to the surface for me and I went online to check flights, making notes of times, dates and prices. When he returned to the lounge, where I stroked a restless little Delly, he was red-eyed. He touched my shoulder so tenderly. I gave him the information of the flights. Then I cried. I mean really cried. Whether it was all the roller coaster of the past months…and the tenderness of his darling face. The unfairness of love found and love lost, I know he adored his father so much. I don't know, but I cried and we hugged each other.

Delly snuggled her way in between us and this little touching act made us smile.

Mahmoud packed some things, contacted his boss and I set the washing machine to slush and bubble its way through his clothes. When the morning came, he had managed to book his seat on a flight with Egypt Air. We refused to say goodbye. His boss was dropped off by another colleague and drove Mahmoud to the airport. I had the horrible job of standing helplessly by as they went through the gateway of our drive. Mahmoud, white, shaky and trying to wave. This time we had exchanged all the info to keep in touch and I had promised to visit Luxor as soon as I possibly could.

Going into the office required strength, fortitude, makeup and dark glasses. How I got through that week without tears in my office is still a mystery. At home was another matter. I called everyone and anyone. Gillian came across the lane to me.

"Sorry, I'm such a nosy cow, I saw Mahmoud go… I hope you won't hate me for staring after the car."

"I stared after him too you know, Gillian."

"You love him, don't you? Darling, don't worry. there are some things I know how to keep to myself and this is one of them."

"More than I can ever say. I will be going to Luxor first chance I get."

"Look, ask me, you daft duck, if you want the money. It won't be a loan; it will be a gift with my blessing."

"You're an unusual woman, Gillian. A lot of people never see the golden heart you have."

"Come over to our house, have a break, darling Gina. A cup of tea with sugar is best for shock. I can always add a little Scotch for luck."

I followed her into her home. Praying I would not start crying again. The hot drink perked me up and we watched a Laurel and Hardy special collection film. We smiled at the washing up scene…but laughter was not on the menu. Gillian nagged me about eating properly and said not to be a silly billy and come over or call her any time.

I had to go home eventually and prayed that Gran would not call round or ring up. I had the horrible feeling I might snap her bloody head off. I made Delly comfy on my bed and snuggled up to her. She, sensing the seriousness of everything, did not purr. But gave my forehead a damn good licking.

To be honest, the office became a lifeline, that and the dinners Gillian insisted on leaving on the little bench outside. Various messages pinned to a spotless towel – 'EAT ME'…and 'I am good for you'…and the one I kept in my drawer forever, 'Eat if you want to remain a yummy mummy.' People who don't really know Gillian now, will probably never know her. Not really. I bought her a huge bunch of her favourite daisies. Yes, they were the large cultivated variety but the hedgerows and gardens are dark and soggy now with early winter fingers tapping tapping, and the evenings chill.

I carefully penned a note to go with the flowers.

'Love and friendship, and let's do a Laurel and Hardy wash up film one day. Gina xxxxxxx'

Mahmoud's father died just two weeks later. I called Mahmoud and I knew by his tragic voice that he would never get over the loss.

I threw myself into work with such a force, I must have looked a bit of a creep to an outsider. But it was helping and the more I did, the nearer the Nice visit and hence the great and wonderful trip to Luxor. The frosty morning air seemed to promise such changes in my life. I knew for a certainty something big was about to happen.

I was tussling with the duvet and a sound of drumming in my ear. At first, I thought it was a branch of a tree tap tap tapping my window. I struggled out and Delly thinking it was some kind of new game, began pouncing on the bumps in the duvet. The dream over, I could hear a loud knocking.

I called, "Coming, coming."

Managed to struggle out of the duvet-Delly combo and into a dressing gown. I went down the stairs with great care and opened the front door, the ever-nosy parker Delly excitedly prancing. Was she a circus pony in a past life?

"Mrs Tantridge, good morning, sorry to get you out so early but it's a special delivery."

"Tony, hello, yes, I'm expecting my passport."

"You have to sign on this funny screen."

"Oh flipping heck, Tony, I'm not with it yet."

"Well, join the club."

"You got time for a coffee?"

He's a country postie and his rounds are a bit off and on through the country lanes. He happily follows me through to the kitchen and I offer percolated best Columbian mild or instant granules.

"Ooh, Columbian sounds the ticket."

I make him a delightful drink and I pop croissants in the oven, grab poor Delly, and he helps me secure the 'Wrath of Khan the Elder' Delly, so that I can administer the last tablet. Thanks to all the fairies in Ireland and any that have popped over the sea, she eventually swallows it. We release her to go off like a rocket and tell the cabbage patch what a wicked vile owner she has.

"What type of cat is she, Mrs Tantridge? She's so feisty."

"Ah, this is a very interesting question, Tony, have a croissant."

"Oh, I don't mind if I do…bloody lovely these are."

"Yes, I would say at the present moment she is a cross between Cleopatra and a mountain lynx, with a small helping of Sussex pony thrown in for good measure. On Sundays she is a circus horse and Mondays a wash and wear."

Tony can't help but laugh.

"I'm glad you haven't lost your sense of fun, Mrs Tantridge. Christ knows you have had enough to test your patience."

"To be truthful, it's the only thing standing between me and a bottle of vodka or three."

"You always did have a lot of courage."

"Thanks, Tony."

"I thank you kindly for the breakfast, I better go otherwise I will be in bother."

"Take care out there."

"I will, byeee."

Delly comes back in after her entomology lesson cum growl at the cabbages.

"Oh, darling little girly whirly, did they treat you very badly?"

Quick to forgive, she tucks into her food with all the appetite of a starved tiger in the north of India.

David rings from Denmark, the quickest of calls. He's flying in tomorrow…the relief is obvious. I tell him just to show up…key in usual hiding place. He's thrilled I can tell…well, it's wonderful to have him here. I drive into town and get stuck into the big supermarket shop.

Delly thoroughly approves of the cat treats and cuddles I give her and by way of forgiveness of pill administration, gives my lap a good soda bread kneading. She could go on that famous baking programme if they allowed cats to cook. We watch my favourite film 'Now Voyager', with the fabulous Bette Davis. Delly approves of my mouthing the lines in sync with Bette.

I make myself a huge supper and tuck into a chunk of chocolate sponge that could have sunk a battleship. Delly watches me make short work of several chocolates that I found in a drawer and then I get the most awful indigestion. Serves and right come to mind.

Hoovering at nine pm is a sobering hobby and a bath followed with an indigestion tablet and hot chocolate sees me in bed reasonably early. I snuggle down with a good book and Delly prowls about looking for imaginary rodents. She always has a certain look about her when on this self-invented mission. A cross between I am a beautiful pussy cat adored by all and a tantrum diva. She will suddenly jump up and scoot sideways.

"Spiders, Delly?"

I feel slightly better as I fall asleep so far from Mahmoud. Now I have the means to go and see him in Luxor, which is slowly becoming a reality.

"Spiders, Delly?"

Chapter Five

Packing for Nice began the evening I was granted the time off from the office by lovely Mr Paul. Of course, as I left his office with resident blackbird singing prettily in the tree outside, some of the youngsters were giving me a knowing smile. They have a lot of imagination. Bless.

That night was a flurry of activity which consisted mainly of Delly going back to her other name of 'Delly get out of the bloody way.' With optional tuts. She had already decided that my wardrobe was an adventure theme park with all the trimmings. She hid and pounced on every darn thing I drew forth. I have only classic clothes with few frills. My childhood time spent in Nice paid off in spades. Learning from darling grandmother Alix which styles suited me as well as tailored but appealing lines. My favourite designer is Coco. I would love all her originals. Alix also knew instinctively what could make you look the town frump; besides, I had Gran's English martyred look to warn me away from that particular horror and how to avoid mutton lamb and clown in equal measure.

Of course, I am only human and do make faux pas. A particular hat is well hidden. Oh, and those old sweaters.

My flight being booked, left only the drive to the airport. David's timing was to be admired. He was delighted to care for the Dellynutkins while I was away and was due late this evening. The schedule was tight but perfect. I had one more day at the office and then lift off. Mr Paul is a reasonable colleague and we had fun working out the schedule. I would fly out Thursday morning and return the following Monday mid-afternoon; this meant I was out of office for the skimpiest of times. I would take the laptop without any sensitive information. Mr Paul would keep me up to speed on any current situations; if any terrible disaster should arise, he would inform me. We were working on a delicate matter, but he thought it would not be harmed in any way by my being 'a stone's throw' from the UK.

If in the event of my requiring more time with the notaire, something would be worked out.

In the end, I had made up my mind and tried to recall the warmer temperatures of Nice in late autumn – ah yes, still warm. So, my clothes were neat and cool. Boring? Yes. Essential? Yes. I did throw in a pretty dress in silk which is Mahmoud's favourite. This had to be carried aloft to the case to avoid the darling little Delly's furry capers.

David came in laughing from the sheer pleasure of getting out of the lab in Denmark and we had the best supper in the world with wine and laughter. A quick call to Japan to include Greta in the merriment. She sounded rather jealous, and was most definitely homesick. Poor love.

Every doggy has its day and today I am a jolly little poodle…and my name is Fifi la Fou. Delly was thrilled to have David 'to annoy', and I left them to play together while I showered. The plan was that David would kindly drive me to London and then when I had booked in on my return flight, he would time the drive back up to London to collect me from the airport. If he did not hear from me at all, he would presume it was signal problems and come up midday anyway and park in the short stay. I would reimburse him this expense later. He protested against this but I was adamant.

From the conversations I had held with the French notaire, I could tell she was a charming lady who had the most delightful sense of humour. We were both looking forward to going through the documentation. She felt confident the outcome would be greatly advantageous.

David was fun to be with as we zoomed up to Gatwick. His jolly company gave me the boost needed to face the flight. My new passport and the strange Euros in with my English money added to the strangeness. My first trip away from home for ages. Last time had been to a Greek island. Crete and all its joys. The food made X-Ray ill but he was a bit of a glutton sometimes. I was alone this time so any lively encouragement from lovely David was most welcome.

He waved me off and got out of the drop-off zone fast. You have to pay to drop someone off and seemingly, this facility allows approximately two point two nanoseconds. Within this time sphere, you must get out of the vehicle, retrieve all luggage, say goodbye and close the door. David is a past master of this. He whooshed off in a flurry of leaves. I gave England a cheery mental wave.

I hurried into departures and then gathered my wits – or did I gather my wits? – and then hurry in. No matter. The general busy rush is catching. Soon I'm

113

involved in all sorts of checking in and depositing mascara and lipsticks into a see-thru bag. Next, my shoes are on, off, on, off, and I am longing for a coffee. When I eventually sit in the area reserved for those that have just made it through security alive and all prods, bleeps and general mayhem is at an end, I risk breathing out. Anyone new to this ordeal is easily spotted. The coffee tastes wonderful. To be truthful, they could have given me anything, it would have been great. The toasted sarnie was a dreadfully yummy calorie-packed meal and I have no guilt. Not yet anyway.

The flight was meant to allow me time to draft all my questions to the notaire. I had learned her name; it was a delightful confection of film star and nostalgia – Suzette Bibiane. I suddenly began yearning for all things French. Childhood memory took over and I only intended to close my eyes for a gentle reminisce but sleep grabbed me with both hands, and I woke up with a most awful snort which would have put paid to any romantic interlude with a French film star – oh, how wonderful those childhood visits were. My grandmother's favourites were Jean-Pierre Aumont and Jean Gabin.

We watched amazing films together and I would get very excited by all the action. My thoughts always worked on the possibility that these films were actually being enacted literally around the corner. All highly believable, and once filled with an octane fuel of screen romance and action, I would hold the poor cat very tight; he understood of course that this was all part of the drama and rarely protested. Although he did tend to run under things at vital gun wielding in dark alley moments.

My favourites were of course stars like Olivier Martinez. He had been raised in the suburbs of Paris; this only added to his glamour. Grandpa would laugh at us both crying over some old black and white film and generally tease us. I miss them still so much. I fully intended to make time to visit my old home and take some photographs.

Suzette Bibiane is a saint. I already love her. With French chic and understanding as well as an enormous fee to be extracted later of course, this good woman had arranged for me to collect a modest priced hire car at the airport – well, when in France and all that. No point in battling against the new life, the joie de vivre of it all. The actual reality was hilarious. Setting the sat nav to take me to the French B and B…in the end, I got out of the car and rushed around until I could find a sympathetic man who put them in for me. I felt a fool but I had to be sensible. Driving on the other side of the road and being spoken to by an unknown French lady who is in no doubt of my ineptitude.

All this is quite an experience for a highly tuned woman of a certain age who is hungry again, does not have a clue where she is going and until she gets her bearings, is likely to have a few hysterical shouting fits at the sat nav.

Well-deserved, I'd say.

Eventually, the clouds did roll back and silver linings smiled down, and after a lot of angry motorists told me of good places where I could go and how I could get there, I got the hang of it. I recommend all people learn *tourne a' adroit* and *tourne a' gauche*. Unless you wish to incur wrath of the French male motorist kind. My happy face was back on. if somewhat reddened by the ordeal. I parked in the b and b's reserved-for-guests only. Oh, what is bliss. I will tell you…bliss is getting out of a small hire car and knowing you are alive in the destination of your choosing and taking a gulp of fresh air and drinking some *eau minerale*. Showing off one's crumpled outfit is optional.

I wheel in my little case and sign in to the efficient service that the hotels here pride themselves in. After my shower, I order food and throwing all care to the wind, drink some wine and somehow show great courage and skip dessert. If I am to walk in my best suit without mishap in the waistline region.

I fully intend to find the notaire's office myself and with a great deal of help from the hotel staff and scribbles all over a pad a lovely man tells me to keep for the bonne chance, I feel the time of my youth creep up over me like a comfort blanket and soon learn to raise my shoulders and say all manner of nutty French niceties that oil the wheels here. *C'est tres bon*. But I still do not care for the

sat
nav
lady

Waking to the stunningly blue skies over Nice in a charming, if somewhat compact room, was so odd, but odd in a great way. The breakfast aromas wafting through the floors – the house was old and quaint, there was the occasional gap – made me hungrier than I thought possible.

The owner's son gave me the clearest idea of where the Cabinet Bibiane was actually situated. However, he was adamant that I should drive there. When I pulled a face, he walked out to the car with me and quietly, politely set up the sat nav.

"Oh, you don't know how helpful this has been for me. I do want to learn this but not when I am due at the notaire's cabinet. Thank you so much."

"Perfectly normal not to know all at once about our little ways. You I know are proficient in your own country. If madam I should come to your town, I would ask for the help also."

"You are the French angel."

"Ah, you are kind. Gabriel, the French angel."

"Oh, I see, you really are the Angel Gabriel…that's wonderful."

"Ah, what a fantastic conclusion… I shall speak to *ma mere* concerning this."

We are both laughing as I drive away and Gabriel who is a merry, lovely soul, pretends to flap wings.

What a superb way to start my day… I could do with plenty like this. Driving on the other side of the road and concentrating on all around me getting warmer and warmer, trying to find some way of opening the window all at the same time, I arrive at the Cabinet Bibiane. I need not have worried about parking; the building was refurbished and beautifully clean. The open court area at the entrance was adequate for my small rental car. I was soon less flustered and found to my relief a cold-water bottle with darling little cups. Sipping slowly to cool off, I knocked at the door and was called in.

The office was chic and I began to wonder at the cost of all the expert advice. No, chic was not the word I would use to describe such a room. Uber elegant comes closer. A painting flashed meltingly gem-like colours over the room. I felt giddy with its beauty.

A tiny plaque near the exquisite frame announced 'Maxime Maufrat 1861-1918'. I must have had my mouth open and was floating above the room.

A voice at my side spoke gently, "Yes, it has that effect. It is charming, no?"

I turned to see a smart woman with a wonderful quality in her manner and the calmest kindest eyes I had ever seen.

"Good morning, Madam Bibiane. This painting is so… I am… I think in love."

"Good morning. We are happy that it pleases you. Please come this way, Mrs Tantridge, we are ready for you."

If this room was charming, the next one was subtle and efficient. Chairs neat and beautifully comfortable, were drawn around a low table. Nearby, a large escritoire graced us with its presence.

"Would you like a *cafe au-late*, Mrs Tantridge?"

A smart man offered me a tiny tray and placed it before me with tiny almond wafers on a pale dish as accompaniment to the dearest little coffee cup in creation. My mood lifted, my head went up and my shoulders dropped. I breathed a sigh of relief.

"Please be comfortable, Mrs Tantridge. We are here to serve you. Please, would you kindly show me your documents as to your identity and the letters of introduction."

"Of course."

I handed over the folder with all my family certificates of marriage, birth and death. My passport and the letters all in the correct dates. Family photographs I had placed as near as I could in the order of age. The old quarter of Nice and its truly lovely Russian Orthodox Church, with tourists in older style clothes held in a fragment of time looking forever at its beauty in fresh morning sunshine drew gasps of admiration.

"This is more than we could have ever hoped for. This will be of great assistance to us. Charming, charming."

They continued to oooh and agh over the lovely family scenes of my beloved grandparents in the old-style French clothes. I am not ashamed to say a tear slipped down my cheek as they came to light in that lovely room. People who loved me.

"My apologies to you, Mrs Tantridge. I told you that we are here to serve you, and yet you have served us. This is a forgotten era for many. The modern life here is fast paced, but in this manner so much beauty is passed by without affection."

I sipped a second coffee and then a glass of water a young girl kindly brought me.

"We have, I think, Mrs Tantridge, the correct information and all we require to access the trust fund. If you will be patient with us a little longer, we can inform the office that is administering the trust fund, and we will contact you at your hotel as soon as we have their permission to allow access."

I stand to go and the notaire's secretary who has been preparing the receipts of permission for the trust offices to peruse these family documents, comes across to me. We all witness and sign the paperwork, and there is a great deal of relief in the air. After all, the foolish Granny Grumplings has been trying to defraud the trust over the years. Now they have the real person who it is meant for, it must be a huge relief.

"Thank you so much, Madam Bibiane. May I be crass for just a moment and inquire as to how much the trust fund amounts to?"

"This is not a crass request, Mrs Tantridge. In the circumstance, you should perhaps sit down just for one moment."

I sat down again and calmly waited. Outside I was the picture of cool, inside my heart was skipping all over the show.

The whispered discussion came to an end and the notaire stood up from the escritoire.

"As close as we can calculate, Euro to Pound sterling, it is in the region of three hundred thousand pounds. Perhaps a little more. Your bank will no doubt choose the most favourable method of exchange rate for you in the transfer."

My mouth is open and yet I can't take a breath. I feel a perceptible shift in the room.

"You are much shocked I think, Mrs Tantridge."

"Yes, I had no idea."

"The fact of your not knowing and the lack of interference has allowed the administrators to continue to carry on the instructions from your parents, and so in this manner, the amounts are doubled and great interest has allowed for even deeper investment. Also, the investments were sound to begin with, so your parents were as wise as they were good, Mrs Tantridge."

When I have recovered a little, I leave the offices. But I am forced to sit in the car. Driving for the present few minutes is out of the question. Who would ever imagine such an amount? Certainly not myself. No wonder Granny Grumplings was trying to muscle in. The notaires have such a strict and very necessary method of proof of identity required, and small wonder when you have old witches like
her around.

I pluck up the courage to tap in a new co-ordinate into the sat nav, and me and the hire car set jauntily off to my childhood holiday home in the old quarter of Nice. I trundle it around narrow streets. Get blocked in sometimes, confused others and for the first time in my entire life, I don't care about revving and zipping about. Then calm down before some gendarme spots me, the maniac without the Inspector Clueso of what I'm doing. I put a cd in and lala laa la to the strains of Pierre Desbois; I am unsure of the words and typically where I am unsure, I don't care and add my own. I find my grandfather's old shop with the lovely apartment above quite by accident. But of course.

Parking as close as the narrow spaces left will allow, I wander over and look up. The old place has had a makeover but thank all the angels in long dresses, a sympathetic one. A shop bell jingles somewhere merrily and I wander over and see although the courtyard is the same, the wall to the front of the yard is demolished and a smart little car leans out as if looking for someone. Its headlights peering…no doubt waiting for a flirty Fiat. Then I see it at the top of the steps leading to the private apartment. My little flower pot with its white sea shell stuck on the side. Still there, still intact. I am thrilled to see proof of our lives there. Truly happy times.

I cross to the small shop. It's not quite a shop. Not quite a grocery store or news store or even tourist trinket shop, but that delightful mix of all three. I set the bell tinkling again as I go in.

A girl of about twelve comes in from the back room smiling.

"*Bonjour.*"

She nods and watches as I give her some almond biscuits and then my eyes alight upon a sort of casket. It is of over-the-top oriental design and has delightful arabesque swirls and twirls. I lift it up and its heavy.

"*Sable du desert.*"

The young girl offers up the explanation like a special magic phrase. Which in fact, to me, it is. I turn it slowly. It is silly, I know, but I want it. The lid bears a turtle swimming – or is it a tortoise? No matter. I check the bottom and see it is only twenty euro. Sold. Or is it *vendu*?

I hand over the money and the sweet girl places it with the biscuits, and I leave with a smile of thank you before I spend any more. I don't feel rich in this particular minute. I am going in and out of phases of restraint and splash out emotions. I am sure all will change very soon.

Back at the hotel, reached by various routes and swearing at wrong turns, I order a nice meal and ask if I can have it in the tiny courtyard amongst the old pots where I spy a lovely area partly in shade. Gabriel is happy and calls out.

"You choose well, madam. Some wine noh?"

I reply, "*Some wine oui!*"

119

Gabriel is a darling chap. He smiles all the time and is the very epitome of what the French so sweetly call *'joie de vivre'.* Add to this a rounded physique that never saw the inside of a gym, twinkling dark blue eyes and dark, curly, unruly hair and you have him exactly. I drink my wine and to keep me company, Gabriel sits with a pastis. We are pals of the new kind. We know enough about life not to feel awkward yet not enough to feel cross about each other's shortcomings.

Gabriel wants to open the casket. To this end, he fiddles with the lock with a hairpin and makes me laugh.

"You are puzzled about sand, Gabriel, how it is made up and what it looks like?"

He laughs very loudly and makes the cat jump. A cat so unlike Delly in looks, cleanliness and temperament, as a pig is to a gazelle.

"I am curious to know if there is treasure."

"Gabriel, the only treasure around here is you and the wine…oh, and the pastis."

"HA HA HA, my mother should be here for this philosophy of the English."

"Ha, that's where I have you, my father, don't forget, was French."

"Zut alors!"

"Also, I spent a lot of my school holidays right here in Nice."

"I am so happy for this, Mrs Tantridge. You marry English and get his name."

"Indeed, but I never lost touch with my ancestry in that I love the French way and the French wine, and more important, most of the French inhabitants."

"Ah, it is open."

We peer into the casket and much to our delight, there is a letter with Arabic script. I pretend to gather it up like an excited pirate and allow the wine to do its work."

"Ah mon amie…ziss iz ze very map I was telling you about it shows the way to the Gobi Desert. Now we will be rich as princes…that is to say those that are rich."

Gabriel is falling about laughing and then hurries indoors and comes back brandishing a sword of indefinite age and category. His mother astonished is on his heels with a look of pure horror.

"Crazy boy, leave our guest alone…you are crazy, *allez-vous en, allez-vous en."*

Gabriel ignores her and continues sword fighting in the Gobi Desert, or thereabouts, with great zeal, courage and pastis.

We finish our drinks and I am called into the reception by a sulky girl.

"Oh, Madam Tantridge, my sincere apologies to disturb your enjoyment."

It's the notaire's secretary; he is a little flustered looking, so I offer him a seat and a glass of wine as my guest. He seems genuinely relieved at such a friendly reception. Gabriel peeps around the door into the courtyard and brandishes his sword in mock attack. His mother sneaks up behind him and clouts his arm; she is too small to reach higher.

The secretary looks alarmed.

"Ah, I will explain, I purchased a casket of sand as a souvenir of my stay here and Mr Gabriel with the help of the pastis has kindly opened it for me."

I show him the paper we found. He is only just short of astonishment at such foolishness but too polite to inquire further into the mysterious other side of French life and entertainment.

"I have come with an important errand from Madam Bibiane, who is most anxious that you are kept informed of the situation. She understands you are returning Monday on a midday flight to London and has managed to get the bank dealing with the trust to peruse and have sight of all your important and vital documents etcetera. To this end, she has requested me return all of them in person. So please, if you will check them and sign this paper to say they are all present, I would be most grateful."

"Thank you."

I check them carefully, but the sneaking feeling is that they will be intact and I have full trust in the Cabinet Bibiane. Smiling, I sign the paper and hand it to her secretary, who sticks to the letter of his errand like glue to a photo in a book. To my delight, he at least has downed the wine. We rise and without another word, he departs with a smart courteous nod. As if he is paid by the word uttered and no more outside of that instruction.

I return to my room and put everything away being sure of the fact that at least things are now really moving in the correct direction. I email everyone and send a particularly hopeful message to Mahmoud in Luxor.

I am very happy.

Happiness is forever challenged in life however. An email comes flying back from Greta who is thoroughly miserable and wants to give up on the whole Japan deal and come home. I reply smartly and firmly.

'Darling, if a degree in Japanese Studies were easy, everyone would do it. Stick it out, write your essay, complete your course there, and yes, that is an order. I am sorting legal family documents and visiting my old home in Nice. Other people are living in our old home here which is to be expected. Have had a lovely afternoon with memories of childhood and drank some strong French wine with the owner's son Gabriel. Have you heard from David?'

The email comes flying back, so she must be online.

'He's okay and up to his eyes in research and essay writing. I feel such a dope. Homesick as hell. I don't want to visit Japan ever again.'

I reply as upbeat as I can manage. 'Understand, you sweet girl…but stick it out, you will be okay and we want you to succeed. Xxxx Mum.'

The message may have hit the right nerve because she goes silent. I shower and look at the evening's menu.

Greta sent me a text message which worried me. 'No Mum, it's no good, I'm packing it all in."

I sat down and thought it through. My first instinct is to protect and cuddle. Yes, but if I keep doing this, she will never achieve anything. I hated myself for my next action but was so determined to save her from such rash behaviour that in the end I replied sternly.

'No, you can't run and hide when you get to the first obstacle in life…rise to the challenge, that is part of a degree course to find your way through the obstacles between you and the prize. Have a nice meal and list all the things you want to achieve. Tough love from Mum xxxxx.'

What else could I do. If she packs her bag now, she will be doing it forever. This was not like leaving a cruel father or brutal unfaithful, husband. This was a fabulous maybe once in a lifetime opportunity for her to shine.

A reply came back. 'I feel horrible, Mum, but I am going to try the meal and list thing. Good to know you are enjoying Nice. Must be good to see the old place. Lots of memories.'

I sent a sympathetic reply. 'This will be a turning point in your life, darling, believe me, you can do it and with flying colours. We will have a huge party and dress up as tarts and vicars or something. Gillian will sing and Delly will wear a flower power outfit.'

The reply was cheering. 'Bags, I will be a vicar and David a tart.'

'But of course.'

Gabriel is in fine fettle and singing some saucy French ballad of unknown origin. After breakfast which was as usual delish, I had a few minutes in the courtyard while it was cool. The weather man promised a fine but slightly cooler day. Gabriel came in full of smiles. God, what a character.

"Madam Tantridge, I would like to drive you and another guest to the Baie des Anges and after a picnic we can go to La Ciotat. How does this appeal to you, *mon amie?*"

"Truly unexpected and you can count me in."

The other traveller was a young man with the most delicate build and features. He was a student as far as I could gather and spoke very few words of English. His name, Raphael, amused me greatly and I sent a text message to Greta telling her I was in a French car with two French angels.

We drove away from the district then climbed a little way out of the town centre and joined a jolly stream of busy traffic all seemingly headed on holiday. Tops were down on convertibles and music blasting out. Not to be left out, Gabriel chose a fabulous selection of rowdy modern songs all seemingly with a theme of love and dangerous liaisons between sexy men and curvy women – oh, and some curvy men were also featured. We soon were all singing nonsense at the tops of our voices. Gabriel turned off the fast road and we wound our way through some of the most fabulous scenery I have ever seen. We found a parking place and tumbled out.

The Palm Cafe was wonderful, the menu bursting with French and intercontinental cuisine. We ordered crepes and coffee. The bill was large but the merriment was even larger and we left in ultra-high spirits. Raphael is a highly intuitive fellow with meltingly fine good looks but so terribly thin he reminded me constantly of the famous dancer. Vaslav Nijinsky who is buried in Montmarte Cemetery in Paris. I visited Paris constantly when young and know Nijinski is in good company with many famous people such as Ludmilla Tcherina and of course the wonderful Francois Truffaut who made such fabulous films for new wave cinema – *Jules and Jim, The Soft Skin*, and *Shoot the Piano Player*.

So much of my life is influenced by the riches of French art in its many and enchanting forms.

Gabriel is in fine singing form and we sing ourselves into a giggling frenzy, so much so that we are obliged to pull in to drink water and try to calm down from the most awful fit of the giggles. Back on the road once more with my jolly

French men, I am soon oooohing and aghing at the bay views which make this one of the most achingly lovely parts of the *Cote d' Azur.*

Our picnic is a hoot and we all take part in entertainment chosen by Gabriel, who clowns and demonstrates with us and some passersby to join in with the farce which would be disgracefully naughty in most circles. It was a form of charades unlike any I have ever experienced but somehow, here, now, and today, belongs in and of the moment. We are practically hysterical by the time we pile back in the long-suffering car and the driving suffers. God, please let all the French Traffic Police be at lunch. Or turn blind eyes. Gabriel thankfully, although nutsy and great fun, is a stickler for the speed limit and keeps us safe, and we arrive eventually at La Ciotat.

I confess to having the most awful aching sides and Raphael is suffering too. In the nicest way possible of course. We manage to find toilets, then set off once more on the second Monsieur Hulot's holiday and yes, it is true his fantastically funny vacation was on the North Western coast of France.

we
are
recreating
art
in
our
own
way.

The hangover was in two parts and the first part woke me up and the second part put me into a semi coma state. The moral of the story is all joy has to be settled with a bill one way or another. I am not going to ruin a perfectly good hangover with further despicable description. Breakfast was served without the presence of Gabriel or the angel Raphael. My packing was still to be done and I had to have another shower to wake up…but hey.

My passport somehow had vanished into the notaire document's file and had to be retrieved…but of course, and the sand casket developed wandering grains. My head thumped and the general consensus was my search for headache relief would be well rewarded. Paying the bill, I was surprised at how reasonable my peculiar jaunt into the Nice b and b experience had been. I left thank you messages for Gabriel and his mother, who was also absent. I asked Miss Sulky where they might be.

"Madame is gone to market and Monsieur Gabriel is stay to his bed with the headache."

"Oh, that makes a lot of sense."

I wrote a message and left it with her. Thanking them both for making my time so pleasurable and fun and that I would tell all my friends of the true hospitality.

Unsure of how to get the sat nav set up. I eventually managed somehow. Battling brave as a tiger against the sadness of going, my head thumping out a tune of pipers now being paid, and a general feeling that a little hurry up might come in useful.

The hire car people went over the vehicle with a fine-toothed comb and in the end decided that the dents it had started out with were still all present and correct and my money left as deposit against other assaults upon its person, refunded. Another miracle. Airports are fun places when you are clearheaded. When you are not…well…

Soon as I could, I dived for coffee and ate ravenously again. What is it with me with France and food? David responded quickly and light-hearted to my text. He would be there and would wait at the coffee shop nearest to the arrivals exit. He was there and smiling…we hugged like bears.

"Oh, so good to have you back, Gina. Are you alright, you look a little green around the gills?"

"Party on the Cote d'Azur…in a car with two French angels."

"Right, what else could it be. Delly is missing you. She wanders from the sentinel cushion to Mahmoud's duvet then to yours…she usually winds up annoying me as a last resort."

"Oh dear, poor little nutkins. Hopefully Greta is not waiting outside the house with pouting lips and a mound of grubby kimonos when we get back."

"I may have overstepped my boyfriend role to be honest, Gina. I told her to sharpen up."

"I very much doubt that. You did the right thing. We both did. Come on, let's find a greasy spoon, I have to devour another hot calorie loaded meal before I can face the office desk."

We loaded my bits into the white van which was showing signs of wanting washing, but it's not my place to say anything. He's a perfect son-in-law-to-be in my estimation.

"Greta is calmer now, she says you gave her courage…and also promised a big party on her return, is that true?"

"Yes, it is, you will be a tart and she will be a vicar. Delly is going as a flower power girl."

"What will you go as?"

"Oh, I fancy it will be whatever Greta forces me to be. Oh look, David, a greasy whatnot, turn up there."

David drove me direct to the office from the cafe, and soon the youngsters were all clamouring for his attention. One good thing about holding a more senior position in the company is I can bring people into the break room to sample the delights of our tea and coffee. The chorus of hello and welcome back was rather pleasant. Mike Kemp came over with a folder and a grin like a crocodile.

"Oh Mrs Tantridge, welcome back. Did you manage to seduce our French neighbours?" I took the file…with a smile. One must show willing.

"Thank you, Mr Kemp. Where is Mr Paul?"

"Called to head office I'm afraid…he will be here tomorrow afternoon. Was there something you needed done especially?"

Derek was heading over and I ushered them both into my office.

"Any direct memos I should be aware of, folks?"

"Yes, Shoreditch is despatched without a reference and he will probably, well, let's not gloat, but he has to sell up. On the dole as of tomorrow…so to speak."

"That's horrible, Derek. He should have been aware of such consequences. He can't expect to get away with such things in the modern office."

"No, and I better get my nose back to the grindstone. The Harriman Report is the most 'keen' to be dealt with, Mrs Tantridge."

"Thanks, Derek, that's appreciated. Tell the youngsters there are two packs of French bon bons in the break room."

Mike Kemp grinned.

"That will be a stampede then."

"Oh, they're a truly nice bunch of kids. I am ultra-fond of them in spite of the mistaken matchmaking which seems to reach glossy mag proportions from time to time."

"Mmmm, they have Penny and myself down for a spring wedding."

While we chatted, I set up my computer and checked emails…nothing much really had gone down…or up or sideways. Except the Harriman thing was very much in evidence.

"The Harriman is looming rather large, isn't it, Mr Kemp?"

"Look, call me Mike, it's easier and I won't read anything into it. Yes, it's hot stuff. We are really pleased that your last investigation into them highlighted so much. You missed only one thing. Most impressive."

"Only one…must be improving in my old age."

"I don't think you had the full dossier then…but now somebody will be ordering the last coffee and doughnut spree."

"Not here in this office surely, please none of ours…we are all so knitted in now."

"No, breathe a sigh, Mrs Tantridge. I don't have it all but as per, Mr Paul is getting his teeth into the last of it now. He thinks we may get some fabulous accounts from the results."

"Oh yes, we felt this might happen. How mysterious are the works of the commercial engine, Mike?"

"Well, you seem upbeat and ready for the fray…must have done you a power of good over there."

"Indeed."

I arrange a meeting with Mike Kemp and Mr Paul for Wednesday, and carry on loading and sifting research data at home. We have less specifics than usual for the Harriman Report. There are aspects to it that sit badly with me…nothing to do with being away.

Life goes on, Nice or no Nice. A decision was made very rapidly last night. Granny Grumplings called the house and in case I ripped her head off with a hasty remark or three, David took the call. He made me smile with all his grimacing and silent pleads for help. He was helplessly impaled upon her remarks by his own politeness. Poor love. This very sweet obedience to the elderly was about to come to an end. A swift and timely end at that.

"Oh hello, how are you?"

"Gina is working at present, is there any message?"

"No, you don't understand, Gina is extremely busy and cannot be disturbed right now."

"Greta wanted to go to Japan."

"I'm not taking a tone with you; I'm merely stating facts."

"You can't blame Gina for everything like this…no, I am not rude, but by God I will be soon."

"How dare you blame other people? You gave Greta the money after all."

There is a seething pause. Delly runs to me and not up the curtain…she gets an anxiety thing at raised voices. I cuddle her.

"It's alright, darling, it's nasty old witchy witch…she can't get you while I am here."

"Gina, I am at the end of a long tether with that woman, she is impossible. All my first impressions about her are totally out of the window. She is horrible. Not only does she blame everything on you, she now states that you are pretending to be more important than you are and that really winds me up. The woman is—"

"A witch. Yes, it takes a while to work out so don't blame yourself. Humour her and look at everything she says and does with humour, and save your sanity, darling. I do. She probably had her broomstick clamped."

With that David comes over and hugs me.

"Goodness me, how have you put up with it all these years?"

"Humour and picking the right battles. Come on, let's have an elicit coffee break on the firm's time."

Wednesday is fabulous. Mike Kemp and Mr Paul have arranged a working meeting at a local hotel. Unfortunately, not the posh expensive one. I have promised a tantrum if I don't get dessert. My poor waistline. David swears I am eating for two… I am keen to point out to him…no, three actually.

Mike is looking smarter than a well-polished Mercedes at a Greek wedding. Mr Paul is ordering the best wine. I am smug as a panda under a tree.

"Ah, I see we are all hungry and on time."

We shake hands, then sit together and enjoy the fussing profusion of waiters. When they leave, I offer my two penn'orth.

"How lovely, it's so nice to be free to talk."

"Oh yes indeed, and eat good food and not have to wash up." Mike Kemp is a single man.

"We are in luck today, Gina, they have your favourites."

"Knowing you, Mr Paul, you phoned ahead and insisted upon sea bream and summer pudding. Eton mess and Mike's favourite, 'waitress ala creme caramel'."

"Ah, Miss Clever Clogs, that's where your wrong, I insist on an apology…they were told that we could always get it at the competitors."

"Works every time."

Mike was busily giving all the waitresses marks out of ten…only for deportment whilst carrying a tray of course.

"What was it he said in Four Weddings, Mr Paul… Ah yes… 'damn fine filly…think I'm in with a chance there'."

We all laughed at that one. Mike blushed up. I am getting naughtier by the minute. Might have a slim connection to coming into so much money. A huge sigh of relief had come over my life. Followed rapidly by 'I am determined not to let X-Ray and Dairyman Dan get their paws on the trust fund that my parents obviously sacrificed things for themselves to set up for love of me'. For love of me. It rings through my mind as we tuck into the most delishus, deeeevvvvvine seabass. Everyone is in agreement. Fantastic.

We all get on so easily together and without the tensions of the office gossip, we can totally relax. Of course, the wine plays a significant role. The Harriman soon comes up and I explain what I want to achieve.

"Mr Paul, I will be able to work on this better at home without a single interruption. It's anti-social, I know, but it's vital in this instance."

"Quite so, excellent idea…do you have everything you need?"

"I would love Penny to assist and to shadow me on all the attachments from day one. Sorry to be so pedantic. Mainframe clearance essential for her on this mission only understandably."

"Password by pass clearance…essential presume?"

"Essential. Any ultra-sensitive material can be passed through me and give her essential 'management specific' clearance level this mission only."

He visibly blanches.

"Christ, Mrs Tantridge, this sounds serious. Mike is sound, Mrs Tantridge, you can speak."

"Sorry to exploit the popular myth about room at the top, but in this particular top, there will be even more room."

It will be fair to say I do gain their full attention. "Not another head-rolling…please…no."

"Oh I am feeling like Madame Therese Defarge, so watch out if you see me busily knitting a bobble hat with initials worked in."

"Is this what is known as guillotine humour, Mrs Tantridge?"

"That, or a healthy demonstration of how to find the exit quietly for a well-known person of stage and screen."

Mike now is visibly pale.

"Would you like dessert, Mrs Tantridge?"

At that we all laugh very raucously. It really is the night of the long knives all over again. Contrary to popular belief, I hate this part of the process. Mr Paul looks really down in the mouth. I want to blurt out who it is and how I found it out, but this really is not the time or the place.

"Can I have Penny? I understand it's asking a lot from Mike's side of the woods but it is crucial."

"But of course. You're getting close by the sound of it, but I know these issues cannot be made public without absolute proof. Am I right when I say investment and taxes?"

"'Fraid so."

We clear up pudding like crows on a battlefield and I for one am glad to get back to the office. The sooner this horrible task is executed – forgive pun – the better. Penny is thrilled and acts the part to the letter. Love her. She hurries to me the second she hears.

"Oh I am so excited…Mr Paul says you asked for me specifically."

"You will be a fellow knitter at the guillotine. Penny, I hope you have a brilliant sense of humour and strong sense of 'for the good of the company'. You are sure going to need it."

I open my front door to Penny at nine am sharp. God love her, she gets into the spirit at once. I had a strong feeling she would. We brace ourselves as we enter the 'Management Only' clearance zone. I look at her and Penny gets it. I mean she really gets it. By ten o'clock that evening, an exhausted Penny retires to sleep it all off in Mahmoud's room. David is a great help in a crisis and seeing that we have a big problem to sort. Makes us supper. Being honest, he dotes on us like a mother hen.

Bless all the fairies and the little people as well as gnomes, Darby O'Gill plus any long dresses not yet worn by French angels, we complete the report. I have the file…this is far too delicate to go on a laptop of any clearance.

I ring Mr Paul from the lounge after my shower, sporting my best dressing gown – well, one must keep up appearances.

"Ah, Mrs Tantridge, how can I help?" Bless.

"We have it. I am bringing it in tomorrow, it's typed and this is a one-time one-copy-only scenario." He whistles.

"That serious."

"It could have been a news editors new Maserati gran turis, Mr Paul. I pray we can save it from that arena."

"We are grateful, Mrs Tantridge."

"We are happy for that kindness. Penny is asleep in my spare room. She is exhausted, poor love."

"I will personally see to it that the pay for you both reflects this work."

"We rather thought you might, but to be clear on this, we don't want any change in our pay for at least three to six months."

"Ah, I understand. Jeez, you think of everything."

"My grandfather was a newspaper man. So clever at working through plots and what is signature to human nature."

"Greed and desire."

"Exactment ba."

The next three weeks were in fact such a challenge. Once Penny and I had delivered the 'Harriman Bombshell', as we called it – not in front of other members of staff naturally – our lives settled into a quite routine. Well, mine did. David had gone back to Cambridge to prepare for his finals. He had given me the timetable so that I could, if I wished, call him and leave good wishes on his answer machine. He was very hard-working so I felt he was sure to do well. His schedule was punishing. Marine science evening exams were taking place on the fourth, sixteenth and twentieth of October.

I naturally assumed he would call his family and Greta and myself when the ordeal was over with. I sensed he would soon be involved in any way he could, the Centre for Industrial Ocean Impacts being high on his list. We had a fine and intelligent young man now within our family. My sadness was that Ray would quite probably never know him. There is always hope.

Greta was settled into the Japanese studies yet again and sending all sorts of wonderful emails and texts telling me she loved me and would I always be this patient with her. I had to reply with great care not to give her the impression I was softening. Oh yes, I know my girl so much better than a year ago. A whole world away a year ago…David of course had made a huge change upon her personality.

He told me he truly loved her and wanted a fine future for them and was sincere. My goodness, what a difference.

Jean and David were travelling in the outback and sent me postcards of the richness of the wildlife and landscape. There was another successful marriage. Thankfully, I had good examples all around me to learn from for next time. Yes, I was ever hopeful there would be one. Then it happened, I had letters from the notaire and the news sent reverberations through the whole of my world. I found myself writing back and telling her the huge decision I had made in the last few weeks.

Everyone was making new beginnings. David and Greta, I felt sure as soon as it was practical and within their power, would be married. Ray was soon to be legally X-Ray and I would be left cuddling the cat…but where? I took a huge dive into my new life the following Monday.

I was rich and so there was no fear of destitution. I called the local estate agents and a man I always called Mr Smooth although his name was Mr Brown – no logic of course…but that's me sometimes – arrived on the Saturday just as I was busy sweeping yet another avalanche of russet leaves, which must have given him the right impression. He parked his car and I offered him mistakenly my gardening gloved hand.

"Ah, I see you're a lady who loves flowers and gardening, Mrs Tantridge."

Delly ran over to make general inquiries as to whether this man had treats or would give her manly caresses. Such a tart when men were around.

"You must be, Mr Brown…from Herricks. This is Delilah but she is known by the sobriquet of Delly or Delly nutkins…you know how it is with a pet."

"I confess, Mrs Tantridge, I have an amazing little Boston terrier called Dude, but we ended up calling him Doodles. Our son refuses to walk with us when we go out with him."

"Children get easily embarrassed by parents. He's a teenager then."

"Oh yes, and don't we know it."

"Come in and we can do the grand tour."

"Indeed, this is a fine property and this area is so much in demand. You won't have it on the market very long, I can assure you of that."

This really was most reassuring and I wondered just how to tell Greta that she would have to marry David now. Or be without a base. We all had to move into our new life which was there ready and waiting.

My plan was to give my notice at work. Penny was already prime to take my place. She had found her voice and was an excellent candidate. I would not of course get the final say on that but I knew I would be able to influence. Being able to 'influence' is a huge step in any direction in the modern office.

I would pack up here and then go to Nice and search for a character property. Within a certain radius. I could drive my car over and if it broke down, I would be able to buy another… Everything in life looks easy on paper. Of course, there would be challenges, I would embrace them – wouldn't I?

The alternative was to stay here and risk X-Ray getting his hands on my trust. No, no, no…I could not bear that he should benefit after he had cleared out our account, and I will never forget that thirty-two sodding quid incidents. Never. Forgive, yes, but not forget.

Mr Brown of course sang the praises of the well-appointed family home wrap around garden. In its own grounds would be pushing the description a little too fancifully, I think. Parking in the drive was alright for two cars, but three really was a pinch.

Still, to my pleasure and astonishment, he came up with five two five…hundred thousand that is. This agent speak is always an irritation…but today I felt rather grand and all irritants vanished· I sent an email to Gillian and X-Ray. Gillian was at my door by three in the afternoon.

"I knew it, I knew it. Darling, I have had the news bell in my head for the last two days. It's him, it is, I know it…Ray…he wants his share. Oh sorry, darling, me and my big mouth."

"Sweety, if I hadn't wanted you here and had not wanted you to know, I would have said nothing and let the removal van speak for me."

"Oh, Delly darling, you're going to move, yes you poor little sausage."

"Have a glass of wine, Gillian, and tell me all the latest."

"Oh, but you're the latest. Do you want anyone to know…well, that is around here?"

"The more the merrier, so chatter and run all you want…besides, wherever I go, you will be coming for holidays. But keep that part to yourself. I really mean that too, my dear pal. Please, not a word."

"Oh, it's Nice isn't it…it's the South of France, I knew it, you are off down there, you naughty little French girlie. Oh, my sainted aunt, I AM SO HAPPY FOR YOU. OH BUT DARLING, WHATEVER SHALL I DO WITHOUT YOU? You're the only one I really love and admire around here."

Gillian's voice had reached fever-pitch, and Delly had zipped up the curtains from the sheer hell of it all.

"Gillian, please help me get Delly down."

I woke up very early probably due to going to bed not long after Gillian had left returning home to make Bob supper. Her parting remark was a grimace.

"I'm trying to cut back on his food portions and leaving longer between meals Gina. I may as well order a ton of ice-cream for all the good it's doing."

"Is he just going out in the car and eating at the local chicken lickin' joint?"

"Got it in one."

My morning was adventurous. I gave in my notice to Mr Paul, who arrived at my office with a blanched and sad expression.

"Is there nothing we can do to change your mind, Mrs Tantridge?"

"It's my desire to leave, it's not my colleagues, who I deeply respect, or the work. It's my marriage break-up. I want to start afresh in France, Nice as a preference. My parents' trust fund is through and I will buy a character property there."

Delly's pet passport papers had arrived. I contacted the vet's to get her through all travel and health legalities. My pal Penny kept weeping. Crikey, am I loved this much? Surprising how we are but just don't realise. I learned many lessons those last five weeks at the company. The house was on the market and I felt an extraordinary wilfulness of nature take over from indecision. It is good…right…it is good. Well, are there any more surprises in my character?

The biggest scare I had was a call to let a family view the property. After this wake up to the reality of my recent actions, there were many rushes round with the hoover and Delly was once more treated to quite new expressions…the latest being, "Yes, I know you are cute in your furry trousers but just get out of the bloody way." Announced in a low mutter, you understand as those poor curtains were truly finished. In the end, I took them down.

Mr Brown contacted me a lot over that hectic month. Gillian became miserable. Then I said it. The thing that would change all our lives at the end.

"Why don't you come and help me look?" Well, I can tell you Transformation City shone on the mossy path. We were fine together after that. Decisions made had to be adhered to.

My leaving party was being hushed-whisper planned and a dog-eared list and card was doing the rounds.

I, of course, saw nothing and subsequently became very emotional when I saw my decisions had set all this in motion.

Gillian was making lists and lists of lists. Bless. Delly was making nuisance rounds of all the rooms, as if saying goodbye to them all in turn. They showed signs of great depletion. I emailed Greta developments and Gran rang.

"Hello, Gran, how are you?"

"Where are you going to live? I spose' he wants his share of the house. I knew he was the wrong type."

"It takes one to know one, Gran."

I ended the call. At work, Penny was constantly with tissue box at the ready and I had to remain calm for both our sanity's sake.

Jean emailed. 'Good for you, good luck.' I constantly re-inflated my sagging resolve. Mahmoud had not been in touch. Sigh. The last day arrived and Mr Paul presented me with a bunch of the most beautiful flowers. Speeches were made, parties buzzed and everyone hugged me. I wondered if I should give a speech. I couldn't, for tears streaming embarrassingly down my face, manage more than 'I shall miss you all'. Which was true.

The time had come for me to step into my new life. During the last hour in my office which Penny now occupied, we could not help but hear the youngsters, who, bless their designer handbags and shoes, were on high whisper mode…which was rapidly reaching full throttle crescendo. Elementary, my dear Watson.

I gathered up the far-too-generous leaving gifts, and the much mangled signed by anyone and everyone leaving card. Which I actually would treasure always. Such is life. Only when you're going do people make you welcome with hugs.

I insisted that Penny come out to visit once I had a sound roof upon the villa…that I still had to find purchase and move into.

Back at the house which was now just that… 'my home' would have to be carried in my heart or by my pals and the dancing Delly for a while. We were appointing various items to the rapidly growing 'French home', cases and boxes, the rubbish pile, the local charity shop bags and as I already had cleared my home once, this task was not taking long.

Gillian was with me telling me what to take, what to do and what to eat. I let her boss me, I loved this naughty gossipy woman with all her bangles and fake tan. I would not have her any other way.

Funny that. Delly sensed that this was an occasion which demanded her to dance everywhere behind us and when we were appointing ourselves the task of unloading onto Gordon Elder all the books I owned apart from absolute favourites, she obliged us all by sitting in his van. He promised to get a good price.

Gordon is a bit of a one. Yes, he had sold my French books. Correction…my beloved Grandfather's books. So, he would get shot of the lurid art paperback books and one or two peculiar subjects. One of the volumes spoke of 'Beekeeping on the Continent.' Gillian, bless her heavily ring adorned hands, snatched it back with glee.

"Oh no, darling, you're going to need this at your chateaux." Oh, the blissful state of future hope.

"Oh yes, now that's a brilliant idea, Mrs Tantridge."

This is from Gordon, who, with the help of 'Delly get out of the bloody way nutkins', is trying to load things into his 'tardis' van.

Ah, the bliss of hope.

Ah, the sound thrashing of reality.

We had to keep stopping and making tea, pouring wine, classed now as an 'evening only' exercise. The first time we had attempted to sip wine while packing had ended up with me answering the door 'trousered', I think the polite description could be, to Mr Smooth – oops, sorry, Mr Brown – with the next best thing to a Quaker family of highly thought of reputation, who gawped, including their children who were dressed like fashion plates from another century.

Gillian thought on meeting them that she had been transported to another age. They were not of course the only visitors during this pack up the house party. Others came and snottily inquired as to if we had a conservatory. They may as well have asked for an orangery and hey, while you're at it, what about 'in its own grounds'. Five two five gets you a walk-in pantry and grizzled but fruit-bearing trees of unknown history. And no, the cat isn't staying.

Gillian was driving down with me to Nice so she had to be back home across the lane and make dinners for a year to feed Bob who could not even peel an apple let alone prepare a three-course dinner. He revered anyone who could cook. His hobby was keeping as round as a pumpkin and shunning gyms.

The day the house came off the market, bought by the people who I thought might be a Quaker family, goes down in history as ultra-strange. I was always prepared in the past for surprises, but what happened that morning would defy any definition of average. I had been careful not to pack certain things until the last minute. Of course, the sand casket was going in last, it had not 'leaked' any more grains, which was good, and I kept it on my dressing table. Oh, I know everyone will say it's mere coincidence, but as I was dusting it carefully, the phone began ringing and it was Mr Brown.

The house was to be sold subject to contract. Well, that was it. Gillian and I had to go now…we left very early one evening…yes…this is our masterplan. We crossed each thing off the famous lists as we did it. Delly was taken in great confusion and many whispered cuddles from me by Megs. Gillian to promote hope and courage was telling her in one delicate pussy cat ear that she was a 'darling sausage'.

"Yes, Gillian, she is…!" was the best I could come up with.

My car was considered too old and bashed to be trusted and so we drove along merrily enough in Gillian's Mercedes – well, you would, wouldn't you?

A good, solid overseas removal company, Beckwood, had been given keys to enter and empty the house and the keys left at Bob's. The 'shipping' costs were high, but still cheaper than buying all new. God forbid. Greta was flying back from Japan to also enter and empty her room, and David was driving the lot up to the new rented property near Ullapool. He was set for a reasonable outcome from his exams. The Ullapool team were taking him on. He was happy, Greta was happy. They were not getting hitched for years as they were unsure of what sort of wedding they really wanted. New horizons.

We get on the 'Road to Morocco', as we laughingly called the trip to Nice, with Megs holding up a wailing all-knowing – she had been left behind and I was going off to unknown destinations to no doubt, no doubt…stroke pussy cats of other breeds and compilations…Delly nutkins. Who really is a most unusual cat!

We have maps, food, refreshment, and more maps and sat nav and maps, and more clothes than we will ever be able to wear. If we have to be rummaged through at any borders, we are in big trouble.

I had already called ahead to alert Gabriel and his lovely mum about our requirements. I was informed all would be ready and they had the best surprise for us. Another one. Phew. We still had to get there and we had no idea where we going really. But hey. We called ourselves romantic hippy names like Gigi and Jo'jo. Anyone listening, hang on to your hats, sanity and bottles of fizz. We drove over tracks that no other Mercedes had driven over. We stayed at places of ill repute, posh repute and downright expensive repute. By the time we had hit the trail into Nice, we were experienced in finding shops selling toothpaste, hand cream, comfy driving espadrilles, headache cures and finding excellent sarnies was the top of the new list.

The old lists had long since been lost out of the window or some such thing.

Gillian had been made a new woman at a beauty salon in Aix-en-Provence. I was astonished at the transformation. Gillian insisted that I get one too and while she waited for me, went to the cinema.

We roared away like skid kids and were stopped by the speed police. I was trying to hide in my seat. Gillian was carefully polite and just so full of regret. Apology and smiles from a glamour queen with a Mercedes can work. We feel only once. Driving with the greatest respect and care after that certainly took the shine off the gingerbread. Calmed us down though.

When we made the last call to Gabriel that we were some thirty minutes away, I really don't know who was most relieved.

Living in the South of France. Pent-up excitement flowed through my veins… OOO lalala. Happy days ahead began with the surprise. Gabriel almost gobbled Gillian up when he saw her, scooping her in a lusty armful, kissing her the required three times and then turning to me and saying, "Oh how wonderful…you bring the angel I asked for in all my prayers."

Protests and explanation, explanations and corrections would be falling on French deaf ears. We followed him with great flourish and ceremony which would not have been out of place in the French Court at Versailles. To a back courtyard I had not seen before, and a gîte, which from its fresh masonry and paint, was a very new addition to the homestead.

"Wow."

"Ah the wow indeed, my dearest friend Mrs Tantridge. Look how the busy we have been in the absence of our lovely friend."

We followed him inside where he hurried to show us the chic interior. Tiny stove and kettle, all the accoutrements for a quick cuppa and the dinkiest fridge ever to grace any room. Twin beds of generous proportion and cute shower over a bath, toilet, bidet and minute hand basin of such newness and neatness with hand towels, dinky soaps and sachets for your hair. All lovingly and comically demonstrated by a proud Gabriel. Gillian was close behind me giggling at his antics and we both found it hard to hold back the laughter. When it came to the shampoo demo, Gabriel pretended to squirt it over his hair and massage with clowning face until his black curls stood to attention.

By this time both Gillian and myself were sitting with splitting sides on the beds, when from the doorway were heard, "Ah! So I catch you at last, you naughty Romeo of the *Promenade des Anglais*, you keep all the most beautiful women to yourself."

My happiness is complete. I jump up and run to Raphael. We hug without any embarrassment. Gillian is gawping.

"Gillian, meet Raphael; Raphael, this is my dearest kindest pal from England."

"Oh, but you have my complete understanding as to why Gabriel is in such high spirits. He always did choose the most charming femme fatal that walk in the designer shoes."

We all laugh and Gabriel leads the way after our cases are deposited inside the gîte – which we would be fools to turn down – back to the lounge where pastis cognac and snacks arrive from mysterious places already planned, of this there is no doubt. Raphael raises his glass to the party and we all sing out, "…to the future."

Raphael takes me to one side and Gillian vanishes in a cloud of mystery with Gabriel. Good God, what's he up to now? Oh well, she is a woman grown and can more than take care of herself. What amazes me more is her willingness to go without protest or complaint.

"Gina, you have been so much in my thoughts and when we planned this gîte, Gabriel and I, well, we had no idea that it would be you and your charming friend who would be the first. Believe me, *cherie*. Can I help you further in any way?"

"Raphael, you have surprised me enough today. When Gabriel spoke of surprises, I had no idea of all this. It's fantastic. A perfect base. I am longing to find a suitable property in this region. Oh Raphael, you have such charm. I had forgotten how lovely French men can be."

"Not all, I'm afraid, some are dangerous…like the gangster."

"You have been so busy; how did you manage it all?"

"We had purchased the land and put in planning permission over one year ago but of course we don't count the cockerills."

"Chickens?"

"Ah yes, you are the best teacher."

"Oh no, Raphael, the worst."

He drew from his pocket a sheaf of papers.

"When you have time and have rested, perhaps you would find these of much interest and I hope great help."

I took them and hugged him again. It really was so good and comforting – yes, I use the word 'comforting' to see him again.

We ate supper quietly together, Gillian and I. Both of us were very tired now and it wasn't long before we said our goodnights and thanked everyone and turned in.

I slept like a log. Gillian too was asleep in seconds so she told me later. After showers, we tried to get our hair to reset in the style that the fabulous salon in Aix-en-Provence had given us. We really battled but I am afraid it fell short. We made up for it by dressing as tastefully as possible so as to create the right impression. Making sure that two very tasty and flirtatious French men noticed us.

"Chanticleer! That's the word I was trying to think of. Sorry to make you jump, Gillian, but I forgot." Gillian was tucking into a mouthful of the most delicious sausage ever to grace a plate.

"Quite alright, sweetie…this food is going to ruin my waistline…but I will think about that when I get home. I am determined to enjoy all the delights that France has to offer. Let me see that list your Raphael gave you last night."

"My Raphael?"

"Er yes…it's as plain as the nose on your face, Gina my love, that the man is crazy about you. There really is no mistaking it."

I feel my face redden, but remain speechless. Handing over the sheaf of papers with a naughty school girl shyness.

"Well, this is a good start, Gina. These are within your price brackets."

I cool down and we look at them together. Raphael really did understand the brief no doubt relayed to him by the more than excitable Gabriel, who although a natural, good humoured, loveable clown, also has a very sound business head on his broad shoulders. Funny, he is so suited in that respect to Gillian…they could have been made for each other except of course Bob is a lovely, loyal, clever hubby and we do him an injustice by not reminding ourselves of this fact.

We do feel better and excited by the prospect of being driven up into the hills on a merry jaunt with Raphael. Gabriel can't go, he is so busy at present. He is pulling faces as we leave and takes out a hanky to wipe crocodile tears away. To my surprise, Raphael is not quite the impoverished student I first thought. He is a dark horse. We set off at three and the sun has come to greet us with all its warmth and south of France splendour. He is driving, much to Gillian's delight, a new Citroen Berlingo.

We set off under a broad blue sky with sun streaming. However, as we drove merrily along the coast, we hit a little sea mist. This added a truly ethereal quality to the scenery. Gillian was enchanted.

"Darling, you are lucky to be living in such a wonderful place. I wish Bob would relax more and maybe, big maybe I know, should just come out here and unwind."

"Perhaps he will…with all your good reports, it's bound to change his views. Would you live here permanently like me?"

"Given a chance, yes."

Raphael turned up to the first house we had arranged with the agent to view; we had others lined up, and as I jumped out to undo the main gates, my heart sank. It was much, much larger than it actually appeared on the photograph. The roof was half gone and I knew it would need a millionaire's income to sort out. Undaunted and as they say, 'on the spot', with an eager agent coming toward us with hand outstretched, there was simply no getting back in the car yet.

'Villa Paulette' was full of history, he explained, and was a survivor – well er, yes – but I don't think you needed any imagination to see a great many euros would be required to initiate its next phoenix rising from the ashes show. Crumbling fountains told tales of wonderful days and sumptuous nights of dancing and fine wines. Once upon a time in fairyland…a land now vanished like the water supply.

Delly would have loved it.

We trooped after him as he danced ahead clutching brief case in true agent style. I had switched off at the illuminated in neon price of near a million euro. Gillian looked at me and sighed audibly. We knew with great reality of the moment; we were wasting time. I was the one to speak to Raphael.

"Raphael dear, dear friend, we have seen enough, it's way out of my league."

He spoke with great courtesy to the dancing while demonstrating agent, who, with great ceremony, pulled faces of sadness. Well, you would, wouldn't you? A handsome commission…*phut*…gone.

The next week was very similar. No house was located and we were simply going through the motions. We lost Gillian who was called home by Bob. Fair enough. She drove off very sadly. We were enjoying the sun and the driving out a little too much. Another week for me in the gîte. Or so I thought. Raphael had a huge proposition. He thought being alone was not good for me. He was right of course, after the lively company and fun with Gillian, and still a lone search for a home ahead, he thought I would be sad. So, he took me to meet his mother!

This was so alarming that I was as excited and enervated as a spaniel at her first Crufts. The family home turned out to be a grand and I mean grand – chateau up in the hills. He truly, just as Gillian predicted, is the dark horse.

Madam Raphael, as I mentally called her, was a slender – I can see where he gets his build from – lady of means. Her voice was cultured and face lovely. She came to me with such warmth I was instantly comfortable.

"Ah, there you both are. My dear, you are so welcome. I hope you don't mind responding to an old lady's whim. But when Raphael told me your plan, I said at once…but no, Gina must not be alone and such a hard task ahead of her. I insisted he brought you here. Please, sit down."

"Thank you, your home is so amazing, I am a little astonished."

"Oh please, you are too charming, I wish only to help and please, no formality…call me Martine please, all my friends do. Raphael, would you call for tea and some refreshment please?"

Call for tea. Oh, my goodness, they have staff. I should have guessed a house of this splendour and size would no doubt have many. I was doubly intrigued.

I sat next to her on a fabulous chaise lounge with so many pieces of fine art around me. I could not even think of what to look at first. There was a little of the showgirl in Martine, her demeanour and flourishes. But a longing behind her eyes which all this colour warmth and beauty could not hide. Her story I felt was of late a very sad and chastening one.

"Your English is perfect, Martine, and I am very taken aback by the beauty of your home."

"Oh, none of that, my dear, we want you to be comfy with us. Raphael says I gush too much and frighten people away. He does not understand that I am lonely, although he is here a lot, when he drives people around showing them French history and all the magical places, I admit I get fidgety and annoyed with myself."

"Oh Martine, with such honesty, you must have so many pals. There must be people fighting over you."

Martine laughs very openly and I can sense that she has had a great sorrow to bear. We both watch Raphael as he comes with a tray followed by a cross-looking maid.

"Madam, I try to carry but Monsieur Raphael will not let me do my duty. He says bring the biscuits." Martine only smiles. I am learning a lot here.

The tray is denuded of its heavy cargo of tea pot, milk, sugar, crockery, buns with currants and croissants with chocolate, and sandwiches with dainty fillings. I am so hungry I dig in right off with Raphael following my example and to my surprise, even the dainty Martine. How the hell she keeps her tiny waist is beyond me. Mine is forcing itself against the fabric of my skirt more and more the longer I eat at the Hotel Gabriel.

"Forgive me, Gina, but may I ask what kind of home you want to buy?"

"Of course, it's all very new at the moment having some money. My wonderful parents were killed in a car accident and they had already set up a trust fund for me to collect when I became an adult. Because I had no knowledge of it until this year, it has matured and now it is sufficient for me to buy a modest villa outright. I have not anywhere near enough for most of the properties around here but I am hoping to spend no more than say two hundred thousand sterling. I have enough left over to decorate and renovate and set up a little business…you understand that I cannot idle about."

"Nor should you, it is bad for the health. I should know. I was a dancer and fell in love with a happy-go-lucky man with a great deal of…how would you say it in English, Raphael?"

"*Joie de vivre*, my darling *mama.*"

"Oh, but Gina."

"Gina has a great deal of understanding of the French expressions…she spent all her school holidays with her grandparents in Nice. The Mouriers no less."

"Oh *mon dieu*, this is amazing news. I said that something good was coming to us this year now, didn't I, Raphael, you must admit I did."

"You knew my family here, Martine?"

"My father often spoke of them and they loved to read your wonderful grandfather's articles about the state of the governing bodies. Oh, how wonderful, to recall my youth and how your family's newspaper would send photographers to me, and I would pose…oh such days."

"You were a dancer of the *Corps de Ballet*."

Raphael came to me with another fresh cup of tea. Smiling at the happiness I was bringing by talking so naturally with his mother, he touched my shoulder lovingly. I felt such a weird sensation at that moment. I could only look into my tea. My goodness what a day this is turning out to be.

Martine held up a tiny cake and sipped her tea.

"No, my darling girl, I was a dancer of the burlesque cabaret. Raphael gets his looks and physique from me."

I almost choked on my croissant and we all broke into laughter.

"Gina, my mother was, and still is to my way of thinking, a delightful dancer and mimic on the stage, and made my father the happiest man in the world. Luckily for him, his parents, who were the most frightful snobs, had already passed on so he could keep his wealth."

He gestured around the room and drank some more tea.

"And marry the girl he loved."

Well, after that peculiar connection to my family, Martine was easy in my company and it was decided that if I wished, I should move into the guest room and my furniture could be stored in the barn. I was unsure of the barn idea until I saw it. The whole place was warm dry and very clean indeed. I contacted Gabriel and he was sad to see me go but agreed that as Raphael was a good man, rich, and with good heart, it was by far the best. It was settled and I soon became used to having my lovely Raphael with me more and more.

Contacting the shipping company, I gave them extra details as to how to find the Chateaux, and told Bob and Gillian, Greta and David of all the new developments. Greta's email tickled me pink. It simply said, 'Go girl.'

Megs was to come out with Delly and I sent her sufficient funds for this. Martine was not scared or allergic of cats; she had a neutered tom of her own called Pueblo. I wanted to inquire one day how such a tatty-eared cat came by such an illustrious name but felt it might be taking my welcome too far. I had shown her photographs of the wonderfully naughty Maine Coon Delilah Nutkins, whose breed had originated from North America, was a chatty catty and an absolute expert at massage of the lower back and shoulders. This description along with the photos had her longing to see her. Raphael hugged me tightly one day when our search for a home was going badly.

"We will find it, my sweet Gina. My mother thinks you are so funny and loves you dearly already."

"Oh God, I hope you're right."

And in true good time, as all things are in the nature of things, we did. But it was how we found it that was so odd. One property on our agent's map was constantly eluding us. Villa Cheval Dansant. We were always trying new ways to seek it out and like some elusive fairy of the mists, it tricked us into here, no here, not there, here. Ah no, no, I am not there, but here. We constantly joked about it.

I even remarked one day, "It's the magic place that does not really exist."

Then, one day, I pointed to a place on a very old map. Insisting that we stop the car just at the roadside and then getting out of Raphael's car, I took a brolly from the back seat and began poking the hedge. Lo and behold, there was a five-bar gate that had been totally overgrown with some sort of rapacious weed. We pulled it away and there she was, my villa. The villa of my dreams. She was so lovely and yet not at all old and ruined, just bloody impossible to get at from any road map we had been supplied with. Local people told us how to use the new road to arrive at the back of the property and we passed converted stables, beautifully made into holiday gîtes of an exceptional style.

Raphael rang the number supplied by the agent. When his call was answered, he broke into a smile as broad as ever I have seen. Then he plunged into old Provence of French, a wonderful dialect. I understood not one word in twenty.

When he closed the call, he began to walk about with me in a very happy, jaunty way. I caught the bug and soon we were like kids in a magic kingdom. We looked in all the windows and ended up at the front of the villa again. He went off to the car for something and I stayed pressing my nose against the pane, peering in at the most stunning wall table – it was probably a reproduction, but I didn't care one jot. Above it a treasure, a fuzzy-with-age mirror which sang out with the sheer joy of being a mirror…displayed around its edges galloping, cavorting, dancing, were beautifully gilded stallions and mares. Believe me it was easy to tell them apart. The curvy bottoms of the stallions were so fabulous and the mares seem to whinny and neigh with delight.

I would have picked the lock to get in if it was not for Raphael's excellent local reputation. He was at my side with slices of apple and we munched happily as we looked at the stunning decor of the mirror and table.

I put my ideas to Raphael and he listened very intently with his arm across my shoulders.

"Now these mares are very happy to see these stallions, yes? Or are the stallions very happy to see these mares?"

"Ah, Gina, it is…how you say…the oldest story of love in the world. This stallion, you see him with the saucy toss of his mane? His name is Raphael, and here, this mare, her name, it is Gina…oh yes, I have all this on very good authority."

We walked to the gate to look out for the agent. Monsieur Babineaux, who was apparently a local legend in many ways, had promised he would be here very soon. He seemed to understand our problem about finding the way in.

Eventually, an ancient automobile turned in and parked next to Raphael's modern, practical car.

This stunning vehicle could not in any way of imagination be called just a car, it was vintage, and had it seemed its own set of rules, engagements, manners and general air of importance. The oldest man I have met in France stepped out as dapper as a prince. He had pure white hair and wore designer glasses. Slow, so slow and gently, he assembled himself complete with papers and a bunch of keys which could have opened the Palace of St James if they had a mind to. These 'keys' were put into use and the door swung in. All the while Raphael and this wonderful Dickensian style gentleman were chattering away.

We wandered slowly, carefully and delightedly from room to room – noh, noh, not rooms here, chambers and salons. The kitchen was a mish-mash of attempts to bring it into the modern era…I loved it all. The only modest sized chamber was the far corner bedroom. There were four massive sized chambers or masters, plus one tiny box room and study. All were clean and no junk cluttered, no mice ran and no birds flew. They could have done because the far corner bedroom sported a small hole and daylight could be seen clearly through to the blue sky beyond. This room I loved. The delicate ceiling decor and windows were wonderful, and a closet with the oldest little basin and stand, cute as cute, with hooks around for towels and clothes. I dubbed it playfully *M salle de bain*, much to Raphael and Monsieur Babineaux's amusement.

"I think the dear English madam has chosen her favourite room in her favourite villa, noh!"

"I love it with all my heart, oh Raphael, it is my dream home…this is it…it's as if I was born here and am returning after many travels in a wicked world."

Without any questions, Raphael spoke to MB as I mentally called him and we all trooped outside to a garage cum stores outbuilding. Within minutes, Raphael had me helping him erect a set of rather sturdy ladders against the wall that corresponded with my ladies' chamber…he went up it like a monkey. MB

146

gave laughing encouragement. I, terrified for his safety, held onto the bottom with all my strength, afraid lest he should fall. Oh, how daring and dangerous these French men are.

So…instant!

Once up, he began trumbling about and a great clunk followed by some dust and another set of clunks and whumps, more dust and then silence. I think the silence scared me most of all.

"*D'accord*, Raphael?"

A cheeky face covered in dust and grime eventually appeared and he gave us both the thumbs up.

"You should marry this young and very handsome man."

I was taken utterly by surprise, and turned obviously mouth open and hair by now very askew, to look at MB, who, not only was handsome himself in a sort of biblical Methuselah way, but had such perfect English.

Well, that's decided then, I wanted to say when the heat in my face had died down to a slight pink spot – or two. I didn't dare answer; anything from me would have broken the spell of the magic villa.

While Raphael did his on-the-spot repair of the roof, MB related the story of this delightful home soon to be mine. Bless all the angels in long dresses, short ones, and medium length culottes on Sundays.

Villa of the Dancing Horse had been built around 1920 by an indulgent but charming horse breeder, who by stint of money from excessive gambling and good luck, produced excellent bloodstock for the racing fraternity ie, the idle and fascinated with racing, rich – any problems with the later wars and Vichy France seemed very far away. Sadly, he became too bold and eventually bankrupt, usual story for those with too much flair and indulgence. Now, after many change of hands, Monsieur Babineaux was in possession.

I asked him, once darling Raphael, a very dusty Raphael, had come safely down to earth, how much the villa could be sold to me for.

MB looked at me then at Raphael. We both waited and I began to tremble with fear and excitement; everything hung on this amount. He spoke in Provencal to Raphael, then promptly as he was aged and tired, returned to the wonderful automobile and sat inside.

"Seriously, do you have two hundred thousand English pounds, my Gina?"
I nodded with pure relief.

"Then it is yours."

"But so reasonable and so and so…"

I was dancing around and jumping with joy and clapping my hands I hurried to the car and shook his hand. I ran round to the garden and laughed and laughed with the sheer joy of living my new life was.

here
it
was
really
here
at
last………

We were delighted with the outcome naturally. Martine arranged a 'finding the dream villa party'. Everyone came from the 'Hotel Gabriel'; they had special cover from a local agency for one night, and the scene was one of naughty charades and wine from various regions. Staff and the big chef from the pretty Hotel Villa Rivoli catered as they were old friends of Raphael and Martine. We were a merry crowd and I discovered how the French of this century throw a party.

The food was excellent, no stuffy sit-down meal – a buffet of truly delightful cuisine! I counted, or rather tried to count, the variety of dishes and gave up. Martine mimicked Eric Cantona, Baudelaire, and Isabelle Adjaine. We were in pain from laughing when she came out in full rig, dressed as the wife of an unpopular politician. Martine was brilliant on tottering heels and loads of badly applied make-up. We were in pain from laughing.

What a night.

Raphael danced with the cross maid, danced with so many people including Gabriel and his mama, and we sported roses in our teeth and did the Argentine tango – well, it was not really the Argentine tango, more a drunken giggling rose-in-the-teeth gaucho moves and all, a hilarious parody.

Who cares?

The films played back over the following weeks made for excellent entertainment. We even put them online. or rather naughty Gabriel and Raphael gave them an airing on some sites. This was our undoing. But of course. The chef from the Rivoli pretended to be drunk under the table with so much good acting, he nearly got dismissed from his job – for all the world. We had to go and explain to his superior that it was acted out as part of a charade. Phew, that was close. He has become one of our closest pals.

Greta rang from England, or I should say Scotland.

"Mum, is this you dancing the tango?"

"I must go and get my lawyer, Greta darling, before I answer that question…and how are you, sweety?"

"Mum, Dad's absolutely livid, he's seen it."

"Oh, excuse me while I laugh out loud."

"Did you see the heading that's on the internet?"

"Hi, life in Nice, no, hi, kickers in Nice party…Argentina comes to the *Cote.*"

"You're in big trouble with Dad, he's fair dancing a jig with fury. Apparently, he—"

"Are you being serious, Greta? I know you're one for joking about."

"No, I am serious. The heading is: 'Nice, Jet Set, Get Tangoed in French Chateaux.'

I'm laughing out loud and can't be bothered to answer. My daughter has turned into her father who is a prude when others have fun, and he is left out.

"The party was thrown in my honour due to us finding my dream home, Greta. Show some happiness for your poor mum, even if you feel like a dope, you're wrong to be like this, Greta, and you know you are. I tried to get in touch with you."

"You're off the rails, Mum, you are really off the rails."

"Good, I always wanted to see what it's like to be on the up side of something instead of the down. You told me to go girl and I went."

"Well, Dad is so angry, because he says you're living the 'hi life' and obviously live in a massive chateau while he is forced to share a tiny flat with his new partner."

"Oh, I am crying for him…don't cry for me, Argentina…"

I began trilling down the phone. Even Greta starts laughing.

"Oh Mum, you are so funny."

"Have you met his partner the milkman?"

"Oh, he's not all there, Mum, some sort of nutter. Has no pals at all and talks rot…makes Dad talk rot too. Has had some sort of council house background, loads of ill-mannered family members."

"That's nice."

"Oh Mum, you're a card, you really are."

"Greta darling, have you forgotten that X-Ray left us without funding and we held a 'boot it all out', and Delly is at the door, I have to go."

"Oh of course, Megs delivered her. Sorry to keep you then, darling! I am so glad you are okay, that's been my biggest worry if I am totally honest. David sends you loads of love and wants to know your moving-in date so that he can come over and arrange the housewarming at the new villa."

"You sound like me, Greta. It's all so marvellous. Raphael has let Delly in, she is in love with Martine's tiny tom cat called Pueblo. They cuddle up together in front of the fire. Raphael is turning photos of them snuggled up fast asleep into greeting and thank-you cards. He's paid for a print run; it's costing over seven hundred euro."

"Wow, I would love one."

"I will make sure you get one. The house going okay in Ullapool?"

"Gradually, Mum, gradually, one room at a time."

"Same as me at the villa. We get the keys in three weeks; I am so excited. The paperwork's going through easily due to total cash purchase and no chain. Also, the owner is a friend of Raphael and Martine. Must go, darling, toodooolooodoodle. Love to David."

"Bye, Mum, take care and have fun."

This,
I
can
comply
with.

The next week we were all of a flurry, and an air of excitement of a very different kind settled over the chateaux. My laughter-filled villa was abuzz with builders doing God-knows-what to everything. Raphael had convinced me that a sensible, practical solution to the main chamber not having a good bathroom was to let the builders make me a Jack and Jill between my chamber and the next. No sooner decided upon than sharp the word and quick the action…as soon as the paperwork was finalised with the notaire, work went ahead.

To say I was thrilled was an understatement. Delly was now in the arms of her beloved Pueblo. On the hour and every hour, they graced window sills on sentry duty. They ate together, they played like kittens, and they took advantage of every bed, table and chair. When it was time for Delly to be groomed and the very important 'up do' of all her feathery long curls wisps and ear…trimmings. This had been my, or sometimes Greta's task from day one. Delly understood this performance. However, now she was a married lady of means with tatty husband, it was considered churlish of us, in her opinion of course, to leave hubby out of this attention. So, we took it in turns to pamper the newlyweds.

So, brush in each hand, we would venture forth and singing softly in French to Delly mostly, to prevent Martine having newly ravaged 'call of the wild' curtains, the chosen hairdresser sallied forth into the fray. We knew exactly how to obtain the very best results.

It was around this time that Martine was to celebrate her birthday. No one asked which one…that is if they wished to remain alive. Raphael drove me into town to choose a lovely gift. We were looking at very pedestrian necklaces for a few minutes when I piped up.

"Raphael darling."

"Oh, you call me darling a lot these days, Gina."

"So you are."

"I like it…you can call me darling all the time if you wish."

"It does suit you rather well."

"Oh, I think under that well-groomed exterior of yours, Gina, beats a romantic heart."

"I think we might get something really exciting for Martine. Do forgive me for being so bossy, but every time Martine has a rest on the couch or sits at her desk, I notice she is always gazing longingly without knowing she is doing it of course, at a dear little white sporty type car. I know they have one at the local car sales show room."

"*Mon dieu*, Gina, you are full of surprises. It will be so expensive."

"Oh, I don't think I want to stint over such a wonderful opportunity to thank her for all her tremendous generosity and kindness…plus, I love you both."

So, as I was quids in now due to all money being satisfactorily located with the aid of notaires and my solicitor in England having given the go ahead to spend my money here, I was never one to waste money on lots of new clothes so why shouldn't I buy this. It made perfect sense to me. The new spoilt to bloody death me, that is.

We found the dealer sipping a hot black coffee. He was warm and brisk in manner. No doubt seeing a definite buyer in the showroom. We put the little car through its paces. Raphael was adamant that the car must be checked thoroughly, and it was agreed that I paid five thousand euros on the spot. This would set in motion change of ownership to Martine, and we supplied all the necessary information for insurance…or rather, Raphael did.

The dear little car was delivered on the morning of her birthday. It was parked in the sunshine on the gravel at the front of the chateaux, but of course, *mon ami*, I had given instruction that it should be valet cleaned and to a high polish. Well, they did not misunderstand the brief…God love 'em. She – I always call cars she unless it's a lorry – she was magnificent. I hurried out and dressed the bonnet with Raphael, giggling fit to burst, partly from anxiety to be caught out before we were ready, and partly from happiness. We intertwined pale blue ribbon tastefully with white flowers over the dainty bonnet.

The result was magical. We were like teenagers that day with our surprise. Raphael had paid for the valet and complete service, break checks etc, to be carried out. Which was rather expensive considering what we had already spent out. But best not be stingy. We placed a card on the front of the car as a finishing touch.

I will never forget her face as we led her blindfolded to the front of the house with all the staff present. We sang happy birthday and revealed the gift.

Martine was crying. I was crying. Delly was crying, and everyone else was laughing.

When she had recovered her equilibrium, Martine hugged me close. I gave her the keys and without as much as a by your leave, she hopped in and drove off. Laughing and waving.

Well, you would, wouldn't you?

"That's the last we shall see of her for two weeks," announced Raphael, which was a shame…I wanted to go with her.

That night I thanked all the angels in long, short and mid-calf dresses for such a splendid time. Martine returned flushed happy and we had a nice family meal and only five candles dare show their faces on the birthday sponge. We all prefer sponge.

The next day Martine was gone early in the car. We were pleased that she loved it so much. I did feel proud to be able to give her something so special, after all she had done for me. This was a short-lived joy. There is an African saying, so I have been told, 'Don't let God see you are too happy…he will take something from you.'

Yes, right, okay…or do something to you or allow someone else to do something to you.

We were looking at wallpaper for the newly-completed bedroom next to mine. My chamber was dressed and painted in stucco. The finish was stunning. I was to paint a pattern with stencils when it was dried out which would take a while. Raphael was with me all the time now and we were as inseparable as Delly and Pueblo. The staff came to me for his needs and went to him for mine. It was an endearing quality in my opinion.

I looked out daily for the decree nisi from England. It was not however the nisi that showed up that morning of great peace and winter sunshine in the house.

We heard the car and naturally thought it was Jan the chef or Gabriel or one of Martine's pals or a delivery for the kitchen. The first surprise was some horrible shouting.

Martine was in the middle of Pueblo and Delly spoilt to death nutkins grooming, one brush in each hand, singing bravely the Marseilles as softly as a whisper. We never knew why this was such a favourite with two very daft and different looking moggies. Life is like this.

Raphael opened the front door and I heard his voice raised in anger. Michel, the odd job man, joined him. Martine and I looked at each other greatly puzzled. Delly sprang to the floor and ran to me, she leapt into my arms as if old nick were on her fluffy tail. We were all alarmed. I heard English and some vile swearing and general abuse. We stayed glued to our seats in surprise. We were now a very spoiled and sheltered set you understand.

Raphael closed the front door and came in. Delly had reverted to her old ways and was sucking the life out of my top. How very odd.

"There is this horrible man outside with the face of the boxer dog bottom. Gina, he shouts your name in a most abusive manner. There is also a man in a horrible cheap hire car. I cannot make heads or tails of such a situation. Who are they?"

I was speechless. I didn't know. Martine took charge.

"Raphael, call the police at once. Tell them to hurry."

Raphael did just that.

Pueblo was demanding permission to join Delly on my top, thinking no doubt it was some sort of new grooming method. I manage to persuade them both on to the older couch in the room. No hope of them staying there of course. Martine came to me.

"My Gina, I have the horrible sensations that this is very much the actions of a husband. You may find if you look out it is him somewhere in all of this. I think his boyfriend has the perpendicular head."

We hurried, followed by the two moggies, to the window and looked out.

"Oh Martine, you are right."

Sure enough, out on the gravel, the pristine gravel of the very fine chateaux which I had called home for some months now was a terribly cheap rental car. At the wheel sat a redfaced X-Ray. Oh, my lord, for all the world. Martine looked at him with a certain amount of curiosity and distaste. Mostly distaste. The lad doing all the shouting and gesticulating was, there was no doubt, the horrid Dairyman Dan. His face most unfortunately did resemble a boxer dog's bottom. Raphael is very good at description…and this time he was spot on.

A police siren wailed up the avenue of trees and two smart French police cars with full complement of passengers leapt to the fray. No sooner had this happened than handcuffs, shouting, more swearing and more rough words and fisticuff ensued, and we all, including the staff, pressed at the drawing room window to get the best view of the action.

Boxer dog was soon overpowered by French efficiency of the uniformed variety. Delly demanded to be hoisted up like a sack of spuds – 'to see' – and Martine was cheering. The cross maid was cheering, in fact. we all gave a sigh of relief when the sirens died away and the bourbon was brought out. Much needed, I should say.

"Well, this won't stay out of the news for long."

Martine sat down and laughed until the tears rolled down her cheeks.

"It is the French Farce all over again."

She managed to say. We all raised our glasses in agreement.

A wonderful calm descended upon the chateaux, but the villa was quite another matter. Gillian called with news from 'The Village'. Her new neighbours, now living in my old house, were as cool and distant as she is warm and lively. Bob, who was left in charge of selling my old Honda, had to drop the price but refused to go lower than three thousand, as although a little scraped from supermarket visits, was in fact a super reliable car. At last, it had sold. I could send some money to Greta and David for Christmas.

154

Gran had turned up as a regular at her front door. Gillian was rather non-plussed but courteous. Why she had descended upon them was beyond my comprehension. I had recently sent Granny Grumplings a lively letter and explained with great care why I had moved to France. My feelings had never been her first concern when I was a child, but I was so happy that I let it all go and wished her well. Gillian, however, was very excited about another new neighbour.

"He's something to do with poor old Mrs B. He's about six-foot-tall and a bronzed Adonis."

"I bet Bob feels he better shake a tail feather and go to the gym."

"Oh. the only thing he shakes, Gina darling, is the sauce bottle."

"Oh Gillian."

"What are you doing, Gina? I hope you're planning happy marriages with the fabulous Raphael. I told Bob all about him, and wait for this, Gina my poppet, he said, 'She should snap him up toot sweet before another woman spots him.'"

"Ah, there might be a legal obstacle with no decree nisi in the pipeline yet. Everything else is in place but not that, and then hip hip hooray, it's only weeks for the decree absolute, which is the one we need. X-Ray drove the very horrible, sorry to be spiteful, Dairyman Dan here and caused trouble at the chateaux."

"Oh no, what happened?"

"The French Police happened. There was a regular brawl outside. With his horrible boyfriend lashing out at the uniformed and heavily armed men who piled out of two cars. The sirens deafening us all. We thought it would make headlines in the local paper. So far, thank heaven, it's been a mere two or three lines."

"Well, sweetheart, you're best off away from him and his new cronies. Ruffians, one and all."

"The shock was the worst of it. We all had bourbon and the staff were tutting for a few days, but a lovely calm has fallen, thank goodness. Martine laughed at the whole shebang…called it a French Farce."

"Oh, what a good sport."

"Yes, I am lucky to be with such people."

"Well, about time. You had it rough here, now this is your new life and if you don't mind my saying…"

"No, go ahead."

"It's been the making of you. We think France has given you a great opportunity. Your area was not affected too badly by those horrific wildfires."

"No, they had three areas affected, but it was more concentrated around Marseille. Raphael has not taken any tourists around there for a while now. We are all donating to rebuilding funds."

"Not to diminish what's happened to the people, but how are your building plans going?"

"We are able to get very local people now. They have completed four rooms. I have a new Jack and Jill. Today I'm here with it all laid out for stencilling patterns and old-style flowers on my bedroom wall. The men are setting up a small-scale scaffold for me as we speak."

"Oh darling, that's wonderful, I know you were very keen on doing that."

"I got lucky and ordered some things locally. A vintage bird and flowers and various Marseille style designs with a super *C'est La Vie* over the bed. It means I can create them over and over in all the rooms. They are very therapeutic. Martine is off today looking for some more things. I don't know what I would do without everyone like you helping me."

"Oh, I'm so jealous…would love to be there. Is anyone booked in yet. Have you seen Gabriel?"

"Oh, we have new cooker, and a table was brought here by the 'oven man'…he's a doll."

"Sorry, lovely, did you say 'oven man'?"

"Oh yes, he is great, he is arranging for us to have some special good laying ducks. Raphael is busy filling the garden pond right now."

"Ducks, oven men, garden ponds, Raphael, X-Ray, police sirens and fisticuffs. You are leading a quiet life, aren't you?"

Peals of laughter keep us from speaking coherently for a while.

"Yes, so staid and boring really. Gabriel is really pining for you and has lost weight or so he says…keeps pulling his pantaloons away from his waistline and going 'POOOUFFF NOTHING POOOUUFFFTY WUFFTY I AM VANISH… MY GILLIAN, OH MY GILLIAN'."

"Oh, bless him, I love him dearly but I can't leave Bob. We are a couple, even if he snores like ten pigs in a sty and jiggles in the bathroom and out of it."

More laughter. I can hear Raphael calling.

"Sorry, my darling Gillian, Raphael is calling me down. I think the ducks have come at last. I will speak to you soon and wait 'til you see our new table, it's from an amazing old villa. Villa Sandrine, I think it's called. Bye, darling, bye."

I go down into the garden, which is being tidied up by Raphael and Michel. Michel is a constant clown and believes in many glasses of good strong French red just to get his engines firing. He calls it laughingly *'allumage moteur.'*

The garden is bustling with loosened ducks. Oh crikey, should they be free to paddle and wander? What if a fox should come? A hundred worries beset me as I hurry in my borrowed finery of baggy overall nipped in with rope – a generous loan from the builders – and my hair tied up with an old scarf around a pony tail of a rather jaunty description. Not chic, not chic.

"Raphael…what about Renard!!!"

"Ah, we have you, my Gina, to frighten them all away."

"No, seriously, I am frightened for them."

The men come out to see what the kerfuffle is all about and set to making big smacking noises with their mouths at sight of our cute as anything ducks of the best laying variety. I want to take them all into my arms.

"I can't bear them to be hurt by wild creatures, please Raphael, don't laugh at me."

But he does, and all the men start laughing. They put down tools and start a picnic of a very lively sort in the garden with the ducks making the most dreadful hullabaloo. I am crying now and they all laugh even harder – going to great lengths to wipe mock tears away.

Escaping to my new Jack and Jill bathroom, I found solace in a warm bath with bubbles and a glass of good rosé wine. Emerging and dressing in my neatest outfit that I could rummage out of my now shabby suits, I heard Martine in the little white sports car roar up the short drive. Breathing a great sigh, I went down to greet her.

"Oh hello, forgive my intrusion, Gina, Raphael rang me and told me. It's these rough men. I have sent them off to sober up. They are typical to the nature of men; I am so sorry. You see they found a couple of bottles of the very strong red in your garage and are the worse for wearing it on the inside."

"Oh, I see, they are gone to sober up."

"*Oui*, they are plastered, therefore they cannot plaster…good English style joke, *N'est-ce pas*." I hugged her tightly.

"Do forgive some of our foolish ways, Gina…we are not long from the mother's womb."

"All is forgiven and forgotten. With such an ambassador to represent them, how could I be churlish? Can I offer you a drink of some kind?"

"Noh! We have the special mission to Aix-en-Provence. I am stealing Raphael's car and taking you on the shopping spree of your life...no if, no but...we do this now or we do it never. Come to the car, dear Gina, I have to tell you many important ideas."

"I won't argue with that, Martine."

"Trust me on this if you trust me on nothing else."

"Forward, Martine, into the battle."

I wanted to say 'man the barricades', but thought it might be in poor taste.

We soon hit the correct roads. Martine is a past master of any sat nav, she is always on the ball with any side turn and does know her lefts from her rights. Thank Darby O'Gill for me when you see him. We are there in a very short time with Martine's shortcuts. We settle for a meal at the Piacere little Italy...literally within walking distance of a shopping mall. I tuck in, then stop due to the sharpest pang of remorse for my waistline.

"Ah, you are the sensible one...like me, Gina...this why I love you. Too much food before we try clothes will not be so wise. Andre, do place this wonderful food in a take-out *s'il vous plait*...Gina and I will enjoy it all later."

We bustled out into the busy streets and found the mall, which was fairly quiet for the present. Martine wanted to find me fun clothes...that was easy enough. we tried on about five outfits giggling like kids. I settled with Martine's great encouragement to be 'bold and fun' on some wonderful maxi skirts with a gypsy top, several wide-legged pants with nipped in waists, which were all the rage there, and fabulous bags all of various sizes prices and colours. Guilt was out the window at last.

I advise strongly any woman who wears stuffy office clothes, no matter how well cut, to chuck them if she wants to live a happy life in a French villa called Dancing Horse.

Shoes and a stunning raincoat which made me blush to look at the label for years later, came next and we broke off for nibbles and coffee...for extra energy of course. The next part of the 'spree' was quite different. We shopped for a wedding outfit for me. Martine explained very quietly the great necessity for such a purchase.

"My son, he will ask you to marry him very soon. What do you think of this? It is your decision."

158

"Oh, how wonderful. Do you approve of his choice? This is a very strange way round, I think."

"It is me that inclines him to consider greatly his future happiness. You are made for each other, Gina, I am convinced of this. We all love you and your life has done the great take-off here with us in France, please be truthful to me...do you agree?"

"I do."

Martine sees the funny side of this and we explode into easy laughter. Finding the top salon for the more sophisticated woman of a certain age, we settle on three fabulous outfits and one in particular is a great favourite. I am blonde and it's a better cut than I had in England. So we choose a dainty tiara.

"This ivory colour is very chic, but Gina, it is your final choice, what do you say?"

"I love the pale peach; don't you think it might give me more colour?"

I try on the peach and look at myself. No, it's all wrong. But the ivory is very elegant and yet a little too cool against my face. The dresser comes to the rescue, she brings a silvery blue. I try it on with a terrible feeling it will be all wrong. I gasp... In the mirror is a stunning woman with blonde shining hair, slim hips and the complexion of an angel.

"Gina, it is out of this world."

The dresser pulls back the waist a tiny amount. She just nods very slowly and pointing to the mirror smiles.

"Oh Martine, it's like it was waiting for me. This is the dress I have always wanted."

We have it measured as it is to be altered so so slightly, then it will be sent on to us by special carrier. All part of the bridal service. I'm speechless with gratitude, and Martine and I dive into a patisserie for a tiny 'pick us up'. We drive back, with me taking the wheel this time. It's decided my next purchase probably should be my own vehicle. There's no rush. I can't wait to show Raphael all my finery. We stop off in Nice town to find a lot of nicely made reasonably priced sweaters for the staff and for me, and naturally, two excellent quality jerseys for Raphael. Loaded to the gunnels as they say, we arrive back at the chateaux in time for food. Both exhausted, laughing, and longing for wine. Waistlines were forgotten for a while.

Two days later, I burn all my horrible stuffy English clothes and the manky much-repaired shoes and the blouses go up in smoke in a metal burning bin in the garden. The tendrils of smoke rise like old ghosts into the French sky…which has decided to be ultra-blue that day. How thoughtful.

Martine is longing to show me off as her daughter-in-law-to-be. I am flattered by this and am so excited that when the builders gawp at me in my long corduroy maxi skirt and neat sweater, I don't turn tail but hold my head high. They are making what they politely call '*Canard maison.*'

I love it and tell them so. All friends again.

The ducks wander over and inspect it, and Raphael joins me as we watch all their antics. He places his arm around me as we watch and although the workmen look on admiringly, they keep their remarks to under-whispers we can't catch. The guffaws have been tucked into bed by the clever interception of an armed and guided feminine missile called Martine.

It must be said. The time that Raphael put his arm around me in the garden was so natural. I felt the truest sensation of love I have ever felt. No pang, or jolt, or fear. I also felt some new sensations. My frozen little heart was thawing from the long winter of English coolness. About bloody time too.

The ducks had their house and we took great pains to close them in for the night and drove over to Martine who was longing to see us.

A great parcel with my name scrawled lazily across it, stood on the hall table. I rushed forward with the excitement of a child at the sight of it. I grabbed it up and danced with it through to the kitchen. Everyone laughed.

Greta rang, "Mum, oh Mum, you're so generous. We just got your Chrimbo gift and David is dancing around. He wants to talk to you so over to him."

"David darling, how lovely, it's ages, isn't it?"

"We are really thrilled about your news, what an email to send and what a gift. Dad, and this is only a pencil in."

"Right, standing by with pencil."

"HA! Dad has just contacted us and he might be your first paying guest at the Dancing Horse Villa…and wait for this…he's bringing his new lady friend. I'm sending you his email, so that when you are up and running, you can contact him if you wish, and he can bring her out."

"Tell him that's excellent news all round! I am really pleased. They are in the middle of sorting out the old bathroom in the west bedroom which has sun from midafternoon, as you can guess by the description, and is ideal for those that love a sunset. The best part of the room is its darling little balcony. We are putting in new French doors, sorry about the pun. The builders have completed most of the work…it's just a case of finishing off and appointing a surveyor later to see if we can sort this kitchen cum lobby area without spending a fortune, and or upsetting the look of the place."

"Oh, how lovely. I will tell him what's happening. Roughly when do you think you might be able to accept a couple of guests who really won't mind roughing it just to get away from tiring jobs and the English climate…oh and sample the delights of Nice?"

"Raphael thinks February is possible. I want all the building work out of the way and any dust settled and cleared, and we are trying to get staff. How is the job going?"

"Seriously panicked, Gina, the state of the oceans is a great worry. The plastic issue. Marine creatures are ingesting those tiny breakdown particles."

"Oh, how horrible. They are in trouble then because of our dirty habits and lack of intelligence. Will you be able to approach the main culprits in industry?"

"Main aim is to conserve and inform and push, push, push to maintain the oceans. We are showing governments the best way forward…but will they really listen?"

"You need more funding, I presume?"

"Always, and informing, but informing with the best outcome for the planet. Gina, I don't need to lecture you on the matter, here's Greta trying to grab the phone."

"Did you get all that, Mum? Hey, you know I have been involved with Japanese culture…well, get this, David thinks it may be a brilliant lever into getting into their media and informing the industries there stop them over-fishing and contaminating. How about that! I will be doing something useful after all."

"You are in the best of company to achieve that. I'm always proud of you both…and that would really set my heart singing. Raphael is very happy here, darling, we were always the best of pals when we first met but now, I can't begin to tell you how it's all going so happily along. The ducks are settling in and laying. Does David's father like duck eggs?"

"Oh, he's up for everything and anything French. He is showing off to his girl all his language skills…so funny, Gina. She's a real card too. Talk about nutty and not a bit as you would expect her to be. Oddly enough, they sort of complement each other…really sweet to see."

"Sounds ideal. I'm glad it's all worked out for him and yes of course they will be most welcome. Ask them to inform us about any allergies or special diets won't you…and I will supply the opening date as soon as we know. Also, we should be able to give him family rates. Sadly, we can't offer anything free as we have spent a scandalous amount and we must try, and I say this with a sigh, try to make it work and create a business."

"Brilliant, we won't keep you Mum, it's going full pelt by the sounds of it all. Very exciting. Oh, Mum?"

"Yes, darling."

"Dad's really upset about all that happened. The authorities still have that awful boy in custody, awaiting trial."

"Oh dear, what a mess, your father has never been involved in anything like this before. It's his mid-life crisis…sorry, Greta, only way I can describe it…where is he now?"

"He came back to the UK on the plane, alone of course, and is now living in a tiny studio in your old village. It's miniscule really from his descriptions. He's mighty peed off with all his choices and how it's all turned out."

"Does he have work?"

"Yes, thankfully, that's why he came straight back after the authorities had gotten a statement or some such thing. He didn't want to mess up his life any more than he has already."

"Well, that's something. He might get a good job now. What is he doing with the money from the sale of the house? Do you know?"

"He foolishly gave it to that awful thug. Mum, the lad had such a strange hold over him."

"Oh, so that will have to go toward the boy's court case here. All frittered away in the system no doubt. I could kick your foolish dad in the butt. What a waste, what a daft outcome. I'm stunned."

"Best forget it all, Mum. That decree nisi should be with you soon, the horrible Dairyman Dan spent a lot of Dad's money on pushing that through with a top divorce lawyer."

"The only good news from that quarter. Thank you, darling. I will tell Raphael. Good bye to you both. Take care my darling girl, miss you, do try to get out here on your Easter break, won't you?"

"Top of the list. Bye, Mummy, we love you dearly, cuddles to Delly and Pueblo, we love their photo. David framed it. He's a softie, isn't he?"

"Not at all… I have one in our lounge. Byeee."

"Byeee."

This phone call shook me to the core. Ray in a tiny studio. I can't imagine what kind of work he was doing. I sent a text to Greta, requesting she tell me about his new career. The answer was quick and frightening.

'Oh Mum, just odd jobs around people's gardens. He is no expert flower grower as you know.'

I found Raphael and related it all to him without histrionics, although I felt like throwing a few. Raphael took my arm in his and we walked through the villa…from room to room…my spirits lifted.

"Darling, he chose that path, you chose this one. Simple really. You took yourself off away from an old life that was painful but applied patience, politeness and good sense. This is the result. A lovely villa…and one called Dancing Horse…surely you see the beauty."

"I see you and you are beautiful, no doubt in my mind there."

"Not too skinny, as they say in England."

"Oh no, since we have been courting." He laughed.

"Since we have been courting, my pretty man, you have filled out and now are like a plump turkey." He began dancing along the passage that led to the main chamber. All the rooms bar one had been painted and there were just two walls left to be stencilled. The builder was moving the scaffolding into position for me on Monday. He drew me into the room and closed the door. He was grinning but in a very new way indeed. I began to feel he was definitely changed. The shyness had gone. Oh, my goodness, he wasn't, was he? Oh, my lordy lord. He was.

We held each other very close and every time one of us tried to wriggle away, the other would snuggle closer. The ducks were quiet and it was this sudden lull that made us smile.

"They are listening to our lovemaking. Oh Raphael, we have naughty ducks."

"Yes, all ducks in France are of this special breed, it is called 'those that listen to lovers make splendid kisses…ducks'."

"We are very lucky to have them. Don't you think?"

I cuddle him closer, his mouth is so handsome…tenderness is in every curve of his sensual shoulder. Tracing my fingers down, down, down. Then wriggle away while he groans in dismay.

"I must make sure these kissy ducks are okay."

"Oh, so ducks come before me, the loved one now…I am sulking forever."

We dress somehow amongst peals of laughter and teasing. Just about managing with many cuddles and kisses to get along the corridor and down the stairway to the kitchen. The ducks are all settled silently in their little house. They look at us very disapprovingly. Well, that's how I read it, anyway. The light has gone from the sky and being sensible little ducks, they think being inside gives them the edge. I check their food and water for overnight and Raphael closes their door and places the strong bolt across.

We walk arm in arm through the garden silent and happy. If sex had not come, we would still be getting married, I know that, but sex is a vital component. We would have stayed together no matter which way we had lived, with or without. This is how we are. We can only be what we are. I am of course vibrating with the happiness our bodies have given us. I would never have rushed him. He is, it thrills me to say, surprisingly excellent in that department.

We pick our way carefully in the dusk looking up at the trees at the edge of the garden along our wall to the once overgrown gate with its rampant weeds now cleared thank goodness. The trees are in need of attention, we have been advised. I don't want them touched but I have to listen to the tree surgeon. God forbid a guest should be hurt by a dangerous branch. We know what we must do and I know we will do it. But just for now, we want to just be in the silence of our home. We are content. Raphael is a good sweet man. I am a most fortunate woman.

The next day brings the builders…we have trouble getting out of bed. Martine calls us to 'check to see if we are alive.'

Some tone in her voice is amused and knowing…she sounds very pleased with herself. Martine is a matchmaker and we would not dare tell her otherwise. Although if we are honest, it is Gabriel who really brought us together with all his crazy antics that day so long ago. It feels like another country. Well, the passport was labelled high risk, and all the money you can spend, oh and a very handsome man will kiss you. Haw hee haw hee haw he haw…or whatever they say in those peculiar and wonderful French Farces. What a world, what a life and what a difference. Indeed…*vive la whatnots.*

Maktoob

To say we are all excited at the chateaux about Christmas is an understatement. The morning of Christmas Eve brought so many trades people including 'oven man' who was thrilled to be involved. Raphael was, I thought, rather on edge. He had recently been placing ads for staff to help out in general and only a few applicants had arrived. With this in mind, I put it down to general concern. Wine is a great resident in the cellars. We had to move sufficient to our needs for the party. So, we all made an effort not to open any…instead, as many as we thought necessary were placed 'closer to the action' in the store room near the kitchen. Excitingly wrapped boxes, parcels and cards piled through the front door with every post and I was enchanted by the thought of a possible decree nisi.

No luck so far. Ah well, in the fullness of time. Martine and I were trying to stop laughing long enough to decorate the dining room. Then, on a more serious note, lay the magnificent table only brought to the fore within the party season. Great white and red clothes adorned the backs of its chairs while cross maid and I donned gloves and polished its broad as a whale's back top…well, mostly the legs. The top had a quick go-over. Spotless cloths were spread and measured. Yes, measured, so that they appeared even from the door. Essential apparently.

Candelabra appeared from a locked cupboard. I was in awe. Martine and I set to with Michel to clean and polish these magnificent additions. A turkey arrived in a huge parcel with all its retinue of trays and cloths, sprouts and parsnips. Raphael and a new helper, Vervain, with her daughter a rather sulky, pretty child of eight or so, called Rosie, trotted to and fro helping in the kitchen. Cross maid appeared briefly at Martine's side; I guessed from the scowl the helpers were not to her liking.

Martine, ever tactful and kind, let her moan and then as she left, looked to me with a shrug.

"We try so hard, Gina. We try so hard."

Nodding, I returned to adjusting my gloves once more and getting the polish out of my elbow…or some such thing. Holly came in and some mistletoe arrived from an unknown source and everyone was all a dither at its arrival. I went looking with a fallen sprig for Raphael. He was peeling potatoes and giggled wildly as I held it above his head. I noticed his eyes flicker nervously around the room.

"I think everyone knows by now, darling."

He went on with the spuds after our kiss. A sullen Rosie watched with the eyes of a malevolent pixie, or was it just my fancy. Yes of course…all kids go through these awkward as hell sulky phases. I did, I'm sure, and as for Greta…well, they only lessened recently if I'm honest.

By the time we sat down to our cold supper with hot toddies, we were exhausted. But the chateaux had somehow sprung to life. The tree still had to have the lights switched on…and we stood by as 'oven man' and Michel threw the lever so to speak. The wonderful branches, so rich and green with their load of baubles old toys and darling tin soldiers, fairy queen and star – all left over from Martine's dancing career – sprang into life, as if from some great book. Not a goblin dare show its face. I added my own touch of our own sweet reindeer from the Christmas's of long ago. X-Ray's special gift to me one year had been a snowman. He went on also. He looked almost accusingly at me. Now I am imagining things.

Oven man was so happy that he could not stop supping and giggling. Martine looked a little worried and took me to one side.

"How can we make him and Michel last until the end of all our party…my darling, Gina…the man is totally squiffy already."

She was very concerned.

"Potato or pasta, Martine stuff 'em full of them and they will sober up."

So she did, and they did. Vervaine said a cheery good night with the trailing 'sulky shoes' as I called Rosie, grumpily following in her wake.

Martine took me calmly and quietly into the study. She opened her safe and said sweetly, "I have a little necklace for you to wear for the party tomorrow. It's dreadfully expensive. Family heirloom in the making of course, my darling one…but oooh la la…it is as they say, a sparkling bit of nonsense…catches the light so wonderfully. Your neck is lovely and will be a fabulous background for it. My neck is no longer right. See, now say what you feel. If you hate it, Gina, please don't wear it."

I took the offered necklace. It was like nothing I had ever worn before. Martine fastened it and offered me a mirror.

"Oh, it is like ice, fire and ice."

"Ah oui, fire and ice, like love itself. It was given to me by a wealthy but rather crazy admirer. He is dead now of course, poor sweet…but the stones still carry the fire and the ice. Don't you think, my darling Gina?"

"I think, Martine, you must have been a totally wonderful and captivating dancer to be given such a gift. I love it and love it and love it."

I danced playfully around the room with the mirror held out like a partner and Martine laughing joined me. We waltzed out of the study and down the hallway.

Well, you would, wouldn't you?

Christmas day was an angelic sky day. All my happiness exploded. I had not seen Raphael all night and did not want to make a fuss. He came in to breakfast with more parcels and was his usual laughing loving self. He must have spent the night with Gabriel. They both festooned the hallway with all sorts of greenery and lit candles. After breakfast we helped clear away and preparation for the party began right after we returned from church. I was in a tizzy. There was so much laughter and guests kept coming. We were all on top form however and the turkey that had been dressed, undressed and placed in the oven very early. Eventually cooked to perfection…but of course…it was brought out to 'rest'…and what a night we all had.

The table groaned with goodies and things appeared as if by magic. Cross maid and I were settling people for the pudding course and Martine was tapping a glass for silence. Her face flushed and happy. I looked around for Raphael. He came to my side smiling and we raised our glasses in appreciation of such fine food and company.

Martine came to me about thirty minutes later and gently touching my arm said, "Gina, would you mind going to the wine store by the kitchen for more of this red? Michel is busy with some of the washing up." One must be kind…he has been very good up until now, so I took the empty bottle of red for reference and sailed off with a saucy wink. Martine is very fond of saucy winks from me.

I removed my shoes as they are very high and new…in other words, okay for sitting down in and general trotting on level ground, but trusting them on steps, however few, *noh, noh, noh, ma chere.* As I oh-so-merrily went down into the store, I saw two figures. In my bare feet, I was silent especially with all the racket overhead. Before me were Raphael and Vervaine in the most passionate embrace, kissing wildly and rapturously. His wonderful hands held her face as if she were some princess in a story. I could not take in what I was seeing…it was quite impossible…the ground came up to meet me.

Down in my dreaming heart, all is light. The warmth of the sun touches my face reaching up to feel its caress upon my cheek. I feel rain…rain in the desert. Music from far away beckons and I turn to walk through the deep sand of the dunes, higher and higher. I am singing out my own little threnody. Just over the next dune is my own Shangrila. I sense this, but the journey may take a little longer. My ankles are decorated by bracelets that chink, chink, chink. The drone of the plane's jet engines is comforting. I feel something touch my face then I recall where I am. My face wet with tears; I don't notice straight away the voice at my elbow.

"Excuse me, would you like some fresh water?"

I take the little glass; no, it is not a glass, but a plastic tumbler. Of course, I am on a flight. A tanned sturdy and rather plainfaced woman hands me the water.

"Thank you."

"They were rather worried about you and if it's not in the handbook of passengers behaviour, they exchange frowns."

"Oh…what was I doing, I thought I was asleep…dreaming…"

"Yelling out more like. Oh, your face is rather bruised, would you like some of this, it's arnica, keep smoothing it on and it will fade out very quickly. My name's Deardra by the way, what's yours?"

"Gina. Is my face still really bad? I had a falling out with some flagstones in a French chateau. They won."

"Oh, those chateaux will get to you every time. Christmas party."

"Indeed."

I sip the water and feel much better for it.

"Look, I'm ordering hot coffee, would you like some?"

"Music to my ears."

Her tanned strong hand flies up and the hostess is there in a jiffy. Very few passengers up this end, I notice. No wonder it was so easy for Martine to book the flight and so cheaply. I only recall dribs and drabs of the past few days, the kindness of everyone. Gabriel's tears – oh God, poor Gabriel – he volunteered to take very good care of Tom and the girls. He would move the house with the aid of 'oven man' to his back garden, the smaller one, and open up a little paddle area for them. Delly happy with Pueblo in Martine's expert care. Such overwhelming kindness.

"Not to worry about anything. When you come back, they will be pleased to see you. Remember, there are those that are genuine and real, who love you like sister, brother and friend."

I remember Gabriel's dear face, his dark curly hair and that sad crinkle of a smile. Martine cried with me. Raphael…was gone. Tears fell again. I must pull myself together. A box of tissues appeared.

"Keep blubbing like a baby…thanks, had a bad shock, you see."

"I think the hostess is very concerned."

I nod. What can I say…nothing…words don't cover how I feel. Disappointed hopes, smashed dreams, a wedding dress which is so perfect and no groom in sight. Gone and gone again. I sip the coffee with great slurps and Deardra laughs.

"Yes, the way I enjoy it is in a noisy way. Your first trip to Egypt…Luxor…and land of the Pharaoh?"

"Oh, it's that obvious…and I thought I could slip under the radar."

"Depends on the radar. I love it out there, just love it. I have new man to make passionate love with. If he's busy, he will send his little brother to pick me up…you can share, best thing for you if it's your first time, otherwise you could be robbed. Ramshackle taxi affair but still does the job. I'm booked in for a few days at the Lotus; which one are you in or are you in an apartment? None of my business of course."

"Thanks for the offer of the taxi…I accept. I'm booked in at the Polo, is it called?"

"Oh no, it's a dump. No clear Nile views. First time out, Gina, you must have clear Nile views, that's a definite…oh and they have the most surly, unfriendly, miserly set-up and the staff, well… Oh, and a mossy infestation 'cus of too many trees. And it's next to a busy main road which will keep you awake all night. Nobody goes there unless they have to. A Coptic man named Misery Guts is the owner. Have you paid any money up front yet?"

"No."

"Then come and share a room at the Lotus with me, that way it's a win-win all round. Don't worry, I never snore, and I will be out a lot with Mohammed."

So, the decision was made for me…you might think me nuts to go off with a stranger. But after all that had happened, to be blunt, I didn't bloody care anymore. Plus, I may even see Mahmoud and that would make life out in the land of the Pharaoh a whole lot more interesting. Let's pray in a good way.

"Thank you, the Lotus is a whole lot better, I presume."

"Excellent Nile views from nearly all the rooms and a pool next to the Nile. Cheery, and the food passable. No noisy road. Staff very comical…always joking with you."

Deardra talked a great deal and I enjoyed her upbeat banter. Rather comforting. She didn't need any real answers…preference for the one-sided chat line was her calling card. Mohammed must be a patient listener.

I would apparently need a Luxor mobile…it would save me a great deal of money to go on the local company signal or some such thing. Made sense. What I was saving on the room could go toward it.

I had money anyway. I had never touched more than a thousand from my share of the house in the village, which seemed a lifetime and a galaxy of stars away.

We were circling now and lights and belts and general bustle kept us busy. The hostess gave us sweets for the landing. Barely felt it…must be excellent pilot. Was this Egypt, was this really that strange ribbon of green slipping like paradise through desert sands for some two thousand miles?

Maps don't give off heat. As we stepped out of the jet plane onto the steps, I felt like somebody had opened the oven door somewhere. Lights, sounds, bustle and hustle, a few passengers groggily tried their legs out on the steps down to the tarmac. A bus drew up and we were speeding to the main terminal building. It was small and rather chummy looking, I thought

We were so very fortunate at the airport; the line for visa entry was long but our luggage came through far more quickly than any of us anticipated and after we had run the gauntlet of airport authority stop and search, we were out in air so hot, at first, I could not breathe.

Breathing became easier and Deardra found her lighter and lit up. I watched with interest as she inhaled deeply.

"Must be wonderful after all those hours."

"MMMMMY goodness, there is nothing quite the same. Ah, it's little Amr."

A small but sturdy boy hurried to us with a smile as wide as the Grand Canyon.

"Madam Deardra, welcome to Alaska."

We were bustled to a rather ramshackle taxi and all luggage dealt with by the irrepressible Amr and his sidekick, a tiny boy of indeterminate age. We were treated to a lot of rather fresh warm air. I was soon feeling better. Deardra chattered away to them in such a happy-go-lucky manner. I made a huge decision there and then. I was going to learn Arabic and I was going to be merry and relaxed.

Yes, yes and yes again. I shrugged off my old life of not quite getting it right.

The hotel was lovely. It sat between two monsters of tourism. I dubbed the one to the right of us the corset factory, and the one to the left, the stocking factory. So dull were their facades. The dear little Lotus was literally that. A sweet lotus between two factory architectural weeds.

We were greeted and ade welcome, and Deardra ordered yoghurts and a plate of snacks and lashings of hot tea.

"Trust me on this, Gina."

So I did and let the cloud nine I had begun floating on carry me to room, shower, snack and bed. Two days later – so I was informed – I finally truly woke up and struggled out by way of exercise one must presume to a paradise that made me stop in my tracks. Very few views have affected me in such a way. A mist was burning the last few strands of its hair over a great wide river. The far bank was festooned with light golden hazes interspersed with violet and pale cream and touches of green. Rose twirls came through and beyond hills of pale grey blue and shadows and shades of sandy terracotta. Palm trees with waving fronds looking totally unreal, were thick and lush. A line of butterflies dipped along the surface of this majestic river. I pointed open-mouthed.

Deardra who was already smoking her breakfast, "We are going to get along just fine, you and I, Gina. They are *faluccas*. It's the tourist boats for anyone brave enough to venture upon this fast tidal river…the longest in the world no less…THE NILOS."

Her arms spread wide for dramatic explanation…she smiled that wonderful closed mouth smile.

"Breakfast?"

"Oh, I could eat a horse, Deardra."

"Try a camel."

We laughed soundly at this thought. Actually, I think I might already have partaken at the Mascara restaurant in Brighton. We supped from what was left in the tiny fridge and then while we slurped the last of the yoghurt, Deardra rang down for omelettes.

"Big or small…Gina?"

"Gigantic."

I quickly showered and dressed in the cool wonder of my real silk dress.

"Wow, that's going to turn some heads."

"Everything else is too hot."

"Don't worry. Do you have enough money to buy some cool cotton things, 'cus I know a shop that will fit you out with a fabulous and totally suitably modest wardrobe for a hundred English. No problem. Oh, you have sandals, that's brilliant for starters. They are a bit plasticky and yuk here…that's life. Still, you might find the odd pair that have escaped mass production. But it's doubtful. My advice is to look after your undies and get a scarf for around your head in the day and one or two for knocking about the knocking shops at night. If a rent boy takes your fancy, don't say how much, just smile and walk on by, point him out to me if you can, and I will make the appropriate inquiry. Oh, and close your mouth sweety."

I laughed out loud and went out to my favourite perch on the balcon – they don't call them balconies, apparently. After breakfast, true to her word, Deardra after calling salaam to almost every man we saw, crossed to the other road and hailed a little battered bus with squiggle writing on. Inside was music as I had never heard it before and I began to cry with joy. I was in a dream…one that I may have had…but now I recalled it sharply as if from some past life that up until now I had not known I had actually lived. We were soon singing along, me doing the best I could, not really knowing the words and eventually we tumbled…and I mean tumbled out into a sprawl of shops, horns, cars, lorries, buses, donkeys, carts piled high, carts piled with children, and empty carts with satisfied trotting donkeys going about their own particular affairs as if they were in charge of all of life in every universe in the galaxy. People, people, and more people. The *souk*. I will never forget the *souk*. Fruits and veg were laid out like carpets over old carpets and the clamour. Well.

Deardre beckoned me and we wove our way like little silk dolls. Deardra was wearing a bright sari type outfit…through the bustle and we ended up under some long dresses and scarves which a little boy swept to one side for us. How quaint. The owner was a jovial, crafty-looking chap with eyes like a great panda, black as black. Oh well. He showed me several things and I liked quite a few – oh bliss, they were light and cool. Also. I loved a lot more. I tried on a few things then got so hot I trusted fate to do the rest and just bought loads. We struggled outside in the midst of tea glasses, which by now were strewn all over. Tea is the oil of conversation apparently here. We laughed at our nutty shopping ideas. I had not even spent a hundred pounds and we found a taxi to take us and our loot out into the surrounding area. Deardra called a halt at a coffee shop and we dragged the taxi man with us…someone else she knew. We settled with shisha and coffee, bottled water, and wafers so creamy and delicious, I decided I had been sleeping up until now in my eating habits. We also tried some lovely savoury food. We did not care. No, let me re-phrase this…we cared very much indeed, but we enjoyed not caring.

Get it…life had begun…no…that's way too glib.

Life is fun…no, this is a poor way of describing such a way of going about…oh forget it.

An old gold Peugeot, the estate type, was circling the cafe block for quite possibly the third or fourth time. I felt a familiarity with it…not knowing why…I strained my eyes in the late afternoon light to make out why I felt so drawn to it.

It is Mahmoud. Is he circling to make sure it is me? There are plenty of places to park. Eventually, he pulls in and I watch closely as he locks it and comes into the seating area.

His hand comes out instantly. I am as surprised and delighted as he is. What a turn up for the books. He sits next to me smiling as wide as a Cheshire cat.

"Hello, dearest Gina, I keep going around then I stay away from you a few minutes then come around again…on the next time, I know it is not dream or trick of the light, it really is you."

"I could not believe my eyes when I saw you staring at this table." Deardra was open-mouthed and silent – bless her, that has to be a first.

"Why you not tell me you are coming? Were you wishing to surprise me? Because I am very surprised. When did you arrive?"

"Monday last… I slept for two days solid apparently. This is my real first day out. Deardra took me shopping because apart from this dress, all the clothes I brought were too hot. You know, unsuitable."

"I understand… This dress is so beautiful. You are staying in hotel or apartment?"

"The Lotus, it's friendly and very nicely built right on the Nile…I love swimming. Ideally, I need an apartment…not an expensive sort, just clean and tidy. I have no linen or towels, you understand."

"You ask for something there is plenty of. Tourists not like to come to Luxor so much…I have man who keeps four apartments…all were empty the last time I spoke to him."

He waves the coffee shop man to come over and I hear shisha and chai. Well, I know what these are already. He picks up his very lovely new mobile and chatters away.

"I spoke to the owner of the apartments. Would you like to see them tomorrow morning? He can't come now because his brother makes a party?"

I nod. The word party makes my heart jump and I recoil inwardly from the pain. Sod, sod, sod. I must stay calm, no tears here. Please don't cry here and now, I tell myself. Mahmoud knows me well, however, and does not miss the wince.

"You are not so well I think, Gina, I know you well and there have been many problems I think for you."

"Yes, I sold the village house and had to give Ray his share, which he has already squandered on that worthless boy. I bought a villa near Nice town and have just come out for a quiet relaxing time after a nasty accident at a Christmas party. You have had your share of sorrow too, Mahmoud, that's easy to see."

"Dearest Gina, I thought I want to die too…my daddy…he is my world. This the reason I not speak to anyone properly for long time. My heart, it is broken. I feel like I have been in war with life. This why, and you understand this is not normal for me."

"I can see the sorrow in your eyes and the way you walk and talk. Life is a cow at times, a fair cow."

"I think I hear this saying in an Australian film."

"Yes, they say fair dinkum…which apparently is good, and a fair cow…which is very bad."

"Your husband made another problem I think."

The next morning there is still no sign of Deardra…no surprise really… I suppose. Mohammed looks an amorous sort of chap.

I have a call from Mahmoud to meet him outside at ten o'clock. I get showered and have a good breakfast…so hungry I could eat the whole breakfast buffet, but naturally do not. Leaving a note for Deardra about the plans and the lucky chance meet. I must not go into detail with anyone about my life in England. It's best that way I feel. I keep it short and sweet. No detail.

We go first to the bookshop and I quickly find the exact little booklet I need, and then hurry outside to Mahmoud who is of course as per usual on his mobile. We zoom off, no, sorry, this is the old gold Peugeot we are talking about…we chug…yes, that's the sound. Chug.

The streets are busy and dusty. We wind through various donkey carts and taxi lines and horse-drawn carriages. The traffic thins and we reach a quiet street…sorry again…*shara*.

A man is outside with a bunch of keys that would have brought a blush to the tower of London keys. He shows us up to a large airy apartment. I get a bad feel from it and say sorry I don't like it.

Then begins the usual mobile calls and address taking. I follow in the wake of the noisiest departures of all time from a residential building. With both men shouting at the tops of their voices, we reach the heat of the sun again beyond massive iron doors.

"Not to worry, I show you the others, this man must go."

We all shake hands again and the owner vanishes in a dusty old car. His car chugs too, I notice. The next apartment is funny. We walk in and then walk straight back out. Mahmoud is hilarious. It's good to see him a little like his old self.

"Where is my Delly, she is in France now or in UK?"

"Delly is married to a dear little French tom cat. Very tatty, due to him being a bit of a fighter in his youth, but they are enjoying great times with my very dear friend Martine at her chateaux."

"My Delly with French cat…me am so jealous."

We both laugh at this. Oh, it is so good to be with someone so warm and sensitive as Mahmoud…he is a tranquil man and I feel better already. Mistakes are being forgotten. We drive to another apartment which is a few steps up and has the best view I have seen. It's a two-bed-roomed affair with modern kitchen and clean linen. The balcon is the best; I fly to the rail as soon as Mahmoud opens the double shutters and doors…so popular here. Oh, my word…

"Yes, Mahmoud, yes, this is the one, I love it. I can unpack my sketching things and watercolours…oh, don't you realise, dearest Mahmoud, that I can actually relax and paint here and be undisturbed…for the first time in…in…forever."

"This is good one, Gina. I will get it for you, no problem. Gina, I have another surprise for you…you can see my kitchen from your balcon."

There are so many places to see here that I sit on my balcon and think…just quietly think. Rest and restoration are going to be the order of the day…running around has exhausted me. A stunning sky so blue that it invites me to enter it like another country, has held me captive. Stool and chai mobile, coffee…still can't track a supply of Rose' de'Anjou…if I had felt more 'with it' at the airport, I could have bought in supplies.

Painting going a little better…was rusty at first but with my eye and hand coming in again, all is coming together upon the pristine acid-free zone at last. The farm and the panorama, dogs scratching out sand fleas, lice, and whatevers, provide me with subjects. I'm content enough and have no needs. Greta doesn't miss a trick however, and cheekily sends an email. 'I have a feeling that the tombs temples and pyramids are not the only attractions in Luxor, enjoy and relax, Mummy darling.'

I reply with a funny face. 'Ah, my darling, you are so right. I have come for the sunshine and the hot spicy inducements. Love, Mum.'

This will set her laughing and no mistake. Glad she is not getting upset about my awful experience in the storeroom plus flagstones plus plus plus. Still cannot bring myself to examine it any deeper. Lessons learned and all that. Soothed by the heat on the balcon, I find myself gradually nodding off.

Shower and dress, and try to get to shops. Ah, the fairies and Darby O'Gill have been here…they also made it by jet plane, bless their little hearts. Sitting proud as Lucifer…throw salt and bury a donkey in gold dust…are three bottles of rosé wine…of which I select three and struggle home with all the booty…good day indeed. I should say. The price must be overlooked as this is a definite requirement for all sanity to be restored. I have a glass of the most refreshing nectar of the gods and my equilibrium comes in from the wilderness.

Mahmoud rings me.

"Darling Mahmoud, where are you, sweety pie?"

"Outside, please to throw down the *muftah*."

Now I have learned several words and *muftah* means keys, I oblige. The fact of not really looking where I am throwing these metal articles escapes me until it's too late. Luckily, Mahmoud puts three and three together and comes up with squiffy. Very bright boy. I hear his long-legged leaps up the stone steps to the door and then he's in.

"What are you up to, my Gina?"

I show him my water colours including the dogs scratching.

"Oh, my God, you are such a funny lady. I love this one, it's so good. Who taught you?"

"Me taught me…want some cool drink or a chai, nibbles, full three-course meal?"

He's in that fridge as fast as a whippet and holds out the rosé like a gun…pulls faces.

To give hive him his due, he says nothing. OOOPS! I am never going to be a non-rosé wine drinker and there is an end to it.

"I have invitation for us to eat in restaurant. Are you ready to come?"

"Two minutes." Well, this will be fun.

I manage to do some 'improvements' to my face and hair. Stick on a pair of 'hide the bloody lot' sunglasses and array myself in the newly washed and pressed purely by luck, silk dress. Grabbing comfy shoes and handbag stuffed with all required kitchen sinks, I sally forth grinning. First mistake.

"Gina, my Gina, you are so lovely."

He cuddles me and gives me a warm kiss. He has some lipstick on now and I don't. I have to remove his with a tissue. He seems not to care about it at all. I wait until I am in chug-a-long Charlotta, the gold car, until I assess the facial damage. Not too bad or maybe it is and the wine prevents full awareness. Fair enough.

We arrive at the front of a noisy bustling restaurant called 'Squiggles' – it's in Arabic, so I can't tell what the name is. Who bloody cares anyway. A lot of very nice people stand up for me and then sit down again, a meal is ordered and I dig in to my bit. The room swims a lot but hey, all part of the entertainment, right? Mahmoud is very jolly and in fact that is how the time plays out…we leave in cool twilight air and go to a coffee shop, which says Lotus Coffee Shop in English above the window. This for no reason at all amuses me. Mahmoud as happy as three or maybe even five sand boys, gives a shrug.

"This my usual place."

We sit and I begin to shiver. Mahmoud concerned, goes off to the car and comes back with a lovely warm shawl-style thingamebobsicals. I love it and make a great deal of fuss about its texture, warmth and colour. Everyone laughs as I snuggle down into it. Mahmoud, ever the smiling gentle person that he is, comes across and says, "Gina, you are still having the wine…in your head I think…I will get you a coffee."

He very much likes to look after me. Bless. More and more people arrive and I have coffee and avoid smoking anything; if I took that route, I would be sick as a dog.

My mobile trills and stops, trills and stops.

It's Deardra. I ring her and the signal connects and breaks. Oh, thank goodness she is okay. The fact that we catch only one word in ten, is of no matter. She is well and that's all that matters. She sends a message, 'Ah I'm still in the arms of my beloved, we are so lucky out here. The hotel said you left. Hope apartment to your liking.'

I manage a reply, tapped out whilst inhibited by handsome man and strong wine. 'I'm good, no, correction, *we* are good…apartment fine. I am in Lotus Coffee Shop, funny, eh.'

To which the ever-patient Deardra replies, "Are you drinking strong wine? If so, good, now make sure you have strong man to carry you home and make love to you."

I reply, 'Okay will do, over and out.'

When in Rome.

My time of reckoning is here. Woke up with a start. Missing the villa – big surprise – Greta, David, Gillian, Bob, Martine and dear sweet Gabriel…Michele, cross maid, oven man, and Tom and the girls, and all lovely French pals who are ever loyal as friends. Even the naughty pussy cats. Beyond this, I dare not go. If Raphael – there, said the name and did not pass out with shock – and it's the biggest 'if' on the largest billboard in Hollywood, if Raphael has missed me, there is no sign of it. Although as some men have said, it does not always follow that they don't want to. Guilt provides a large fence for such airing of emotions.

I can't stand it another minute. I shower and get out of the apartment after half a cup of coffee. Huge plans are afoot and I aim to be the one taking part in them. First stop is to get my hair cut beautifully. The first salon is packed to the door with laughing bridal and bridesmaids. The next looks as dirty as a hole in the ground – er, no thank you kindly. The next street – correction, *shara* – brings all the treasures of the east and the west. A new looking salon and a charming receptionist. I am in the door and sat down with a magazine having my horrible hair day turned around before you can say Delly's whiskers.

"Would you like a conditioner treatment?"

"Yes please, oh and you know you said to find a style that might suit my face and this wonderful heat, what about this?"

I hold up the perfect model with a feathery and ultra-flattering cut.

"This will suit you very well...much better than your present style...which is too heavy for your face."

Amira, the stylist, also throws in a make-up session to bring out my eyes. Well, if I can have the bags, shadows and lines removed, all the better. I use my own lipstick, the colours the Egyptians use are anything from lurid to pure Gothic...which is a huge surprise. I leave the salon a new woman. I am walking on air. It was the best move.

Hailing a taxi which is the easiest thing to do in Luxor, I ask for Karnak Temple, because it's the only one I have really read anything about. There's a little coffee-cum-chai and whatever nibblers are left nearby. I order chai and something like a lumpy wrap. It's the falafel and salad. Oh God, big risk. No need to worry though, it's a sort of workman's café. So they grin encouragingly at me as I dig in ravenously. Cheap as cheap. I am charged the same as the men. We all cheer as fresh food is planked down on a low trestle table and we stuff more goodies in. I am the centre of attention. It never bothers me. Men are fairly basic. If you are reasonably attractive, female, you are worth smiling at. Egyptian men are no different; in fact, I would go so far to say they are more kindly. Although, stories have provided me with other realities. Ever the diplomat and used to the board rooms and meetings of my old company, I plunge on.

The ticket office provides a rather strange list. I don't want a guide, I soon decide, due to the one that's on offer and is hovering with a hopeful leer. He wears a white headdress, which I am very jealous of, or rather the fine wrapping skills involved. A long white dress demure to the throat, and the finishing touches of the leer aforementioned and two large prominent teeth that could have swung a hammock. I know I am being offensive and rude. But those attributes can be left at home, this is a romantic tour I wish to take alone.

When the present world takes the heart out of you, the ancient one can give you a new one. It's just a case of going through the right door and seeing the right view. This is my day.

I am softened now. This fabulous temple with its glimpse of sky and a world so far into the past. It has brought me full circle and I am.! ried by a golden warm fuzz into the here and now. The movements and conversations around me fade away and a clarity of lightness takes the place of sadness and car fumes. Words are feeble here. Feelings are paramount. The temple site is such a fulfilment of all desire to praise a divinity, the ancient people's dreams come into being. Great columns, so mathematically aligned, they transport. I feel that I am in a great and wonderful ship of stone.

I am dwarfed by the architecture's dreams. The design exudes a power that I feel I can participate in.

The ancient gods transfer power. We can either accept or ignore. This is how I begin to feel. I have never felt this before. Sitting to one side on a massive fallen pillar, I look along the avenue of the sphinxes. I am so stunned by the beauty of the place. A stone hits me; it's a child grinning, slightly hidden. Not for long, an armed guard comes from seemingly another dimension…the boy vanishes.

Gazing upon these ancient people's possessions, I am in awe. With awe comes inspiration.

Mahmoud never talks of all this wonder. Why not…for it is the ancient cultures of this remarkable country that draws visitors from every corner of the globe…not the modern one. If this is true, and the feelings I have right now are that it really is, why is it not spoken of? Maybe it is a jealous view. So stunning is this civilisation, they cannot better it. They make people afraid with the threat of expulsion. Believe or die. Ah, I see the trap. My romantic view…of course the great Pharaoh ruled with all sorts of powers I have no idea of. Beware where I mentally tread.

Was this built for giants to enter? Was it a house inviting the greatest striding gods and goddesses? The little book tells of Isis. She has these wonderful winged garments around her. Could it be her that is passing through upon the breeze?

I trace some of the wonderful carvings upon the columns…the language of a people who cannot imagine us. Or maybe they could. This was certainly built to be present thousands of years hence from their time upon the earth. I shiver with the excitement of it all.

Colours drift, settle and mutate…the wind is coming from the River Nile, faint as a whisper. I head to the entrance. It takes a long time; this is a grand arena for the gods and Pharaohs to play mind games with you.

At the entrance, I am soon brought up like a galloping horse into the here and now with my mobile shrill and demanding to be answered.

I find a quiet call to answer; it's Mahmoud, God love him.

"Gina, I look for you at your apartment and become nervous all your shutters closed so tight. Where are you?"

"I am at the fabulous Karnak Temple, by the ticket office gate thingymebobsical."

"Stay there, I come for you two minutes, okay."

"Okay. I will wander to the little cafe."

But he's already gone. Very abrupt is Mahmoud when he has a plan set in motion. Watch out. He has some Taurean attributes and they dash suddenly at what they want apparently. I order a cool drink and sip it as the sun slides over the horizon and the light begins its magical descent into the Egyptian twilight and then dusk. I am told this is the moment when the gods are most active. Thin wisps of golden orange fade down into purple, deep cerise then an eerie green. The desert has claimed its prize of the sun for yet another night.

"Gina, you look so fantastic…I am staring because I am unsure if it is you. The light plays tricks here."

"Thanks, that's a real compliment. You like my hair?"

"More than you will ever know."

My favourite saying. Oh, how am I to leave this amazingly exotic land with Mahmoud and all this light and warmth. After a quick conversation with one of the guards outside, Mahmoud takes me to where chug-along Charlotte is waiting.

"My carriage awaits…see…hello darling, Charlotta."

"You speak to the car, my Gina. Why…she answer you?"

"We speak another language to the normal one, Mahmoud."

He laughs at the idea of a car speaking any language at all. I pat her dusty interior with great affection.

"Yes, this good car…my mum wants to see you…we eat there and then go to a special coffee shop way outside of Luxor. I have friend for you to meet. I am so proud of you Gina; you look totally good."

"Glad to hear it. Won't your mum be a bit cross if you are supposed to marry a local girl that they have chosen for you?"

No answer. Maybe that idea is under review but I doubt this. I have never been under any illusion concerning the culture of the Egyptian higher classes. To marry outside the culture is likely a taboo rarely gotten over.

We trundle and chug along…the streets quieter as we reach Mahmoud's area which seems to have the houses nowhere near as crammed together as in other parts of Luxor. We park in front of an imposing house. I am slightly aware of being observed by someone. Then shake it off. A very large lady in black from head to foot comes to greet me. Her warmth quickly dispels any nerves.

181

"Hello, Gina, at last I meet you. Mahmoud was very happy at your house in England. Thank you for looking after him so well."

"Oh, he was the best. I have a daughter called Greta, perhaps he told you…and Mahmoud was absolutely no trouble at all. Not like Greta who is a great deal of trouble indeed. We loved having him with us."

This made them all laugh. Which is good, it breaks the ice somewhat. I could in their minds be dragon lady extraordinary. I am not of course, but they may think him under my spell. Perhaps he is.

Mahmoud, I notice has coloured ever so slightly. Quite right too. Some little figures enter the room silently…his sisters…! I meet everyone it's all terribly formal compared to England. I drink a fabulous homemade squash its lovely, so refreshing. One of his sisters wants to go to art school and we sit looking at some of her work it's in childish style crayon I notice…not the easiest of mediums to get tonal quality.

"Well darling, if you can work this well with this medium…oils should be a doddle for you." Everyone laughs at 'doddle'. Mahmoud is soon bustling me out the door and we are back in Charlotte before I can get my breath.

"That was short and sweet."

"Sorry, but I promise, my friend…to meet him and it's a long way."

"I'm very hungry, Mahmoud, can we stop somewhere for a takeaway…?"

"Don't worry, I will make it all good for you…please relax, my Gina."

I don't think it's me that's nervous. Mahmoud seems a little wary of too much exposure to the family. Ah, but it's all imagination…the mobile trills out and he hands it to me.

"My mum need speak to you."

"Oh hello, Mum, you, okay?

"Yes, yes, I will tell him, thank you for your hospitality, Mum…speak soon."

He looks at me very oddly.

"Mum wants to see me again soon."

"Yes, she will steal you away from me. This what happens to the woman out here… The family want her. My sister wants you all for herself. This is the way. They love you."

"Oh, I see."

I rub his shoulder affectionately, as we are out on the top road out of Luxor heading toward a new destination for me. My goodness what a day it's been and there seems to be more to come. How will I ever settle at the Dancing Horse

Villa now with its quiet lane and multitude of trees. All in need of pruning. I have learned one must not touch your fellow here with people watching it's another taboo area. All manner of things must be observed.

Life!

Our journey out to the coffee shop which was, seemingly, a big thing for Mahmoud…he was playing 'our' music full blast as we continued on the top road. I like this area and to be frank I would have liked it a lot more if it was not a backdrop to high volume male American vocalist. So loud I could not think. I indicated to Mahmoud by pointing at the Bruno voice emission and my ears. He grinned and turned *it* down a mouse whisker's breadth. I pointed again then to my ears. What is it with noise and the young? I must have been just the same. This of course is one of the generation factors.

We arrive, thank God, me with some hearing left. He gets out and gestures.

"Come on, Gina…big surprise."

"I hope one of the surprises is a quieter one."

"Look who is here."

"Deardra! How fantastic, thank you, darling, thank you."

Bless her she jumps up and runs to greet me. We hug and chatter at each other.

"My God, Gina, when Mohammed said you were coming out, I did not believe him."

We sat down and ordered everything. I love this crazy spontaneous lady. While the men nattered and grinned and hailed every passing car…we nibbled on wonderful food of all kinds…very healthy food, burnt to a cinder on the outside chicken being the only exception. They love it out here and devour lorry loads. Salads which are so nutritious you try to remember the recipe from the plate. A small bottle is passed under the tables and behind chairs and tiny thimble glasses. We all hid the whiskey and sip its fiery forbidden message to the heart. Taboo, taboo, taboo… Anything forbidden is delish. Why pray is this.

The evening is one of the best of my life. It goes up there in neon lights for me as fabulous. Mahmoud is happy and has temporarily forgotten his torments grief and woes. We live for the now.

Now, may be all we ever have.

"Gina, how do you fancy a trip up to see the pyramids with me. Cheap flights up or is it down to Cairo are all over the net at present. We could also think about Siwa Oases when we get to Mersa."

"Mersa Matru sounds wonderfully exotic."

"Gina, it's nothing compared to the Siwa Oases…Siwa Lake and all the wonderful history. You know The Oracle of Amun?"

I look suitably puzzled.

"You know Amun?"

"Umm, I saw something to do with Amun at the Temple of Karnak."

Mahmoud snuggles in closer… Must be the whisky.

"He is very big god to the Pharaonic people, Gina."

"There is an oracle to him there…Siwa was a very important oasis, it still is, of course.

"We better go there then. Are there sand dunes…?"

Everyone laughs at this remark. It's obviously something very daft that I just said.

"There is a flight up to Cairo Friday."

"Well, we better be on it Deardra, don't you think?"

As we hoped the taxi man is her fellow, but of course, so no money changes hands. We fly up to Cairo and stay in a shabby chic hotel which has seen better days and nights, I'm fighting fit but poor Deardra begins to look a bit pale under her wonderful tan. I put it down to change of air, water and well anything and everything. We get out by taxi to the Giza pyramids and once I close my mouth in awe, scramble through the crowds to the camel man. We want camels there is no other way to see them in this stifling heat.

The camel man is beaten down by Deardra's fierce haggle – crikey, she can be amazing. I know it's an act so I stay out of it and let her do her stuff. We climb aboard. My camel has been on baked beans for the last year. I call out.

"I think this one is about to take off…phew don't get down wind of him."

"Yes, she do this 'cus she love you so much."

"Oh really, well, I wish she didn't, well, not quite so much."

"What's her name?"

"Queen Nefertiti." I should have known.

We set off like the whacky races and soon the keeper or camel man is trying to keep everything calm and under control. Mine sets off at a fair old whack and we are half way round the great pyramid when breathless he catches me up on another camel and grabs my rope or rein or whatever it is. I'm happy as they come and not at all nervous. Deardra is nearly falling off of her camel which is led like a nervous old lady across the road…but we all get around the great pyramid of Khufu which we managed more by luck than judgement. Having to navigate through stray, heavily unfit perspiring tourists and things and more gazers on the beauty of such amazing structures. Words do not express. By the time this unruly outing has also navigated Menkaure and Khafre, we are sweating buckets and Deardra is looking decidedly unwell. I manage by shoving and encouragement to get alongside of her.

"Deardra, you look a bit green."

"Crikey, you are good on a camel, Gina. Who taught you?"

"Oh, am I? It just came natural like. I'm getting the thumbs up from Charley boy the camel man so must be doing something right."

"I should say. Feel bloody awful, so nauseous."

"Want to go back now?"

"God no…I got the deal of the century for us and this is the best camel I have ever seen out here old but trusty, not so dusty."

"That's good. Mine must be living on beans the noise from the back of the bus is almost as loud as those from the front of the bus, if you understand my meaning."

And I'm off again. We do a little waggle run and the Charley Boy owner man starts a special temper dance in the desert.

"COME ON, NEFERTITI HABIBI, LET'S GO BACK BEFORE HE CALLS THE POLICE."

We return reluctantly to the others. Charley Boy is incandescent, but hey. We dismount with Deardra laughing and crying at the same time. Sadly, it is the last time I see her laugh for some time.

"You good with this camel lady, but she is never like this very quiet camel…how you make her do that?"

"Oh, it's this dream I keep having I am Bedouin in the desert all dressed up in dark blue with pyramids on the skirt and bangles and jangles on my ankles. It's an amazing dream you must understand."

He looks at me thunderstruck. Well, I must come across as a crazy white woman from some far-off planet. Which I do. I am happier than thirty-three sand boys on a spree. Poor Deardra in the meantime is helped off of her lovely old trusty mount who belches obligingly as she dismounts. Correction, is helped off by two, no three of the camel men. They gaze in awe at me. And give me a little 'in crowd' salute. Well, I am so amazed, that's a new skill.

I wondered when that dream would crop up again. We just about make it back to the hotel room when Deardra skates to the bathroom and throws up her breakfast, dinner and every meal since last Tuesday. I go in and hold her head and apply cold wet flannels and such to her burning skin. I manage to get her out of the mucky clothes poor love, and into her nighty. We scrabble for the bed as it is so tightly made and I yank and pull until she is able to flop in. I call reception and get lots of bottled and sealed water delivered. Plus, my lunch as I am ravenous as a hunter.

She must be ill poor love she has not smoked for ages. I wonder if this is just the heat. She may be pregnant. This we can only wait and see about. It is always a possible when it comes to ladies of the childbearing age.

I ask reception to kindly launder all of our clothes. The chap that comes up has a bag ready to put Deardra's ruined attire in. Good thinking. They obviously have done this kind of service before.

Deardre looks so pale and shaky I take the law into my own hands and ask reception to send a good local doctor. He arrives within the hour and I whisper to him that Deardra may be pregnant.

He's a dear man and nods appreciatively. I am on standby at the bedside, clueless but willing. He chats away to her in Arabic which obviously helps. She has another vomiting episode while he is there and so the handy bowl does make an appearance.

He gives her an injection and settles her down with a wet towel to her forehead. He has a quick rummage in his bag and I have a quick rummage in mine for the fee. We exchange paperwork I get a prescription and he the required fee.

"The injection will provide time for her body to rest and reduce nausea. We must work with the idea…as you rightly say that Deardra may well be in the first trimester. We *won't* think of this as acute hyperemesis just yet but she clearly is most unwell. I will deduce that it may so far be only a combination of change of climate, water or some bad food ingestion."

"Thank you for your advice that I should return her to her home in Luxor when she is better."

"When she is no longer dizzy. This will reduce the symptoms. Once the system has cleared itself, we can go the next examination. No milk or fats. Just juice and water. Avoiding dehydration is the first step."

I find the oats and show him.

"She might manage to keep these down…what do you think?"

"Oh yes just make with water and a little sugar…no milky things."

He goes, and I sit down with a cup of oats for myself on the balcon. I take tiny quiet steps once in a while to check on my poorly friend.

What a nice doctor and what perfect and expressive English. I nip out to a pharmacy and on my return thank the reception staff. They are most concerned.

Deardra feels a whole lot better next day and begs me to order some food. I tell her not to have milk or fats.

"Doctor's orders, darling girl."

She nods and makes inroads into a bland omelette. Very plain bread and a chai. She perks up in the evening. Thank goodness.

"I think we should forget Mersa…I am so sorry, Gina…all my idea and all that. My body is telling me get back to the flat asap."

I get on line and find two flights back the next afternoon. Cheap as cheap. We manage to keep her on the fat free and the hotel taxi man helps us out and down into the reception. After settling the enormous bill…but of course…we head out gently, gently, I keep telling him, to the airport. Poor Deardra, we get her into a wheelchair. No point in risking anything. I pay extra to get us through and on the flight. We land okay and I text Mohammed as we wait by the luggage carousel. He will be with us quick as quick.

Deardra sits head in hands at the airport cafe table near arrivals zone. I ask Mohammed to call us as soon as he is outside. It's a well-oiled machine between us.

The mobile trills out and Deardra gets to the toilet just in time for another session. Poor kid.

"Mohammed, I hope to wheel her out in ten minutes but you must promise me to drive slowly and carefully no swerving around…do you promise?"

"Oh my God, Gina…I am so frightened for her. She very sick."

"Not if you are slowly slowly."

"*Shwai shwai*…yes, yes I will do."

It amuses me how we always double up on words to make a point. A very human habit, I think. Mohammed is a peach and an angel about all of it. And glances nervously at Deardra. He obviously loves her. No sign or text or call from Mahmoud. Charmed, I am sure.

We arrive outside an extremely old property which could have been built in the reign of Tutankhamun…so delicate is the blue of the washed walls. Deardra perks up and we get her undressed and into bed. Mohammed makes off with a shopping list and some money. I sit by her bed with a hot chai…

"You look better already, Deardra."

She nods and sinks back into the clean pillow…after a few sips of the hot chai.

"Did you tell Mohammed I might be pregnant?"

"God no, that's for you to decide about between you. I would never interfere."

She nods off thankfully and I explore quickly find a shower and cool off under it. The television tells of freak floods in Paris. Bloomin' heck. Other cities are told to take this seriously. The pictures of the Seine surges are very frightening. The world's weather is certainly changing. David is right. I email everyone and keep them all in the picture. One darling email comes flying back from Greta and David. 'Darling Mum…miss you terribly. Can we come to the Villa…with David's Dad…as planned?'

I think for a minute and then reply…give me a week…a friend here who was most kind to me…is unwell…as soon as she is better, I will fly back, love mum. You can go to villa anytime even if I am not there you might have to do a few things for yourselves…but Gabriel will give you the keys etc. Love mum. I miss you all so much.'

Martine's message makes me cry. 'Come back Gina my friend please.'

I hide my tears from Deardra it's not her fault that she is ill. Mohammed returns with loads of things for the fridge and gives her a back rub. Sweet. We make a meal and poor little kid she pecks at hers more to oblige us than anything else. Mohammed is a good nurse so I let him take me back. They need to sort things. I hope she gives him a chance and informs him about the possibility of this being a baby on the way. His baby. I stay out of all of this of course. Mahmoud calls briefly, he is busy. Right, my mind is made up. I send him a text with all the details of Nice and the villa. It's up to him.

The last week flies by and Deardra's sickness has settled down now. We have a quick call by telephone the day of my flight. She says, she will let me know as soon as she gets the six-week test completed or something. Modern women are more *in* the know than ever I was.

Mohammed is silent on the way out to the airport. I dare not ask about Mahmoud. He has not called to say bye or anything. I ask Mohammed the terrible question that I perhaps have no right asking.

"Mohammed, does Mahmoud have any feelings for me?"

"He likes you a lot. But must obey his family. There is talk of an arranged marriage. He has no choice you understand me, I think you are clever lady, Gina, and know…we don't have the same way here. Our way is different. I want be married to my Deardra. We can live together in her apartment. Take secret Nicka Urfy marriage. You understand this, I think. We go to man but he not tell all the peoples, authorities…you understand why."

"Yes."

"Mahmoud would do this with you if you ask him, just ask him he say yes. He is very confused at present and his father died so he must make the company…if he not make the company his family not have future, his sisters not marry. His brother not marry, his mother not have her life. They are rich but this is not enough for future. You understand…"

"I think so."

We hug our goodbyes at the airport and he hurries back to be with Deardra.

While
I
Get
on yet
another
plane.

We go on many journeys…this is the age of Jetting. Jetting here Jetting there. We keep all the same problems and must still resolve them. They start to peck like hens at the mind. Happily, I am undisturbed on this Jet flight back to my refuge of the Villa of the Dancing Horse.

Ah! I see Darby O'Gill and the little people have been doing their stuff. At the arrivals gate I am thrilled to see a huge notice with. 'WELCOME BACK, GINA'…lots of hearts kisses and smiley faces. The two main smiley faces being Martine and the irrepressible Gabriel. What will they get up to next?

The hugs I receive turn into a cuddle dance and we nearly fall over with the rapturous feelings. I never got anything like that in Egypt.

We all bustle into the car, and my luggage vanishes into corners. Everyone is talking at the same time. But of course. Martine can't let go of my arm and I am laughing so much my sides ache. One thing is for sure it will take wild horses to get me to leave here again.

At Gabriel's, which we visit due to his hotel being so close and filled with food aromas. His mama gives my face a good kissing and is complaining of all aches and pains. She points to Gabriel who is clowning.

And declares with great French passion at the injustice of it all.

"Take him off my hand, Gina, rna chere…take him. He biggest pain in my derriere. He more pain than all pain."

To which the reply from Gabriel, complete with tongue well out, is a raspberry.

Yes, oh how good it is to be amongst friends…and loved ones. Delly and Pueblo are still madly in love. Oh, I should have such luck, and Michel is back on the sauce and Lilian [cross maid] is in the process of packing her valise and departing yet again. Martine explains the hilarity of it all.

Michel complains he does not get sufficient affectionate embrace and Lilian says she wants marriage before she will give sufficient to his needs. He meanwhile holds his own with promises which Lilian responds to with loud tuttings and rudeness which cannot be printed on the page…for all and sundry.

The saga will continue in Greek tragedy proportions. No doubt to the end of time itself. No doubt.

When they open all the gifts the ooohs and ahhhs are sufficient thanks. I meantime have checked delivery of my mail which I intend to sit down in front of eventually and with a large glass of Rose de Anjou…or my name is not Mufflewafffle Murganzers. Yes, I know my name is Gina…but hey.

Fed, refreshed and having checked out Tom and his ladies which Gabriel will deliver as soon as his van – he always refers to 'oven man's' transport as '… he's funny, that…softee.'

I announce cordially that I have some aftershave for 'oven man'…to which the resounding reply from all is: "HE NEEDS THIS."

Mama is most kind to me and so sweet she comes over in a quiet moment and thanks me for thinking of her…I bought her a lovely light flower perfume… I get up and give her a cuddle she has tears in her eyes. Oh bless… My stay at

Gabriel and Mama's is enough to refresh without over…egging the guest pudding. So to speak. I have to buy a car and so take Gabriel with me. He looks at so many I sit down and say 'oh Gabriel' over and over to which he pulls faces appropriate to the task. He then makes a beeline…he's awfully good at those…to a dear little Honda which although not the prettiest car on the forecourt is a cheaper deal than most and he announces.

"We have found the one."

I am overjoyed. I love Honda and this one, although it will not replace my trusty old thing in UK. Is a bloomin' close second and is newer. Not the favourite car of the French, it is lacking in something to them. I manage to arrange payment from the bank and the next day we get rolling on insurance and fill her up at the pumps and hey presto I follow a delighted Gabriel to the Villa of the Dancing Horse. Oven Man…is waiting outside with a suitcase. I am not expecting him to move in and thank me in any sort of amourattating manner for the aftershave so I get out and greet him with a handshake and a certain amount of apprehensive surprise.

"Post…"

He announces proudly. This is about all the verbal you can honestly expect from Oven Man…even on a good day. Although I have it on good report, he is a chatterbox amongst men. Kel surprise. I go in and am delighted by what I can honestly call home again. Home for real – within the refuge of beauty and light. All is well for the time being. I go through and Gabriel and Oven Man follow in a short space with all the luggage and lots of groceries and milk.

After refreshing my dear friend's tummies and heads with omelette aux herbes and red wine. Crikey how do they cope out here with the driving. Ah! It is the way I suppose. I settle into a routine of sleep alone and answer correspondence and email everyone. Greta, David and his father are coming soon…but the girlfriend is no more. Ah best not to mention anything there then.

I unpack my holiday cases gradually and try not to get upset about Mahmoud. Not easy, but reality must be faced. I pull out the sand casket and decide that I am going to do something about this problem of the translation of the mysterious writing once and for all.

I drive into town and place an 'ad' in the paper.

'Arabic translation required…for papers found in sand casket. Apply to Gina Tantridge…local person…'

My email address sits daintily alongside the request. I then carry on with normal shopping and go home. Blissed out in the study with wine and nibbles lined up, responding to everyone as the emails come in from Gillian and Bob…who are coming out. Wow…Bob is on the move. Flags out.

I get a hysterical letter from Gran who has not a clue about anything or anyone and Gillian God love her won't spill beans sufficiently. Good for Gillian. I get a lovely email with all the right credentials from a nutty professor of French who wants to wine and dine me over special translation…probably of the "Kama Sutra' if the amount of drool is anything to go by. No thanks. The only other response to the ad is one from an, Amr Bedoiu. Now, this looks right. I tell him to call me and pop in my telephone number. This sounds good. I sip the glorious nectar out on the balcony of my home with all the leisured air of a woman who has been through something but is not quite sure yet what that something is.

Close to the bottom of the suitcase of post are two very official letters. Yes, it is the oddest thing. Now their contents no longer matter or have any bearing on my plans the sodding things turn up.

I don't panic, no need anymore. But read them carefully, decree nisi…decree absolute. Poor Ray, he is without his boyfriend who is 'banged up' I think the modern expression is…in a French secure unit.

Serving a long sentence. Attacking French Police equals this outcome apparently…what is it he has against their uniform? Ray now has no exec-clothes, no exec-car and certainly has no need for the very expensive laptop he used for his very well-paid job. History solves mystery. Those yoghurts have a lot to answer for.

It would appear I did rather better. Revenge, cold, and hindsight…but the wine is so wonderful and slips down rather gurgly and pleasantly.

I drive into town in my little car I call her 'hurly burly' on account of I am as daft as two brushes and this little angel car takes me back into the hurly burly of it all in Nice town whenever I feel the need for it. Get it. I park and look at pots, ceramic ones. I have the feeling my rooms are not as aesthetically pleasing as they should be with the stampede of guests expected. I engage in a conversation with a woman who certainly wears a lot of very heavy make-up most of which is in her eyebrows and on her teeth. I cannot keep a straight face with this animated over-pricing clown so dive down side streets by way of escape. A young lad in clay spattered overalls is throwing a pot and singing happily. Today is the day I meet Felix…

Who

will

change

everything………

Amr turned up with a smile as broad and warm as the wonderful sunshine of his homeland…Egypt. The temptation to ask him if he knew Mahmoud was forced to one side. He held out a neat brown hand that reminded me of Deardra. The kitchen was a shambles with all the guests arriving the next day. Lilian had been delivered like a parcel of giggles and swearing. Martine had called me and begged…

"Take her for a few weeks please, Gina, I am begging. I cannot stand the quarrels between her and Michel another second. Please darling they are testing my sanity."

So naturally I allowed myself a secret smile of amusement and got on with chores.

Luckily, at the sight of pleasant faced Amr…walking through the hall…Lilian was intrigued but calm at present…she brightened up…taking me to one side…whispered eagerly in my ear.

"He is like the George Clunies C!"S!.l oh."

"Oh Lilian, 'I only call her Cross Maid in my heart you understand.' He is Amr, and an Arabic translator."

I may as well have said he has come to massage my back…for all she believed this, and guffawed in the way that only Lilian can guffaw. Such is my life. Accusations were flying from her receding figure. I carry on into the lounge and lay out all the tools of translation for Amr. He sits at my desk as if he was born there. I give him the sand casket and a hot coffee and some little madeleine cakes, which the bad tempered but slowly defusing Lilian has made. She has the perfect touch…you must understand…her secret to employment… Certainly a temperament such as hers defies description. The book she will write in her dotage will be, 'Passion and Patisserie'.

I peep at Amr…not out of desire but of general…you know concern…mixed with real curiosity.

He was head bent working away when I had returned from the garden terrace. I had arranged with Felix at his ceramics workshop to come out to the villa with some truly reasonable pots. He was an eager, lively character with a quick mind.

We had gone together from room to room holding aloft various bowls and vases and now I had settled accounts with him. He asked if he might come and repair my truly lovely old garden jardiniere and look over the place for pots and he would give me all the details and a breakdown of the cost. He would keep it to the minimum in return for any truly broken shards he could find. I agreed. He was a nice little soul and rather in need of the income. Nice had suffered due to rain and the problems of Paris flooding had changed the tourism. I felt a bit puzzled why this should be. Adding it to the fires I suppose people were put off. The 'season' was still new of course. I had plenty to do for now anyway. David had created an internet site for me and given me a brilliant domain.

The idea came to me that I might be able to get a helping hand from Felix. He was doing badly, not from lack of trying or skill. I put it to him and he said he would be delighted to draw up a schedule with me.

Lilian was peeping through the door jamb with a very soulful expression…she visibly jumped. As I returned from seeing Felix off.

"Oh Gina, oh madam…"

"Oh dear Lilian…"

I replied laughing and teasing. I went to Amr's side and he looked pleased. He'd done it all and handed me the results.

"Love poems by Rumi."

"Oh God, how marvellous. Well done!"

He smiled rather awkwardly…must be the effects of the cakes.

"How much will that be…you must have a fee or something."

"Oh, I could not take anything…please the cakes and coffee you know…Rumi…such a pleasure to see this…"

He waved a hand generally around the room…the sand casket…seemed to positively be alive with its golden contents like a dishevelled woman. I took up the translation, and while he nibbled on the patisserie, I read slowly and quietly.

"Rumi…

'Oh beloved, take me, liberate my soul, fill me with your love and release me from the two worlds.

If I set my heart on anything but you, let fire burn me from the inside. Oh beloved, take away what I want, take away what I do, take away what I need, take away everything that takes me from you."

I felt very shaken by this stunning work…so famous I could see that…what a delightful idea to place the poem locked inside a casket of sand.

"It must be older than I first imagined, this casket?"

"Perhaps, I think just turn of the last century."

"I bought it very cheaply in a little back street souvenir shop. Right here…well, in Nice town of course."

"It is not of any intrinsic value."

"But the sentiment and the Rumi poem…surely."

"Oh, of course, priceless."

"True love like this is the highest price that heaven can pay."

He looks at me and nods…there is sad, vague, other-worldliness about Amr… I feel he could have easily been conjured from the genie's lamp just to translate this and is about to vanish back into it again.

"Do you need work at all, Amr? We have guests coming tomorrow…my daughter Greta and her boyfriend David, oh and his father a French chap in fact. We need help if you are able…or perhaps you have other prior arrangements?"

I can tell by his frayed cuffs that he has not. I don't want to condescend to him. He is a secret well of academic knowledge. You would need a lot of buckets to plurnb, his depth. Luckily for us he nods. Eager to eat in the future no doubt. The sand casket looks different in the light of the lounge. When Amr drives off, I tell Lilian we have two more helpers. And hoping I am doing the right thing go upstairs to return the casket to my bedroom. On the way I look out of the window. To my astonishment I see a figure jump back as if they had been watching the house and alarmed at my looking out had pulled back out of sight. Probably my neighbour. Who, is a solitary and rather curious one…so I am informed.

The week that followed was the best and the worst of my life so far. We had all the food in hand but the wine would constantly get drunk. I feared for my bank balance. Happily, at the end of it, Greta produced a wad of notes. They all reported the most fantastic time. No doubt Gabriel had supplied much of the merriment as they had vanished off to his restaurant quite a lot. I settled back into the idea that not only did I have the help of the dear little Felix…who I noticed…indeed who could not…that Greta was more than a little attracted to him. Amr, shy diffident and not at all in your face…was a strict out of sight behind all the scenes worker. Lilian begged me to take him on full time.

The thought came to me that murder might be done. Michel is not known for his non jealous approach to love, lovers, and all matters of lust. If my employing the dear, calm, academic should prove the pinnacle of passions for all the women…I saw Martine's interest also. Just like life to throw the love spanner in the works. Oh it's cupid… that's right.

Cupid's spanner.

I saw Greta, David and his forlorn looking dad (girlfriend trouble apparently), off at the airport. They were happy but truly wanted to stay. I would too. All the food and wine you can consume…and the lively Lilian to keep us all in tears of laughter as she swooned daily over Amr, who is as oblivious of his looks as the flower that blooms unseen at night in the desert.

He hides all his lights under a very dense bushel. However, I have been fooled before by the supposedly quiet and shy male of the species. Beware all women and heed this.

Lilian has a huge crush on Amr. Cupid's spanner, wings, saucy matchmaking and lustful arrows are very much at work at the villa. Nothing much can be done about it. Martine calls me daily to get an update.

"How are the staff. Lilian seduced him yet."

"Hello darling Martine. Lilian is in the middle of the 'Catch 22'. She is really the lover of Michel. Correct."

"Oui…but she refuses to marry him because he drinks too much and he drinks to 'soothe his own sadness' because she won't marry him."

"At about midday last Thursday where was Michel?"

"Missing…no one can find. All the cleaners and laundry people were here for the big clean up and not one saw him…heard him, or caught him in a cupboard with a bottle."

"It is my thinking that when you cannot locate darling Michel, he is spying on Lilian best way he can…from the bottom of the garden through the trees."

"Mon dieu…this is too sad. The poor fellow. Please let me tell you my idea."

"Oh anything my darling, anything."

"I call Lilian and explain to her. This exact truth. I also tell her Amr…is how shall I say…

"A cool academic…like a cold choux pastry come from the fridge…and she is a hot smoking tasty haddock."

Laughter down the phone, as Martine tries to work this out.

"Yes, it is true, oh it's too funny. Yes, we can try. Let it come from me. I know how to keep a giggle out of my voice most of the time. We do not want to send one of them over the hedge."

This is Martine all over. I am still working on her perpendicular head. Love her so much.

We leave it at that and Felix bless his Jesus sandals has arrived to get cracking on the rooms. He has a helper and they trundle off to engage with hoover and cloth. They sing loudly and we will know all popular French hits very soon. Lilian is spying on Amr. Sigh. Her mobile goes off.

"Man the barricades."

I say to Amr, who like me, is steadily working through all the billing and general correspondence emails and the like. We exchange glances waiting for the crash of crockery, and swearing fit for a drunk stevedore to use. Silence. I listen with one ear while I type. Felix and his pal have devised a method. They shout timber and Amr or myself go and get the linens and towels from the bottom of the stairs. We stuff it in the two machines and let them gurgle and munch, swish and swirl to their hearts content. Silence from Lilian and I know Martine has dropped the anti-cupid bombshell. I look at the innocent Amr who is frowning over a letter from Gran. He is well versed in replies of the polite nature so he begins at once to type a letter back to her. He has permission to engage in his own demure scholastic cool as a cucumber manner. Literature and language. Praise the angels in long, short, flowered, sequinned, and gold lame dresses. From Derbyshire to Timbuck bloody tu!

Lilian is in the garden we can see her and we know she wants us to see her. Amr has secretly with pleading dark eyes of the seriously bedroom variety, explained the awkward side of things. He sensed the situation almost at once. Not knowing how to engage her in conversation…he is strictly an 'on paper only' sort of chap. He did all his appeals through looking at the ground and various careful avoidance methods. He was never interested and never led her to think he was. Sad as hell, but hey. She is really crying now, so upsetting. I went into the garden just as a 'TIMBER' rang out through the villa.

"Quite."

"Lilian, oh Lilian what has happened?" Red eyes and soggy hanky tell the tale.

"Martine is so cross with me."

"Noh noh…she wants what only is right for you and your future happiness." Her dark eyes engage me with such misery.

"But she say Madam Gina that Amr is a cool sugary choux pastry and I am a hot smoking haddock tasty and spirited. They cannot really sit comfortable on the same plate."

I feel the plate edition or addition to be genius. The perpendicular really has its uses. I do not smile. I put myself in her place and Lilian cannot be blamed for cupid. I get an idea.

"Cupid makes mistakes darling Lilian. He is not the perfect one. I should know."

Raphael puts in an appearance in both our heads…Lilian cuddles into me.

I walk her back into the little world that she knows… The sight of a partially stuffed chicken with legs akimbo…was not one I really planned. But life is full of these moments. Dealing with them is just how our lives are tested and we move forward, back or sideways. Or, as in my case down, on very hard flagstones.

In this instance, I make Lilian tea and gaze into the pantry hoping and praying that Derby O'Gill will save the day. He does. Sitting on the shelf are some dainty biscuits. I take it all into the kitchen and lay this little break from the routine out. I make her tea exactly how she likes it. Sit with her while she tearfully tells me all of Michel's horrid drinking and that wonderful Amr, sober as a judge but not interested etc. Life is a puzzle. She eventually calms down and not a plate was broken or a cup dashed. All the biscuits are gone… Small price I would say.

She mops tears for now into a hanky…another one. 'TIMBER' rings through the villa again and Lilian…seems to wake from a drugged sleep…where she lived on the planet, 'love in a mist' for a while…

"The boys will be hungry noh?"

I nod and leave. Never, never, change a good and positive outcome I always say. Of course there were other tears and it would take a while but at least now Amr can pass her without her running tearfully away. Poor Amr…poor Lilian…bloomin' stupid cupid.

I explain carefully to Martine as we stroll on the fabulous warm beach at Nice. We are on a special-girls-on-the-town behaving like French-tarts-outing. We feel we have earned it.

Bob is bringing Gillian out for an unspecified amount of time. They are to be given the honeymoon suite…due to the wonderful attentions from Felix. He is so wonderfully romantic. Bless him… He designed pots with hearts and I gave instructions and ideas to Amr who is making a few very lovely calligraphy designs…he is so gifted. Lilian does have excellent taste, if somewhat off the route of her own needs, comforts and happiness of the heart. Amr is wonderful at designing art and love but not delivering it. So it would seem.

I feel very blessed with my life at present. No doubt cupid or chaos will show up again soon… But for the time being… Tom and the girls are the only sexual antics we shall witness. At least we have eggs.

Gillian is coming and I am thrilled I will of course give her generous mates rates. My bank balance would not survive too many handouts. I want to pay for everyone. Staff however comes first.

Bob and Gillian are given star treatment. They spend two nights with Gabriel and mama. Gillian wants Bob to experience the full treatment. Gabriel shocks everyone by being on his best behaviour. Not a naughty word to be had. He must be sickening for something. I have an idea he truly is in love with Gillian.

When they finally arrive at Villa of the Dancing Horse…we make a huge party and Mama comes out with them. We all get terribly squiffy…which is how it should be. Felix is proud to show them to the honeymoon suite as we like to call it. His decor is much praised. Praise to Felix is like cream to the cat. Martine brings Delly and Pueblo to join in the fun. A little bird tells me she has a secret desire for one of my staff. I am unsure as to what the next step will be. Excitement, wine, good pals, and handsome men that carry good food about always in style.

When everyone was chatting laughing and generally shouting at each other in joy. Mama came to me with an earnest look on her sweet face.

"Gina, I want to look around, properly…can you show *me?*"

"My pleasure, darling Mama."

We walk gently around the villa and while Mama nods approval and we say nothing just let things explain for themselves…what they are and what their function is…our love for each other is like a delicate and lovely thread…we connected quickly Mama and I…there is a treasured understanding.

We walk the grounds and I sit down with her on the nice wooden bench Amr found for me…he's so like Oven Man in this respect. We say nothing just sit…after a few minutes Mama hugs my arm close to her. She is crying a little…

"Mama, are you ill, is there some malady?"

"Noh, my dearest girl…I am so happy."

We sit on a little longer just happy to be in each other's companionship. We are like this Mama and I. The shadows lengthen and I take her indoors for a hot tea. Generously splashed with brandy the way she likes it. I call Gabriel. He comes straight to the point.

"Where my love where my Gillian my heart breaks. The stars in the sky they know my sadness. Where my Gillian give the phone to her please Gina."

Handing the phone over to Gillian I can tell by her stifled giggles, Gabriel is in a naughty mood. Bob like most men from the English stock seems oblivious of his own wife's allure to other men…simply carries on eating. I worry for him…he is so obese.

All good things come to an *end,* and I drive Gillian and Bob to the airport. We cry and Gillian says she wants to come out in about six weeks if that is convenient. I drive back with mixed emotions. I miss her and Greta terribly but each one must live their life. I park in the drive of the villa and Amr comes rushing out.

"Gina, Gina…it is Deardra calling from Luxor."

I run in and grab up the telephone from the hall. "Darling girl, are you alright?"

"Oh Gina, please *don't* be angry, but it's about as bad as it can be. Mohammed tricked me into buying a fabulous apartment…made every excuse to prevent *me* from going there to see how it was coming along. He left out a vital piece of information. I said nothing to him and one day went there out of the blue to see how the decorating and furnishing that I had chosen was coming along. I spent a lot to make it a really nice place you understand. He didn't want me to go there after the first few viewings…because he wanted to surprise me…well he certainly did that. The girl his parents wanted him to marry is his wife and she is living there, it was all lies…she is in my apartment."

"His Egyptian wife do you mean, oh just get your lawyer to write her a letter and order to *go.*"

"Yes, I have instructed him to do just that. I was livid…she's strutting about in there like it is hers. I told her…it's not Mohammed's apartment, he did not buy it for her. I bought it for me and his child."

"Crumples, I bet that went down well."

"She is simple in the head…and does not believe *me.*"

"The lawyer will persuade her otherwise. *Don't* worry he will get her out."

"Yes, and best of all, my lawyer is Coptic Christian and put a clause in at my request…he thought it vital as some Egyptians are so slippery. I have a line in the contract of purchase…that it will be for my sole use and my child or children and no other only those I choose personally…you know to stay there."

"Thank goodness you did that; he is a good honest lawyer by the sounds of it all."

"My landlord here, thinking I was moving soon has now let this place and I have to go. He made up some daft story…which has a ring of truth."

"Which is…"

"The shara does not approve of a woman on her own expecting a baby…rather conservative if you get my drift. I know BLOODY MOHAMMED IS BEHIND ALL THIS ROT. It's just so unfair. He wants me to be pushed out of Luxor so that he gets the wife and the apartment. He won't be able to due to the clause. He knows nothing of the clause."

"Is he on the contract. Sorry in, the contract in any way shape or form?"

"Is he hell. No, it's all my money and all my lawyer."

"Do you have nowhere to stay while the lawyer gets this sorted."

"No, luckily I am as fit as a jumping bean now the sickness has stopped."

"Get on a plane with an open return ticket. Deardra it's the easiest and safest way for you and the baby. Mohammed might get unpleasant with you…you know once he hears about the clause and he has to go… Due to the law of his own country."

"Good of you Gina. I am a little worried in case he cuts up rough."

"Just pack up and show up. We will sort it all out. If the worse comes to the worse you can have one of the lovely new gite places at the end of the lane. Three of them are empty… We have excellent maternity clinics in Nice. So no worries there."

"Thank you, dearest pal. You're a diamond. I will text you all the flight details."

"Good Gabriel will come and collect you to help with your cases. We will take good care of you, don't worry. He's a good soul."

"Shukeran habibbi."

I hurry to the kitchen and tell everyone. We all discuss what can happen next. How we can deal with the room situation. Things will alter a lot here very soon…I placed an ad for a new chef…due to Lilian being back now in the bosom of the Chateau.

Deardra arrived with a flurry of wind rain and the biggest guest invasion so far. I say invasion because there were two children which were allowed to run riot. 'I wished Gran were here' being my mantra for the two weeks. Deardra had all the hand luggage required for an overnight stay and little else. Poor love.

Amr and I settled her into the quietist corner we could manage and then set to interviewing staff for the chef position. I have learned life delivers a lot of help in the nick of time. Amr thought like me that; Claude was the very best of them because he smiled so cheekily and was the oldest. In this instance we were right on the money.

The menu already on the tables became a thing of the past. History in the baking…I called it. Claude did what he wanted and we just sat down and said oooh and yum. He came from a huge expensive hotel and they had 'let him go'. All due to the age thing. How mean and spiteful is that. He was grateful to be away from the factory floor of cookery the shouting and swearing scuffles and back-biting. He was brave coming out here with certificates and his utensils, cooking notes, books, and…well everything he owned in the whole wide world. Bless.

I liked his spirit. Amr…thought him a great personality and we should give him the chance. I had done this before with great result. We ship of misfits and fools that we are. All thrown on the winds of fate. We had all washed up here at 'The Dancing Horse Villa'.

Amr and I really had got it right on the money. Deardra adored Claude and they became close companions of the sink…and bosom pals of the oven. Singing together in every language, not always the correct words, they gave us meals fit for two kings a prince a starving dog and a pernickety duchess. I wanted Deardra to rest, but after she said…

"I would feel stupid just mooching about with my belly protruding…" I pulled back on the nagging.

We rarely had a quiet moment…but at least the euros were flying into the bank account to pay all the staff and buy in the best quality food. You cannot make good meals without excellent fodder Mantra two. Deardra and I grabbed ten seconds in a lull, which are as rare as gold rabbits or rather Or' de Lapin around here.

"Jeeze Gina, this place is the dogs dooferpompoms."

"I knew I had got something right in my life."

"What's with the darling Amr. He's a looker and no mistake."

"He is such a help to me…like you. I don't know how I managed in my life before."

"Very self-effacing though. The women swoon around him."

Yes, very little can be done about that. Martine's maid Lilian cried buckets over him…

"Hand me a pail. Wow…this is such a unique place and if those children were elsewhere, the little darlings, it would be paradise. I love it all. Claude is the father I always wanted. Felix well, I would marry him tomorrow in a coal shed and live with him covered in soot and kisses."

"But of course, mon ame'."

"How did you leave things in Luxor. Mohammed help in the end?"

"Ah…a duck would be more use at a Jewish wedding. He kept himself in Hurghada, rushing around pretending to work. His wife, poor cow…yes bitchy, but she is…came to me and said sorry. He has left her anyway…that was plain as the nose on your face."

"I am so happy that it all turned out well with the apartment. Brilliant clause that. Your lawyer must have demanded quite a fee."

"Nothing's perfect. I am so relieved. When I have the baby, he wants me to allow him for free to get people in to tidy it for the baby to live in."

"Just the baby."

"Yes, funny wording. You are carefully avoiding the Mahmoud subject Gina."

"He makes no contact at all…what to do. He has to make a company…and his brother must marry first."

"How do you feel about him?"

"Love his sexy body and miss contact with the same sexy body. Warm kisses not thick on the ground here. Unless you count the bear hug from Gabriel the other day…love working and getting on with things."

"He is moping around for you. I saw him at various spots in the souk shopping and once in the Lotus Coffee place. Head down over the game of dominoes with some fellow. Grim…" "Oh don't. I have dreams about him and we are laughing."

"How wonderful… I have a dream where I am above Mohammed with a bucket of fish guts just about to empty over his conniving thick skull."

"Have a madeleine darling, bury your sorrows."

After the last guest has departed and the worst child has gone screaming into the car with his doting mother and father. The calm descends like a curtain of fine silk. We are all hushed by exhaustion. Never will we get the like again. We hold a staff party and enjoy not answering shrieks or bells whistles and yells. Our nerves soothed by a lovely year for red wine. Oh it is bliss with that first red kiss of fine wine. We talk in subdued voices, eat Claude's wonderful food, and leave the dining room door open…now that the fine still weather has returned. A cat walks in and stands looking at us with a certain amount of black cat amazement. 'Humans are very few and far between in the French countryside'…she seems to say. Although at present I cannot tell if it is girl or boy but the following day brings no quiver of the tail or horrid odour so we feel that she can stay. Claude calls her 'Pudding.'

She is as thin as a rail so I guess it is irony at its best. I miss Delly Nutkins but it would be cruel to separate her from Pueblo and Martine…she loves it there. 'Contentment' is written in letters all over the loving couple.

Pudding is on probation of course. Yet another fool for the good ship… My old life in the village and the office in UK. Cooking for Greta… Sleeping with a cold hubby, is so far away. Greta and I email each other still. Her final year next year and she is ill-prepared. Admitting this fact openly does not make it any better. David wants to go with her to Japan to inspect waters, and the wonders of the deep etc, Japan has a bad record with whales, I think he said.

We have few guests for a while. A honeymoon couple who rarely leave the stunning suite that Felix has designed. The view from this exquisite suite is right over into a painterly distance into the blue paling to soft lilac though the evening light. This must be holding them…but of course…

Claude and I are out on the town in 'hurly burly' and it is a momentous occasion. We are shopping for an outfit for him to wear to a wedding. Half way through the *'Season'* Deardra and Felix came to me with excellent and not really surprising news. Felix had asked Deardra to marry him and even though there was no coal shed or soot…there were apparently many discreet kisses.

Deardra had moved out of Dancing Horse Villa and was gradually clearing Felix's bachelor crash pad, or as she laughingly called his flat above the ceramics shop…the bachelor trash pad. Baby being due any time now there was a definite mood of a rush on. We found her an outfit… The new look of new *mum's* today is big round and sassy. What a bloomin relief. Pun's a plenty for hire here. Comfy shoes were her biggest problem and, in the end, the only things she could get on with her poor little swollen mummy to be feet…were white frilled ballet pumps. She joked as usual…so blissed out with all that was happening.

"*I'm* the biggest sugar plum fairy of the Dancing Horse Villa Troupe." I try not to laugh…but it is true.

Now we were doing the rounds and Claude is to give her away. I am chief bridesmaid…and have the perfect dress…as we all know. My world is too happy to worry about such niceties as *it's* a dress meant for my own wedding…ohay.

We manage to locate a chap doing a good line in suits for gentlemen that have enjoyed a few dinners, suppers and let's not stint…breakfasts as well. Claude beams in his finery and I buy him the gloves and tie…as a special thing. Amr, already has a smart suit. He modelled it for me and I almost swooned with wonder. Fly me to the moon now…please.

We all arrive at the wedding with flowers and Deardra is beaming. We have a few minutes to wait outside the pleasant 'Council offices of the Maire' and we all get ready with straightening bow ties and realignment of flowers in button holes. I have the most delightful bouquet. Amr, is smiling at me all the time and whispers…

"Perhaps, you and I can go in after, noh?"

I am silenced into a red-faced walk with head high and the stoic's determination of not falling over in these treacherous heels. I have a spare pair of flat ones tucked neatly away in my clutch bag….Who does not.

When the official registrar asks boldly and seriously… "*Prenez-vous cette femme pour etre votre femme.*"

Not only was I blushing with a mixture of happiness shock and the heat…boy it was a hot day. But I was crying at the sweetness of it all. Deardra was radiant in the last throes of pregnancy. We might have to deliver more than a wedding cake at Chateaux Martine. The ring had to be really 'eased on'. Savon was mischievously whispered, and the paleness of the groom who was smiling bravely through tears with his mother glaring from the side lines…who bore the look of one who expected nothing less. Mothers of grooms who choose to marry unknown pregnant persons…requires a look of mixed emotion crossed with a Pekinese's brother-in-law twice removed. Or, as in this case. The mother-in-law to be who knows she has met the one that is loved unconditionally by her son… One must take real life into account. Cupid is always at work and he does it all best in the naughtiest fashion. C'est la vie.*rn*

Claude is trying not to cry but the flow is not unlike those in the little house when Alice does the eat me drink me. All is wonderful. Lilian is casting seething with desire looks in Amr's bewitchingly handsome direction… Michel is staring with a trembling, protruding bottom lip in same direction. I am shaky…hot, and very worried I will put a foot wrong…literally. Weddings make you think of your own predicament. Odd that.

Outside after the emotional ceremony we are all alive and hugging, crying, laughing, and looking at each other in total disbelief. A perfect wedding. I wished Greta and David would…ma'U' get wed here.

Felix is red in the face…flushed with success one might say and will not let go of Deardra's brown hand. The ring is held up for all to see and we eventually manage to get into cars and drive with a great deal of hilarity, wrong turns, honking horns and shouting out of windows. Our hot sweating bodies crammed together…off…to the wonders of the reception.

Martine is treating the couple to a grand Salon Style reception. They are thrilled. We, that are single mingle and life goes on. Champagne bubbles tickle noses and we all congratulate each other. The speeches are too tearful to be understood. Gabriel is of course fully understood with a ripeness and juiciness of humour. Everyone laughs. Nobody cares anyway. Deardra sneaks to my side.

"I just remembered something."

"What is that, newly married Mrs Felix Durand…"

"How funny I must have looked on that camel by the pyramids." I hugged her very gently…taking the bump into account.

"Well, you would look a lot funnier now my sweet friend."

Our laughter made the whole room look round…and that made us laugh even louder.

Amr was a constant companion after that and we strolled out into the grounds as the night drew on. Martine was happily engaged in very deep conversation with Claude…and Deardra was having a nap, exhausted no doubt. Felix came to us, every once in a while, bless his heart. To thank us for everything. Mostly, for Deardra.

"Gina, my friend if you had not asked Deardra to just pack and turn up. Oh my life would be…still incomplete."

"My pleasure Felix…it's all turned out marvellously…"

Now I am returned to the place where it all began and ended. Raphael is far away now and I don't know any more about him than when I first climbed into the car that day when Gabriel took us off on that jaunt. I am hand in hand with a clever but finer feeling man. Amr is content just to be with me. He wants to marry me that has been made very clear. We want just to be quiet. I have withdrawn from showiness. Understanding a quieter sense of myself and the facts of having created true friendship with Amr. We are getting to know each other as work pals first. Seeing each other's rough edges so-to-speak. I am not suffering from illusions any more.

Our lives take these sudden paths. Which one is the right one…well, we have to saunter run or stumble down each one to find out.

Felix was very high spirited and we could see he was getting boisterous. We have to understand he is…over the moon with happiness. Deardra is sitting in a crowd of guests all clamouring for her attention. She looks exhausted.

"Amr, go and rescue her while I get the car and park it out front…"

They are both going to the ceramic shop tonight. They are not really in a position financially or physically to go on planes for fancy honeymoons. Deardra has done wonders with the little flat and the plan is to go directly there… Martine is signalling to me frantically as I head for the door.

"Gina, oh thank God you are sober…Felix is busy being a witty groom in front of his friends…it's probably the only chance he will get so let him enjoy it while he can."

"Amr is off to rescue her poor love, she looks all in." "Oui, oui it is all too crazy. Will you take her to the flat?"

"That is the plan so best stick to that, don't you think? Ah here she is."

"Gina, please. Amr says you are taking me to the ceramics shop. Felix, is clowning and won't listen to a word I say."

Martine helps us get a very tired Deardra settled into the car.

"Oh Deardra, do you have your keys?"

By way of reply she holds up her handbag. Amr ever practical takes it and shouts, "keys present."

I call out…

"Car…present. Gina present…Amr…"

"Present."

"Deardra."

"Present."

"Thank you, Martine darling, see you soon." Martine is laughing and waving us off.

With the roll call over we all go laughing off down the drive headlights blazing in the midnight light, or rather the lack of it.

We manage with a few scuffles and several attempts with the key in the awkward lock of the shop and with many giggles and loud whispers to get Deardra inside and I pop the kettle on for hot tea…we are all so thirsty. Amr comes shyly to me.

"Gina, I am a little nervous…Deardra wants me to help her out of her shoes, she can't bend down that far."

"Ha, ha, I don't suppose she can, you take over in here sweetheart." Deardra is flumped in a dishevelled heap. Face hot and generally bothered.

She looks relieved to see me coming to her aid. "Come on darling."

I look on her as a daughter and am well qualified to remove clothes from helpless young women without shyness. Poor Amr he must have almost died of embarrassment. I bundle her into the shower and when she emerges wrap her in a towel. Once she is tucked into bed and as comfy as the bump allows. I take a shower. It's such a hot night…and we all end up on the bed laughing and drinking tea, eating toast…it's gone one o'clock in the morning and excitement flushes our faces. Amr proposes a toast…

"To love and lovers, marriage and happiness."

I am as surprised as Deardra and we all clink cups.

We let her fall asleep and then wander into the lounge. The flat comprises of a large bedroom and tiny study…now turned by Martine's magic wand into a very upmarket nursery with all the lovely things that Raphael once owned as a baby. That is of course if a baby actually can own anything.

The lounge is small but sports a couch. We make ourselves as comfy as we can. I am not leaving her like this…anything could happen after all the excitement. Amr and I are suddenly shy of each other. Amr is simply not the sort of chap you can…you know. Not like Mahmoud who is a lover through and through. Initiative taking was ever his strong point. So, we talk about the wedding and Felix and fall fast asleep.

I wake up to a buzz in my head and the doorbell clanging or some such thing. The day after a wedding is such a muddle don't you think. There is a sort of free entry to the land of mess, fuzzy heads and blurred visions. Coffee is high on my agenda always. Luckily, Deardra is up and swinging into action. She laughs when she sees me.

"Oh darling, you look better than Amr, he is shaving and having a shower."

"I might join him."

I find Amr and slipping out of my horribly creased dress. I am so happy I throw all care to the wind and join him in the shower. The shrieks from joy and embarrassment combined. Deardra comes in with her smart phone.

"Gotcha."

"No, no, no Deardra please."

We are helpless in soap suds and laughter. I get out and pull on a bath robe I found.

"We are turning your innocent home into a house of ill-repute, Deardra darling."

"Oh please do…it's not seen much groovy action of this kind for some while."

"Are you feeling chipper today…you were like a dead duck last night."

"Oh Gina, it's my bloody feet they will swell up so. Can't wait to have it now."

"Oh your so close…where is Felix?"

"You may as well ask about the atmospherics on the ruddy planet Venus for all I know. I have left several messages."

"This is normal for here…you know French etiquette for the groom etcetera he's probably locked into a bathroom somewhere in Portugal by now…or even a bawdy house in Aix-En-Provence."

That sets us laughing and I am ashamed of myself instantly.

"No don't, you make my baby laugh too Gina."

Amr brings a tray in and is handsome as ever with a clean face and fresh aroma of aftershave…no doubt nicked from Felix toilet cabinet.

The phone is clanging off its cradle and Deardra can't quite get up so Amr answers.

"Felix, ah mon *ame'*…*yes,* yes we are here in the flat and we have Deardra safe and sound…D'accord D'accord…we will wait here for you…but *don't* be too long we have work to do…D'accord…I will, yes I will."

He rings off and looks at us with the look of a man who is about to break news of the mischievous kind.

"Ah, it is the simple explanation. He is in a house where there are many people and all is well, he is safe and sound. But…"

"What is the but…please Amr…don't stop *now.*"

"His friends have stolen his clothes he has only a bed sheet to wear home."

"This is too much; I shall have the baby from laughing at this rate."

"What does he want us to *do,* collect him take him clothes what exactly?"

"*No,* the people of the house are amused and very nice about the whole thing…they will help him and lend him things to wear… They will drive him here as soon as they can."

"How did he get into such a pickle…no *don't* tell me he was so very squiffy…oh well he only gets married once. So we must forgive all these pranks! His friends are behind this. We will have a lot to talk about for the rest of our lives that's for sure."

I cuddle her and try not to laugh.

"Deardra my dress is in an awful pickle do you have some things for me to wear home."

That does it and we all laugh until our sides ache. Poor Deardra looks like she might pop. Rubbing her sides, rocking gently…saying over and over no, *no, no, no,* no…enough.

Felix arrives about an hour or so later sheepish and reserved. A huge sorry expression on his cute face. His hair is dyed with orange and blue streaks and the remnants of sequins adorn his eyebrows. Amr and I leave the lovebirds to it. I manage to take their photo…which will make excellent Christmas cards for the next few years.

Amr and I escape to the streets, still quiet with early morning. A few workers were gamely getting their act together for the day ahead. It was going to be another hot one. We drove to a side street and found a workman's cafe…I have always classed myself a working woman although the problems now are so few…and I am in a beautiful setting. My 'villa'…I say it to myself a lot these days 'My villa' my home. My family…Darling Greta and David…although, more and more I see Mama and Gabriel, Martine, Cross Maid, Michel, Oven Man, dearest Deardra and Felix, Amr, and lovely Claude as my new family…people in the UK are friends…but I feel sure that if they came here, I would see them also as family. Gillian is the best pal any woman could have. Bob is a terrible worry. I have an awful premonition about his health. He must frighten Gillian. He eats constantly.

There will be a new addition soon, a little babe…how wonderful to see life renewing itself. Names are being bandied about. I think this little one will be petite. Deardra is stocky and not very tall.

Amr orders us a lovely breakfast we only managed coffee at Deardra's before the errant groom arrived many hours late for his own honeymoon. Deardra was patient, although, another dirty stop out night of this kind would lead to rolling pin humour I should think. They embraced as if they had been parted for a lifetime.

We sit with our bowl of latte, supping its wonderful depth Amr is as creased up looking as me and we are getting looks from the amused workmen. Who, wink at him and make the odd joke?

I say nothing although I want to. Amr's a dear person to be with. In the next few minutes plates of food arrive and we tuck in with the appetite of wood pigs. Probably sound like them too.

Amr is grinning broadly. I nudge him smiling.

"Do you know the date of the baby coming Gina?"

"Ah I shall look into my crystal bowl and see…yes, it is here…" I gaze into the coffee bowl, Amr is giggling.

"Are you making fun of me, Gina, because if you are I shall have to be very firm with you later."

"Who is this I see approaching…ah it is a little figure in a nappy it is I think a little brown eyed child with very curly hair…she is the little Queen Nefertari."

"Collette is a lovely name don't you think Gina?"

"Yes, you are spot on with that one."

I send a text message to Deardra, not expecting one in return they are on honeymoon after all.

"It's very exciting I worked out the dates…if Deardra and Mohammed were 'together' at the end of last November…and I offer this in the name of unbridled lust of course."

Amr is blushing and grinning…there is hope yet for him.

"Then and this is only a rough calculation the baby may be due if all follows natures full plan…about the first week in August. Every babe is different and every pregnancy individual, so I may have got it figured way out."

"Oh, of course you met her when she started feeling sickness."

"Yes, she had a rough time poor kid."

"Do you want more children Gina?"

"That's a big question to a woman who is tucking into a fried *egg.*"

"I would love a child."

"I hesitate to pry into your life Amr, but are you married still…where is your wife…you don't have to answer me of course."

"I married a long time ago, to a French woman but she was afraid of everything. We divorced some three years ago."

"Afraid, what of you of childbirth…life."

"Yes, everything from the morn until the night made her nervous."

"Oh dear Amr, I am so sorry, so…you have no children, oh poor love and I can see you would be a good, kind, patient husband and father."

"Perhaps, you Gina would consider me in this role with you…I would like one day to call you wife…I am not so young I know but I would be fair and just and would work very hard to make a life with you. There would be no playing games with you. I know you were treated unfairly before. My loyalty shall speak for itself. I am not good at this, sorry Gina. Women want to be swept off their feet…and made love to. I think this is in films only…and not sincere; marriage should be sincere. Just my opinion of course."

"You are a little academic and plain in your approach…but yes, sincerity is the best way of starting but when I think of a romantic lover…well

I have had them and look how that turned out…although I think perhaps Mahmoud was slammed down by his culture."

"You have a lot of feelings for Mahmoud I can tell."

"Am I that obvious?"

"No, it is just that you speak of him when we talk of marriage."

"Ah…you are clever and logical. Is this what you really want Amr, we are friends I know and work really well, no that's not true, we work more than well together we make an excellent team. Not the romantics in the poems style of course, but we are complimentary…crumples I am as cool as you are about all this are you sure we could make a go of it… We are a bit…"

"Perhaps cool and logical can win over hothead Gina. Hot heads lead to sudden quarrels and divorces…Lilian is hotheaded, I know she thought of me as husband for herself but the truth and the reality would have proved me right in that instance…you must let me be right sometimes."

"I saw that right away Amr, Cupid should have taken a vacation."

We laugh at that outright. The workmen look at us and smile and wave. One points to his wedding finger which sports a handsome gold band. Then to our utter amazement he and his pal a swarthy giant of a man points to us and they both nod in our direction.

"Surely Gina, a poem written when man and wife are growing old together is more proof of tenderness and not just the rush and excitement of being young. Young lovers can part so easily."

I nod and wonder if this is true. Excitement is one thing; it does not last of course. Yet, I do want to be swept off my feet…I see this. I have missed out on years of warmth.

"Amr, you see the trouble is I had a cold husband. I would snuggle into him but he turned his back on me so often that after my Greta was born…we, we never made love again."

Amr is surprisingly tender and covers my hand with his. He can't do the rush at the woman and wrap her in passionate kisses. I have a strong feeling he can stay the courses though. All of them. He has for some reason chosen me. Perhaps because of my not drooling over him like all the others. Not agreeing to every syllable he utters. Downright cross he made me sometimes when he would dreamily write loving and kind letters to that despicable Gran of mine oh God it's me, I am sooooo sooooo angry, I finish the food and Amr pays the owner, they are very jovial with him… He is I also notice a real man's man…when needs be. Oh I don't know. I have chosen two lately from the heart.

Both bad moves…both gave me great loving, but the bedroom is only part of the life. But it is the most exciting part of the life of a couple…isn't it? *We,* for goodness sake, have a bloody honeymoon suite…up at the villa…it's one of the most popular and lucrative incomes so far. Oh damn oh damn oh damn. I am crying…yes it's all coming 'out like a river. Oh no, no, *no,* not now. Not now.'

It's a horrible crying jag. Embarrassed to hell in a scruffy what should have been my wedding dress.

Untidy hair no proper make-up and Amr is there holding me we get into the car and I really let rip.

Amr drives me to a quiet place and I blub horribly. Tears and a runny nose mess and muckiness. He holds me to him saying over and over…

"Let it out Gina, let it all out…it's the best way. You will feel better soon…I know I did."

I am jabbering incoherently into his neck. Poor man. He will be soaked through at this rate. One thing stands out as clear as clear he is not saying unkind things like pull yourself together or just pushing me off and driving on. He is letting me get it out of my system. I stop as quickly as I start. He pulls up by a pharmacy and runs in…he comes out with a box of wet wipes and a rose in a box.

He places them both in my lap. The rose is soap shaped cleverly and is rather a shock.

I look at it in a daze. We drive back to the villa without another word spoken. Silence heals. Martine calls me a week later.

We are planning a secret birthday party for Claude. He knows of course that Martine has invited him to the chateaux to an evening meal with her. He is totally unaware of the reason for me slipping off now and then for several hours to make and apply marzipan and icing to decorate an old-style fruit cake. He is of the old school and our delicate sponges would not excite. Fair enough.

Amr is going to add the essential writing and candles. I told him if he had any doubts on the matter, he should call Greta as to my lack of decorating skills in fine written messages on expensive cakes.

Deardra is at the villa with Felix daily, upon my insistence. Felix has left a little lad in charge of proceedings. Felix does not want to close his shop he just wants to earn money. The tourism is slowly picking up we have two guests who are no trouble at all. They go off all day with their car…and explore. Ideal people I should say.

The correspondence pile has grown and the day before the party Amr and I sit in the study cum whatever we want it to be at the time room…and just as expected Gran has written a letter pleading for news. Amr, fingers poised above the typewriter about to send a sweet loving missive full of the joys of summer is stopped.

"Amr, I swear to God if you write to that horrid old witch on her horrid old broomstick, I shall empty the contents of the refuse over your delightfully handsome head." He being of sensible turn of mind goes off to find other jobs in the house. A good man knows when a woman has truly reached her tether end.

The great day is here and Claude is in the kitchen against our wishes, he loves to make breakfast for everyone. My poor waistline…he is opening all the cards and there are a lot. We applaud him, kiss him, and generally make him laugh. He takes me to one side.

"Will it be alright with you Gina if I slip upstairs later to get ready for Martine's little supper for *me*."

"Of course…darling *man*."

What he does not know of course is that we are all leaving just twenty minutes after him. We are even taking the guests to the party. They, are thrilled to be going to a real-French chateau and are under strict promise not to breathe a word of the real plans for the evening.

The plan goes ahead and Deardra has her little hospital case with her. We drive slowly she is in misery with her rotund body. Felix is excellent with it all. Good choice Deardra. Her feet are slightly better now I have located slippers of generous girth…she says they are blissville. Oh poor girl.

Martine pulls us all in and we love the look on Claude's face. He knows now there is something afoot.

Martine waits for us all to settle and tapping her glass signals to Felix, who, blows on a little trumpet like a fanfare. Oh how funny. A piano is wheeled into the room and it is followed by a dapper music student in straw boater, bow tie, and sports coat. He makes a huge entrance to loud applause the champagne corks explode and he plays a lively piece. We are thrilled once more when Martine flings off a drab dress which I was most surprised to see her in and reveals the sauciest outfit ever to grace a stage. We gasp, and whistles cheers with bawdy good humour make a raucous setting. This is a mixing of…all the styles and when she and the pianist whisper urgently, much nodding and giggling goes on. Martine stands back picks up the mike and announces with a husky lisp.

"La vie En Rose.
Des yeaux qui fait baisser les miens Un rire qui se perd sa bouche
De L' homme auquel j'appartiens. Quand il me prend dans ses bras II me
parle tout bas
Je vois Ia vie en rose.
II me dit des mots d'amour Des mots de tousles jours.
Et ca mefait quelque chose.
II est entre' dans man Coeur, Une part de bonheaur
Dont je connaise Ia cause. C'est lui pour moi. ·
Moi poour lui dans Ia vie
II me L'dit, L'a jure' pour Ia vie Et des que je L'apercois,
Alors je sense n moi Man Coeur qui bat."

The silence after this fabulous song sung with such feeling. I knew then that Martine is a wonderful person. No wonder the rich man of the chateaux wanted to make her his own.

Claude is up and goes to her and they embrace. He is a very tender-hearted man and wipes his eyes thanking her over and over. We manage to restore some semblance of order and the pianist strikes up Happy Birthday. We sing and shout our heads off. All the love in the world goes into that party.

The cake is wheeled out and is cut with great ceremony, we actually enjoy its richness.

But it is the song the stunning Edith Piaff number. The Little Sparrow song that is the greatest success. I am proud to know and be amongst such people.

It is well past midnight when I drive the guests home, the rest are staying of course. Martine hates to end a party, what energy she has. I love her dearly, dearly pearly. I love all my new family.

Tucking the guests in with hot chocolate…their request. I go through doing my last checks. Amr is the one to do this normally but he is chatting to Claude, they are firm pals. In the shower I count all blessings. Sleep is swift to come and the next morning I prepare breakfast for the guests and then wash up while they pack for the airport.

We are enjoying the peace and harmony of the villa in its almost empty state. I take a break and sit with Pudding who is now resembling her name a little more closely. The phone trills…

"Gina, oh I have such news. Deardra had a little girl she is the sweetest angel ever, like a little princess. We wanted you to be the first to know."

"What time was she born?"

I can hear him checking with the staff.

"Ah five this morning. I have no sleep I am so tired Deardra is sleeping now will you come with me this afternoon…I shall slip home for a few hours…I am done in and Deardra is exhausted."

"Of course, I will be there at three this afternoon it's the 'Polyclinic Santa Maria Maternite' have I got that right?"

"Oui, oh dearest friend we are like children walking on the moon."

"Congratulations darling Felix. I will be there…three o'clock."

He rings off and I dance with Pudding around the room she is used to all our odd antics now and is not in the least put out by these antics.

I go upstairs and tell the guests the good news. Then shower and change into a clean dress and comfy shoes.

The maternity section is bright cheery and very clean. It's expensive here so Deardra will only be here a few nights. Felix's mother insists that Deardra stays with her. I told Deardra this is excellent and I add…

"If she becomes dragon lady, text me and I will bring the cavalry of one black cat and Amr to rescue her and the baby."

Deardra is feeding the babe as I go in and I kiss them both on the top of their heads.

"Congratulations, Deardra darling, how do you feel now?"

"Oh fantastic. You know, Gina, it's often true…apparently that if you have the lousiest of pregnancies."

"Which you did."

"Yes, I did, didn't I? Well, you get sometimes get this quickest labour in history. God it was like shelling a pea. I don't know how we made it in time it was like a scene from the keystone cops or some such thing. I love her so much oh look at her Gina. Oh and we are calling her Felicity Gina Collette. What do you think about that?"

"I'm honoured."

"We took ages getting it right but the name Gina, your name dear pal." She covers my hand with hers momentarily.

"Well, it had to be in there if it wasn't for you none of this would have been possible. Well, this little angel would be here of course but Felix and, and, and the marriage."

"You are better now I can tell because you are back to your old verbal self. Welcome back Deardra."

"I have been thinking that you and Amr should go to my apartment in Luxor. I have the keys. It would be a small thank you for all you have done and I will think up other things as well ofcourse."

I don't want to tire her out so we agree for me to come the next day so that we can arrange for more photographs.

I text Amr, who calls back…at once, delighted of course.

"What weight is the baby?"

"Oh I forgot to ask. Deardra is exploding practically with joy. The baby looks about six pounds. Thank goodness it was no bigger. I don't think Deardra would have survived. I'm on my way back…where are you Amr?"

"At the villa, the party didn't finish until after four. Claude and I slept up in one of those massive rooms."

"Oh the fancy one with the two big single beds and all the canopies…its great in that room. I slept there a few times too."

"Claude was out like a light when I left. Forgive him Gina but I think he may have the hangover of all hangovers."

"We call those a 'Gabriel', hangover."

"Oh he went just after you because Mama is not feeling so well at present." A pain like a knife went through me.

"Oh God, no, not mama. Amr, I beg you, please hold the fort at the villa, I am driving straight to Gabriel's."

I manage to find parking – there does seem to be more activity at present around the hotel and then head to the reception desk. Sulky girl looks at me very askance. Then wordlessly points to the private curtain that sections off the private rooms for Mama and Gabriel.

"Gabriel, are you here, Gabriel?"

"Oh *mon amie*, what a sight for my eyes. Mama is so unwell."

I follow him through. She is in bed and looks pale under her lovely, tanned old face. Her dear lovely face so sweet. I hug her tenderly as I dare.

"Gina, I am so pleased you come to me…of all the peoples you are my angel to bring me well."

"She has been saying, do you think Gina will know about this will she come she is busy but will she come."

"Oh darling Mama…I came the instant I heard. Of course I did. Do you have a pain is there something the doctor wants you to have?"

"Oh what he has in his bag dear one cannot make me well… I am come to old age with all it brings in its entourage."

"You will outlive all of us."

Every little bird has its beak.

***

Gabriel had made tea for me and as soon as mama had fallen asleep, I joined him in the little garden where once Tom and the girls had sported and splashed. It all seemed so long ago.

"Mama has nodded off."

Gabriel has bags under his bags. Eyes tired from partygoing and worry.

"Gabriel, do you think it's time to employ help in the kitchen. I know it's not my affair but Mama will not get younger."

"My thought exactly Gina. I have placed an ad in the local paper. The main problem is she hates people in the kitchen that are not aware of our standard of good food."

"I know and of course she is of an age when they really do know what French people like to enjoy as well as visitors."

"Exactment, my hands were tied but now I have come to it by the round the house and bush method."

"Do tell."

"I will insist that she goes to stay with her sister for one whole month in the cool of the hills." He beckons behind the town. We sip our tea which is so refreshing in the heat.

"Then, while she is there, I personally will train up someone to our method and when Mama returns the poor soul will be more or less resistant to her scolding."

"You are not just a pretty face Gabriel."

He throws back his head and laughs one of his special all-encompassing of the planet laughs. We wind down with chit chat and I shop for a few things that Claude has asked me to bring in and return to the villa. We will be going through a lull according to the bookings. We don't particularly wish this but it is what it is. I grab two lovely things Amr and a tray of food and wine...tea for him and yank him away from his desk *for* five minutes.

We stroll to the farthest corner of our garden and sit on a bench which Felix has rounded up from some unknown source...more than likely the outcome of nefarious activities with Oven Man. He has also repaired two rearing horses which I presume were dumped along with a great deal of junk in the garage. These horses he has patched lovingly and although they have a sort of cock-eyed look about them...they are high on the list of the 'much loved' at the villa.

Amr snuggles close in the shade with me, the surrounding trees here were never lopped like all the others on the main path, so the light is dappled...sort of gentled down, my favourite kind. He lights up a tiny cheroot...a habit learned from guess who. Deardra is safely ensconced with Felix's mum and so far, there have been no calls for the cavalry to rescue. Pudding has decided to grace us with her enlarging daily presence and the three of us enjoy the peace.

"Mama is having an enforced rest and while there is a lull here, I thought we could take advantage."

"Oh, go to Luxor, you mean?"

I nod glad that Deardra has already dropped clanging hints to Amr when I'm not around.

"Yes, it is an excellent idea all the more that we have a residential address which is in a good area. The authorities at the airport are not keen on Egyptians just drifting around in these tense times."

"While we are there I want to go to an oasis. I have been reading about the very old routes that the Bedouin people followed routes by star formation and certain features in the landscape, the moon and sun. They were totally self-sufficient. I would like to look deeper into their lives, *it's* a dream of mine."

Amr was very quiet and I soon discovered why. He had already given up at the first hurdle. Apparently, he had been informed that due to the instability of the Egyptian permits and border controls regarding free movement he may not be allowed back in to France. So, he unpacked his things and went off on a sort of aboriginal walkabout.

Claude, ever the soothsayer these days was very gentle about it all.

"This is not of our making Gina; you are generous to a fault with people of all cultures and creeds but the International politics are tricky."

I nod and put the old tatty maps away and sit with Claude and sip tea. We are great sippers in the villa. Champagne may be quaffed, wine gulped, coffee slurped, but we tend to sip hot tea with the air of stoics.

"I'm still going but I will get an up to the minute map of modern roads. A compass and any books I can lay my hands on about famous oases routes."

Claude chuckles…I love this about you Gina, you get hold of the idea and hold on like a little terrier with a bone."

"As it has been said before. I always say if you find a wall in front of you barring your path go out and buy dynamite."

Claude thinks this hilarious and for the last few days of my packing, map perusals, and general odd pre-flight behaviour he gives me meals with the headings of…

'Dynamite Soup.' 'Dynamite Sorbet' and my particular favourite… 'Meringue Dynamite with Strawberry Topping.' One has to admire such elongated humour. Claude is always cheerful and we get along just fine. I am proud to have him here. I don't see anyone anymore as staff we are all family.

This is proving to be ideal to all our personalities. Deardra has had enough of the 'baby talk prison' as she has dubbed living with Felix's mum and shows up out of the blue complete with all she needs for baby for the day. Felix had remonstrated that she must not work. I chorus this. She offers the argument,

"I can answer the phone and write messages, reply to emails and generally make a muddle of *Amr's* filing system."

Amr not being here gives the opening, and although we know he will be back sometime. When, is an open question and who am I to take him to task. I am secretly sorry for him he is a failure in so many ways. Books and scholarly pursuits it would seem have their limitations in the world of making one's way in the capitalist jungle. He is from a repressed culture. No personal freedom.

I would not like to question any single person on their belief nor would I like my own challenged. We all live in a muddle of a world where politics borders and visa control are concerned. I the free to move one, cannot understand a religion that causes such grief.

The day of my departure brings everyone to the villa Claude is still playing with menu titles and dishes of a wonderful oriental and middle eastern flavour have been gracing the table. He states it is to 'prepare my palate.' I thank him most sincerely, what a chef he is. Yummy and gobble it all up are the order of the day. I probably won't get such good food as this in Egypt so I eat it with relish.

Amr calls and is very upset he is staying away because he cannot bear to let me down. He also would have loved to see his Egyptian family. He has been away from Egypt for more than five and half years. I tell him that I am sad he can't remove such obstacles. I am going anyway. He sighs audibly and I move on quickly to the subject of holding the fort in my absence...he states he will come back and help generally. I had already spoken of Deardra taking calls and ordering supplies. We are without guests until the beginning of October apparently. I am happy to follow the Bedouin and then I will return complete with sand in my flip flops or whatevers.

The flight is wonderful and I manage to sleep, eat and generally enjoy all that the modern traveller in a little seat in the sky can enjoy. Wine was in the picture. The funny antics of a little girl who kept wandering up and down the plane kept me occupied. I even brushed her hair and told her stories about some bears that went to a wedding in the sky on the cloud formations. This is what can happen when you give women of a certain age wine on flights into Luxor. Happy days.

Her mum turned up at one point and thanked me very nicely. Gave me her number and email address. She lived in Luxor and would be happy to meet up with me if I had time. I thanked her and we did a great deal of waving goodbye at the Luxor terminal.

If I thought Nice warm, it was nothing compared to Egypt. We all stepped out of the air-conditioned plane into an oven. Like a slap in the face. I loved it and stood on the top step and stated…wine still activating attitude…

"Hello Luxor."

Then scuttled slipped and struggled along with the others down to the waiting airport buses. We were scooped up and herded along like flotsam and the other one, until we reached visa purchase where the touts tried with the usual inventiveness of the greedy to pull us into their pits. I waited and paid the exact price of entry and stumbled out into the dusk which was warm, heady, and pale purple in the distance. A flurry of drivers and tour operators came gliding to the surface from a mirage of heat and I managed to see the timid chap I knew from the Lotus. His hand holding a card saying Mrs Tentridge… One cannot nit-pick at such moments.

"Welcome Mrs Tentridge, you are coming with me…please the taxi is over here."

Happiness was in that moment. Pure and lovely… Tears of it welled up in my eyes. I could say nothing but followed him artless little chap that he is to the white Luxor taxi. I wanted Mahmoud to be there more than anything in the world and the poignant realisation hit me hard.

We zoomed along in the new car with its purring engine and whoosh of air. I could sense a cold coming if he didn't turn the air con' down and indicated for him to turn it down.

"Nice is also very warm, so I don't mind a little of the heat."

He nods. It's a bad move and he turns it to a whisper and I nearly melt. Me and my big mouth. Once registered and 'in' my room I look at the shower with longing. I wash away dust yes dust. Where does it come from oh yes, there is a desert of hundreds of miles of it either side of the thin green magical ribbon…called Egypt.

A bed was never more welcome or sighed in before.

The breakfast room overlooking the Nile was buzzing with waiters calling and orders floating past on little trays. Great flourishes and scrambled things. Cakes seem to be very popular in Egyptian hotels for breakfast. I had two days to sort the Kharga oases requirements. A tour was being assembled as we speak. I had to report to the office at an unearthly hour to be part of the convoy of trucks with police and a machine gun or three. Tourists from various parts of the globe would be my companions as we, romantically, or in our own heads at least joined the footprints of those ancient ones which the stars looked down upon.

I swam like a dolphin…well in my head I was. Freedom from everything is a great aphrodisiac. Reminding myself after the poolside waiter God love him brought me a tea…that both mobiles were still on charge in my room upstairs. If I squinted against the fiercest light, I could just make out my tiny balcon. Returning with great reluctance to the room, I found the best message ever. Shanuda, Deardra's helpful er lawyer had left a list of things he had carried out at Deardra's apartment.

Managing to get dressed in the coolest clothes I ordered a taxi and thankfully, the young cheeky faced driver was a reasonable chap and did not overcharge me. I persuaded him to stop on the way at a place called 'Forty Market.' Let's not pretend here they had everything. Wine stood beckoning me from twinkly bottles along a whole section. Rose' prices were high but I had to sip the nectar. Paying at the desk I knew I must draw more funds to take to the office for the Kharga trip. Still no word from them. Between us with a lot of giggling we managed to get the key in the front door, it was all new. *There must be a story behind this*, I thought.

"Beautiful, madam this is very good place, how long will you stay?"

"Oh thanks, it's not mine it belongs to a friend, I may be here for two weeks, it's all a bit open at the moment."

"I would like to give you my card. Mumkin, you take time to see Luxor with me I charge small price if you like, not force you."

"Thank you, will do just that, leave me a couple of days and I will be in touch."

"You promise?"

"I promise…what is your name. It's in Arabic on the car…" He took it back with another flashing smile.

"I will write in English."

I gave him a pen and he carefully scrawled 'Mr Peaches'. Then the numbers he wrote on with great care and a great deal of frowning concentration. Bless.

"Thank you."

I gave him a note and he was pleased with it and left blowing kisses…well you would, wouldn't you?

The apartment was well aired and had a light fluidity of contemporary styles mixed with Egyptian decor. I must say she did a good job on the colour choice. Soft clay colours merged with ochres from the paler end of the spectrum and palest orange almost peach with dark blue vases against the walls. The lighting suffused and tiered for maximum romantic effect. I placed all the shopping away and hung up a dress in the wardrobe. Two small bedrooms and a nice kitchen with the basics, a bathroom and lounge completed the tour. I checked every window and left quietly. I did not want to go back to the hotel just yet. The Sharas were quiet in the heat of the early afternoon. Walking as slowly as possible in the heat I traced my way back and noticed to my joy the hair dressing salon that had made me look so fantastic before. I drew a map of where it was by shops and colours and went back to the hotel room with a great weariness coming over me.

Still nothing from the Kharga tour operator so I asked reception to check it out. They chatted merrily enough and I was starving waiting for the English bit to kick in. Impatience does not serve well so I breathed slowly and waited.

"It is all ready, they will wait at this office." Points to address on a map of Luxor…

"At five tomorrow morning."

My evening meal was a merry one. There were a troop of dancers just booked in from some far-off country where they make laughter an absolute must. How did I know they were dancers; well the sudden bursts of twirls and jolly moves were a huge clue. Remind me to go to the Ukraine. Now my holiday really was beginning. I ate like three pigs on a spree with extra portions. Why had my appetite suddenly developed, especially as I had decided to lose weight? I will never be a stick insect that's a definite. I sneaked away with all the cakes that had been on the side plate hidden in my bag in paper napkins. Gawd knows when breakfast would be tomorrow. Five am loomed out of the ether writ large. I placed a wakeup call the desk.

The following morning my phone jangled me into fire drill action and the taxi man laid on for me was the dear little man who had met me at the airport. The dancing troupe were snoring loudly in Ukrainian and I tiptoed out into very cool air. This is a first. I don't ever want to leave Egypt I had decided. My rucksack is heavy with all the things I might need. I have tucked the contraband cakes into a corner and lo and behold the hotel give me a huge box…it's in the place of the hotel breakfast. I hump that along as well.

The pure white taxi drifts along the empty sharas speedily and then suddenly slows for the speed bumps. Jeez I shall be sick as two dogs a cat and a pigeon named Ralph if he does this driving style too much. At last we arrive. I offer him money he says.

"All paid with the ticket."

"Oh thank you…how sweet see you later." He speeds away in his white whooshing car.

The tour consists of two drivers and one of them is Mr Peaches. I can't believe it and he breaks into a wreath of smiles and rushes to me brandishing papers while a group of some six or seven South Korean girls all laugh with joy.

"It is me Mr Peaches, you are most happy and I am so happy ana sahiddi habibi."

We are a wickedly funny set of characters after this wonderful surprise. Mr Peaches has a smile as wide as a bunch of bananas from wherever the biggest grow on the entire planet. I love it. We joke and lark about all of us in our given seats in the minibus. My companion is named Yunme and her smile is genuine. Once on the road for real so to speak (we had to run the gauntlet with an armed guard for a few kilometres due to some activities of the fundamentalist kind). All is revealed about the trip, I thought camels may come into the picture somewhere and Mr Peaches assures me they will.

"If they not have the bloody camel Madam Gina…I personally will make the bloody camel."

Well, you can't say fairer than that, can you?

We all pull into the usual tourist trap restaurant for breakfast and I have my box but the hot tea on offer is fantastic. We all laugh and chatter. What luck to have such jolly young people with me, they make you feel so good. I love it. Mr Peaches is soon beckoning us with his paperwork once again.

We pile into toilets…and I manage to brush my hair up and put on the Bedouin scarf. Mr Peaches soon reties it and I sit glam as is possible so early in the day with lipstick and sunglasses and the most amazing headgear. In the front with Mr Peaches. I hope this does not mean we are engaged or anything. No need to worry, everyone gets a turn in the best viewing seat.

Birds fly up out of the bushes once we hit the desert roads. I am in my element and point to them as they rise high into the blue in front of the car, their wings like sparkling jewels of gold light in the Egyptian sunshine...

"Oh how lovely."

"Yes, Allah is so clever and every little bird has its beak."

We are on an exciting journey to Kharga in an enchanted land...!

Thanks to the safe driving of Abdou and Mr Peaches, who kept going through all sand road and lack of roadside signs...do they follow the stars as the Berber once did. We 'sailed' through the night under a sky so beauteous and bountiful with constellations that it was truly like a dream. This was, I felt sure where my dream may at last be fulfilled, if so, it was a rare experience and I refused to miss any second of it. Sleep stole me away and I awoke with the change of rumble wheels of the desert roads to the music and reflections, lights and sights of Kharga.

We were booked into our hotel which had a fabulous little facade and exquisite reception area. Smiles were free around here that was for sure, and my feelings that it would be barbaric and destitute of comfort were a little overplayed.

My room was next to the Korean girls and they were a merry bunch...I fell into the shower then into the dining room where the hilarity of the corridor outside my room was carried on. We sang songs to the television and Mr Peaches arrived to give us our schedule for the next day. He carried

off certain long goodnights with his usual humour complete with a banana smile and big-eared good nature.

What a character.

Abdou was a little in the background. I felt still waters might run deep.

I slept like a baby. Waking to indigestion and thirst. Foolishly drawing back a heavy curtain I was leapt upon by the fierce lion of the golden sun. Diamonds of splintering light filled the room. I soon closed the curtain.

Kharga was once an infamous last but one stop for the merchants who plied an horrific trade in people. The history is as strange as it is also significant. Slave traders would rest up here on the route between North Africa and the tropical south. There is a temple to Hibis two kilometres to the north and this is our destination today. We are advised on the schedule to carry water and cover our heads against the heat of the sun. I nab poor Mr Peaches who ties my Bedouin headgear for me once again.

He calls it his, 'special job'.

We head out with another guide and he is a lively one, it isn't long before we stop for an armed man who salutes us all. Nice of him…then on we go…I was glad the camels had been forgotten for a while the heat being so dominating and penetrating. We arrived and stumbled almost blinded to the entrance, where we saw the dark interior what a welcome it was. I understand these wonderful moments of respite from the sun. Hibis ancient and wonderful was built on the site of other holy temples to the 'Hebet'…plough…in the ancient Egyptian language…which is so valued to grow food. We are surrounded by a palm grove and one wonders about the usual underground water tables…to sustain them.

Located on what was once a very dominant position of the old city of Hebet…which during the Persian occupation 525 BC to 404 BC…King Darius I expanded the earlier Saite period temple instructing his artists to carefully renew the inscriptions and then added a gateway which is finely decorated. During the reigns of Achoris (c 390 BC) and Nactanebo 11(c 380 BC) … Additional structures were added.

The Ptolomeic Dynasty brought more changes with Ptolomy 11 Philadelphus building the 'Great Gateway' (c 282 BC).

We are in awe of everything and wander with necks craning through the temple. We reach the third hypostyle hall and I admire the painted decorations on the columns carried out by Darius rt.

It's all so magical. We are guided through other scenes and my head starts to spin with it all. Yunme has stopped to massage her neck, it's aching from looking up. We are rewarded by the West Wall, where a scene of the king on his throne with Thoth… (Dijuty, Tehuty) baboon and Ibis god of the moon. Thoth overcame the curse of Ra allowing Nut to give birth to her five children…with his skill at games, and Horus – the son of Isis and Osiris…tying the cords around the base of the scene of the mysterious 'Sematawy' ritual.

The entire North Wall is covered by long hieroglyphic texts – an acclamation of the King as Horus.

We leave the temple in two very differing moods…one that we would love to stay longer and the other that we are all tired and overheated and a little hungry. We walk about like zombies in the heat and I wonder what Derby O'Gill and the little people would make of all this magic.

Kharga in Arabic means 'Point of departure' in opposition of Dakhla 'Point of entrance', which lies further to the west. The population exceeds more than one hundred thousand people. The population of the people are Berbers with roots back to the time when the oases was a station on the famous Forty Days Road between Sudan and Egypt. It has a horrific history connected to the slave trade.

We were all unaware of this until now and we are a subdued little group as we get back into the bus. No one alive today can be blamed for this…but it is a very sobering thought. We talk in whispers on the bus.

Mr Peaches attempts to lighten the mood with jolly music but we are all very quiet. I whisper to Yunme as I massage her poor neck…she is really suffering poor lass.

"What about all the poor slaves that had to work in all that heat…we have an air-conditioned bus and hotel to recover in…it takes some thinking about."

She gravely looks at me.

"I am so fortunate with my life." I nod.

"Yes, me *too*."

Back in the hotel I manage to get online and send messages to everyone. There is another from Gillian…funny as usual… 'What's it like sitting on Mr Pharaoh's knee? …we are okay here Bob has been talked into a diet of sorts, doctors' orders, and I have to watch him like a bloody hawk…he is so sneaky. Have fun and passion while it's not on ration'.

I reply with a cheeky retort. 'The knee is a bit uncomfortable due to the heat out here at Kharga Oases. We have all just learned about the slave trade route that came through here. The temple itself is just a couple of kilometres from here and is very fine in parts apparently it was named after the plough…Hibis…and is well worth seeing. The depiction of a bird with the most amazingly artistic wings really caught my attention so I have a photo or two to show you. Post cards are so plentiful though so will stock up on them…also have a bracelet for you to dance in…love to all. XXX Gina ps. good luck to Bob tell him to try water cress and grapefruit.'

I send more or less the same to Greta, Martine and the others. Amr is still sad according to his email. So rather than rub his nose into what he would have, should have, seen and experienced…poor man…I carefully avoid any glamourous detail. I don't know what else to do. He, the Egyptian cannot come to this, his own history. Without risks.

Meeting up later I notice that now we have shared some history of great tragedy as well as beauty…that we are a closer-knit group. I tell them of my dream of being dressed up in a costume of the ancient tribes' people that lived in the deserts the Berber Blue I think it's called. They, to my utter amazement know a shop that sells all sorts of things. We ask Mr Peaches if we can take a detour there…just briefly…he, ever ready and willing to please pretty women of all colour, culture, and creed…obeys instantly and Yunme shows him the 'on line' map to it. My God you can get anything these days.

We roll up outside the brightly lit shop much cheered up after our sombre history lesson… The shop is so expensive it takes all of Mr Peaches and little Yunme's charm and haggling efforts to get the merchant to part with a rather simpler version of the Berber look. Fantastic as it may seem it looks just right…unlike the other glammed up touristy styles it is a bit worn looking and washed out…Yunme alights on this and I am standing back in horror as the merchant shrugs and throwing my outfit to one side goes for a more or less frightful copy in a modern material. The one I want…the cast aside garment has the little pyramids on it and I must have it. The neckline is small but I manage to put it over my head and am looking at it in the mirror…when the merchant comes from his interior den of genies and starts to wind an old washed-out cloth around my head, places ear ornaments upon me and loads bracelets and anklets with the help of the others.

When he has finally finished everybody gasps. I am taken to the mirror…for once, my height is in my favour and the woman that stares back at me is a total stranger from another life, another time, and world. The world of travel through desert under stars. I don't know myself and yet…I know my true self for the first time. There was much discussion about the price. I cannot pay out such prices for the bracelets. I have some anyway the gold on the heavy bands is probably not real· But the effect is stunning of that there is no doubt. A great many photos were taken.

Mr Peaches does not need to do much more haggling. The merchant is much more pliable when he sees the results of great happiness on my face. I am astounded by the transformation as is everyone else. For the first time in my life in this wonderful garb I notice the upward tilt of my eyes…like the cat. We end up paying about fifty English for the ensemble but the bracelets have to stay. My purchases are placed into very pretty bags and I march out with the others who also have had some fun with headscarves and ankle chains…! Well done Yunme and Mr Peaches.

We are heading off to a party in the desert and any thoughts of me dancing in the dunes are quickly laid aside. My time probably has come and gone. The venue is pure tourist and we soon forget any gloom of the temple and history and are raucously joining in with a modern style of music which would make a Bedouin blush.

We probably shall never know what we ate drank and danced to in the pretend to be Bedouin for one night under the stars but the actual lack of romance did not really upset us. It was great, great fun. Mr Peaches has fallen for Yunme big style and they are sitting close together laughing at everything they say to each other. Sweet. And the other girls melt away with various groups and I get the opportunity to walk out of the camp and stand quietly alone looking at the great tall palms with their fronds moving like fingers against the night sky. A breeze springs out of nowhere it seems and everyone starts talking about a possible dust storm.

The party is soon broken up…out here it can be deadly to be caught off guard apparently. We climb like little weary bundles of dust and giggles back into the mini bus which takes some starting…another sign of things to come. We are soon witnessing a very different Kargha. In my room I lay out all my purchases since our arrival. I am much surprised… A lot of fruit and some darling little cheroots have crept into the luggage along with bracelets and anklets of dubious manufacture…oh who cares! I am having the time of my life. I text Greta and David and tell them.

I am
now
Bedouin
woman.

I send the photo that Yunme took. Mrs Yunme Peaches sounds good, I think.

A wind as shrill as any banchee of Irish lore…is seeking a way in and we all get woken up every few hours by its racket. A mixture of fine dust, gritty sand and litter has descended upon us…the hotel staff are shrill with anxiety of trying to clear it from their precious rooms and corridors. The mystery is how it gets in every little crack.

A meeting is held about the planned trip to a camel station…did I…get that right…I'm the oldest of the group by a long way. Give them all their due they take me under their wings as part of the whole party. South Koreans I have learned are willing to learn anything about anything. Curiosity, is a gift which must be carefully looked after. Answer its need and remain involved and anything can happen. Some of the things that happen you might not be ready for but hey *ho*. We all step out into brilliant sunshine and discuss the night before…we all had dreams…the girls inquisitive as kittens turn to me on the bus…

"Gina, what did you dream about…I had this weird one about being in the Wizard of Oz…"

"We sure aren't in Kansas now Toto…"

Sang out the whole group. I don't think I can follow such vivid imaginings.

"I had a dream I was painting cranes…the birds, you know the ones I mean."

"Ooooh, that's a good dream."

"Thank you, but the one that finally woke me up when the wind was really loud…well that was horrible. I was in a deep blue sea with all these horrible floating bleached bones and a landslide took away people's homes."

Yunme came over and hugged me.

"Oh that is a nasty thing to have but it's out now and you will never dream it again."

"Thank you darling, you make me feel better already."

One of the girls had a dream about some lovely children that turned into wolves. This brought laughter and accusations of too many games.

We set off through the dusty streets that were certainly worse for wear. Palms were struggling for breath, their fronds coated with the horrible gritty dust. When we had arrived at the camel compound the camels looked at us very oddly indeed, as if to say, 'haven't you got food to munch like us and good water to slurp and do you have to leave your safe beds to come and bother us'. They have a point. I love camels and soon hoist myself onto the peculiar saddle. More like a pile of old colourful rugs really. They have tassels and they communicate with an alphabet of grumbling gurgles which they exchange between them when they get up. It's as if they are saying… 'crikey, what a lump this one is, too many chocolate bars and no mistake.' My camel boy turns to help Yunme who is Deardra all over again when it comes to the finer art of camel riding.

So, I take advantage and urge mine with some dignity to round up the others and generally frolic about.

The boy is most put out and I make everyone laugh by turning my camel this way and that to dodge him. In the end he shakes his head and gives up on the whole circus. We file out like Lawrence of Arabia and his men…well in our minds…correction, in my mind. I am on the spree of all sprees. I have great satisfaction at my camel's speed as I tear off like a Bedouin hoodlum.

Our lead camel makes horrible noises up front so we overtake him come back and shout 'whhhheee' if I am told off for this lark I do not care. The lead camel deigns to allow us to be
alongside and his rider who looks about nine and is a dab hand at the game of camel trooping, smiles at me with great happiness.

"Where you ride camel before…madam you are very okay with this camel."

"Round the pyramids at Cairo."

We soon get a good stride going and the poor girls are trying to keep up with us there is a great deal of giggling and shrieking. To these noises the camels twirl their ears and make corresponding noises at both ends. It's like an outing for the totally nuts.

We head out into small dunes but they are not worthy of dancing and singing on top of. If I am guilty of anything on this holiday, please let it be sheer foolishness and childlike behaviour. When we stop for a break, it is at a tiny Oases, all of us are thrilled by it. In the distance the shimmer of the mirage provides a back drop we all go down and back again with the boys helping us. The tents and funny tea kettles tell their own story and we take photos as if the whole thing could be a dream. It is for me and I wish for the impossible. That Greta was with me.

I am not normally maudlin but for some reason I miss her dreadfully at this precise moment. She would have loved it, I am sure.

We return to the camels' compound with great reluctance and I say lots of goodbyes with tears at the corner of my eyes…my camel treats the whole thing with a sort of dignified contempt.

Mr Peaches leaves Yunme's side for all of two seconds and comes over to me.

"You are more Egyptian than the bloody Egyptian Madam Gina."

"Mr Peaches…I take that as the best of compliments."

We drive back and have late lunch at the nearby restaurant… Our hotel is having problems with deliveries of supplies…so we enjoy a buffet…I sample the lovely hot dishes. They are utterly delicious. I try to work out the flavours.

Claude would know all of them he is such a good chef when it comes to exotic food.

Too soon, way too soon, the visit to El Kharga is at an end. I pack with great sadness and we troop out very forlornly to the waiting mini bus, waving at the staff and management. They had a lot to put up with after all…Korean girls certainly laugh a lot. Bless them.

The journey is orderly and Abdou does a lot of the driving. I have a feeling Mr Peaches has been furthering the cause of cultural niceties with Yunme…he is subdued and I see them exchange, 'telltale glances of a hidden secret life'. How great it is to be so young…oh and rich.

Once I am dropped off at the Lotus…we wave tearfully and 'never forget us' rings in the air. Yunme is very upset and I think it's not just me she is reluctant to part with.

The hotel is the best place for me at present. I know the apartment is free to stay in, but I will face its lonesome newness tomorrow after a swim in the pool. Lovely decor cannot replace all the pretty girls and their wonderful humour. I really will never forget them…

I eventually bite the bullet and pack up all, goods and chattels and settle the bill at the Lotus. I call Mr Peaches fully expecting him to be out of service for a while…but no, he picks up the call quickly.

"Madam Gina, you miss me already, that is good."

"Yes, I miss you Mr Peaches, I am moving everything into the apartment today…you know the one, don't you?"

"Oh my God, yes. You want go there now?"

"Well, yes if you are available."

"Two minute and I am with you…wait there, okay?"

I wait there. He rolls up with the flourish of a magician. Where does he get his good humour from? Smile as broad as ever.

"I am good for schedule, yes."

"Yes, I don't know anyone better and service with a smile like a bunch of bananas."

We pile everything in lithesome load. Off we go and if he had one of those American horns that play the Dixie or whatever it is. I would not have been surprised.

At the Forty Market he helps me to find things for a good supper and I get him to find the spices that are missing in the cupboards. We soon get back on the road again and unpacking all this stuff takes a while… Without a word he sorts the gas cylinder for cooking and the kettle is washed out and filled…we soon find cups and make chai. We are just adding sugar one, and half for me and four or five for him when the doorbell tringles out like a couple of birds with laryngitis.

I open it to…Mahmoud!

Well feather and knock

down…

These split seconds of our life prove the butterfly effect. I wanted to shout, I did not, I wanted to hug him, I did not. Instead I opened the door and walked into the kitchen…and made him chai. The icebreaker being a spoonful of sugar…one might say. I could hear them back slapping and greeting in the brotherhood manner of most Muslim men, a club, women never enter. To be angry would serve no purpose but to drool over would be worse.

I am happy with the thinking time allowed, from delving in the units to add extra rice and water to the pot which has luckily only just come to simmer. The lamb shanks will stretch to three and I take some biscuits and wafers through on the tray with the chai.

Mahmoud engaged my eyes with such frankness and tranquillity all my doubts fade. I felt my old-world slip behind me as I offered wafers and pushed the sugar pot closer to his hand.

"Ali tells me you are very good with a camel."

An odd way to greet a woman after months of separation…a woman much loved…or maybe not.

"I didn't know, I was a natural…it's been a shock I can tell you. Mr Peaches you didn't tell me your name was Ali…you gave me the taxi number with Mr Peaches written next to it."

"Madam Gina, I am sorry. We all have little nicknames here in Egypt."

I am sensing an awkwardness between us all. I am not going to turn out Mr Peaches, he has helped me by every method. He is staying and yet his presence seems to totally unnerve Mahmoud. Perhaps that is a good thing he needs to be shaken up a little. We sip tea and make small talk about the apartment…

"Very beautifully decorated Gina, did you choose all these things?"

"Not at all… Deardra directed all the scheme…she had the devil's own job getting it back from the cheeky woman that moved in on her property. Deardra has had a lovely baby girl in Nice, we are calling her Felicity Gina Collette."

I wanted to add put that in your pipe and smoke it. But kept my tone polite and quiet. It never pays to rile anyone. I am still peeved about Mahmoud not getting in touch but make myself behave about the past. He has lost his father and that must have caused a long term hurt. He is so much more subdued than before. I am made aware that all that chirp and cockiness of youth is gone forever. He is just not the same person. I know how much he loved his father and so take all of these tragic events into account. Poor Mahmoud…

As for Mohammed well thank all the angels in flowery dresses that he has not shown up, that would have had me chasing him down the shara with a broom and no mistake.

"I will need to put more roz in the pot, Madam Gina."

I have done that already…would you mind taking it off the heat…I don't know the new pan, it might stick."

Thankfully he gets up and the awkwardness goes with him to the kitchen and stays there. Mahmoud gets up and comes next to me and in one movement kisses my cheek.

"I missed you more than I could bear. I have been on the West Bank for seven days in our company office…I drove to the Lotus today and they told me you were gone to your apartment. They said Ali is taking care of you. He is a good person but not understand our situation… Not know our story."

"I never discuss our love affair with anyone Mahmoud. It's between us and no one else."

"Still you love."

"Of course, I do not think of anyone else in the romantic way ever. Truthfully, I have had an offer of marriage but I didn't take it up. I would be going against my own true feelings and you are the one I love until I die. There, it's said."

On a weird turn of the fates Mr Peaches walks back in and holding a large wooden spoon coated with rice, sorry roz…he flourishes it in our general direction.

"The lamb she cooks good the salad she cooks good and the rice not stick."

"We need to make a gravy of some kind. I am sure Mr Peaches that we have some of that special mix somewhere…"

We find the granules and I make it up. Mahmoud used to it from life in the UK is smiling…but Ali Peaches is bemused at the miracle of domestic science and hot water. He is an instant fan.

The meal saves the day it is utterly delicious and luckily Ali knows all about Mahmoud hating hot spicy food. Very fortunate indeed. Mr Ali Peaches gets a call and dives out the door. I call after him about the fare, he didn't get it. He calls back up the stone steps in the echo chamber that is the internal stairwell…

"Not from you dear lady, you are special friend of me and Yunme."

"He is happy to call you friend and the meal is the first real one he has had for a while."

"That company you know, the office tour company thingameebobs they are very hard with them I think."

"Yes, life hard here for taxi men…all job now very tricky if you don't, you know…"

"What jump through the higher hoops."

"Ah you understand…"

"Same in the UK. Also same in France darling…I am employing several people now and I treat them like family. I know what it is like to be used in a cold hard way. Remember Gran."

"Oh my God, she is so wicked with you. Is she same now?"

"Keeps writing, wanting to know all my affairs…I have warned Amr."

"Who is Amr?"

"A very clever academic man, oh yes Amr, you guessed he is Egyptian."

"You have Egyptian man work for you at the villa…for how long?"

"He does all sorts of odd jobs and helps me with the desk work correspondence and translating languages. He translated the Rumi poem in the sand casket. He was writing very sweet letters to her until I told him that she is horrid old witch to me in my childhood and if he continued, I would empty the refuse bin over his head/"

This for some reason cracked Mahmoud up.

"Oh my God Gina, you get strong now this is a good way for you to be. Strong women are much admired in Egypt."

"Well, that's good because I needed to get some gumption…that's for sure."

"What happen with your husband?" I shrugged…

"Oh you not see him ever again…he is still with the funny boy."

"Good choice of wording Mahmoud but I don't think of him being funny…far from it. I would rather take a gun and shoot the miserable yob. He ruined Ray's life. Mine has improved from such interference to such a degree that I do not and I repeat do not know myself anymore. Our lives are altered forever…and all because of extra deliveries of yoghurt at the back door. Sunny Day Dairy and Co are the turning point in my life…apparently. As are you."

"I like to hear I am in your life, thank you."

We cuddle up in bed together and our lovemaking is more tender and sweet than it ever has been before… Bitter sweet understanding. It is all fine again. Our future decisions hang on all this. I know the age difference. I know the cultural strangeness, if anything, I know too much. And yet I know nothing.

In the here and the now we can be. Life outside may have other plans, but here and now we endure…the question is 'we'…will have to learn slowly how we make our way forward.

I do not trust the lap of the gods.

Greta sends me a text message which startles me.

'I have just had a dream about you Mummy darling…you are very happy."

How right you are sweet girl….

We became 'roof top in the morning people'… For some reason the new apartment is a little too stuffily warm at that time of day. We love the cool sting of air on the roof and Mahmoud would carry up the heavy tray god love him…while I brought up the coffee pot.

There is an immeasurable stillness to this part of Luxor, and we enjoy the odd car horn and dog bark while all the other people snoozed on. Now and then a street trader would trundle a hand cart or donkey conveyance through the shara below. Enchanting to me. This is where we would whisper our well-worn phrases of happy times and recall my garden with its familiar speckles of light and shade. We feel we have a history.

When Mahmoud drives to the company office, I wash up quickly and assemble my water colours on the roof. Each day attempting a new panorama. I use a lot of water as it seems to dry out quicker each day. As the sun progresses, I flag accordingly and, in the end, give up and trundle the bits wearily down and say goodbye to the little rooftop birds who come for crumbs.

We are at peace and it is a wonderful feeling. Ours is a good union. No coldness, all affection. It is a wonderful and new experience for me. I feel sorry for Ray for the first time. He has emotional issues. I thought it was me…it never was. Greta is in constant message mode. They are off to Japan she's flunked her essay…again. My student daughter is showing real signs of wanting a baby and not going in pursuit of the career that she was shouting from the rooftops that she must have. Life is a lesson in understanding it seems where our children are concerned. It's her life. I can't make her become a Japanese Cultural Attaché…which was her dream. Not so much a dream I see that now, but the sounding of the title all through her teens must have impressed.

Her partner David is the brains of the duo. He is a hot potato in the marine conservation world. My pride for them both knows no bounds.

Oddly enough it is Greta who will be helping him in Japan. So not a wasted education after all. I am happy that the relationship has blossomed for the good.

Mahmoud is away the day I get the awful panic call and so I had no choice but to take this turn of events at the villa on the chin alone. Is there any other way, I ask myself.

I answer the call swathed in towels after a long cool down shower. Deardra is frantic.

"Darling Gina. is that you?"

"Yes Deardra, what's going on you sound frightened."

"We had a guest cancel his autumn booking and ask to come this week instead. We saw no harm in it as everything was prepped and ready…the room lovely and clean."

"Yes, I saw to it myself…it would need only light dusting."

"That's right. He seemed okay the first two days then he started to complain and threw food across the kitchen."

"Excuse me."

"He threw food at Claude and you know how mild Claude is, we were taken by surprise but then he began to barricade himself in the room and shout abuse to anyone who came. He threw things out of the window. We called the police twice but they are up to their eyes in paperwork and the security measures dealing with the terrorist threats."

"Amr is good at all this sort of thing, did you ask him to remonstrate with the fellow, what's his name?"

"Amr tried and was sworn at and called horrible names. We pleaded with the police they said it would be two days before they could give it their attention. Felix put a ladder up to the window against my wishes and called out Mr Deeson, Mr Deeson you need to come out and speak properly to us."

"What happened?"

"HE THREATENED TO PUSH HIM OFF."

"Oh the sod."

"Yes, what a swine of a man. In the end hunger and thirst drove him out and we had to manhandle him out to the drive and place all his things out there. He made the rudest gestures as we closed the door on him. Michel came over from the chateaux and all hell broke loose for a few hours. Now this dreadful Deeson man is in the garden with a sort of makeshift tent. He spends most of his time just sitting on the little bench with his radio at full blast and intimidating us with threats and yells."

"I am flying back."

I left a note for Mahmoud and told him to come any time he wished to Nice, but that I had been called back on an emergency, my apologies and love. I was ultra-lucky with a cancellation booking and stepped in on that with great haste, it was very cheap too as it was a last day cancellation or some such thing. I packed with the speed of light and Mr Peaches promised to attend to everything. He knew I was not the kind of woman to act so quickly without due causee I tried over and over to contact Mahmoud…he was probably in court with a client.

One minute I am in bliss villa with Mahmoud next thing I am snoozing lightly on the plane to France and goodness knows what trouble lay ahead. The taxi driver the other end did not know what hit him I told him of the emergency and he really took it seriously. As soon as we drew up at the front of the villa I jumped out of the taxi and called to him.

"I have a plan…please stay and have a drink at the kitchen."

During the flight I had hatched a plan of such hilarity it would bring me either fate or fortune. My dander was up and I felt cool and very, very, furious that such a sod of a man could come to our little family» our little escape from the rat race and behave in such a vile way. I was dressed nicely and not too dishevelled from the flight so I would not be very scary…shame. I went through as the door opened and my astonished loved ones watched with great interest as I changed into my house shoes marched through to the refuse bins picked up the potato peeling and slops container which would serve very nicely thank you, then selected a strong yard broom.

The swine was sat with his back to me…good.

I stalked up, with the radio at top blare he could not have heard several horses at a gallop…good. Placing the broom against our obliging tree, I swung the slop bin complete with vile contents over his daft head and forced it down…good.

It made a delightful to my ears squelching sound…double good.

Then I picked up the strong yard broom and proceeded to swing strike swing strike the bin with a very satisfactory sound. Never in all my life did I get such satisfaction. I turned off the radio and called to Amr.

"Amr...I think the gentleman wants his things put into refuse sacks and placed outside the drive gates. Please would you."

My open-mouthed friends all rallied as if they were scalded cats! The taxi driver could not stop laughing and Claude was cheering. I love to see Claude cheer.

The noise from the slop bin was most unusual it was half cry, no, that's not quite true. It was one third choking gasp one third yell and one third something not in any known dictionary. I washed my hands, a thoroughly messy business all round *I'd* say. Then headed for the teapot and poured a steaming mug of tea. I plonked in milk and one sugar and a sweetener for good measure. Deardra and Felix came back with exploding smiles and hugs. Little G was brought out of hiding for cuddles. Claude was hugging me and little G together and Amr was washing his hands after piling the offending guest's things into bags with the help of the taxi driver. They had deposited it all at the end of the drive. The stupid Deeson fellow was red-faced, mucky, oh and silent...For a change. He never returned. I managed to get through to Mahmoud and relate everything. The only thing he could say in the middle of laughing was.

"Oh my *God.*"

We had a party to end all parties. I am home, and a very quick return it has been.

After the...dustbins in the afternoon...incident. We all decide that we must write a full report in the most truthful manner and put it in a drawer. Fresh in the mind being a lot easier to clarify than trying to recall later. We also redecorate and redesign the room with colours daisy fresh. All reminders removed, we make the villa ready for the lively sets of guests coming and life settles to the routine which is so welcome.

Mahmoud is coming at Christmas and I have plans to make a special meal with him in mind. Dancing Egyptian style included. Mama returning from the hills like a bandit insists Gabriel visits me first and I take her into my arms and we have a tearful reunion. Gabriel is delighted to leave her with us overnight. I sit with her in the lounge as the guests are all out on various trips and we have the room to ourselves.

Deardra brings us tea and cakes it is a very wonderful occasion. My first act is to hand her the bracelet and another gift that I know will please her.

"Gina, you are the daughter I never had."

I hold her hand…tears slip down my cheeks, tears of happiness.

"Thank you, Mama."

"When I first see you in our little garden, I know…the way you know about a good melon."

"An unusual description but I like that…I love you with all my heart Mama, both you and Gabriel were with me and on my side with every step I took when I was learning everything out here." She nods gravely, unties the parcel which hides a cashmere cardigan.

"Oh mon Dieu… This is too much."

"Noh Mama, it is never enough. I want only to see you smile and be happy…"

Helping her into it for a fitting I add the bracelet she is beaming and gets up to see herself in the hall mirror. We put it away again as it's a warm day…although this will change soon as high winds are expected. Amr is already in the little garden busy with the stakes to tie up the more vulnerable of the plants. Felix is in the area beyond the garage which is hidden from the house and main garden.

We walk out there, Mama and I. My arm under hers, she seems more frail than I remember. Laughing and joking about the good looks of all my staff which I call family. They are all so belonging to this place just as I belong. If only…oh but it's no good wishing one's life away.

"This is the best idea don't you think Mama to plant legume and such, look we have started a little fruit tree area…what do you think, are we going about it the right way. We need you to tell us honestly."

"*Yes,* yes my little dove you are right to break the earth with the pomme de terre. I am always happy to see this way, it is the correct way."

"Thank you, if you see us go wrong you will tell us."

"You go wrong…not often my dove. I heard about the horrible man who make the problem. You are as brave as the what her name. Ah, lionness the brave! Grrrr when this horrible man come to harm your cubs…grrr up with the weapons refuse and broom."

We laugh as we walk on and enjoy our time together. Gabriel comes to collect her the next day and she is tearful as we part…I cry unashamedly and we decide to meet on Sunday after the present group of guests have departed. My love for this dear old lady knows no bounds. It is true that she reminds me of my darling grandma Mourier. She always will. When mama goes the old style of French woman will die out with her. All those that knew true hardship and survived so much and still kept love in their hearts. It will be the end of an era er<:J in France that is only in the hearts of those who truly understand the old way, the laughter, and the deprivations.

Deardra is in the kitchen again with Claude they are discussing something quietly…I pop my head in…

"Are you wishing to discuss something privately, I can come back."

"By all the gods and saints…Madam Gina you are welcome always…we talk about the police."

"Oh God, no they aren't coming, are they?"

"I'm afraid so…they say at eight something like this…this evening. They are mindful that you have guests and don't want to come in the middle of the meal…"

"Oh that's very obliging of them…well that sounds hopeful."

Nevertheless, I am concerned and check the paper work on the incident is still at hand. Thankfully, it is.

We have all cleared up the main meal of the day and guests are either in the grounds, no doubt giggling over the cock-eyed horses…which often get a big mention in the visitors' book along with Claude's cooking, the cleanliness of the rooms and politeness of our staff. This list of niceties makes my pride swell I can tell you. At least we have got something right…or they may be planning the next day when apparently three of them go to the wonderful Lascaux caves near the village of

Montignac…This reminds me suddenly and painfully of Raphael who took tours there. My curiosity is still piqued by any mention of these places. The constant association of him with French history will always draw my attention. Unavoidable.

The police come just as we are sitting out in the kitchen after we have cleared and had our own meal. Felix by far the most smiley of us is thrust forward and we wait with drumming fingers to be called one by one. My turn comes and the gendarme is polite and friendly so I don't hesitate to guide him from the hallway to the kitchen and offer him refreshment.

"Madame Gina Tantridge, this is correct noh."

"Oui this is *correct.*"

"You are the owner *of...*"

Looks at papers.

"Villa of the Dancing Horse."

"This is also correct." He sips the hot coffee.

"We were unable to attend your staff the day in question…but it has now been settled with great satisfaction noh…"

I nod and gulp.

"I must tell you that this man has no business to do this in our country to our citizen. He has already caused the similar problems in Aux-Au-Provence…we have full dossier upon him and we will arrest on sight. If this pleases you madam:

"Ah I see, I am not surprised there was something about him."

"No doubt the pomme de terre trimming upon his clothing n'est-ce-pah."

My face is bright red. I find myself nervously shuffling the papers with all our reports.

"You must not alarm yourself Madam. I know everything from the village. We are always aware of any visitor to our country not knowing our little ways. You are the exception as you know us so long and understand that the broom is a useful tool to sweep up the ordures. We commend you."

And with that he finishes the coffee, salutes, and taking up his mobile and notebooks walks smartly grinning broadly to his car. Of course everyone was hiding next to the kitchen stifling giggles and now we all explode with laughter…I go to the wine room and draw out some red white and of course Rose'.

We get out the glasses and take everything into the garden Little G is fast asleep in her pram and we wheel her out also. Deardra and Amr light up cheroots and Claude pours the wine. Felix stands and we salute the wine. Then each other…then last but certainly not least…

"*Vive
La
France.*"

Tom and the girls were very noisy about something so I hurried out to see what was going on fearing a return of the dreaded dustbin incident. All our nerves were still a bit jangled. Pudding hurried out too she is becoming such a clever

243

and dear little soul. I miss Delly Nutkins but a decision has been made. Her happiness is paramount.

"What is it Pudding do you know?"

Always talk to a cat is my motto. There in front of the pond was Raphael. My heart leapt at this sudden meeting. Having not seen him since the flagstones whacked me in the chops. I was able to just say,

"Hello Raphael."

What a dope…I should be reaching for brooms and co. Not greeting in this polite manner…but hey ho. He turned slowly and was sporting a very black eye.

"Oh you look like you have been in the wars."

"Gina do forgive me just turning up like this. Mum wanted me dearly to see all the fabulous changes you have made. I have a letter from her for you."

"Thanks…does Martine need a reply right away?"

"Noh noh it is to help me make the much-needed apology. I am so sorry for all the hurt I caused. My feelings were in turmoil, and well, it's still inexcusable."

"Why don't you come in and share a coffee, no hard feelings, water under the bridge, and I am very curious as to how you got that shiner."

He touches his utterly divine handsome as ever face. There should be a law about men looking this good *in* fact even more sort of wonderful with the black eye. The dashing corsair…almost. No, I will not succumb I will make coffee read the letter and send him on his way. My feelings were not as they once were over him…but I am still in a little danger. Playing with fire… I think they call it. They, being all sensible reasonable women of sound mind and judgement of men…that is. I may never totally fit into this category.

"Why were Tom and the girls so stirred up."

"Perhaps they remember me. Also I used to feed them a lot…with you if you recall."

I wander in like dopey Dora doll on a bad day. Oh god oh god oh god. He's so…oh he's so wonderful, to look at. The memory of bed does come to mind sharply.

I pour coffee… Uncle Claude has taken Little G for a nice walk before the guests return for the main meal. We are having a fabulous 'filet de boeuf en croute'. My memory of the last one still lingers with a happy sign over it. We will never be vegans here. Although we are trying very hard to find the best in vegan recipe' but mama with her explosive laugh gave a good detail as to its foolishness. My thoughts are more passive. We need to cater for special needs of certain guests. It's a puzzle at present. Claude is most ruffled by the thought and we love him dearly.

Raphael has been walking about, and now returns to the kitchen. I pour him a mineral water.

"You are as ever the charming hostess."

I nod with a closed mouth smile, easy does it, old girl he flatters before he comes in for the kill…remember.

"How did you get the black eye."

"My own foolishness as usual…you know all my weaknesses Gina. The husband did not care for my overtures to his charming young wife."

"Not learned yet then."

I said it out of real earnestness but it came out blunt and sarcastic. Well it would wouldn't it.

"Maybe, when I am grey and wrinkled, the lessons will come thicker and faster. I am so sorry after the event. At the time of the event though as you know I am caught up so very alarmingly and stupidly with the excitement of the chase."

I walk around the table to his seat and take his head between my hands and with real desire kiss him.

Mahmoud would not be pleased.

Raphael is so taken aback he says nothing. He is astounded.

"I know that did not thrill you Raphael, something tells me you only get 'excited' when it is taboo." He blushed and turned to the mineral water as if it held all the secrets of the earth in its sparkling depth. I stepped forward and did it again slower and longer. Kissing him deeply and unashamedly, passionately, and with true intent of giving him a run for his money…to be totally vulgar. I always think these days a little vulgarity may prevent falling into any real trouble. Gabriel's influence.

Please do not judge. All the angels in long, short, and mid-calf dresses know I am no temptress…but if you see Raphael the way I see him. Go, stand in my shoes now all you ladies in your early forties and tell me he is not the most sensual and wonderful man you ever saw…go…slip them on.

"Gina, you are so bold and adventurous. This is a side you kept hidden from me. II

"Oh I have learned a few things about 'life', you know what a teacher it can be. We only live once. Right I have to shoo you out now and help Claude prepare the meal. Our guests cannot be kept waiting."

He leaves but not until he has appraised me with those dark mystical eyes. I am thrilled to the bone. But pretend a light-hearted cockiness of manner and taking up my apron shoo him off.

He stands and salutes me with a smile that could melt an iceberg.

I clear the table and as I do so I hear the pram trundling in. Deardra is upstairs trying to rest. Gawd in heaven she looks peaky. I hope she is not pregnant again. It's a torment for her. I do watch Raphael walk down the drive with many a backward glance. He gets into his car and drives off slowly and carefully. No doubt to savour the moment. No doubt.

"Mmmm; well Pudding that's enough to make a cat's tail curl."

I stroke her delightful black coat glistening now with health. Claude and I wash our hands and he looks at me very mischievously and sideways for some minutes.

"You have a twinkle in les yeux. I have the feeling that the car that is now leaving has more than a little to do with this…"

I smile the indulgent smile of the winner at poker. You know, the one in all those films of glamour and fast cars women in see-through dresses and men in those Calvin Klein trunks, modern, essential, black. Why stint!

One by one our little villa family turns up to aid Claude in the kitchen. Guests show their pleasure of his food, which is amazing, by leaving scraped clean plates. Felix is back from selling the complete sets of ceramics to the department store buyer and is mighty pleased. He waves the cash with a cheer and a whoop of joy. Amr makes him put it in the safe. Wise move. Deardra still peaky helps me clear up.

"You feel better hon after the nap."

"Oh yes it's the disturbed sleep…you know how babies are when they get that first tooth. "Not another one on the way…I was very worried."

She looks at me with a grin which is lovely.

"No darling Gina, we are doing the family plan thingy. I am not at my best as you well know sweety when in the pudding club."

With that Pudding jumps down and comes over expecting treats.

We all laugh at that one. In all the excitement and bustle I had forgotten Martine's letter. Why a letter…she is a great lover of talking to me on the phone. I open it and Amr is by my side as I read out to him…

Dearest Gina,

I am going to Italy for Christmas just for ten or so days. My school friend Marie has just had the most terrible shock with her husband…he had a heart attack…and she cannot stand to be alone for the holiday. You dear one will understand I know; I will come to see you before I go of course. Michel and Lilian will be here to take care of things but it will be closed up for the whole of the holiday. Please forgive me. I love to throw parties as you know. My friend was there for me when I lost my darling…you see…you do understand don't you?"

I sat down with Amr at my side and between us we composed the correct and most gentle reply. Poor Martine. This must be drawing up all the sadness of her own very great loss.

Oven Man shows up late in the evening with Gabriel. They are having the verbal tussles they so love to have. I take them into the kitchen. Our guests being in the lounge watching some peculiar play.

We pour a little wine and make tea. Gabriel is very closely watching my face. He's up to something and I don't know what it is. Then a sudden thought comes to me. He has seen Raphael. They are both making comments of the most odd sort.

"It won't be the first time. "Noh."

"He has a way that is clear. He is totally…"

I interrupt.

"You two are acting most oddly. What's happened."

"Oh we talk of the possible new venture that you might, with our help…if you so wish, to return horses for guests to ride here. Your *voisin* has land he may want to sell. This can be done nicely. And why not. Dancing ponies return to the villa…this makes a nice little marketing picture *ne'est-ce pas*."

My head is in a whirl with all that's happening.

Before meeting Martine, who wants to see me in our 'happy place' – a rather rough and ready coffee shop which sells the best homemade cake this side of heaven, and coffee which can melt the heart of any dieter – Amr is coming. Due to the Christening shopping we have to buy him a shirt, and I am taking a beautifully designed card to Martine inviting her to be Godmother and of course to the Christening. I think this is a wonderful idea. As soon as she returns from Italy, we are having the Christening celebration and Little G will officially be a very blessed child. Claude has been chosen to be Godfather, a role he has already taken most seriously from day one of Little G coming into his world.

We are a happy trio as we meet in the car parking area and make our way all talking at once to the 'happy place' …Amr slips off to find a shirt and Martine and I hug again.

"Oh Gina, it's so good to be out in the sun again. To be with you. I am foolish to lie down in dark rooms. It's too much, I am meant for jolly moments."

"I think you had to go through that to come to this conclusion."

"Ah you know my heart. I am happy again and it will be a trial to be in Italy but it is one I must go through. My dear friend suffers so. I am the one that knows so much this suffering. The best news is what you bring me."

Martine never one to stint on those she adores, gets up and comes around the table to bear-hug me. She is terribly thin. Too thin. I have a strong feeling those dark glasses although 'chic' and very French they hide dark circles.

"We are all very pleased that Deardra and Felix made this decision. Claude is a natural choice as are you."

"Ah it is the best thing in a long time to be chosen to care about this little one. We are now all one family with this move."

"Yes, did you hear about Gabriel and Oven Man."

"Oh noh noh you still call him Oven Man."

"Sorry, it's stuck now, and he did bring me the oven. They want to find nice riding horses for the villa."

"Ah, I recall those funny times and Tom and the girlies. Oh, how funny those early days for you, dear Gina. And you and Raphael…"

She stops herself and takes my hand.

"Forgive me, I am gone foolish in the head, it is all that's happening and it just slipped off my tongue as you know this can happen, please forgive your Martine. Horses to ride, yes, it makes perfect sense dancing horses return to dancing villa…*oui oui*…why not…brilliant idea."

"Nothing to forgive. Anyway, I kissed him black eye and all when he delivered your letter."

"Noh, truly you do this. I understand it all now this is why he looks very happy when he comes back. I told him all the way through he is lucky to know such a tender-hearted woman…he is full of regret foolish boy that he is. Sadly, he will not change I am his mother and feel this from my heart. Don't be taken in. At first, I think yes, he is settling now and will be able to leave mild flirtations behind and be good husband to my Gina. But noh he is still the spotted leopard. Lilian has nicknamed him little leopard from the very beginning"

"But he is your only son and it is right you feel this way that he will change, become good and not kiss married women and get carried away. His looks are his downfall as well as his blessing."

"This is true…ah here comes the divine cake…let's eat a really grand slice and not care."

"Martine you can afford to add an inch, me noh, noh, noh."

We laugh ourselves silly and then after settling the very small bill for such wonderful food, we trot to the shops and look at dresses. Always, always go to the shop with Martine, she will never let you put a foot or waistline wrong. We select a cool rich navy for me and a cream sheath for her. Also for fun, we choose two enormous hats one in creamy white for me and the other in a mysterious navy for her. The outcome is a fashion statement to end all fashion statements. We think we are on the covers of Vogue and don't care what remarks we hear.

'Well, who the hell do they think they are!' was the best one.

Martine insisted she bought my hat. Cripes, it was so expensive, and the dress due to its clever, plain, cut looks rich with it. I am satisfied. We leave the shop very smug indeed. Chanting out loud and laughing…

"Who does she think she is."

"Who does she think she is."

Once we are around the corner we double up with hysterical laughing. We call Amr, he is already waiting back at the car and sounds peeved.

"Who does he think he is!!!"

And we are off again. Martine who is happier and almost her old self again grabs up my arm and we manage to hold each other and all the shopping, laughing at our silliness.

"Gina…don't marry Amr. He is the only one who will benefit…you need a strong man who is able to go into the world, hold up his head, clever and sexy and with a little bit of you know what…"

"I think you are right."

"He makes the argument for you sound good and clever, and the answer to all your prayers for husband. But there is something very lacking, the 'give it away', it's in his eyes."

"Ah you have seen that little flash of dynamite go across."

"Oui just so…this is the sign of one who wishes to control all outcomes…and when you are married to such a man your every look and step will be judged by him…"

"Oh and there was me hoping it was a flash of passion."

"Noh, noh, do not go there. Passion is felt another way when you are close to a passionate man…you know he wants to take you to bed and make love to you. A warm fuzzy glow darling Gina a warm fuzzy glow."

"Oh no I don't ever and have never felt like that in Amr's presence. You are right I had a cold husband before I don't want another."

"This is your first thought."

"Mmmmmm, 'fraid so, the minute I met Amr…I think a little too controlled and yes scholarly but cold somewhere…hard to put a finger on it…an excellent work mate and friend…but not husband material."

"In this you are one hundred and twenty percent correct."

We are however near the car and feel that we must not be unkind.

Amr, forever a gentleman in other ways, opens the doors for us and we pile in with all the shopping.

"Big hats."

I offer as the excuse for such huge packages. He nods and yes, I do see all that Martine has said is true. Secretly, he does not approve of such extravagances.

Once back at the chateaux we unwrap all the finery in Martine's bedroom and laugh our way through a whole bottle of champagne and not the cheap stuff either. Lilian shares with us the hilarity and the champers with much amusement. Lilian and Michel are invited of course but Lilian wants to look for a saucy affair to wear and that will take a little longer. My feelings for her are always sad, she is looking still to tempt Amr. So very strange is life. We have invited Raphael but it is beginning to look like he will be away in Northern France attending some historical events.

When Amr, who refuses all spirits to my knowledge…another thing I cannot get used to. Never to get your nose tickled by champagne or imbibe the glorious nectar of rosé in my view is an insult to the life given to us. The vine is the gift of the gods. To me and everyone I know. Mahmoud never says anything although he does pretend to tut. He however, only tuts in jest. His motto being live and let live. I love this about him. Cannot wait to see him. He is flying into Nice, Cote d'Azure airport two days before Christmas.

Such
pleasures
to
come,
n'est-ce pas.